S0-AAA-259

Bridle Path
Press

ALSO BY M. K. GRAFF:

The Nora Tierney English Mysteries
The Blue Virgin
The Green Remains
The Scarlet Wench
The Golden Hour

The Trudy Genova Manhattan Mysteries
Death Unscripted
Death at the Dakota

THE EVENING'S AMETHYST

A Nora Tierney English Mystery

M. K. Graff

The Evening's Amethyst is a work of fiction. Names, characters, places, and incidents are the products of the author's imagination or are used fictitiously. Any resemblance to actual events, locales, or persons, living or dead, is entirely coincidental.

Copyright © 2021 by M.K. Graff

All rights reserved.

No part of this book may be reproduced or transmitted in any manner whatsoever without permission from the publisher except in the case of brief quotations for purpose of critical articles or reviews. For information or permission contact:

Bridle Path Press, LLC
8419 Stevenson Road
Baltimore, MD 21208

www.bridlepathpress.com

Direct orders to the above address.

Printed in the United States of America.
First Edition.
ISBN: 978-0-9908287-3-0

Library of Congress Control Number: 2021939781

Book Design by Elizabeth Ryan Cole
Cover photo by nesneJkraM/istockphoto.com

FOR ARTHUR

We're Still Standing

AND FOR AVERIL AND MARTIN FREETH

Gone too soon

Great Britain
Cambridge
Woodstock
Oxford

Cast of Characters

in order of appearance

JIM ROBSON — Pharmaceutical salesman

NORA TIERNEY— American writer living in England

MR. TINK — Nora's house painter

TYPO—beagle puppy

DECLAN BARNES—Detective Inspector Thames Valley Police, Criminal Investigation Dept., St. Aldate's, Oxford; Nora's fiancé

CLAIRE SCOTT—Nora's stepsister; graduate student at Exeter College, Oxford

CHARLIE BORDEN—Home Office Pathologist

BEATRICE JONES—Dead graduate student, Exeter College

TREVOR WATKINS—Declan's sergeant and right-hand man, St. Aldate's CID

PATTI PHILLIPS—Undergrad student, Exeter College

JACK SOONG—Undergrad student, Exeter College

BENEDICK JONES—Bea Jones's twin brother; ordinand, Ridley Hall, Cambridge

DR. ERNEST JONES—Bea and Ben Jones's father; Director, Choral and Organ Music, Christ's College, Cambridge

SEAN TIERNEY—Nora's son

SALLY WELCH—Vicar, St. Giles Church, Oxford; Nora and Declan's neighbor

SAM WELCH—Sally's son; Sean's playmate

SIMON RAMSEY—Nora's children's book illustrator

DOUGLAS MCAFEE—Newest sergeant on Declan's CID team, St. Aldate's

CATHERINE (CAT)—Secretary to Superintendent Morris, St. Aldate's

PAUL MORRIS—Detective Superintendent, Thames Valley Police, St. Aldate's

JULIE WATKINS— Sgt. Watkins's pregnant wife

NICOLA MORTON—Undergrad student, Exeter College

SERGEANT DAMEN—Uniformed desk sergeant, St. Aldate's

DENYS CURSHIK—Computer technician

ANNA—Charlie Borden's morgue assistant

CHAD BROWN—Exeter College Shakespeare tutor

DR. PETER HAMILTON—Exeter College Literature tutor

PHIL COOK—Christ's College, Cambridge, porter

MARGARET SMYTHE-JONES—Bea and Ben Jones's mother

VAL ROGAN—Nora's best friend and a textile artist; runs the Oxford Artisan's Cooperative

SOPHIE JORDAN—Val's partner; archivist, Oxford University Press

DORA ROBSON—Jim Robson's wife; mother to boy known as Digger

LAURA HAMILTON—Nurse; Peter Hamilton's wife

LILY GEORGE—Civilian analyst for St. Aldate's CID

SHEILA O'CONNOR—Scout for Stairwell 10, Exeter College

JANNA—Waitress, The Star Inn, Woodstock

CHRIS BREEN—Proprietor, Antiques at Heritage, Woodstock

REVEREND DR. JOHN-MICHAEL CROTHERS—Academic Dean, Ridley Hall, Cambridge

ALVITA BROWN—Former teacher; Chad Brown's mother

THE HONOURABLE MR. GARDINER—Her Majesty's Coroner

WILSON—Exeter College porter

NEIL WELCH—Nora's neighbor, married to Vicar Sally, father to Sam

WINSTON MORTON—Nicola Morton's auto mechanic brother

DEIRDRE CURSHIK — Dora Robson's sister; Denys's mother

STEFAN CURSHIK— Uncle to Denys Curshik

RHONA CURSHIK—Aunt to Denys Curshik

CAROL and PETER MCAFEE—Parents of DS Douglas McAfee

THE EVENING'S AMETHYST

" . . . Now again she flies aloof,
Coasting mountain clouds and kiss't
By the Evening's amethyst."

—Robert Louis Stevenson
"XI. To Will. H. Low,"
A Child's Garden of Verses and Underwoods

"What the heart loves, the will chooses, and the mind justifies."

—Thomas Cranmer

CHAPTER ONE

Cumbria

Spring 1992

It was a warm spring day, with bluebells carpeting the roadside verges as Jim Robson drove past drystone walls and fields dotted with sheep. Wordsworth's famous daffodils, their heads drowsy, swung in a light breeze as he made his way along the A591 through Windermere and turned off onto the A592.

He drove into the quaint town of Bowness-on-Windermere, past the east shore of the lake. Tired of his wife's whining about their childlessness, he needed a break, even if that longer route would take him home later than she expected. Dora would complain anyway, so what difference did it make? He remembered the sweet and gentle woman with a core of inner strength he'd married in Glasgow, those halcyon early days of their marriage and their move to Cumbria. Most of all he remembered how disappointment had changed her happy moods, a creeping wall of ivy that had taken hold of her joyfulness and throttled it.

After visiting a large hospital and carrying away a terrific order for the new infant formula, Jim decided to reward himself with a drive past the lake. Salesmen were always on the go; why shouldn't he take a few minutes for himself? He stopped on a whim on his way out of town for a pint of cider, the roadside pub calling to him. He took his pint from the gloomy inside to the sunshine outside, where he sat at one of the garden tables behind the pub, mulling over his life, and how it had fallen from his expectations.

That's when he'd noticed the dingy playpen with the little

boy, quietly playing with a stack of blocks. Jim looked around the garden. No one else was out here today. Where the hell was the mother, or for that matter, the father, and what were they thinking leaving a little toddler all alone out here? Anyone could snatch him and be gone.

The thought returned to him over the next weeks as Dora's depression grew and her crying jags increased. He loved Dora, had hoped to always make her happy after they'd met and she'd charmed him, despite the decade between them. He knew he would be considered old-fashioned, a real throwback, but Dora's overriding desire even then was to be a mother. Unfashionable for some, but he'd supported her. He'd welcomed the idea of having a wife at home waiting for him, their children clean, dinner ready, and everyone happy to see him.

These years of failure had taken their toll. Their marriage suffered when one fertility treatment after another hadn't worked. Dora turned sullen and depressed with the adoption wait taking forever. Jim was at his wit's end. He wanted his wife back.

He returned to the same pub on his next trip through a few weeks later, the sun warmer now, spring fully taken hold, and there was the child again, that poor lad. Sitting in a soggy nappy, even he could see that from where he sat, and maybe full of something else, too. The boy looked up at him and smiled, uncomplaining, his two bottom teeth shining in a face grubby with snot running down to his top lip. Jim took out a clean handkerchief and cleaned off the boy's face as best he could. The lad lifted his arms to be picked up, and it was all he could do to restrain himself.

He'd had enough, and when he returned his empty pint glass, he asked the bartender about the boy.

"Donnie?" The man hooked a thumb in the direction of the darkest corner, where a skinny girl with bad teeth and lank hair sat draped over an equally skeletal man with inked arms extending from the cut-off sleeves of his denim shirt. "Works here evenings when we get busy, spends her days looking for a new baby daddy."

They looked like addicts to Jim. He had a hard time reconciling that smiling boy with these two as he thought of the dirty nappy and face, the grungy pen. Donnie deserved better, that little boy, a proper mum and dad to care for him.

As the idea took hold, he deliberately drove past the pub on his next trip. He couldn't stop again for a pint or the bartender would remember him. But each subsequent week he drove by and slowed down. And each time, he could see that dirty pen and the little lad trapped inside.

He decided to be sensible, and if things fell into place, well, that was a sign, wasn't it? He made preparations at home. He applied for and received a transfer to the company's Woodstock branch. Why not? He was one of their best sellers of infant formula and pharmaceuticals, and the Woodstock office was happy to have him. Dora brightened right up and fell in with the move when he told her that the transfer to a more densely populated area brought a better chance of adoption. The waiting list in Bowness had been long; they'd been warned they might have to wait years in a rural area. It made sense that Oxford might bring a child faster, but in any case, Dora chose not to ask too many questions, for which he was grateful. She focused on shopping for items to furnish a nursery. He let her.

They had their first really good weekend in years, traveling to find half a terraced house on a nice Somerville street with a small front garden and a larger one out back, all for a price they could afford. They finished packing up their Cumbrian rental and moved to the Oxford suburb last week. This morning he left Dora putting the finishing touches on the nursery. He was on vacation time and knew he'd never return to Cumbria again. It was a small price to pay. Soon his new life would begin in earnest.

Jim pulled up far enough away from the pub to check things out. There was the playpen, unattended as usual. No one sat at the tables. One car, the same one he'd seen before, stood parked haphazardly outside. It had to belong to the same couple.

Could he do this? His heart started to beat wildly. He looked in the back at the car seat, belted in place and ready to go. He'd picked out a toy from the box Dora had accumulated at home, and even had a bottle of apple juice and a clean bottle ready to fill. He'd estimated the boy's size, and had nappies and wipes in the footwell, plus a soft blanket for when he fell asleep on the long drive to his new home outside Oxford.

He'd covered everything but the act. His stomach churned and his legs quivered as he rolled the car slowly down the side road toward the pub without turning the engine on. Jim pulled up near the yard. He was certain his legs would fold under him when he stepped out of the car.

He hesitated. There was still time to change his mind.

At that moment, Donnie looked up and saw him. The boy's face broke out into a wide smile, and he pulled himself up using the mesh of the filthy playpen.

Donnie stood there, swaying, and held out his arms.

CHAPTER ONE

Oxford

Friday, 1st December

9:30 AM

Nora Tierney stood at the library door of Haven Cottage and scrutinized color chips with her painter, Mr. Tink. The lanky man towered over her petite frame while she bit her lip in indecision. Once this room was completed, she and Declan, her fiancé, would have the house finished in time for the impending holidays. The last boxes would be unpacked from their move three weeks ago, and she could strip the drop cloth off her desk to start work on the next book in her children's series. And write her next freelance article. And concentrate on plans for their small May wedding.

Somewhere in there she needed to buy and wrap Christmas presents; decorate the house; plan, shop, and cook the meals for Christmas Eve, Christmas Day, and Boxing Day; all while she parented her young son and trained their new puppy. And sleep. She would definitely want to cram in sleep. She blew away an auburn curl that fell onto her face.

"Take your time." Mr. Tink sat on the stairs to the upper floor. "Where's the lad?" He looked around as Typo, the beagle Nora had adopted, promptly rolled over at his feet. The painter pushed his painting cap back on his head, revealing a shock of white hair; his gnarled hands gave Typo a good belly rub. "He and this rascal are usually together."

"Sean's at the creche St. Giles holds in their undercroft. The vicar keeps an eye on him, along with her son, Sam. Sally says they both need the socialization." Nora had worried that at 14 months her son might be too young for the nursery, but since he'd been there, Sean had thrived, with his precocious speech improving.

Mr. Tink shook his head. "Still can't get used to women vicars. Church of England's gone to hell with itself."

Nora smiled, having heard Mr. Tink's views on most things British. He considered it his job to inform her American roots that she lived in what he called the "new" England. His views encompassed his general feeling that the "old" England he'd grown up in was clearly better.

She heard Declan whistling upstairs as he finished dressing, and her smile widened, even as she perused the chips. The Oxford detective had been in a very good mood lately, with major criminals and murderers taking a holiday of sorts, which allowed him to use some of his plentiful accrued time off to help her. They'd had the upstairs bedrooms painted before the move so they could all sleep comfortably. Declan plunged into helping Nora unpack as each room was subsequently painted, and Nora grew to admire his organizational skills and suggestions. Mostly. She was a list-maker herself, so that part of them clicked. That was not all that clicked.

She pondered her color choices, stalling to look around the main room of the renovated cottage. The previous owner had opened up the downstairs without losing the house's charm in a renovation sympathetic to the period feel of the home. With cozy upstairs bedrooms, the timbered home had dark beams downstairs. Haven Cottage formed a V-shape around a gothic-arched front door, while thick window ledges showed the home's age. Light flooded in from tall French doors that stretched across the back wall of the kitchen and dining area, and looked out onto the garden whose fence was masked by thick green hedges. The lack of interior walls made the area feel larger. It already felt like a real home to her nascent family, and with the holidays looming, that effect would be further enhanced. Nora felt a rush of satisfaction.

She turned to the paint chips and frowned; she'd have to live with these decisions for a long time.

Mr. Tink had Typo on his lap now and rubbed the dog's velvety ears. "Have you decided?"

"In the words of Hamlet, Mr. Tink, that is the question." Declan Barnes came down the stairs, adjusting the knot in his tie. He neatly sidestepped man and beagle and stooped to check his image in the antique mirror that hung over a console table inside the front door. "It depends on the hour, trust me. Can I go on record as saying I've never heard such ridiculous names for paint colors?"

"Don't start, you two. This library is important to me," Nora scolded. "But I think I'm ready."

"Note the 'think,' Mr. Tink. Just like the downstairs loo under the stairs, where you dithered for days, Nora. What was the one you ultimately chose?" Declan raised an eyebrow.

Nora pursed her lips and reminded herself not to tell him how sexy she found that arched brow. She opened her mouth to answer, but the painter beat her to it.

"Elephant's breath," Mr. Tink supplied. "No idea how they figured that one out, but the pale grey looks very nice. Hint of lilac with the light on."

"I *have* decided." Nora tapped the color card. "Remember we talked about painting the inside of the bookshelves to break up all the oak and bring a spot of vibrancy to the room? Radicchio will be perfect."

Mr. Tink nodded, a look of deep concentration on his face. "Vibrant."

Declan stifled a laugh. "Radicchio sounds like a salad, Nora."

Nora ignored them and pointed to another chip. "And for the ceiling between the dark beams, this white that has a hint of blue to it."

"Which is called?" Declan kept a straight face.

"Blackened." She saw the grin that passed between the two men. She hurried on. "For the walls, this soft green-blue called Teresa's Green."

Mr. Tink scratched his head. "Who's Teresa when she's at home?"

"Darned if I know," Declan answered.

"That's enough, Laurel and Hardy—you two are worse than a bad comedy skit. And I'm not saying who's who." Nora handed the painter the color cards. "I've put a giant X on those three. You're clear where they belong?"

Mr. Tink stood and took the proffered cards. "Green, blue, cranberry. I'll get right on it." He saluted and left for the paint shop.

Nora moved towards Declan to straighten his tie, looking into his grey eyes. "Really, the two of you are incorrigible together, Declan."

"Yes, but I think he loves you just a tiny bit, while I love you a whole lot more."

Their kiss was interrupted by the almost-simultaneous ring of their phones. Nora headed to the kitchen where she'd left hers on the island; she could hear Declan as he answered first.

"Suspicious, McAfee?" said Declan to his youngest sergeant. "Sounds hellish. Watkins on his way? … Good. Tell the sergeant I'll walk over and meet him there."

He gave more orders as Nora grabbed her phone and saw it was her stepsister, Claire Scott, enrolled in a master's program at Exeter. "Hi, Claire." She heard sniffling on the other end while Claire composed herself enough to speak. A thread of anxiety ran through her. "Are you all right? Is it your dad, or my mom?"

"I'm fine, but my friend Bea isn't." Claire choked back a deep sob. "Please come, Nora—Bea's dead!"

CHAPTER TWO

9:44 AM

Declan entered the kitchen, trailed by Typo, to tell Nora he had to leave.

"Nora, I had a call that concerns Claire—"

"That was her on the phone just now. Her friend Bea is dead."

"I'm on it. Claire found her. Watkins is with her now."

"I'm coming with you. I told her I'd be there shortly. Give me a sec to sort Typo."

He watched Nora hurry to the mudroom off the kitchen, the puppy at her heels. She fetched a chew bone, while he considered the wisdom of allowing Nora to come with him. She flung the bone across the yard and yelled "fetch." As the puppy raced to retrieve the treat, she placed his water bowl outside and closed the door.

Declan saw the set of Nora's lips and heard her tone. He decided not to argue; it might be helpful to have her there when he spoke to Claire. Finding the victim made Nora's stepsister an important witness and, unfortunately, a suspect.

In the time since the young woman's death, his sergeant had called out a forensic team and the coroner had arrived. Declan thrust his arms into his sport coat while Nora stuffed her keys and phone into her jeans and grabbed a denim jacket off one of the hooks inside the door. "We can walk over to Exeter and meet Watkins there."

"Fine. I have plenty of time before I have to get Sean." She rummaged in her purse and added a packet of tissues to her jacket pocket. "Mr. Tink has the spare key." She rooted around in the drawer of the console table for a pad and scribbled a note she left on the bottom stair. "Just to let Mr. Tink know I had to go out."

Declan noted she wrote the names of the paint colors and where to put them on the message. "Not taking any chances?" He held the door open for her.

"He's been perfect so far. Don't want to tempt fate."

They walked out into the crisp day and down the drive, where the house was hidden from Woodstock Road by a stand of tall hedges. A curl of smoke from a few blocks away in Jericho showed someone had lit a fireplace this cool morning. Turning left, they passed the rectory, made of the same pale Cotswold stone as the Norman and early Gothic church, where Neil and Sally Welch lived with their young son. Declan followed Nora on the uneven path that ran up the side of the church, bordered on one side by an ancient graveyard, and let them onto the Banbury Road.

They turned right and onto St. Giles and waited for a break in the heavy morning traffic to cross the broad road, then walked up St. Giles to the Martyrs Memorial, threading their way through a tangle of students and tourists.

Declan saw Nora draw her jacket closer around her. "Cold?" Although the sun shone brightly and the sky showed a clear blue, studded with fleecy clouds, winter was in the air.

"Just a chill." She grabbed his hand. "Claire was so upset, Declan. She said Bea fell from their stairwell, and she found her at the bottom. There was nothing she could do."

"Do you know Bea Jones?" Declan held her hand, transferring his warmth to her cool fingers. Students leaving exams, still wearing their sub fusc, passed them on the street, their black academic gowns billowing around them. They mixed with the ubiquitous gaggles of visitors who came to the ancient city year-round.

Exeter, founded in the early 14th century, was one of the university's federation of separate colleges and was one of Declan's favorites. The ivy-covered buildings exhibited Victorian refurbishing and charm, crowned by an enormous chapel modeled after Paris's Saint Chapelle, and featured a William Morris tapestry. He'd first met Nora while investigating a case that revolved around Nora's best friend, Val Rogan, and involved them both interviewing an Exeter don. He recalled his first impression of Nora; though she was slight in stature, she was obviously a strong, determined young woman. His notion hadn't changed in the time he'd known her.

Nora shook her head. "No, we never met. But Claire mentioned her often, and I recall Val said Claire brought Bea to the co-op once." The textile artist, Nora's best friend, helped run an artists' cooperative in town. "Claire said Bea fell from the stairway. How could she fall?"

"I don't have many details yet, but we don't know the woman's state of mind."

"You're thinking suicide?" He felt Nora shiver.

"It's one possibility to rule out. We need to know more facts and see the scene before we focus on anything." Declan guided Nora left onto Broad Street past Balliol College. He could feel her tense up the closer they drew to Exeter, a block down. "Watkins said this entrance was closest."

Exeter stood on the corner of Broad and Turl Streets, with the round, domed Radcliffe Camera behind its other side on Brasenose Lane. At the far end of the Broad Street entrance, a mortuary van had drawn up behind the redundant ambulance.

"Claire's room is near that entrance, staircase 10. They use Roman numerals, so she's at X. Sounds awful—X marks the spot." Nora looked up at Declan. "I'm babbling, aren't I?"

He dropped her hand and squeezed her shoulder, catching the juniper scent of her perfume as a breeze lifted her hair. "Certain you're up to this? I could have a patrol car bring Claire to the cottage once I've interviewed her."

"No, I'll be fine." She straightened her spine. "Claire asked me to come. She might be a stepsister, but she's the closest I have to a sibling, and I want to support her. I'm happy she called me. I wish it weren't for such an awful reason."

An only child himself, Declan understood her reasoning. Blue and white police tape closed off this entrance. A crowd of students and onlookers had been pushed back to gather across the street, phones clicking as they took photos. He could never understand why people's misery figured so highly with the public, but he'd learned there were many reasons for their interest, from straight prurience to relief the awfulness had happened to someone else.

Declan's mind was already in overdrive, mentally listing the steps they would need to take as the case unfolded and he learned more details of the death of this young woman Nora's sister had known. Did she have a boyfriend or lover and they'd argued? What was her state of mind? Could this have been an unfortunate accident? Was there anyone in her life who could have wanted to harm her? His team would have to answer all of these questions and more.

He took the proffered clipboard from the officer guarding the entry, who logged everyone who entered or left the crime scene. Declan signed them both in, then handed it back. "What's happening, constable?"

The constable took the clipboard. "Sir. Sergeant Watkins is inside the first door on the right with the witness. Forensics have been at work for a while, and Dr. Borden is finishing up. Three students are waiting upstairs to be released. The tutor, a Dr. Hamilton, is waiting near the body until it's moved. The porter came on duty after the incident, but he said the scout for this stairwell had a sick day today." Scouts were college housekeepers responsible for a set of rooms.

"Thank you for that comprehensive report." Here was another officer keen to be a detective, and Declan noted the man's name badge. He ushered Nora under the tape into the curved-ceilinged entryway. They were immediately plunged into a cool darkness, with daylight on the other end of the entrance which led to the quad and the back of the chapel on one side and the rector's lodgings, offices, and don's rooms on the other.

More crime scene tape closed off the stairs to their left, while a white sheet draped the victim, whose body sprawled half on and half off the lower steps. A man wearing an Exeter sweatshirt and shiny joggers stood outside the cordon, watching over the activity. This must be the tutor Watkins had allowed to stay as a college representative.

Declan guided Nora to the stepping plates forensics had put down until they came near the white-suited medical examiner, Declan's friend Charlie Borden. Charlie had already drawn a white plastic sheet back over Bea Jones and closed up his bag. One of the young woman's hands, enclosed in a plastic bag, lay outside the edge of the sheet, the fingers curled in supplication. Charlie leaned over and gently tucked her hand under the sheet. Several other suited crime scene investigators continued to gather evidence in the stairwell; the photographer stowed his video camera.

The home office pathologist's beard and ample belly gave

him the appearance of a cuddly bear and belied his meticulous practices. "Hullo, Dec. SIO on this one?" He tilted his head. "Hi, Nora."

Declan heard the question in Charlie's voice. "Nora's stepsister heard the woman fall and was first on scene. And yes, I'm senior investigating officer, and since you deemed this suspicious, Watkins had the area forensics manager send a team to get started."

"Covering my bases." Charlie pointed his chin toward a door that opened off the ground floor. "Sorry for your sister, Nora. She's resting in there with Watkins." He looked back at the body. "Pretty gal. I always associate Exeter with the last of the Morse books, when he has his fatal heart attack here." He shook his head. "Now even John Thaw who played him and Colin Dexter who created him are gone. Life is transient. Look at this young woman. A tragedy."

"Any ideas?" Contrary to television pathologists, Declan knew Charlie would give him whatever information he could with a minimum of speculation.

He scratched his beard. "Since we have a witness, we know the exact time of death for a change. Nothing obvious yet to say if she fell accidentally—or something worse."

Beside him, Nora stiffened. "You don't think she threw herself down those stairs? Are you thinking murder?"

Charlie raised a hand to ward off her questions. "No idea, Nora. But it seems a tough way to commit suicide, I must admit. The stone stairs are steep and have sharp turns. Forensics tell me they become wood after the first landing. Wouldn't be a sure thing, and there are easier ways to duck out of life." He pointed up the stairwell. "She had to have hit the railings and stairs on her way down. Most of her limbs appear broken."

While Nora drew in a harsh breath, Declan set his lips in a grim line. "Any idea when you'll get to the post, Charlie?"

Charlie pursed his lips. "I'll come in and do her tomorrow so they can set up a timely inquest and you can get going. Need to have a formal identification, too." He ripped off his white suit and thrust it into the forensic waste bag set to one side.

"McAfee told me her parents live in Cambridge," Declan said. "Local officers delivered the notice. Expect them down later today."

"Then I'll definitely put her on for tomorrow. Come see me at nine, unless I see you later at the ID." He stood to one side and nodded to the mortuary men.

As the men stepped forward, unwrapping a fresh body bag, Charlie and the tutor stood at respectful attention. Declan nodded to the tutor, and the man entered one of the nearby doors as Declan turned Nora away toward where Claire waited. He knocked and entered without waiting for a reply.

Watkins stood by the window where he must have seen them arrive, watching the crowd across Broad Street to give Claire Scott room for her grief.

Claire sat on the side of the bed, barefoot, wearing sweat pants and a faded University of Connecticut sweatshirt, her slender frame wrapped in a shiny blanket from the medics. A cup of tea with a white film stood on a side table, half full. She stood and raised her tear-stained face when the door opened. Her eyes sought Nora.

Nora brushed past Declan to hug Claire, who burst into tears. "It's so awful, Nora."

"I know, sweetheart. Sit down. Here's a fresh tissue." Nora sat on the bed next to Claire, rubbing her back and talking quietly.

While Nora comforted Claire, Declan conferred with Watkins. "Where are we?"

"Heard back from the Cambridge officers who did the notification. The father called the brother, who'll drive them down to make the formal ID." Watkins checked the time on his phone. "Should be here well before noon."

"We'll meet them at the mortuary. What else do you know?"

"Three undergrads and two graduate students live in this staircase. The victim, Beatrice Jones, was one of the grad students, the same as Claire Scott. We've kept the other three students upstairs. The tutor arrived back from a run right after the incident, a Dr. Peter Hamilton. I told him we would speak with him later at some point for background if needed. He was the victim's advisor and knew her well."

"He was hanging around until they took the body," Declan said.

Watkins shook his head. "I was hoping it would stay quiet until the baby arrives." Watkins' wife Julie was due any day with their first child. Every time the phone rang, the detective jumped.

"Maybe we'll get this wrapped up quickly." Declan looked around the nicely appointed room, with its large bed and work desk. "Whose room is this?"

"A tutor on sabbatical this term."

Whoever usually slept here would be happy he or she had missed the death on their doorstep. "Ask the porter to give you the contact details for the scout on this stairway. We can talk to her or him Monday if need be." He knew scouts often kept students' secrets and turned a blind eye to their hi-jinks.

Nora had given Claire two more tissues before she finally

appeared cried out. Declan caught Nora's eye and she gave a small nod.

"All right, Claire?" he asked. "Feel up to answering a few questions?"

Claire nodded and twisted her bare feet over each other.

Nora spoke up. "Declan, she must be freezing with these stone floors and nothing on her feet. Could we go up to Claire's room?"

"Watkins, check with one of the SOCOs would you please? They won't appreciate us trekking through their scene."

Watkins ducked outside and Declan took the opportunity to distract Claire. "Sergeant Watkins and his wife are having a baby any day now. He says she's as big as an elephant, so I've given him Nora's sage advice: Never tell a woman she's waddling like a duck." He saw a tiny smile lift the corner of Claire's mouth.

Watkins opened the door. "We can go up if we stick to the plates along the far side of the stairs. We're not to touch anything on the way up or on the landing."

"Follow Watkins, Claire." Declan ushered Claire to the doorway. She stopped at the threshold.

Nora patted her arm. "It's all right, Claire. Bea's been taken away."

Claire nodded and followed Watkins up the stairs, with Nora behind her. Declan brought up the rear and watched as Claire kept her gaze steadfastly in front, trying not to glance at the white towels that covered the pool of blood left behind on the stone floor.

They made several turns on the landing as they passed the first floor. As Charlie noted, the stairs became wood. They reached the second floor, where Claire's door at the top left of the stairs stood ajar. A scene of crime officer measured the distance from the railing on the right to the floor; both areas had already been dusted for fingerprints. On the stairs to the third floor, a young man and woman waited. The man's thick, black hair needed a trim; he had a stuffed rucksack slung over one shoulder. The leggy woman with bleached, short hair and a silver ring in her eyebrow had a bulging overnighter at her feet and an annoyed expression on her face.

"Finally," she snapped, her white hair quivering. "Can we leave now? We've been trapped here literally for hours while the bugs did their thing." She gestured to the investigator in her white Tyvek suit.

Nora and Claire stopped outside her door. Two doors opposite stood open. In the one directly across from Claire's, another SOCO sealed evidence bags in what must be the victim's room. In the far room, Declan saw a young Black woman with a multitude of beaded braids standing by her window, gazing at the back of the chapel. She played with one of the beads at the end of a braid, rolling it between her finger, over and over.

"Your names?" Declan asked the students on the stairs, knowing Watkins would make a note.

"Patti Phillips." The blonde shifted from foot to foot.

The young man offered, "Jack Soong."

Declan addressed the woman. "Miss Phillips, forensic work takes time and is vastly important. We could easily keep you upstairs for days, or have you removed by a fire truck ladder if we wanted."

Patti had the grace to look chastened. "Sorry. But it's ghoulish being stuck here when we didn't see anything, and we all have exams coming up."

"Perhaps, but at least it's temporary and you get to leave."

Declan hit them with the harsh truth. "We'll need you to come to St. Aldate's station and give statements later today, so don't stray too far. Also, we need your contact information before you leave here, as well as where you'll be staying for the weekend and end of term."

Phillips nodded. "Anything to get away from here for a few hours."

Soong dipped his head in agreement. A man of few words, Declan decided, or else the blonde ruled the third floor.

Watkins pointed his thumb at the two students hovering on the stairs. "Guv, I'll get their info and then head in to speak to"—he consulted his notebook—"Nicola Morton." He spoke to the SOCO. "All right for them to leave after that?"

The tech pulled back her hood, revealing a crop of glossy brown hair sporting a pink streak. "Measurements and prints are finished and I am, too." She shot the two students a dark look; Declan had the feeling Patti Phillips had been giving the forensic team a hard time. She issued instructions. "Stay on the walking plates and don't touch anything."

Declan led Nora and Claire into her room, where a poster of Ed Sheeran graced one wall. He glanced at Claire's laptop, open on her desk under two narrow windows. The screensaver was a wedding photo from when her father, Roger Scott, married Nora's mother several years back. He recognized the Scotts' porch on their Connecticut home he'd visited a few months ago. In the photo, Claire and Nora, both wearing cocktail dresses, flanked the couple. Everyone held champagne flutes and genuine smiles. He hit the space bar; the screen sprang to life. A fleeting look showed him a Word document; he caught the names Wordsworth and Dickinson. The windows looked out onto Broad Street, where the ambulance and mortuary van had gone, as had most of the onlookers. He turned to watch Claire move about the insignificant attached room, her sleeping space. A scent of lavender lingered in the air.

Claire knelt on her bed to root around the shelves behind it to retrieve a pair of fleecy socks. While her large sitting room had the perk of a fireplace, and the windows let in a fair amount of light, that generous room made up for a second room so narrow her bed resembled a cot. It was pushed up against a recess with open shelves on one side and a rod for hanging clothes that formed her closet.

A tiny sink, attached to the opposite wall with a dorm fridge next to it, held a tray of mugs with tea things on its top. The tall gothic-arched casement window gave a view of the rear side of the chapel; its wide ledge held Claire's toiletries strewn across it as a makeshift vanity. A bouquet of dried flowers was arranged in an empty wine bottle, while a round hanger on the wall next to the curtain dangled a jumble of colorful scarves.

"I'll make tea to warm us all up." Nora waited for Claire to leave the tiny room. Declan watched her fill the electric kettle at the sink and turn it on, then rinse three mugs and drop in bags of PG tips. He moved away from the window and desk, trying to decide where to sit.

Socks on, Claire sat behind her desk and closed her laptop. Declan chose the couch and immediately wished he hadn't. He knew Exeter began in 1314, and this couch felt like it was an original piece from then, lumpy and hard. With his long legs, it would be a tough crawl out. Nora moved a single chair next to Claire's desk.

Declan took out his notebook and pointed to Claire's laptop.

"That essay for your coursework?"

"It's about how Emily Dickinson and William Wordsworth could be considered nature poets, even though Dickinson is often classified an early modernist and Wordsworth a romantic."

Declan watched Claire warm to her subject as she went on. They'd met a few times: when he visited the Scott home in Ridgefield, where he and Nora became engaged; and a few weeks later at Sean's first birthday extravaganza at his English grandparents' Cornwall estate, when she'd already started at Exeter. Nora wouldn't be happy to think Claire was on his suspect list, but that couldn't be helped. Procedure dictated that the person first on the scene always had to be eliminated as a suspect. He'd have to tread carefully here, but be fair. While he could juggle with the best of them, his first allegiance was to the victim.

Claire's hazel eyes had rims still reddened from crying. She wore her wavy light-brown hair pulled back in a messy bun that had half fallen down. Her arched eyebrows, a few shades darker than her hair, framed a square face with high cheekbones.

The kettle shut off and Nora rose to busy herself making their tea.

"Let's start with yesterday, say the afternoon." Declan had learned that if he brought a witness back to a calm time before the disturbing event, they'd often have clearer, more accurate memories. "How did you spend it, and did you see Beatrice at all?"

"Bea and I had our last meeting with Dr. Hamilton, a wrap-up, really, as the semester is over and it's exam week for the undergrads. We just need to hand in our final work. That ended near four, and we spent an hour so in the Radcliffe Camera cementing final research. Bea was finished, but she wanted to check at few details, she said." Claire scrubbed her face with her hands. "We dropped our things and walked to the King's Arms for an early meal. We had tickets to a concert I'd given Bea for her birthday, which had been last Sunday, but she doesn't stick around on weekends. We saw Daughter, an indie-folk trio she likes." She grimaced. "Liked. It was a great evening together."

Nora handed out the teas and Declan allowed her to smoothly insert a question. "What did Bea do on her weekends?"

Claire stirred her tea distractedly. "She went home to Cambridge for a nanny job. She'd arranged her coursework this term to have Fridays off, and left right after class Thursdays. She'd usually come back early Monday morning, said they needed her on weekends." She raised her head and met Declan's eye. "Bea was so kind; it was typical of her to arrange her schedule like that."

"Any idea of the name of this family she worked for?" he asked.

Claire thought a moment before she shook her head. "She never said, now that I think about it, except for the little girl. Verity. Her name is Verity."

CHAPTER THREE

10:47 AM

Nora stirred her tea. "Verity means truth. That's a sweet old-fashioned name."

Claire agreed. "Bea talked about her nonstop over dinner Thursday. 'Verity will walk soon; Verity is starting to talk.' We stopped at Blackwell's before the concert and she bought her a book. I'd already given her one of yours for the child." She sipped her tea. "You would have liked Bea, Nora. She was so very kind, and passionate about children's literature, especially Roald Dahl. She spent last Hilary and Trinity terms and all summer in Wales on a fellowship, researching his life for a biography. She was due to graduate soon."

"Bea was ahead of you in the program?" Nora asked. She'd learned Oxford semesters were based on eight-week terms: Michaelmas, the current fall term, then after the holidays, Hilary term until March, and after a spring break, Trinity term that ended in June.

"Yes. She would have graduated last June but took that term for the Wales thing. She's—she was—a year older than me. We both love to read and had a thing for Ed Sheeran and became fast friends."

"And after this concert last night?" Declan asked.

"We were both tired when we came back here, so we said goodnight. I hugged her and she thanked me for the concert, but if I'd known …" Claire inhaled to stop fresh tears.

"Did you sleep then?" Nora put her cup on the edge of Claire's desk, aware Declan was allowing her to ask the questions. He'd jump in if she missed anything.

"I should have, but Marco from my Shakespeare class came under my window and called up, wanted me to come out." She blushed. "He calls me Julietta. I didn't feel like going out so late. After we'd chatted a bit, the cold night air gave me a second wind. I decided to reread my thesis for yet another round of edits."

"I know how that goes," Nora said. She was anxious to move Claire's story along for Declan. "How late did you work?"

"It had to be way after two. That's when I took a break on the couch." She shifted in her seat. Nora thought this was the dicey part Claire didn't want to recall. "I slept hard at first, then dreamt I heard this hissing sound I thought was a radiator. I started to wake and turned over, but the hissing kept up, and then there was a scrabbling noise, a kind of shuffling. And then suddenly a horrible scream from Bea's voice, shouting something—" The color drained from Claire's face.

Nora jumped up and put an arm around Claire's shoulder. "It's all right, sweetheart. Take a deep breath. Good. Now another."

Declan leaned forward. "Claire, you're doing great. This is the toughest part. Try to picture what happened as if you're watching a movie. Close your eyes and tell me what you saw, and if you can, what you heard shouted."

Claire took a deep breath, then closed her eyes. Nora kept a steadying hand on her arm.

"I ran to my door, and when I opened it, Nicola was in her doorway, too, a robe over her sleeping things. She said she heard the scream. Jack was on the stairs, yelling something like, 'What the hell was that?' and Patti shouted down, 'What's happened?' I looked over the stairwell and had a rush of vertigo—" She gulped. Her voice dropped to a whisper; she kept her eyes closed.

"Bea was down there, her feet on the bottom steps, her head and upper body twisted on the stone floor." She opened her eyes. "You saw her, Declan. There was blood …"

He nodded while Claire continued, her words tumbling out. "I yelled at the others to call for help and ran down the stairs to check for a pulse. Jack started down behind me until he saw Bea and stopped. Then I held her hand while we waited for the ambulance. By then Dr. Hamilton came from the quad entrance, sweaty from his run, and yelled, 'Bloody hell!' He told Jack to go back upstairs and tell the others to stay there."

Claire was lost in the memory now as it became real again. "I remember feeling cold to my marrow, and I had to grit my teeth to keep them from chattering. Bea's hand still felt warm, but one eye stared at me, blankly, and I knew she was … gone. Dr. Hamilton barked things on his phone, and when the medics came, he helped me stand while they covered Bea. They gave me that blanket. Sergeant Watkins was there by then and took me into that side room. Dr. Hamilton's wife brought me sweet tea for shock, and he said he would stand by Bea and watch over her, but it's all a blur after that until you and Nora came." She raised her head, spent and quivering.

"Just one last question, Claire. What would you say was Bea's state of mind?"

"Blissful. She would get her degree and probably have her thesis published in book form. She positively glowed with this light of happiness."

Declan stood. "I think that's enough for now. The porter told Watkins there are no more classes due to end of term revising. Why don't you let Nora help you pack some things and stay with us for a few days?"

Nora shot him a grateful look. It was what she wanted to suggest. Claire nodded and started to gather her laptop and papers. Nora took their tea things back and rinsed the mugs. She saw the casement window was ajar to let in fresh air and opened it wider. It screeched on its hinges as she looked out at the view Claire had. Without screens, she could look right down onto the cobblestoned ground behind the chapel. If Bea Jones had wanted to commit suicide, all she had to do was jump out her window onto those stones.

Nora pulled the casement closed and turned the old-fashioned handle, securing it, not that anyone could get in this high up.

"I'll head out with Watkins after I look at Bea's room, Nora. He'll drive me to get my car." He squeezed Nora's arm, then turned to leave.

Claire leaned on her desk. "What happened, Declan? How could Bea fall over the rail like that?"

Nora saw emotions cross Declan's face as he decided what to say.

"I don't know, Claire, but we'll sort it out."

Claire started for her bedroom, then stopped at the door. She turned to look back at Nora and Declan, her brows furrowed, her expression tight. "I know one thing for certain. Bea would never, ever have jumped."

CHAPTER FOUR

11:06 AM

Benedick Jones kept the speed steady in his VW Polo on the journey from Cambridge, where he was an ordinand in seminary at Ridley Hall, to Oxford and the John Radcliffe's mortuary. The last thing he needed was to be stopped for speeding, today of all days.

When his phone had vibrated with a text, he'd been in a serious discussion with several other ordinands about how to handle confidential information shared by parishioners. He had his reasons for exploring this question. He'd glanced at the phone, annoyed by the interruption, and his scalp prickled when he saw the text from his father: *URGENT! Take call in 2 mins!*

He'd excused himself and paced the hallway, waiting for his phone to ring, his mind ruminating on what his father would have deemed urgent. If the call had been from his mother, it could have been anything from asking what he wanted for Sunday dinner to complaining her altar flower delivery was delayed. But his father rarely bothered him, too busy with his own work as music director and don at Christ's College, and he never used the word "urgent."

Ben came to a sudden halt. Maybe it was about his mother. Perhaps the old cow had been in an accident or had a heart attack. She exasperated him most times they met, with her supercilious manner and ridiculously antiquated ideas about social strata. Still, he was fond of her on a good day. She was, after all, his mother.

He'd almost dropped the phone when it rang, startling him

from his reverie. "What's so urgent, Dad? What's happened?"

There had been silence for a few beats; then a quick intake of breath, accompanied by sniveling, and with a shock, Ben had realized his father had been crying.

"I've had a visit from the police. Your sister had an accident at Exeter. They think—" he had stumbled over his words. "They said Bea is dead."

"What? NO!" Ben realized he'd shouted. "What happened?" Not Bea, not his sweet twin sister, please God, let there be a mistake. His chest felt leaden with fear; he broke out in a cold sweat.

"A fall in a stairwell. I don't have many details." His father had cleared his throat. "The thing is, someone has to formally identify … her. The police offered to drive me, but I can't bear driving close to two hours with strangers, and I don't think I can drive myself right now. Could you?"

Ben's thoughts were all over the place. A formal identification? He had another call to make straight away. "Let me make a few arrangements here, and I'll get the car and pick you up in 20 minutes."

A shuddering sigh had come down over the wire. "Thank you, Ben. I'll look out for you."

"How did Mum take it?" He could picture his mother fainting.

His father had sighed. "She refused to believe it's Bea. Said it must be mistaken identity. She's gone off to a church meeting."

"What! And make us do this alone?" Ben brought himself up short. He was supposed to be forgiving of people's actions or, at the very least, not be judgmental. "Look, perhaps it's better if we do this together, just you and me, Dad."

"Just come."

In the hour between then and now, he'd first explained the situation at Ridley Hall. There had been a few moments of upsetting but well-intentioned sympathy from his colleagues, with entreaties to help and offers to drive him and his father, which he appreciated but refused.

Then the other call, as he ran to get his car. If he felt gutted, so did the person on the other end in Oxford, who had heard the news. After a brief discussion, it was agreed Ben and his father would do the formal identification. Today the Jones men stood united for their girl.

He'd spent the first half of this drive thinking of Bea, dear Bea, light to his dark, white-blonde hair in braids or loose and blowing in the breeze. Even though they were the same age, when they were young she'd depended on him to check under her bed for monsters. He remembered the time they decided they'd been adopted and plotted for a new family, then realized they couldn't leave Dad alone with Mum. And the way she'd borrow his rugby shirts. Her love of reading as a child had developed to her life's passion. All of her plans for the future were gone. What would happen now?

Most of all, how would the confidences he held be revealed once her death became common knowledge? He wished he knew more about the teachings of how he should behave. Was he Bea's brother or her confessor at this moment? Her confidante or her priest? Or were they the same? He had a knot of anxiety in his stomach he tried to ignore. Time enough to talk to the people involved and figure it out. The rest could wait.

He reached out and tapped his father's hand. Ernest turned to look at him. The sorrow on the man's face had etched the grooves on his forehead and along the sides of his nose into deeper, sharper, craters of pain.

"Penny for them?" Ben checked the satnav. They would arrive before noon. Best to get the tears out now. His father had been told several students who knew Bea were nearby when she fell. There seemed little chance his mother would be right.

"I was thinking how close Bea came to her dream, getting this degree, teaching and writing, all of her enthusiasm, all the hard work she put in these past few years. Dr. Hamilton thought her thesis was good enough to publish as a book, maybe even through the Oxford University Press. She'd been absurdly happy these last months, did you notice?"

Ben's breath caught. "Yes, she was happier than I'd ever seen her." That was a gross understatement. Ben felt his cheeks ruddy with shame; his father didn't notice.

"It's cruel." Ernest shook his head. "Merciless to have your dreams within your grasp and have your future yanked away by an accident. This is the part of God's grace I grapple with."

"I do, too, Dad." If only he'd gotten further in his talks today, he'd be better prepared to handle his own questions about grief and heartache.

And secrets kept or told.

CHAPTER FIVE

11:20 AM

Declan stood in the doorway to Bea's room. He looked around carefully before donning the shoe protectors and gloves the CSI tech had left him on a nightstand inside the door. Bea's phone and laptop from her backpack had been taken into evidence. Other contents would be collected by one of the team still working downstairs after he was finished.

When he'd said goodbye to Nora and Claire, he'd known from her whispered "we'll talk tonight when we're alone" that she was quite aware Claire was on his suspect list. Asking Claire to stay with them he could explain as remaining close to a suspect to see her behavior, if the need arose. He didn't think he could fool Nora, but Claire seemed oblivious that she was a suspect. Nora agreed to his plan and left to escort her stepsister to their home. He could only imagine what pillow talk tonight would entail. Perhaps in the meantime he'd make headway in the case before Nora could do it for him.

Early in his career, a DCI had taught Declan to use his eyes first. Before sifting through Bea's personal effects, he wanted to gather a sense of her personality and how she had lived in this room.

Unlike Claire's room with its large outer room and tiny sleeping area, this was one moderately-sized room, with the bed's headboard against the same wall as the door, the single bed jutting into the room. The bed was neatly made with a duvet cover in a pattern of blue and yellow birds perched on thin tree branches. A wardrobe and dresser stood against the far wall, and on the right-hand side under the window was Bea's desk, with a small bookcase standing next to it. Her open backpack, tossed on the floor next to the bed just inside the door, spilled its contents from the partially open zip.

Declan knelt by the backpack to check the items: several items of clothing, a small toiletry kit, and a child's book in a Blackwell's shop bag. He went around the bed to inspect the desk. Over the low bookcase, four Roald Dahl quotes, written on thick creamy paper in purple ink with elegant lettering, hung in thin gold frames in a row. Declan used his phone's camera to capture a shot of them.

"I think probably kindness is my number one attribute in a human being. I'll put it before any of the things like courage or bravery or generosity or anything else."

"If you have good thoughts they will shine out of your face like sunbeams and you will always look lovely."

"Kindness—that simple word. To be kind—it covers everything, to my mind. If you're kind, that's it."

"We make realities out of our dreams and dreams out of our realities.
We are the dreamers of the dream."

Bea had obviously rated kindness highly, as Claire had remarked. He studied a row of different colored and sized seashells that lined the deep windowsill and took another photo. The desk had a bare rectangle where Bea's laptop usually stood; the charging cord rested on the desktop. A thick folder held several hundred pages of manuscript, a printed final draft of Bea's book on Dahl. With extensive footnotes she'd titled it *Roald Dahl: Imagination on Fire*, with a frontispiece quote from *The BFG:* "Don't gobblefunk around with words."

Declan inspected the bookcase next, where volumes on children's literature and editing shared space with well-thumbed copies of Dahl's popular books. He took each one out and shook the pages before re-shelving. *Fantastic Mr. Fox, My Uncle Oswald, James and the Giant Peach, Charlie and the Chocolate Factory, Danny the Champion of the World*, and others all shared space with two DVDs of *Willy Wonka* (Gene Wilder and Johnny Depp as Willy); a DVD of the London version of *Matilda*; and a first edition of *The BFG*.

When he shook the latter, a note fell out with the notation: *Yours will be the definitive Dahl! XX.* The handwriting was the same ornate printing as in the framed quotes. A gift from an admirer?

He snapped a photo of the note and turned to the dresser. The top surface held a photo of Bea, her smile wide, eyes radiating happiness, one arm out of the frame as though it were around someone's waist. She wore a loose flowing dress in pale blue with an embroidered bodice that brought out the color of her eyes; she could have been a Scandinavian princess. Her other hand grasped whatever hung from a gold necklace, obscuring it. Sunlight behind her lit her pale hair; it glowed like a nimbus around her head and shoulders.

At the back of the top drawer, under a pile of panties from Victoria's Secret, he found a bundle wrapped in pink tissue paper. He opened it to find a small pink infant outfit, decorated with satin bows. A pair of handknitted booties and matching sweater with more satin ribbon threaded through them lay underneath it. He took another photo and carefully rewrapped the outfit.

Was this a gift Bea had bought to give friends once their baby was born?

That was one explanation. But Declan could think of others.

CHAPTER SIX

11:22 AM

Nora kept pace with Claire's longer stride as they walked back to Haven Cottage. She had Claire's laptop case slung over one shoulder. Claire wore a bulging backpack and carried a flowered overnighter in one hand. Bus and car traffic increased at this time of day, their fumes mixing with the crisp December air.

Nora decided her stepsister had answered enough questions for now and kept away from asking about Bea Jones as they walked. She'd been happily surprised when Declan had suggested Claire stay with them. Nora had read enough detective novels to know that the person who found the victim was automatically on the police suspect list. Claire wouldn't remain on that list for long, not if Nora had anything to say about it.

Claire looked outwardly composed, but very tired and lost in her thoughts. They dodged a tour group outside St. John's before crossing St. Giles and heading up the Woodstock Road to pass the church and reach Haven Cottage.

Nora broke their silence. "That window in your bedroom has a nice view, but no screens?"

"I know, weird to an American, right? I asked about that. My scout said they don't have many flying insects here, being an island and all, and the windows are old. I leave it cracked for air at times."

"Downright scary, if you ask me." Nora guided Claire past the graveyard on their right at St. Giles. Some of the headstones were lichen covered, so old their engraving was illegible. Sally Welch had said the church's youth group considered mounting a campaign in the coming spring to wash them. Thinking of Sally reminded Nora of Sean as they walked up the drive and approached the front door of Haven Cottage.

"I have to retrieve Sean from the creche shortly. Let me get you settled first." She let them into the house where she heard Mr. Tink whistling in the library when she opened the door. It was Sean's favorite, "Yellow Submarine." She poked her head in the doorway to find the man painting the insides of the empty bookshelves—grey.

"I'm back, Mr. Tink." She smiled brightly, wondering if she needed to wave the color card in his face.

"Right-o. Priming these shelves for that dark pink color." He dipped his brush into the can. "Need to use a grey primer for dark or bright colors." He continued whistling and Nora turned away, chastened.

"This is my sister, Claire Scott, a student at Exeter. She's spending a few days with us."

Mr. Tink looked around, tipped his hat to Claire, and resumed his whistling.

"You've accomplished so much in a short time." Claire looked around the ground floor. "I appreciate you having me here with all you have going on, Nora."

"Nonsense. Come up and stow your things, maybe have a nice hot shower."

Nora led the way to the guest room next to the nursery. She gave Claire a stack of fresh towels from a linen press standing in the hall. "Let that hot water do its trick, and I'll make us lunch when I get back with Sean." She shooed Claire into the guest bath after removing Sean's yellow ducks from the tub's rim. As she came back down the stairs, she heard the shower turn on.

Nora let herself out the front door and made a conscious decision to leave Sean's buggy behind. Sean had been kidnapped a few months ago, the worst days of her life as she waited to find if she would have him back unharmed. While she tried not to hover over him, at times she did like to enhance his closeness to her. He was toddling along well now, and there would come a day soon enough when he wouldn't want her to hold him.

She strode down the drive and over to the church, then down the stairs to its undercroft, where a few others milled around, waiting for the end of the session: mums, two dads, and several young nannies. The sounds of sweet young voices finishing "Row, Row, Row Your Boat" reached her. She stood on tiptoe to peek inside the double doors to the large space inside. The last song of the day varied and was sung by all the teachers and little ones. Babies held in arms were swayed in time to the music, while Nora saw Sally, priestly collar above her purple shirt, holding hands with her son, Sam, on one side, and with Sean on the other as they sang. When the song ended, everyone clapped, and one teacher opened the door. The older children rushed out, while Sally helped her two charges toddle to Nora.

"You sounded grand today," Nora told the boys. She stuffed Sean's arms inside his quilted jacket and zipped it up. Others around them gathered up children in coats and made their way up the stairs.

"We make music!" Sam bellowed, echoed by Sean's loud "Moos!"

"And very well-behaved boys today, Mummy." Sally's eyes twinkled from under her cap of short bouncy curls. "No biting, no hitting, lots of sharing."

"Good sharing. Well done you!" Nora lifted Sean and gave

him a kiss, then snugged him on her hip. "Quiet day for you now, Sally?"

"Is it ever quiet with an active toddler?" She tucked a curl behind one ear. "Parish committee meeting after lunch and I get this one down for a nap so Neil can keep writing. Once Sam wakes up, he's all Neil's till dinner, while I work on my sermon. What's new at yours?"

Sally's husband, Neil, was on sabbatical from his teaching position, writing a long-planned novel. He consulted Nora often about writing resources, once he'd learned his journalist neighbor had editorial experience and was the author of a popular children's book series.

Nora chose her words carefully in front of the boys as she telegraphed the accident at Exeter, adding that Claire was spending a few days with them.

"Poor woman, to witness the death of a friend. Let me know if you think she needs to talk." Sally prided herself on her pastoral counseling expertise. "Try to get her to speak of happy memories of her friend. It helps to balance the darkness."

"Good suggestion, I'll do that." Nora jiggled Sean on her lap. "Let's get you home for lunch and a lie-down. Auntie Claire is visiting."

"Tica!" Sean crowed.

"I love how he extrapolates names for people in his orbit." Sally had wrestled Sam's arms into a down vest and snapped it shut.

Nora said, "The same way he calls Auntie Val 'Tiva.'"

"Tiva!" Sean obliged, giggling.

"I'm off, but don't forget what I said about Claire." Sally pulled on a bulky cardigan. "If she needs to talk, I'm just on the other side of the hedge."

"That sounds like the title of a book." Nora followed them up the stairs and into dappled sunshine. The day had warmed; the sun shone through the trees. They waved to Sam and Sally, who disappeared into the rectory. Leaves crackled under Nora's feet as she continued down to the sidewalk and approached her drive, hugging Sean against her. She took a deep breath of his baby smell, thinking Bea would miss this lovely day and all the ones that came after. She felt sad, even if she hadn't known the young woman. She could only imagine Claire's grief.

Sean chattered a jumble of words and noises while Nora pondered hedges, an automatic response when an idea presented itself for a storyline. Her children's books revolved around a band of fairies from Cumbria's Belle Isle in the middle of England's largest lake, Windermere. Her illustrator and close friend, Simon Ramsey, had urged her to take the fairies to France, an excuse to visit there with his girlfriend to paint the landscapes that kept his bills paid. The idea for a title, "The Other Side of the Hedge" beckoned, and Nora couldn't wait to put her library to rights. Meanwhile, she'd note the title in the small notebook she carried everywhere.

"You are getting heavy, young man," she told Sean, and reluctantly put him down at the foot of their drive to meander up the gentle slope while she held his hand. His rolling gait, feet spaced widely apart for balance, made progress slow, with only a few stumbles. At the top of the rise, he suddenly sat down and reached for a handful of grass, which Nora dissuaded him from eating. They made their way to the front door, opened by Claire.

"Tica!" Sean cried, and raised his arms for Claire to pick him up, which she did.

"Hello, buddy. You have fun at nursery school?" Claire nuzzled his neck. "Little ones smell so good, don't they?"

"Usually," Nora agreed. "You should get a whiff after sweaty play in the garden with Typo and Sam." To her eye, it looked like the shower had done Claire a world of good. She'd tied her wet hair in a loose braid that hung down her back and wore clean leggings and a long Exeter tee. The idea that Claire could have had anything to do with her friend's death was absurd. Nora would be certain Declan saw that.

Nora ducked her head into the library. "Lunch, Mr. Tink?"

"No, thanks." He was making good progress on the insides of the bookshelves. "Want to get these done today to dry. Then I'm meeting Mrs. Tink for an early dinner." Mrs. Tink used to clean for Declan and had followed them to the new house.

"Tell her I said hello—and thanks." She followed Claire and Sean into the kitchen. "Go ahead and sit him in his chair, Claire." Nora pointed to the highchair at the middle of the table that had elm and rattan bistro chairs at either end. The far side held a long banquette that ran under the windows. Nora took out a bag of cut-up veggies from the fridge and put a few on Sean's tray, while Claire fastened a bib around his neck. "Now I can let the dog in." Typo had been leaping at the back door since he saw Sean. Nora took a dog biscuit from a jar on the counter and opened the door. The puppy ran straight to Sean's chair and stood up against a leg of it to be petted. Nora handed Sean the biscuit. "What do you say?"

"Si-typo," Sean proclaimed. The dog promptly sat, quivering for his treat. Sean leaned over and the dog carefully snatched it from his hand, and sat under the high chair, chomping away while Sean giggled.

"That's hilarious." Claire's smile, the first of the day, was genuine. "What can I do to help?"

Nora pointed to the fridge. "There's leftover quiche we can have. If you'd stick it in the oven for a few minutes, please." She took two plates off the Welsh dresser and added cutlery and glasses.

"Which oven?" Claire held the foil-covered dish and looked at the three doors in the forest green Aga in confusion. "And there are no knobs."

"The lower right is the baking oven." Nora set a timer. "I had to watch a tutorial on YouTube to learn how to use this properly, but I love it. An Aga is always on, with different temps for the ovens. And those large hobs on top with the closed lids? One's a boiling plate and one's a simmering plate. You regulate the temp by how much of the bottom of the pot is in contact. When you see the tops standing open on an episode of *Midsomer Murders*, you know the stove isn't really on." She became aware she was blathering in her effort to distract her sister, and put ice in their glasses, then pulled out a sippy cup for Sean's juice. "Water or juice?"

"Water, and I'll fill them."

Nora screwed the cap on Sean's cup and put it on his tray, then added small pieces of turkey and apple. Sean started to feed himself with his fingers, stopping to take a drink from his cup.

"Jooz," he said.

"Yes, lovey, juice." Nora cut up a lemon for their water and sat down; Claire sat at the other end. They sipped their water for a moment. All was still. "Blessed quiet."

"Between Sean, Typo, and this new house, when you do get your writing done?" Claire squeezed lemon into her glass.

"Mornings, if he's at creche, and most afternoons when he sleeps. There's marketing and emails to answer that take almost as long as the actual writing, plus I still do freelance assignments for *People and Places*. I always have a notebook with me when we walk to the shops for jotting down ideas, too. That reminds me." She rummaged through her backpack and withdrew a small Moleskine book, where she wrote the title she didn't want to forget on a fresh page. The timer dinged. Nora used a mitt to put the warm quiche on a trivet that contained a scene from the Minack Theatre in Cornwall. "Help yourself. And don't tell me you're not hungry."

"I'm famished." Claire helped herself to a wedge, then stared at it on her plate. "It feels almost disrespectful to eat."

Nora looked straight at Claire. "It's okay to be hungry, Claire."

"I suppose. Sorry I couldn't control my crying earlier. It was such a shock." She looked down at her plate. "It feels wrong to be feeling hungry, or something at all, when Bea won't ever feel anything again."

"I know." Nora remembered Sally's advice. "Eat up and tell me how you met Bea."

Claire forked in a mouthful and chewed. This time she was able to talk about her friend without crying. "We met the first day of my classes when she showed me how to get around. We shared the same tutor, but it was our love of literature and reading that bound us." She cast her eyes back in remembrance. "Bea's pale hair matched her sunny manner. She was thoughtful and humane, too, loved children and animals." Claire shook her head. "I'm making her sound saint-like. She could be fun, too, and was into music, but her work always came first."

"She sounds lovely." Nora ate and glanced at Sean. He pushed food into his mouth and around the tray, and she pretended not to notice him hand Typo a carrot.

"She was so very smart," Claire continued. "Roald Dahl was her idol for his imagination, and her master's was a biography that detailed his work. She believed, as Dahl did, that children's literature framed the world for little ones, and had a much bigger influence on them than most people recognize. Her thesis was good enough to be published as a mainstream book, Dr. Hamilton said." She shook her head. "She was over the moon when he told her that."

"He's your supervising tutor?"

Claire nodded. "He's the one who came back from a morning run just as I found Bea's body. He was so upset. He saw Bea's potential and was so proud of her." Claire put her fork down. "But here's the thing, Nora. I've been thinking about this on the way here, and in the shower. There are only two ways this accident could have happened."

Nora gave Claire her attention. "I'm listening." Was Claire going to clear herself? Then Nora realized if Nicola Morton saw Claire come out of her room, the woman's statement this afternoon should do just that. Nora relaxed.

Claire sat up straighter. "Bea could have slipped and fallen, I suppose, but I don't see how she'd end up all the way down with the turns in the stairs. Or she could have been pushed over the railing. I know for certain she wouldn't have jumped. Last week she said to me, 'I'm just on the brink,' and when I asked of what, she said, 'Of everything.'"

Nora pondered Claire's statement. "What did you think she meant by that?"

Claire sighed. "I don't know; she wouldn't elaborate. She said

I'd find out shortly. I have no idea what secret she was keeping, but I know one thing for certain." Claire leaned forward. "You have to help me, Nora."

Nora bit her lip. Did this mean Claire realized she was a suspect?

But Claire continued with her thought. "This secret meant too much to Bea. I can't let her down. I already told Declan she would never have jumped. We have to find out what actually happened."

CHAPTER SEVEN

Oxford

Noon

Declan drove them in his classic MGB toward the John Radcliffe's morgue to meet with the father and brother of Beatrice Jones. The restored car was his guilty pleasure and he enjoyed driving it, despite the engine noise. Watkins held on for dear life as Declan took the corners.

"How come you didn't have to get rid of this beauty when you and Nora got together?" Watkins scanned the narrow space behind their seats. "You can't fit a nappy bag much less a car seat on that back ledge."

Declan glanced over at his sergeant. They'd worked together for years and developed an easygoing friendship. He trusted the man's abilities and intuition more and more as time passed, which made Watkins' nervousness over becoming a father that much more surprising. "The key is two vehicles, one bigger. We use Nora's Volvo estate if we go out with Sean."

"Oh."

"Julie pushing for a bigger vehicle?"

"Says we need a 'family car' now, whatever that is, and her Fiat won't work for long. I told her there were no Range Rovers in the future of a lowly detective sergeant."

Declan knew Watkins's red Vauxhall Corsa was the closest he'd come to a sporty vehicle and figured his sergeant didn't want it to be replaced. "There are plenty of other cars around that have room for baby equipment. Her Fiat will work while you look around for a trade-in." They'd had this discussion once before. Something else was bothering his colleague, and then he twigged. "Julie still insisting on those fancy names you hate?"

Watkins groaned. "Peregrine for a boy. Can you imagine? He'll be bullied from day one." Watkins insisted their baby was a boy and lived in abject fear of a little girl. Julie had refused to learn the sex of the baby, wanting to be surprised.

Declan kept his eyes on the road. Laughter would not be appreciated. "You could call him Perry."

"And what if, God forbid, it's a girl? Then she wants to use her maiden name, Beasley. What the hell do I call that when it's at home?" He shook his head. "After this case, not Bea, that's for sure."

Declan negotiated a turn smoothly. "Let's hope once labor is over, Julie has a change of mind."

Watkins harrumphed and waved the subject away. "McAfee texted to say the student across the hall from Nora's sister, Nicola Morton, called to set up a time for her statement this afternoon. She's gone to stay with friends for the weekend and left her number. I'll call her in when we get back."

"Good. You do that one, please. When Patti Phillips and Jack Soong from upstairs come in, we'll let McAfee handle those. You do Claire Scott."

"Sure. Have to treat her same as everyone else. I took their contact info before they scattered. None of them knew much, if they're to be believed." He shifted in his seat. "Must be tough having Claire as a suspect for Nora. How's that going?"

"Been around me long enough to understand, or so she says. Hasn't been awkward so far, but it would be nice to have Morton confirm she saw Claire leave her room."

"I'll make a point to pin her down."

"They all lived in close proximity to Bea Jones. They may know more than they think." Declan liked to use his victim's name when he could. The term 'victim' always struck him as too impersonal, and by using names, they became more real to him and his team, and, therefore, became more important. He wished he knew more if this fall could be an accident. Claire had seemed so certain Bea Jones wouldn't have committed suicide. He hoped Charlie had some ideas.

He pulled the MGB up to the mortuary of the John Radcliffe, or the JR as it was often called. The autumn sun glinted off the British racing green exterior as he parked and locked it. When the detectives entered the waiting room, Watkins rang a bell and a morgue attendant soon appeared.

"Dr. Borden wants to see you both before the family arrives." He ushered the men in, past the viewing room and several autopsy suites, where Declan could see two other pathologists at work, one a woman. He'd always wondered what would draw a doctor to choose pathology, and asked Charlie once. His reply had been, "I want to find the story they can tell us when they can't speak any longer."

Charlie's small office always had the odor of microwaved popcorn, his favorite snack, and was crowded with cabinets and towering stacks of files, despite being computerized. The man waved them inside, then clicked off on a report and hit "send" before he stood and gave them his full attention.

"Declan and Watkins, my two favorite detectives. How goes the baby incubation?" He peered at Watkins over his glasses, his bushy eyebrows raised.

"Waiting game." Watkins stood nearer the desk and lowered

his voice. "She gets these contractions where her uterus goes hard like a basketball and cramps up, but she insists it's not labor."

"Braxton Hicks, my boy. The body in rehearsal for the main event." Charlie slapped the sergeant on the back. "Any day, I expect. No turning back now."

Watkins nodded miserably.

"Two things, gentlemen. I've put Miss Jones on the schedule for nine tomorrow, so I'll see you then. Giving up my Saturday lie-in for you, Dec, and I hope you know I mean to collect down the road on that." Charlie sat on the corner of his desk, his scrub top tightening across his belly. "I took a cursory glance at her body when she was being prepared for the identification visit. There's a thin line of bruising around the back of her neck that wasn't apparent in situ, as I arrived so close to the time of death." He gestured to the nape of his neck.

Declan frowned. "Only at the back of the neck?"

"Yes, so not an attempt at strangulation, or it would have been around the entire circumference. No petechiae, either. This is the kind of mark that would appear when something was jerked hard against the skin, abrading it. Like the chain from a necklace, not that forensics found one on the floor or stairs. I'll have photos tomorrow. If you find something later on, you can enlarge them for the pattern."

Declan remembered the photo in Bea's room, her hand clasped at her neck. "We'll ask her family about it."

A bell rang in Charlie's office. "That'll be them now. Don't envy you chaps your job. See you tomorrow. And you owe me a pint, Declan."

After years working together, Declan knew he would initially talk to the family while Watkins would jot down information, then add his own questions.

Through the door's window, Declan read acute anxiety in the two men's faces before they noticed him. The older must be the father, Dr. Ernest Jones, dressed in slacks and a button-down shirt, open at the collar. He ran a hand through thinning fair hair as he paced the small area. His son, Benedick, stood a few inches taller with his hands stuffed in his chino's pockets. Bea's twin had dark reddish hair, but his face was a masculine version of hers. He stared out the window and rolled his shoulders, turning when he heard the door open. Declan was surprised to see his orange tee shirt had Gothic lettering across the front that looked like a Bible inscription, but on closer inspection read: "On the eighth day God created bacon."

Declan did the introductions. "We need to ask a few preliminary questions today; the rest can wait until tomorrow. I'll ask you to sign a permission for us to access your daughter's phone and laptop before you leave. Would you prefer to make the formal ID first or after?"

Benedick Jones turned a sickly pale color and deferred to his father. Dr. Jones answered. "Please, call us Ben and Ernest. From what I understand, there's little doubt this is our Bea, and this process is a legal formality."

"I'm very sorry," Declan said, "but that's true, Ernest." By acknowledging and accepting the man's request, he hoped to reassure both men that he had Beatrice's interests at heart.

"Then let's get that over with and you can ask your questions after. I want to see my daughter."

"Certainly." Declan opened the door. The four filed into a room with muted lighting. He gestured for them to stand before a curtained window and hit a buzzer.

CHAPTER SEVEN

Low classical music piped into the room made Ernest look up at the speaker. He nodded in approval. "Handel's 'Water Music.'" He drew in a deep breath as if to gather his strength, and nodded to Declan. Ben moved closer to his father.

Declan pulled a cord on the left side of the window; the curtains parted smoothly. On the other side of the glass, in a circular room, Beatrice Jones lay on a stretcher next to the window. She was covered neatly up to her neck with crisp white sheets; her fair hair had been brushed and fanned out across the pillow. Her face and lips were pale; otherwise, she might have been sleeping. A morgue attendant stood silently next to her body as if guarding it.

Declan watched the two men. Ernest stared at his daughter, his face white with tension. Ben focused first on the cream walls and terracotta ring of indirect lighting that ran around the room near the ceiling. The room was set up as a nondenominational chapel, with a basic altar holding a vase of flowers. Ben inhaled as he geared himself to look, then dropped his gaze to his sister.

Ben's eyes welled up instantly, and he put a hand up on the glass. "Bea ..."

Ernest put his arm around his son. "Yes, that's my daughter, Beatrice." He looked at Declan. "When can we take her home?"

"Let's sit down and we'll talk about that." Declan guided the men back to the outer room, where a tray of tea and water awaited them. They took their seats.

Ernest's face had gone whiter. Ben helped his father to a chair and sat next to him, hastily wiping his tears with the back of his hand, his concern for his father evident.

"We're very sorry for your loss. We'll do everything we can to establish what happened today." Declan pointed to the tea. "The teas have sugar; it helps with the shock."

Ernest nodded and sipped the tea.

Ben reached for a tea, gulped half down. He sat back in his chair. "I don't know how you do this on a regular basis. Makes me question if I'm in the right profession in seminary."

"Some days I don't know how we do it either, Ben." Declan's honesty appeared to help the young man, who nodded curtly. "We try to think of families like you, who need our help."

Ben's lip quivered. Declan explained about the necessity for a coroner's inquest before Bea's body could be released for a funeral, and that she might be held longer if there was a prolonged investigation.

Ernest placed his cup back on the tray. "We need to call your mother, Ben."

"She can wait, Dad."

Declan caught the hint of annoyance in the young man's tone and had to agree. As difficult as this process was, it was something close family members often chose to do together. There was apparently a mother in the picture. Why hadn't she come with them?

Declan twisted the cap off a bottle of water and drank to give the men time to compose themselves. Watkins drew out his notebook. "Do you feel up to answering a few questions?" Once Ernest nodded, Ben did, too. Declan decided to start where he'd seen the annoyance flash. "Where is Mrs. Jones, if I might ask?"

Ben answered. "She uses Smythe-Jones with a Y and an E. Mother lives in a world of her own creation, inspector. She's self-centered, and at times she's clueless."

Ernest grimaced. "My wife has a history of depression and has learned to protect herself. She couldn't accept that Bea could be gone and chose to think this might be a case of mistaken identity. She stayed in Cambridge, and I am choosing to believe she's in denial."

Declan thought that was an interesting way to phrase it and wondered if the man's marriage was in trouble.

Ben stared at him. "She let us come down here alone, Dad. She always puts herself first."

"People handle things differently, Benedick. You of all people should be learning that." Ernest touched his son's knee.

Ben leaned into his father briefly. "Bea got her kindness from you."

"I understand you're in seminary at Ridley Hall?" Declan asked Ben.

"For my sins." A ghost of a smile flitted over his face. "Second of three years. Dad's right; I should be more magnanimous. It's difficult after seeing Bea in there."

"Your sister looked up to you, and you feel you've let her down."

Ben's eyes grew wide. "How did you—?"

"As I said, I've been doing this a long time." Declan directed his next question to the father. "What can you tell me about your daughter and her routine? I understand the author Roald Dahl was her area of interest?"

Ernest's face became animated. "Her tutor said her thesis on Dahl could be published as a mainstream biography. She explored how losing a young sister to appendicitis when he was only three, and then his father just a month later to pneumonia, affected his life and his writings. She even addressed his controversial anti-Semitic comments, didn't give him a pass. It all gave great texture and background to the writer he became." He looked down at his hands. "Bea was on her way to great things, degree in hand soon."

Declan waited a respectful beat, then asked, "Did Bea usually wear a necklace or chain?"

"She had a gold chain with a charm she never took off."

Ben shifted in his seat and frowned. "Is it missing? Could it have come off when she fell?"

"The chain was long enough to rest inside her blouse. I thought it was a cross and she was being discreet." Ernest smiled. "When I saw her in October, I asked her what was so special, and she took it out and showed me. 'It's my heart, Dad,' she said, and it was, a gold heart with a small amethyst in the center. She wouldn't say more about it." He shook his head. "I have no idea where she got it."

"It wasn't with her when we found her," Declan explained. "There's physical evidence it might have been torn off."

Ernest winced. "I don't know where it could be." He met Declan's eyes. "Can you tell us how this terrible accident happened?"

Declan blew out a breath. How to answer? "That's one of the questions we hope the post mortem will help us answer." He watched Ernest shut his eyes at the thought of his daughter being carved up. Ben started to whimper and cleared his throat noisily. "I assure you I personally know the doctor performing Bea's autopsy. He considers this a type of surgery that will give us clues to her death. She'll be treated with the utmost respect."

"I don't understand. There's no question of Bea throwing herself down those stairs." Ben stood. "She had everything to live for!" He turned away abruptly and walked to the window.

"If what you say is accurate, then I need to learn about Bea. Can you think of anyone who might have wanted to harm her?

Or had a grudge against her?"

"Harm?" Ernest leaned forward. "What exactly are you telling me, inspector?"

"Nothing I have clear answers for, sir. I promise you, as soon as we have more information, I will share what I know with you and your family."

"Certainly. We want to be kept informed." Mollified, Ernest sat back and Ben took his place next to his father. "No, I can't think of anyone, not one person who would have wanted to harm our Bea." He looked to Ben. "Can you?"

Ben shifted in his seat. "No one at all." His firm answer belied his uncomfortable bearing.

There was something here that Declan would need to return to at a later date. He moved on. "Her classmates mentioned Bea had a weekend job."

"You mean at the Radcliffe Camera?" Ernest asked.

Declan was confused. "Radcliffe Camera? I was under the impression Bea went home to Cambridge every weekend to be a nanny to a family near you."

The shock in Ernest's face was not mirrored in Ben's. Declan would definitely need to get the young man alone at some point, or have Watkins call him when he was back at Ridley Hall. He was hiding something about his twin sister. Whether it had bearing on her death was another matter.

"A nanny? Who told you that? Bea hasn't been home much since she returned from her spring and summer project in Wales." Ernest closed his eyes briefly. "She's been working as a research assistant for undergrads needing extra help this term."

Declan was at a loss. Claire appeared to be certain about Bea's nanny job. He would have that question asked and corroborated—or not—by Jack Soong, Patti Phillips, and Nicola Morton in their afternoon statements.

Claire's information came directly from Bea Jones, yet her family had been told a completely different story.

Who had Bea Jones lied to, and more importantly, why?

CHAPTER EIGHT

1:20 PM

When Nora saw Sean's eyelids start to flicker, she knew it was nap time and brought him upstairs where she changed his diaper. The nursery was done in a soft blue-green called "Skylight" even Mr. Tink approved of; Sean's godmother, Val, had painted a mural on one wall with rabbits, dogs, chipmunks, and deer cavorting in a forest. An owl winked from an upper branch where bluebirds nested. The older and taller Sean grew, the more creatures he would discover.

Nora tilted the blind to soften the light, wound Sean's musical mobile, and gave him his favorite stuffed bunny. She crept away to the tinkling sounds of snippets of classical themes mixed with nursery rhymes. When she came back to the kitchen, Claire had cleared their lunch away. As she shut the dishwasher door, Nora saw the circles under Claire's eyes had deepened. The young woman's exhaustion had caught up with her.

"Have a lie down, Claire. Sean usually sleeps for 90 minutes or so. When he wakes, we'll walk to St. Aldate's and you can give your formal statement."

Claire agreed and followed Nora upstairs, where Claire paused on the threshold to the guest room. "Thanks for everything, Nora." She closed the door quietly behind her.

Nora checked on Sean, who slept on his back with Peter Rabbit clamped under one arm, mouth working an imaginary bottle in the soft light. His mobile had tapered off, and from the guest room came the staccato beat of Billie Eilish's "Bury A Friend."

Satisfied her charges were stable for the moment, Nora checked on Mr. Tink's progress in the library. Typo napped under the painter's ladder, which stood open. The man stood near the top, stirring the color for the ceiling. Thankfully, this side room had lower ceilings than the rest of the house. She saw he'd finished the primer on the bookshelves.

"You're working quickly today." Nora tried to picture the grey areas painted in the cheerful cranberry she'd chosen. The bookcases looked drab and she hoped she wasn't making a huge mistake. Then she thought of Bea Jones, and of Claire's distress, to say nothing of the young woman's family coping with her loss, and decided paint was a very minor thing that could always be fixed.

"They went fast once I started. Having the closed cabinets on the bottom meant I didn't have to get down on my knees." Tink loaded his brush and drew it across the boards between the dark beams that ran across the ceiling. "Thought I'd start here by the window so you could see this color in the bright light."

Nora waited for him to do a few strokes, then peered up to scrutinize the boards. "What do you think?"

Tink nodded. "I like it. White with a skosh of blue. Still no idea why it's called 'Blackened.' Keep going?"

"Is 'skosh' a painter's word?" Nora teased. "Yes, keep on. I'll take this guy out of your hair." She patted her leg as she called the dog to her. "Typo, come."

The beagle picked up his head and trotted after Nora into the kitchen, where she chose several balls from a basket, then took him into the yard. Ten minutes of training practice for "stay" and "come," then a few more trying to learn to "fetch," running after a thrown ball, soon had the puppy panting. She gave him a cool drink and brought him over to the corner of the yard she was trying to cultivate as his business patch. Her phone rang.

She was happy to hear Simon Ramsey's voice. Early on in their relationship, she'd thought herself in love with her illustrator, soon after the untimely death of her fiancé when Nora was newly pregnant with Sean. They'd since settled into a loving friendship that endured through her meeting Declan, Simon's sister Kate's marriage to a Cumbrian detective, and several cases together at Ramsey Lodge, the inn he and Kate ran in Bowness-on-Windermere.

"Simon! So good to hear from you. I owe Kate a call to see how she's feeling."

"Just starting to show. Odd to think my sister will be a mum in the spring. You should see Ian rushing to do things for her. You'd think she had a disease. How's Sean?"

Nora laughed. "At least Ian's being helpful. Sean is growing and chattering away like a little monkey. How's the renovation going?" Simon and Kate had flipped their personal quarters so Kate could use the small nursery that had been Sean's for most of his first year.

"They're settled in, and right now I'm having skylights put in the barn I'll use for a studio. Maeve is redecorating our other rooms and having fun with that. She said to tell you she scored some Nina Campbell wallpaper for our bedroom that you'd like. How's the house on your end?"

Nora was happy to see she had no jealous feelings left for the slender Maeve. She watched Typo throw himself down in a patch of sunlit lawn. "Tell her that's quite a coup. We're almost done, last room being painted. Listen, glad you called. I had an idea for the next book with the title 'The Other Side of the Hedge.' What do you think?"

"If said hedge is in Provence, I'm delighted."

"Thought you'd say that. Send me those photos you took when you were in Aix-en-Provence last time, and I'll start work on a storyline as soon as the holidays are over."

"If I know you, you won't be able to wait that long."

They chatted for a few more minutes, and Nora explained about Claire's brief stay due to Declan's new case.

"I liked her when we met in Cornwall." Simon's crew had met Claire at Sean's birthday party. "We're all still talking about that extravaganza the Pembrokes threw for Sean, plus putting us all up for the weekend. Expected the bouncy castle, but the pony rides were over the top."

"Harry and Muriel are very generous," Nora agreed. "Simon, I'm worried about Claire. She has to be on Declan's suspect list for now because she found her friend."

"You mean you're already working the case too, right?" Simon's warm laugh came down the line. "I know you too well, Nora. You'll be tracing the poor girl's nearest and dearest before the week's out. Declan and Ian both say the more they learn about the victim, the more they learn who would have had a reason to end their life, if this turns out to be murder. Please give Claire my best and my sympathies for losing her friend."

"I will, Simon. And I think you've just given me a place to start to help her. Talk soon."

She clicked her phone off and left Typo lying in the yard in a pool of light. Simon had given her an idea she needed to follow up on while Sean and Claire napped.

In the kitchen, Nora moved her laptop from her makeshift office at one end of the long dining table over to the kitchen table. Simon had given her a concrete place to start.

Forty minutes later, Nora finished her notes and tapped her pen on her notebook. Simon was correct that trying to learn about Claire's friend was the logical place to start, but Beatrice Jones had one of the smallest social media footprints Nora had seen for someone in her mid-20s. Her Facebook page hadn't been updated in over a year; she'd stopped tweeting around the same time. She'd closed out her Instagram account, too, and didn't use Snapchat or have pages on any other sites Nora checked.

Old-fashioned Googling didn't go much further for new details. Oxford's Exeter graduate program page showed Bea as their student, on their list of expected Michaelmas graduates with an MA in English Literature. Her undergraduate work, where she'd also read English, had been at Downing College in Cambridge, where she'd graduated with honors.

Nora sat back. Interesting that Bea had been at Cambridge as an undergrad but moved to Oxford for her master's, and that she hadn't attended Christ's when she was an undergrad, despite her father being a don there. Was there something more about it, or did Exeter simply offer the kind of program that would allow her to specialize in Roald Dahl?

A Google page from years earlier that contained her name noted Bea's father, Dr. Ernest Jones, had been named Director of Choral and Organ Music at Christ's College, Cambridge. The college newspaper mentioned the twin siblings, Benedick and Beatrice, with a coy reference to *Much Ado About Nothing* and their mother, Margaret Smythe-Jones's apparent love of Shakespeare. The accompanying color photograph showed the twins as young teens, flanking their parents outside the chapel at Christ's. Bea had her father's blond coloring; Ben had his mother's auburn hair. Margaret's hat was so large the brim dwarfed her face, and her husband had to stand a foot away.

For a young woman to drop out of social media was certainly unusual. That age group carried their phones as if they were glued to their wrists, even if Bea had been that rare gal who was not heavily into social media. Nora made a note to ask Declan if Bea's phone had been recovered. When he came home, she would bring up what she'd found. She started one of her famous lists in the slim notebook she carried everywhere.

What could have happened that would have made Bea Jones decide to almost entirely eliminate her social media presence?

CHAPTER NINE

1:43 PM

After setting up an appointment to see Ernest and Margaret tomorrow after the autopsy, Declan and Watkins shook hands with the two men and watched them leave to make their way back to Cambridge. Declan insisted he and Watkins gulp down a hasty lunch before they headed back to their office at St. Aldate's Station. Over shepherd's pie and chips at the Old Tom pub, he brought up the discrepancy between what Bea Jones had told Claire and what she'd told her family about where she spent her days off.

"I'll check that with Claire and Nicola Morton when they come in for their statements," Watkins said. "And we'll ask if Bea Jones had a boyfriend or partner."

"Make certain McAfee knows to ask Soong and Phillips as well. And when you do Morton, clarify that she saw Claire leave her room. I want to remove her as soon as possible from the suspect list."

"For Nora's sake or yours?" Watkins said with a smile.

"Both." Declan pushed his empty plate away. "Interesting that the father, daughter, and son all use 'Jones' as a surname, while the mother hyphenates hers."

"Pathetic, more like it. Putting on airs, my mum would say."

He made a noncommittal noise. His sergeant's feelings about others in positions of wealth or power were well known to Declan. Watkins would never be seen reading gossip of the royal family, although he did have a fondness for the queen, whom he thought remarkably dedicated to have stayed in her job so long.

Back at the station, the detectives noted that the three undergrad students waited in the reception area to give their statements. A brief meeting with other members of their team brought everyone up to date on the death and the family interview. Declan took a question from Douglas McAfee, their junior detective.

"We're leaving it suspicious until after tomorrow's post?"

Declan nodded. "We should have more information then. However, after seeing the stairwell angles, and considering the idea that a necklace might have been torn roughly from this young woman's neck, I'm leaning toward a deliberate act and so is Dr. Borden. If the inquest supports it, we'll be full-on. I'd rather have us starting to look at things that way so we're not playing catch-up and allowing important evidence to escape us."

He explained the family would decide if they wanted a family liaison officer, who would be assigned by Cambridge police, and asked several others on the team to start background checks on the list of names he put on the whiteboard at the front of the room.

"McAfee, I'd like you to take statements from two undergrads, Patti Phillips and Jack Soong. Make certain you clarify what they know about Bea's weekend job, and ask if she had a boyfriend. Watkins, you'll handle Claire Scott when she comes in, and in the meantime, start with Nicola Morton."

The briefing broke up as a young uniformed constable appeared in the doorway and motioned to Declan.

"Sir. The super wants to see you."

"Curtains, boss." Watkins broke out in a huge grin. "I'll start my statements while you get the chop. I can see that Range Rover in my future yet."

"Happy to be the one to put you in a good mood, Watkins. Anything for a friend."

Declan didn't worry about seeing Superintendent Morris. They had a decent working relationship, improved these last months with Declan's immediate superior out on leave after a heart attack. He had a feeling he knew what this was about.

"Go right in." Morris's secretary, Catherine, known as Cat, kept the office running smoothly, dressed well, and refused the many offers of dinner and drinks she'd had at the station. Her air of mystery made her even more attractive. She gave Declan a quick smile and brought her concentration back to her computer screen, fingers flying over the keys.

Declan had no doubt Cat knew what this meeting was about. He just hoped she wasn't typing another memo on further budget cuts to his already bare-bones team. "Thanks, Cat." He knocked once and opened the door.

"Barnes, come in. Shut the door behind you, please." Paul Morris put aside the sheaf of papers he'd been reading. His erect bearing spoke to early years in the military, before joining the police and rising to the rank of superintendent. He had an easy smile, and with his full head of white hair, uniform jacket off and shirtsleeves rolled up, Morris looked like a policeman who kept his fingers on his team's pulse. "I brought us coffees from the canteen. Let's sit over there." He gestured toward a couch with chairs arranged around a low coffee table that held a plate of shortbread cookies, as well as two large mugs of steaming coffee.

"Thank you." Declan took one of the chairs. This was serious if it included coffee and biscuits.

Morris took the other chair and adjusted the crease in his

uniform pants. "I hear you have a new case on. Suspicious death at Exeter?"

Declan explained about the turning stairwell and Charlie Borden's feeling supported by physical evidence that a necklace had been torn from the victim's neck shortly before her fall. "Father and son made the formal ID; Charlie agreed to come in tomorrow and do the post."

"Good of him to come in on a Saturday. And you and Watkins will be attending?" At Declan's nod, he continued. "McAfee is coming along nicely, but he's too new to handle this one."

"I agree. I do want to mention that one of the first witnesses on the scene is Nora's stepsister, also a student at Exeter, who knew the victim." Best to be upfront in case it came out later and he'd not mentioned it.

Morris waved him off. "TIE and keep going." Morris referred to trace, interview and eliminate, which applied to actions for witnesses and suspects. "I can't see that as a conflict of interest, unless foul play is determined and you find evidence that makes the sister a suspect."

"I haven't seen anything to indicate Claire Scott was involved, but I'll keep an open mind."

"As you should." Morris sugared his coffee and took a sip. "Keep everything well in hand and well documented, as you always do."

Declan felt relieved. He didn't want to be taken off this case for a conflict of interest. The idea of Claire being a real suspect felt unlikely. Yet Declan had caught his superior's undertone. "Am I missing something, sir?"

"I had a call from the deputy chief constable. Apparently, the victim's mother, a Margaret Smythe-Jones, is a distant cousin. She's called him to insist, and I quote, 'That we pull our finger out and discover exactly what happened to her daughter.' I didn't have to assure him we were on top of things—he knows our record—and once I told him you were SIO on the case, he felt better."

"Thank you, sir." The DCC knew his name? Declan couldn't resist adding, "Did the mother mention that she refused to believe her daughter was dead? The twin brother and husband drove down to give the formal ID. The husband said his wife has a history of depression and was in denial."

"Perhaps, but I'm quite certain she didn't tell her cousin of her actions, reasonable or not."

Morris dunked a cookie, while Declan, still full after his late lunch, took a sip of what must be his fourth coffee of the day. Was that it for the meeting?

The super took a large gulp from his mug. "Better. Now on to the two reasons I asked to see you." He took another bracing slug and put the mug back on the tray. "I'll get right to the point. John Reid has handed in his resignation. His heart's mended well, but his wife has convinced him it's time to call it a day, to see the heart attack as a wake-up call of sorts. Their daughter in New Zealand is expecting twins, and they want to move there to help out."

This was what Declan had anticipated. Yet now the moment was here, he still didn't know how he felt about it.

Morris continued. "I'd like you to consider taking on the role of detective chief inspector. You have an excellent clear rate, you lead your team well, and the staff respects you. Plus, I feel I can work well with you. There shouldn't be any difficulty getting you past the board review."

Declan felt his ears grow warm and cleared his throat. "Thank you very much." This would be a huge promotion. The problem was, did he want it?

"It means a different routine for you, in some respects, but then I don't picture you as one who stays behind the desk all day, although there are increased reports and conferences involved."

Declan replaced his mug before he spilled it. "May I have a few days to consider it?" He needed to talk with Nora and go over the details, as well as to examine his own thoughts.

"Of course. You can check the salary bump online. I know it comes with an extra week's holiday time. Then, too, that would leave your current DI position open."

Declan didn't hesitate. "Trevor Watkins is my recommendation, if I do decide to move up and have any say in the matter. He passed his inspector's exam with high marks and covers me now when I'm on leave."

"Good man, Watkins. That would allow the two of you to continue working together. He'd be a good mentor to young McAfee, too. Perhaps if you agree, we can allow you both to act up to your new positions while we wait for the formal board to convene."

Declan knew that "acting up" meant he and Watkins could perform their new roles with "acting" before their titles. When they did come before the review board, they'd have clear examples and cases to demonstrate their abilities. "Absolutely, sir. And thank you for the offer. I'll have an answer for you Monday."

"Fine. Now on to the second issue." Morris consulted his watch. "I hate to dump this on your plate, but when I made this determination, I didn't know your new case was suspicious. The other team is involved in stakeouts with that drug ring around the clock." He steepled his fingers. "Cast your mind back to 1992. Does the name Donnie Walsh mean anything to you?"

Declan did a quick memory search, then shook his head. "Sounds familiar, but I was fourteen then."

"And probably not greatly interested in the nightly news. In that year in Cumbria, 13-month-old Donnie Walsh was kidnapped from his playpen in the garden of a pub, just outside Bowness-on-Windermere."

Declan pursed his lips. "Now that you say that, I remember my parents talking about it. I don't remember details."

"You will, soon enough. I've asked Cumbria to send us copies of the file." Morris shifted in his seat.

Declan raised an eyebrow. Surely this was for the Cold Cases Unit?

Morris continued. "A young man walked in here this morning claiming to be Donnie Walsh."

Declan gave a low whistle. "Why does he think that?"

"He's the right age, 20s, and found documentation after his mother died that led him to suspect he's Walsh. I had McAfee tell him to return around three this afternoon with everything he'd found. I know you have this new case, but I'd like your team to look into it."

"A bit of juggling goes with the territory, sir. It might be the sort of thing for McAfee to look into."

"Good man. I hoped you'd see it that way." Morris stood, indicating their time together had ended. They walked out of the office and Morris told Cat he'd return shortly. The super accompanied Declan down the stairway and they stopped in the hall just before the main desk. "I'd like you to take this position,

Declan, but I'll understand if you don't. In any case, my door is always open to you." He put out his hand.

Declan shook his hand firmly. "I'll give it careful consideration, sir, I promise."

The two men parted. Then Morris called out, "There's just one small thing, Declan."

Declan turned back. "Sir?"

"It's time you called me Paul."

CHAPTER TEN

1:50 PM

While Declan had his interview with the super, Watkins checked for messages that had come in during the briefing. There was one from Julie marked NOT URGENT.

His finger hovered over the button. He knew she'd have called him directly if her water broke, but his stomach still knotted in anticipation. He decided after he called her, he would clear his in-tray, do the interviews to get the statements of Nicola Morton and Claire Scott, and head home at a reasonable hour. They wouldn't have too many more nights alone before their lives would change forever.

While he dialed Julie, he thought about the young woman he'd talked to at Exeter, Nicola Morton. Her intricate braids must have taken hours to complete. How did she reach the back of her head? In the unlikely event his child was a daughter, would he be expected to create such elaborate hairdos? And how did she get those beads on the ends? He hoped hairstyles would be Julie's provenance and he didn't care one jot if he looked sexist on that score.

"No, my water hasn't broken." Julie's voice held a smile when she answered the phone.

"You said not urgent. How are you feeling?" Watkins pictured her gamine face with its bit of bloat these days. He couldn't believe how casually Julie handled the idea that she would soon bring a new life into the world. He'd be bloody scared. Even if he wasn't the one facing labor, the thought made him queasy.

"I'm all right, but it will be a relief to see my feet again. Listen, would you bring home a Chinese takeaway tonight?"

"Course. Too tired to cook?"

"One of the websites says Chinese is often good for starting labor."

"All right." Watkins knew if he looked like a stuffed kangaroo, he'd do anything to bring labor on and get back to normal, too. "Do you know how to braid?" Julie wore her curly hair cut to her chin, and he'd never seen her do more than pull it off her face with clips or a headband.

If Julie was surprised by the abrupt change of topic, she hid it well. "Trevor, my hair's not long enough now, but I braided it all through school when it was long." She giggled. "Thinking of growing a ponytail? Only I doubt Declan or your super will appreciate the look."

"Very funny. There's a witness I have to interview next who has these involved braids with beads on the end. On the off chance we have a girl, one of us should know how to braid, that's all." There was a long silence at the other end of the phone. Then he heard a peal of throaty glee.

"Trevor, will you give it up? You'll be a fine dad to a boy or a girl. The braids you're talking about are usually done by someone else, too hard to do yourself. Remember when my sister went to the Canary Islands and came back with hers done up that way?" Julie caught her breath between bouts of laughter. "We have years before we need to worry about hairstyles."

"Easy for you to laugh. You're the one didn't want to know the sex."

"Laughter is all I'm good for right now. Big as an elephant, can't reach to shave my legs or paint my toenails, tired and cranky. I don't know how you put up with me." She sighed.

Watkins rushed to forestall tears, aware of Julie's sudden mood swings. "Now, let's not get your hormones in a bother. You're beautiful to me in any shape when you're carrying our child."

"Even big as a house?"

"That question has no good answer."

"Neatly sidestepped. Just bring me my food and I'll see you later."

1:59 PM

Once he'd settled Nicola Morton in an interview room and resolved to stop looking at her hair, Watkins opened his laptop, at the ready to take notes and transcribe her statement. Her coffee-colored skin glowed; a vanilla scent reached him across the table. She'd dressed in skinny jeans and a bright yellow blouse, and stowed a huge purse and a thick cardigan on the empty chair beside her.

"I remember from this morning you're in a master's scheme." He always started with a few easy questions to relax a witness, a trick he'd learned from Declan. "What's your area of concentration, Miss Morton?"

"I prefer Nicola, not Nick or Nicky. It's Shakespeare. I graduate this spring."

"Behind Beatrice Jones but ahead of Claire Scott."

Nicola nodded. "And different degrees. Claire's concentration is a Masters in Poetry."

"Dr. Hamilton is one of your tutors?"

"Yes, for poetry and literature, but Chad Brown tutors Shakespeare. He's a renowned Bard scholar." This was said with a touch of pride, as if she'd had something to do with the man's credentials.

"Were you and Miss Jones close?"

Nicola's dark eyes filled with tears. "Please, can we call her Bea? It makes her sound so stuffy, and she was anything but."

Watkins sat back. "What was Bea like?"

"Jessum peace!" At Watkins' puzzled look, she explained. "Sorry, that's like your 'Oh my gosh!' My mommy doesn't like it when I sink back to Jamaican patois. I'm at Oxford now and I worked hard to get here." Her beads clacked as she nodded. "Bea was as kind as she was attractive, and smart, but didn't lord it over anyone."

"Anything else?"

"The sort of person who remembered your birthday with a cute card pushed under your door that morning, or asked after your mum if she knew she'd been ill." She snatched a tissue from the box on the table between them. "Very well read in all genres, and there was nothing about children's literature, and especially Roald Dahl, good or bad, she didn't know."

Watkins smiled. "You said not cheeky with it."

"Never. But if you asked her a question that had anything to do with Child Lit, she'd go off on a tangent." Her smile lit her face. "Not to impress you with her knowledge, but because she loved her subject and assumed you did, too. Children's stories teach them lessons without them knowing it. Dahl was a master." Her hands fluttered and her nod set her beads clicking gently again.

"I see. When was the last time you spoke?"

Nicola closed her eyes briefly. "That would have been yesterday, late afternoon. She came back to her room after her last tutor session, asked if I wanted to have an early meal with her and

Claire Scott at the King's Arms, but I wanted to work on my revising."

"No distractions for you at the end of term?" He posed it as a mild guess.

"I need to get my work done to leave for the break." Her face shone. "Chad helped me obtain an internship at The Globe."

Enamored of this Dr. Brown? "That was the last time you saw Bea?"

Her look darkened. "Yes. This morning I heard a scream and came to my door. Claire came out of her room, too, and looked over the rail. She yelled to me to call 999 as she went down the stairs, and then I called the Porter's Lodge, but no one was in yet."

"Anyone else around?"

"Jack Soong and Patti Phillips both started down from the third floor. I think Jack went down farther but I didn't want to look. I went back to my room, and when I heard sirens, I got dressed. Then a while later I heard Patti arguing with the forensic people. Then you arrived." She lifted a shoulder. "Time dragged, but went quickly, too."

Watkins finished typing and made a new paragraph. "What do you know about Bea's weekend job?"

"That she worked in Cambridge as a nanny. She'd zip out Thursdays after class and return early Monday morning."

"Any idea of the name of the people she worked for?"

"She never said." Nicola widened her eyes. "I do know they had a little girl she talked about, with an unusual name." She paused and looked up and to the side.

"Verity?" he supplied.

"Yes! That's it." Her beads swung furiously in agreement.

"Do you have any idea why she would spend her weekends there?"

"I remember her saying the mother traveled a lot, and a grandmother pitched in during the week and needed relief."

"Nothing else?"

"Nope, that's it."

"What about a boyfriend?"

"Not that I saw."

Watkins thanked her and had her wait as he finished typing, his index fingers flying over the keys. He had her read her statement, then asked her to sign a digital copy.

"I expect you'll be able to return to your room by Sunday. Where will you stay for the weekend?"

"With a friend from class. My room at home is being renovated right now." She dictated the address of a friend who lived locally. Once he verified her number, the young woman rose and left the room without a backward glance.

Sergeant Damen at the desk called up to say Claire Scott had called and would arrive for her interview later in the afternoon. In the meantime, Watkins would send off Morton's statement to the rest of the team and log it into the case file. He'd let Declan know that Nicola Morton's story matched what Claire had said about the nanny job. Bea must have been hiding something—but did it have any bearing on her death?

CHAPTER ELEVEN

2:46 PM

DS Douglas McAfee, the youngest member of Declan's CID team, scrutinized the young man who sat across from him. Jack Soong's shiny black hair was scraped up in a man bun at the back of his head. This gave him the appearance of a modern, albeit stick-thin, samurai warrior. McAfee, who kept his own hair short, had slight misgivings about a male who grew his hair to his shoulders, although he knew better than to base his opinions solely on looks.

They'd gone through his particulars: second-year undergrad with a concentration in Poetry and Literature; avid chess player; tutor, Dr. Hamilton. McAfee circled to the events of the morning, and Soong recounted how he'd dashed out of bed after hearing a scream, finding Nicola Morton and Claire Scott in the hallway below him. He'd started to follow Claire down the stairs, only to be met by Bea's body in a pool of spreading blood. "Dr. Hamilton told me to stay on the staircase. Once we knew Bea was dead, I went back upstairs to tell the others."

"The others being Nicola Morton and Patti Phillips?"

"Yes, Patti had come down to that landing and stayed there with Nicola."

"When did you last see Beatrice Jones before that?"

"You mean before she fell? The afternoon before. We passed each other on the stairs and said hello. We didn't share classes, so I didn't spend a lot of time with her ordinarily. But she was tremendously kind and encouraging when we did talk about our work."

There was that word again: kind. "What makes you say that if you didn't spend a lot of time together?"

Soong shrugged. "We lived in the same stairwell. Sometimes we'd chat at breakfast. She was supportive." He looked McAfee in the eye. "Do you know how easy it is to be teased for liking Shelley and Byron, or reading *Beowulf*? Bea took my interest seriously, told me if I'd found my passion to hold it close. She suggested the topic for the essay I'm revising now and it's brilliant!"

The young man launched into a story of how Bea Jones had advised he recount the game played during a storm by Shelley, Byron, and Mary Wollstonecraft Shelley, where they challenged each other to write a ghost story. Mary Shelley's *Frankenstein* came out of that event. "Shelley had her write the story into a novel. The whole title of the book is *Frankenstein; or, The Modern Prometheus*. It's been called the first science fiction story. Most people don't know that."

McAfee nodded. Literature lived far away from his world filled with serious crimes, and he'd never cared for science fiction when he did pick up a book. Nonfiction was more his thing, especially biographies, but he had to admit this story behind the story was interesting. "I see. To sum up, your daily contact was limited, you were friendly enough when you did see her, and would consider her a mentor."

Soong sat forward. "More than that. A huge supporter. There was this weekend competition at Christ's College, where the OUCC play." At McAfee's puzzled expression, he explained. "The OUCC is the Oxford University Chess Club, the oldest in the UK. At this championship I played in 25 rounds, knocking others out, until it came down to the last game between me and a guy from Cambridge, which I lost."

"And Bea Jones came to your competition?"

"No, she wasn't around most weekends." He shrugged his shoulders. "When she came back Monday and found out I'd lost, she left me a huge chocolate bar and a note. It said something like, 'Don't focus on what you didn't do. Focus on what you DID do—played and won 24 games in a row. That's a winner in my book!' Isn't that amazing?"

McAfee nodded his agreement. He restrained himself from asking what kind of chocolate Bea had left. "Very supportive. Do you know if Bea Jones had a boyfriend?"

He shrugged. "Not that I know of." Soong frowned. "You know that stairwell at Exeter is said to be haunted."

"No, I hadn't heard that." McAfee shifted in his seat. His fingers paused on his laptop. He would not be adding that to Soong's statement. Things to do with the supernatural left him uncomfortable, but he did pick up one thing Soong had said. "Do you have any idea where Bea Jones spent her weekends?"

"We never spoke about it, but Patti said she had a nanny gig in Cambridge."

3:12 PM

After taking a brief break to compare notes with Watkins, McAfee moved on to Patti Phillips. The young woman with the spiky hair asserted it was "common knowledge" that Bea went home to Cambridge to work a nanny job on weekends.

"I don't remember who told me. Probably Bea herself." She

fiddled with a small silver hoop that pierced one eyebrow.

McAfee was grateful the piercing wasn't in her tongue. "Would you say you were friendly?"

"Mmm, I wouldn't say we were besties or anything. She and Claire had more in common. I'm just a lowly second year." Patti turned her head to one side and looked at McAfee through very dark lashes, which contrasted with her platinum hair. She wrapped her long legs under her, despite the heavy boots she wore, and slouched down in the uncomfortable plastic chair.

McAfee didn't think Patti Phillips considered herself lowly in any area. She exuded a pugnacious attitude that begged to be challenged. "Do you know if Bea had a boyfriend or was dating someone?"

She shook her head. "Never saw her with anyone."

"And your area of concentration, Miss Phillips?"

"Call me Patti, everyone does. I'm into the women in Shakespeare. I might rewrite the plays from a woman's point of view, relegate the men to the secondary roles." She examined her green fingernails. "Dr. Brown likes the idea. It's just one I'm considering." She flashed him a smile. Was she flirting with him?

Another Dr. Brown fan. Her militant aura would suit her plan very well. Hers would be one play he would skip if it were ever produced. "Would you please recount the last time you saw Miss Jones, and then the events of this morning."

"Aye, aye, sir." Patti sat up and saluted him.

This was not a game they played; he felt his annoyance rise as he waited for her response, his fingers hovering over the keyboard.

"Let's see. I saw her in the shower room yesterday morning, coming out as I headed in." She pursed her lips. "Yes, that's right. Don't think I ran into her after that." She bit a cuticle. "Then this morning I was totally in a great dream—I won't bore you with the details, but I promise, if I was that into sharing, you wouldn't be bored at all!" Her smile dropped at his lack of response. "Anyway, I got jolted out of that by an awful scream. I ran out to the landing and Jack—that's Jack Soong, who was in here before me—was halfway down our stairs. Nicola was outside her room, too, and Claire looked over the rail and swooned. I thought she would faint but she grabbed the rail."

McAfee didn't think he'd ever heard anyone use the word "swoon" in speech. Maybe that's what happened when you read Shakespeare all day. Patti kept on with her recitation, hands with flashes of green punctuating her speech.

"I guess Claire got dizzy looking down. I mean, I would have, too, with what she saw." Patti scrunched up her face as she concentrated. "Then she shouted to Nicola to call for an ambulance—wait!" She held up her index finger. "Claire also told her to call the porter. Such a charming American accent she has, but I don't catch every word when she speaks fast. And then Claire ran down the stairs, and I leaned over the railing and saw her check for a pulse. But I saw blood by Bea's head and I pulled back." She relaxed her shoulders. "That's it. Then the place swarmed for hours with those bug people fingerprinting and measuring, and they made us stay in upstairs forever."

"Bug people?"

"Ugh. Those techies in the white suits. Remind me of larva."

"All right." He wouldn't be putting that in his report, either. "You never came down the stairs yourself all the way?"

"No. Dr. Hamilton told Jack to go back up and for the rest of us to stay away, so we did."

McAfee couldn't think of anything else to ask. "I think that will do. I believe we have your contact details?"

"I gave them to the older guy this morning, but here's my phone again."

She recited a number while McAfee reflected that Watkins, only in his mid-30s, would not appreciate being called the "older guy."

CHAPTER TWELVE

3:24 PM

With Claire's help, Nora navigated Sean's buggy over a kerb on their way to St. Aldate's. The nap had served her sister well. She told Nora she'd dozed off after listening to music and remembering her time with Bea the night before.

"It must feel like a lifetime ago." Nora pushed through a knot of German tourists, happily chatting away as they consulted maps on their phones. One of the things she'd come to love about Oxford was the mix of town and gown alongside international visitors.

"It's hard to believe Bea and I went out last night and now everything's changed forever."

"My father used to say 'time changes everything,' and as I get older, I see he was right. Someday it will be nice for you to have that memory of Bea to hold onto."

"I suppose. We'd only known each other a few months, but we had an instant rapport. I'll miss her. I'm not usually a crier. I guess I was in shock this morning."

"I don't doubt that."

Claire looked around the busy streets. "I was surprised when I first came here by how crowded Oxford is most days. I knew there are tons of colleges, but the traffic! I would never attempt to drive in this town."

"I agree." A bus turned in front of them, belching acidic diesel fumes, and they crossed the street from Cornmarket to set off past the ancient Covered Market and Carfax Tower down St. Aldate's. "I avoid driving locally whenever I can. Too many one-way streets and little parking. Better exercise to walk."

"I don't blame you one bit."

A breeze swirled a few crisp leaves by their feet, twirling them around and into the gutter. "My fairies could hold onto a leaf and get anywhere they wanted if they could control the wind."

"You must eye things with them in mind. When I read your first book, I was surprised by how human they seemed."

"You read my book?" Nora's surprise was genuine.

"Sure, when you sent it home. Your mom was so proud. And I bought one for Bea to give to Verity, remember?" Her smile had a hint of wistfulness about it. "The tiny fairies, Dove, Tess, and Sky, all have individual characteristics. Little boys could imagine themselves as the strong gnome, Logan, or even the troublemaker elf, Cosmo."

"I'm pleased you liked it. I modeled the head of the troupe, Daria, after my mom."

Claire giggled, a welcome sound to Nora. "I promise I won't tell her. She does like to orchestrate things."

"She's definitely an organizer. I get my list-making from her." Nora wanted to ask Claire about Bea and her lack of social media presence, but didn't want her to think she'd been prying. But then Claire had asked her to help find out what had happened to Bea, and Nora couldn't do that if she didn't use her investigative skills. Her own goal was to clear her sister's name. Claire didn't seem to realize she was a suspect. Best to keep that information to herself for the moment.

Nora ran the morning's events through her mind. If she truly discounted that Bea's death wasn't suicide, which Claire assured her was nonsensical, and if a fall seemed unlikely, the only possibility Nora could see was that Bea had been pushed.

No wonder Claire was so upset. Nora waded right in.

"Claire, while you slept, I did a little looking into Bea's background. She appeared to drop off social media soon after she came to Oxford. Know anything about that?"

Claire shrugged. "She mentioned one time that she didn't 'do' social media anymore. She thought people could learn too much about you and your movements, and she didn't want the hassle. 'I'm a private person,' she said."

Nora considered this. "It's so unusual in this day and age."

"Guess so. She was so into her work. Getting her degree and having this book published were very important to her. She saw it as paving the way for her future writing career." A frown creased her brow. "I remember one time we were talking about careers and families. She said she guessed most mothers were tougher on their daughters."

"What do you suppose Bea meant by that?"

Claire watched a group of students walk through the arched cloister at Christ Church. "Her mother apparently pressured her to find the right husband, and often questioned why Bea needed all this schooling and degrees if she wanted a family. Bea said she planned to have it all."

"Her mom sounds old-fashioned. The 'find a man who'll make you happy and take care of you, dear' sort."

"I suppose. Bea brought her mother up last night. She said, 'Soon Mum will see I've had my ducks in a row all along, and won't she be surprised.'" Claire shrugged. "I assumed she meant getting her degree with honors. Then she said my mom would be proud of me. I was a good person she'd helped raise, and that meant more than any grades I would get here."

"She's right about you," Nora said. "You were 13 when your

mom died, right?"

"We knew it was coming, but at that age I prayed for a miracle. I didn't see how I could get through life without her." Claire stopped for a second as a wave of emotion swept over her face; then kept walking. "My mom was great. She'd have these long talks with me during her last months, tell me I could do anything I put my mind to, and that she would always be with me, in my heart. I think on some level I put so much emphasis on my work to do well so she'd be proud of me."

"Maybe that's why we rub along so well. My father had the same kind of faith in me. I was 16 when he died, and I carried guilt for years because I went on a date instead of going sailing with him when he drowned."

Claire nodded. "After your mom and my dad got together, she told me about that. She said it took years to get over your survivor's guilt, and she hoped you'd conquer it to find a good man." Claire smiled. "When you brought Declan home to Connecticut and became engaged there, they were so happy for you. Me, too." Claire reached out to squeeze Nora's hand on the buggy. "I've never had a sister before. It's a nice feeling."

"For me, too. I notice I've stopped telling people you're my stepsister and just say 'sister.'" They passed the tall Tom Tower, almost at the station. When they reached it, Nora bounded up the steps to look inside. "It looks fairly quiet. Want to avoid any crazies, but the desk sergeant will be very unhappy if I don't bring Sean in for a hello." With Claire's help, Nora bumped the buggy up the few steps to reach the reception area inside.

Manning the desk while he jotted notes on a duty roster, Sergeant Damen appeared crisp in a uniform that looked as if he'd just put it on. His florid face lit up when he saw Nora with

Sean. "About time you brought the lad in for a visit."

Everyone at the station felt they had a vested interest in Sean's welfare after the events in October, when a psychopath had kidnapped the child. When he'd been found unharmed, the entire station had a whip around and sent him a toy train set.

Nora unbuckled Sean and lifted him up for closer inspection. She sat him on the high counter in front of Damen. "More teeth, sergeant. Show him your cheesy grin, Sean."

Sean obliged with a Cheshire cat-like smile that had Damen clapping. "Well done you!"

Nora turned to Claire. "This is my sister, Claire Scott. She's here to see Sergeant Watkins for a statement."

"Right-o. I'll call and let him know you're here."

"I take it there's no baby news from Julie Watkins?"

"Not as yet. Don't know who's more anxious, Julie or Watkins."

Nora saw Declan enter the hall with Superintendent Morris, another fan of Sean's. The men shook hands and exchanged a few words before coming out into the entryway. Sean noticed Declan and put his arms out.

"Da!" Declan took the boy from the counter while Damen called the detective's offices on the top floor.

With Sean's biological father presumed dead, Declan was the only father Sean had known. With their engagement, they hadn't discouraged the boy calling Declan his dad. The truth would be made known when he was older. Whether Declan would legally adopt Sean was a matter they could decide after their wedding. Nora had developed a fond relationship with Sean's UK grandparents, Harvey and Muriel Pembroke. That made it a tough subject, as Sean would eventually be heir to their large estate, but Nora compartmentalized that issue for now and was happy to do so.

Morris tickled Sean's cheek and told Nora, "Growing in leaps and bounds, I see. I expect we'll see you at the Police Ball at New Years, Nora?"

"Wouldn't miss it," she said, thinking she would miss the soggy canapes and dry chicken if she could.

As if reading her mind, Morris said, "We have a new caterer this year to look forward to. And by then, you two may have something else to look forward to." He clapped Declan on the back and left, giving Watkins a nod as they passed.

"Here's the boy." Watkins smiled at Sean, who had a shy moment and hid his face in Declan's neck, then peeked to see if he was still the center of attention. He was.

Watkins pulled a silly face at the boy, which made him giggle. He turned to Claire. "If you'll come this way."

"I'm going to walk back up St. Aldate's to keep Sean occupied. If I'm not here when you're done, I'll be down the block at Alice's Shop," Nora called after her sister.

Claire followed Watkins. As they turned a corner for the elevator, Nora felt sorry her sister had to revisit the events of the morning, even though Declan's earlier questioning had paved the way. "What was that all about with Morris?" she asked Declan. She took Sean from him and buckled him back into his stroller. She dropped her voice. "I have a few things to tell you."

"Been investigating already?"

"Now you sound like Simon. He said the same thing." She briefly recounted Simon's call.

"He knows you too well."

A young man carrying a folder entered the station and approached the desk. "I have an appointment with Detective

Inspector Barnes."

Declan turned to the man. "I'll be right with you."

Nora held the door and waved goodbye to Sergeant Damen.

Declan carried Sean's buggy down the station steps and gave Nora a swift kiss. "We'll talk tonight."

CHAPTER THIRTEEN

3:41 PM

Declan shook hands with the gangly young man with a mop of fair hair, who introduced himself as Denys Curshik. He settled him in the station's best interview room, with two bottles of cold water and the folder the man had brought on the table between them. The room had been recently refurbished, and still smelled lightly of fresh paint. After his days with Nora and Mr. Tink, Declan suspected the pale green of the room he would normally have called "Sage" was more likely to be labeled "Early Lichen" or even "Jane's Algae."

After asking permission, he set up the recorder, explaining it would leave his hands free from taking notes, and that the tape would eventually be transcribed for the new file they'd started. He spoke the date and time into the tape, and started off asking Curshik to state his name, address, and date of birth.

"Denys Marek Curshik." He spelled out the names as his hair flopped over his forehead. He gave a Somerville address and a date of birth: "February 7, 1991." Bony wrists stuck out of his long-sleeved shirt as he brushed the offending hair away in a nervous gesture.

The young man probably had difficulty finding shirts with long enough sleeves. "What do you do for a living, Mr. Curshik?"

"Denys, please. I have my own business repairing computers. Perhaps you've seen the advert that comes with your local paper? CompuTechs?" He fidgeted in his seat.

"I believe I have seen your ad." Declan recalled a glossy paper stuck in amongst the flyers in the weekend paper. "Last Sunday?"

"Yes, that's me."

"Do you live alone in Somerville, Denys?" These early questions, while eliciting information, also allowed Declan to take the measure of the man.

"No, I married last year. That's another reason I'm here. Me and Pam just found out we're having a baby, and there could be medical history we'd want to know. But it's more than that." He twisted the cap off one of the water bottles and drank thirstily.

"Congratulations."

"Thanks." Denys smiled.

"Let's talk about what's brought you here today."

"See, it started as something strange at the back of my mind when Pam and I married. Before my Mum died, she'd given me a file with important papers, and on my birth certificate it had 'DUPLICATE' stamped across it. Then when we sorted out Mum's things, Pam pointed out there were no photos of me as a baby. None until I was about two, and we'd already moved here from Glasgow."

"All right. I understand something's come to light that makes you think you might be the missing child Donnie Walsh from Cumbria."

"That's right." The man's anxiety was palpable, from his nervous gestures to the sweat that had popped out on his brow. He took another drink.

Declan knew some people had difficulty talking to the police, even if they had done nothing wrong. He took the cap off the other water bottle, mirroring the man, and after taking a sip, sat back casually as if he had all the time in the world. "Why not start at the beginning, and we'll take a look at what you've brought in today."

Denys gave a curt nod and inhaled. "After Mum died, I inherited her Somerville house. I only vaguely remember living there, mostly grew up in Headington. Mum and Dad rented this Somerville house out when we moved to Headington. After he died, she moved back here. Made a killing selling the bigger house, and that gave her a cushion financially."

"Only child, are you?"

He nodded. "Pam and me, we've been cleaning and painting it up, fixing things, doing updates. We put a bit into a kitchen and bathroom renovation. The rest is just paint and putting things to right. We moved in a few weeks ago and only have the secondary bedrooms left. There's good room for a family, with a decent garden, too."

"Sounds ideal."

"It will be, if I can ever get Pam to stop gawking at her granite countertops." That same grin lit up his face. "One of the last rooms that needs sorting is a small bedroom my mum used as an office. Pam wants that for the nursery, and she decided Mum's old desk would make a good changing table if we put a pad on top, and she could use the drawers for nappies and such." He tapped the folder. "When she cleaned it for painting, she found these in an envelope caught in the back of a lower drawer. I'd missed it when we did our clear out."

Declan opened the folder to several sheets. Each page had a Xeroxed story from a Cumbrian newspaper about the kidnapping of thirteen-month-old Donnie Walsh. He skimmed the headlines:

Baby Snatched in Pub Garden

Distraught Mum Begs for Donnie's Return

Where is Little Donnie?

"I have the originals at home." Denys swiped at his hair again. "We made copies on our printer, so you can keep these."

"Very sensible." Declan closed the folder and tapped it. "You think your mother kept these because you might be this missing boy?"

"Why else keep them? And there's the name. If you knew a kid was used to hearing his name with a D, even a little kid, you might keep that same initial. Donnie, Denys. Plus, those articles say he was blonde. I was even lighter when I was young."

"Anything else?"

"Besides these articles and the lack of baby photos?" He looked down for a second, then back up. "Mum was always vague about meeting my dad, when I'd ask as kids do. Now I think she was hiding something. And she didn't like to talk about Glasgow, where she's from." He leaned into the table. "Listen, they were great parents, the best. I don't want to dishonor them. But I keep thinking about our baby on the way and worry about if there are any medical issues. And how maybe that mother and father in Cumbria felt excited like we are now, and then to lose him, not to illness or an accident, but to someone taking him ..."

"It's upsetting and you need to know."

At Denys' grateful nod, Declan continued. "Tell me about your family growing up."

"I mostly remember the Headington house. We always had a dog around. Dad was an accountant, a real numbers whiz. He used to help all the kids on the block with their maths. He was born in Poland; his older brother emigrated first and still lives in Scotland. Haven't seen him in years. He sent a nice card and wreath when Mum died."

"And your mother's family?"

"Mum was from Glasgow, where they met. She said they moved here for Dad's job, and to be closer to her sister. Her parents are long gone. I remember going up to Scotland once to meet them when I was young, my uncle, too. Bitter cold and windy is mostly what I remember."

"Have you thought about asking this uncle or aunt about your origins?'

Denys blushed. "I don't feel close enough to my uncle to ask him, kind of a gruff guy from what I recall, but then I was a kid when I saw him last. Mum talked about her sister once. I don't remember her. Mum said she died young."

Declan sat back. "Do you have any photos of your parents, Denys?"

He nodded, eager to please. "Sure, at home. Want me to bring some in?"

"Here's what I'd like to do. We'll need to do a DNA test on you; we can accomplish that right now if you're willing."

He nodded. "Pam said you would."

"The file on Donnie Walsh's kidnapping is being sent down here. I'll assign a detective to examine it over the next few days. We'll see if Bowness did a DNA profile then, or if there's any evidence they kept that might contain it. It was early days for DNA, so they might not have done the test since they hadn't found something to compare it to." The word "body" hung between them. "In either case, we still have to wait for your results, and since this isn't a new case, that could take a while. If you'll come in next week with the photos, by then we should have a better idea if there's a way we'll be able to figure out if you could be Donnie Walsh."

Denys nodded. "Thank you for taking me seriously."

"Sit tight and I'll have an officer come in and take that swab." Declan stood and they shook hands. He left to arrange the DNA test. With Bea's probable murder on his plate, he would delegate reading through the files to McAfee as he'd discussed with Morris. They had to see if there was any evidence this young man he'd been talking to could be a child kidnapped over 20 years ago.

CHAPTER FOURTEEN

3:56 PM

When Nora left the station, she pushed Sean up the street, strolling slowly as she knew the shop that was her destination was tiny, and she had time to waste.

Past the Music Faculty buildings of Christ Church, through black wrought iron fencing, she could see the broad expanse of Christ Church meadow by Broad Walk. She lingered by the fence; up sprang a happy memory. The meadow along the River Cherwell been the site of a particularly fine weekend over a year ago, one of her trips back to Oxford from her temporary Cumbrian home to see Declan, after Sean was born.

With the infant strapped to her chest, they'd picnicked on the grass during a rare weekend free for Declan. She knew people around them that day had seen a perfect little family: father, mother, baby boy. But Sean's biological father was dead, or purported to be by Her Majesty's Government, and Declan had stepped up to fill that role in a way that had surprised them both. Nora knew she would wrestle with how to explain her son's parentage to him years from now. For today, it was enough that they were both well loved by Declan, shared a home and a life, and were planning a spring wedding to fortify that love.

Nora roused herself back to the present to give Sean a drink of water. While she rooted around in the insulated bag for the water bottle and poured a few inches into a sippy cup, she thought of Claire. Five years younger than Nora, Claire would return to Connecticut when she finished her degree. This was the time for them to cement their relationship, and Nora planned to capitalize on it. She hoped Claire was holding up well, and knew Trevor Watkins would guide her gently through recounting her awful morning again.

As Sean guzzled the water, Nora turned to Bea's last moments. No matter how she ended up at the bottom of that stairwell, the woman's last moments had to have been full of terror. Claire said Bea's twin brother was named Benedick, the pair from *Much Ado About Nothing*, so one of their parents must be a Shakespeare fan. Nora didn't envy Declan having to tell any family their loved one was dead. She'd been present with him and Watkins when they'd traveled to see the mother of a different victim, Val's partner at the time. Nora had never forgotten the look of dread and terror on Bryn Wallace's mother's face when she realized the reason for their visit. Janet Wallace had managed to deal with her grief. She and her neighbor had each lost a daughter and bonded in their grief. It had to be an experience only another parent who'd lost a child could fully understand. Now there was another family who'd lost a daughter.

Nora decided her father's words had indeed been true. Time did change everything, whether it was new love or getting a handle on grief. She hoped Bea's family would eventually find a way to hold their good memories of the woman close to them.

Thinking of Bea made her remember her earlier research into the young woman. She decided not to wait until evening, and took out her phone to send Declan a quick text: "Bea: little to no social media presence."

That was another thing that had changed with time. Where early on in their relationship Declan had become annoyed when Nora tried to assist in his investigations, now he resolutely accepted she meant to help, even if her role was often limited.

Her phone dinged with a reply: "Thx, will put civilian analyst on it. Xx"

Nora wiped Sean's face, and offered him a string of plastic keys he promptly chewed as they set off again. Her brief conversation with Paul Morris led her to believe the super's hint meant Declan had been offered the DCI position. Declan had mentioned the possibility weeks ago, when his current DCI stayed out longer and longer on sick leave. They'd spoken briefly about what that promotion would mean for their family, then shelved the topic until it became a reality.

Nora doubted it would give them more time together, but it would certainly advance Declan's career, and he deserved to manage the Criminal Investigation Department instead of just his own team. She also knew he was touchy about her inheritance from Sean's father and wanted to support the family on his earnings.

"What do you think, Sean?" She mused aloud as they walked. "Should Daddy be the new main man?"

"Da!" Sean looked around him.

"No, he's still at work, lovey." She crossed the road by Speedwell Street when traffic slowed. The bright red sign on the corner of Rose Place and St. Aldate's was locally known as "The Sheep Shop." It was here that real-life Alice Liddell would buy her barley sugar candy before river trips with Charles Dodgson, who would immortalize Alice in his writings as Lewis Carroll. In *Through the Looking Glass*, Alice visits the shop and is served by a bad-tempered sheep. Today a teen stood in the red-framed window, hanging a string of twinkly white lights. Soon the entire town would be decked out for the holidays.

Leaving Sean's buggy outside, Nora held Sean on her hip to

browse the small shop. No sheep behind the counter today, but the small store was crammed with all things Alice, including the Red Queen, the Mad Hatter, and the other characters that still charmed children. The shop was jam-packed with tourists buying Alice tea towels, hot plates, and the famous candy. Nora sidled between people and tables, keeping an eye on Sean's wandering hands. For the moment he cheerfully looked around the colorful displays with eyes opened widely, and waved to the occasional person who smiled at him. While he was too young for the Alice stories, they'd numbered among Nora's favorites growing up, and she was still a Lewis Carroll fan. She planned to read Sean the books in a few years when he could understand them.

These little things we take for granted, Nora mused, that Bea Jones would never know again. The sight of a child's awe and happiness; the bright colors of the shop and its history; the chance to ponder about future jobs and family. All of that lost in an instant. Nora hadn't known Beatrice Jones, but just the same, she mourned her brief life, cut short.

"There you are." Claire excused her way through the crowded shop to Nora's side.

"Tica!" Sean squealed, making people close to them laugh.

"How did it go?" Nora grabbed Sean's hand before he could pick up the candy that caught his eye.

"Fine. It was easier to talk about Bea this time. And Watkins is so calming."

"I never pictured Trevor Watkins as calming, so that's a new side to him. I know Declan rates him highly." She checked her watch. "Let's head over to the Covered Market on the way home. I'll pick up some chicken to throw on the grill for dinner. Sound all right?"

"Shicken." Sean clapped his hands and made the sisters laugh.

"That's a vote of confidence," Claire said. "But can he have a piece of barley sugar now?" She pointed to a bag of candy that had been prepared in small amounts on safety sticks for young children.

"Sure, if we keep an eye on him as he eats it."

Claire fought her way to the till and held out a handful of change for the woman behind the counter. Nora made her way out of the shop, relieved to see Sean's buggy intact, while she tried not to shudder. She'd never had a problem leaving it outside a shop in daytime hours, but seeing it empty still reminded her of Sean's kidnapping.

Claire opened the bag and took out a stick of the candy and handed it to Sean. "Should I put a bib on him?"

"Don't bother. He'll play in the garden with Typo when we get home if the weather holds. We can give him a bath after."

"Typo!" Sean shouted with glee, then replaced the sweet treat in his mouth. They started back the way they'd come, toward the market.

"Watkins said it would be helpful if I could think what Bea cried when she fell," Claire said. "I know I heard something, but haven't been able to figure it out yet."

"My advice? Stop thinking too hard about it. It's like when you forget the name of an actor in a movie and hours later 'Tom Hanks' will pop into your head."

"Tom Hanks?" Claire gave her a sideways look.

"What? I like Tom Hanks. He's a great actor."

"If you'd said Tom Holland I could understand."

Nora bumped the stroller over a kerb. "My point is, stop thinking so hard about it."

They'd reached the High Street and made a right to head into the Covered Market when Claire touched Nora's hand on the stroller and brought them to a standstill.

The look on Claire's face made Nora ache when she saw the downturn of Claire's features, her dulled eyes.

"Nora, right now I can't picture a time when I'll be able to stop thinking about it."

CHAPTER FIFTEEN

4:50 PM

Declan read through the copies of the clippings Denys Curshik had given him, then did his own Google search. Besides these reprinted stories, he discovered several from the national news. There wasn't more he could do until the file from Cumbria arrived.

With duty done to Morris, he called up the interview statements Watkins and McAfee had taken from the four Exeter students and read through them. Nicola Morton agreed with Claire that Bea usually left college Thursday evenings for her nanny job in Cambridge. Both undergrads, Patti Phillips and Jack Soong, backed this up as hearsay about the job and agreed she left for long weekends. Then where did Bea's parents get this idea Bea worked in Oxford at the Radcliffe Camera? He'd have their civilian call over and verify whether Bea had worked there or not, and made a note to have Watkins ask Benedick Jones which version of events Bea had given him after they'd checked with the mother tomorrow.

McAfee knocked and stuck his head around Declan's open door. "This came for you, guv." He handed Declan a stack of papers gathered into a file. "Sent down from Cumbria as an email attachment. Their civilian printed it out."

"Thanks, McAfee." He took the proffered file. "Sit down a minute." It was quiet for a moment; time for him to get to know this team member a bit better, while he delegated as he'd told Morris he would. "Heard of this case? You're probably too young to recall it."

"I'm 27, guv, was only a babe then, but when Curshik came in this morning, I read up on it. Snatched from the garden of a pub outside Bowness, it said."

"Yes, and a body never surfaced." Declan was pleased McAfee has shown initiative and curiosity, two hallmarks of a good detective. "I'm handing this over to you, McAfee. Make a copy for me and take this home. Give the file a read this weekend, and when Curshik comes in Monday, look at the family photos he's bringing, see if there are any clues there to be found. Comparing his DNA to Donnie Walsh will take a while."

"Thanks, guv." McAfee smiled with pleasure, then instantly sobered. "Poor kiddie could be in a grave that's not been found, or alive and well in another family altogether. I'm adopted, but my mum has proper records."

Here was a bit of the young sergeant's personal history Declan hadn't known. "Any siblings?"

McAfee shook his head. "Mum always said I was enough for her and Dad. They told me about being adopted when I was quite young. 'Not from my body but right from our hearts,' Mum liked to say."

Declan flashed on Sean, and the day he'd have to tell the boy he wasn't his biological father. Would it matter to him? "Ever thought of contacting your biological parents?"

"Not really. My parents have been enough for me."

Declan nodded. He hoped one day Sean would accept him fully as his father. Leaving this file to McAfee was a good decision. He had the postmortem tomorrow, followed by a visit to Bea's parents in Cambridge; he'd be lucky to have Sunday at home. "With Watkins going out on family leave any day now, I'll depend on you more, McAfee. Might as well get up to speed from the outset, and see you keep me posted on your findings and your thoughts."

The sergeant took the file back. "I'll be back with your copy in a jiff, guv. And thanks."

He left, and Declan sat back. If he accepted the DCI position, he'd best get in the habit of trusting his team to keep him informed and their computer records up to date.

He turned back to his computer, thinking of the text Nora had sent him. It did feel unusual that someone in the age bracket of Bea Jones would have such a small social media footprint. He trusted Nora's information on that score, but knew Lily George would enlist a civilian member of his team to work that angle if she didn't do it herself.

Before he went home, he would finish reading the witness statements from the Exeter students. What was the real story about Bea and this Cambridge nanny job, and why did his instincts tell him it would prove to be important?

CHAPTER SIXTEEN

9:03 PM

Nora topped up her wine glass. With Sean asleep and dinner cleaned up, she could relax properly. "Let's take these in front of a fire. A refill?" she asked Claire.

"Maybe just two fingers. I'll fall asleep." Claire held out her glass.

The night had turned chilly, and Declan rose from the table. "Wouldn't be the worst thing that could happen. I'll light the fire after I pour myself a scotch."

They moved to the living room furniture grouped around the fireplace, where Nora turned her Bluetooth speaker on low. "Any requests?"

"Play some of that soothing vintage jazz you like by what's-his-name," Claire said.

"Chet Baker. I would have named Typo after him but Sean beat me to his name." She described how the Welches next door had been fostering the beagle when he'd escaped from Neil and run through the hedge when Nora was viewing Haven Cottage. "I'd been talking to Val about editing and typos, and Sean, always one to parrot words, saw the dog and shouted, "Typo!" When Neil found out I was a writer, too, he deemed it the perfect name, and it stuck." She took a seat on the soft leather couch that had been Declan's and rested his glass of scotch on the coffee table. Claire chose Nora's floral wing chair on the other side of the large fireplace and dangled her legs over one arm as she lounged.

Nora watched Declan light the fire, admiring the way he went about it with assured motions. With his shirtsleeves rolled up, the light glinted off the hair on his arms in a way she found incredibly sexy. How lucky she was to have this man in her life.

Typo moved with them and settled himself on the rug in front on the hearth. The fireplace was one of the elements that had attracted Nora to Haven Cottage the first time she'd seen it. The stone surround and thick mantel, perfect for Christmas stockings, would soon have greens along its top with the glittering animals she'd been collecting to create a forest scene.

"Declan, when we moved in do you recall where I put my cartons of holiday decorations?"

He looked up from his task as the fire crackled and took hold; the scent of fresh wood burning reached her. Declan leaned over Typo to close the fire screen curtains and came to sit beside her on the couch. "They had been in your storage unit. I remember you said not to store them in the attic as we'd need them soon."

"That's right. I shoved them in the kneehole of my desk in the library under the tarp." Nora handed him his scotch and snuggled back against Declan. They all watched the fire as the flames rose and changed color.

"Spellbinding, isn't it?" Claire's look was intense. "I love watching the flames dance, their colors striated in gold, red, blue." She looked around the room. "Where will you put a tree, Nora?"

"In the front window, away from the fire. This will be the first Christmas Sean may remember. I think he'll adore the woodland creatures on the mantel, with deer, chipmunks and squirrels, even a few hedgehogs."

"I love hedgehogs." Claire tucked a strand of hair behind her ear. "Despite their quills they're so darn cute."

"Your parents will be here for Christmas," Declan said.

"I'll be happy to see Dad and Amelia. I guess I should call them at some point and let them know what's happened. Dad worries so ..." Claire's voice trailed off.

"Oh, I don't know, Claire." Nora sipped her wine. "After all, he didn't know Bea."

Declan chimed in. "Nora's found the less she tells Amelia, the better. Keep the calls for the good stuff."

"They can't do anything across the pond, so why upset them?" Nora added.

"You're right. There's nothing to tell them they could do anything about." Claire looked into the fire, mesmerized by the flames.

"Claire, I wanted to mention that Val and Sophie are supposed to come over tomorrow night for dinner, but if you'd rather not have company, I can easily cancel." Nora drained her glass and handed it to Declan, who placed it on the side table.

"Please don't. I need to revise during the day, but I enjoy them both, and I could use the distraction."

"Val is certainly distracting." Nora smiled. Her best friend had a great sense of humor and had been responsible for finding Nora this house. In return, Val and her partner, Sophie, were subletting Declan's modern flat.

"Sophie's nice, too." Claire put her glass on the small table next to her chair and leaned back. "They make a good pair."

"She's very pleasant and very smart. She has to be to keep up with Val. I'll leave it be then."

Claire tucked her legs under her. Nora watched her sister's eyelids grow heavy; soon they closed.

"This is nice." Declan rubbed Nora's arm. "Your instincts about this place were spot on. It's so cozy and comfortable."

"I'm glad you agree. We owe Val for finding it."

"A fact she will be certain to remind us of." Declan laughed and dropped a kiss on the top of Nora's head.

She turned into his chest, where she could feel his heart beating through his shirt. She inhaled his scent with its hint of cedar. Nora glanced over at Claire, who dozed in the chair, and whispered, "I don't want to spoil the moment, but I do recognize that Claire is on your list of suspects."

"I'll need to treat her like the others, Nora, in terms of eliminating her from our enquiries. Morris is aware."

"You do know she didn't have anything to do with Bea's death. I'm not saying that because she's my relative. That's okay. I'll make sure you find out it couldn't be her."

Nora could picture Declan rolling his eyes.

"I have her staying with us. Do you think I'd invite her here if I felt on some level she was involved?"

"Better the devil you know?"

"You don't need to get involved. I'll clear her and soon."

"But I am involved. She's my sister." Before the mood could be ruined, Nora changed the subject. "Did Morris offer you the DCI position? Is this a good time to ask what you're thinking about it?"

Declan exhaled. "It's been at the back of my mind since he spoke to me today. I'm in two minds about it."

"Congratulations on being asked. You should list the pros and cons," Nora urged. "Talk it through."

"All right, let's see. There would be an increase in pay and vacation, and my regular time off might be more fluid, especially on days when we didn't have a new case."

"Those are pros." Nora held up two fingers on her left hand.

"More paperwork."

She held up a finger on her right hand.

"Some reports I could probably do at home in that sweet office I have."

Another finger on her left hand.

"More department politics, but my open spot would allow Watkins to move up."

Nora added a finger on each hand. "That's four to two so far."

"What do you think? You're a part of this equation."

Nora already knew her answer. "I think you are a great leader who the team looks up to, and that's worth a whole handful of fingers."

Claire suddenly woke, eyes wide open, and swung her legs to the floor. "That's it!"

Nora sat up. "What's it?"

Claire looked at them. "That hissing noise I heard. It was whispering. There was someone else on the landing with Bea."

Now Declan sat up, too. "That's great, Claire. Anything else?"

"After the shuffling sounds, when Bea screamed, I know what she yelled." Claire gulped. "She wailed 'VERITY!'"

CHAPTER SEVENTEEN

Saturday, 2nd December

8:44 AM

Over the roar of the MGB on their way to the JR mortuary and their meeting with Charlie Borden, Declan told Watkins about Claire Scott's recollections from the previous evening.

"I thought about what she meant yesterday by 'hissing' when I got to the scene," Watkin said. "When she mentioned a radiator, I checked the one on that landing. It wasn't turned on."

"Good man." With his observant nature, Watkins would make a great DI. He could also be discreet. He hadn't asked Declan about his interview with the super yesterday. "Now to see what evidence Charlie can find to support that Bea Jones wasn't alone on that landing when she fell." At least one detective usually attended the post mortem of a victim on a case, and today he and Watkins were traveling on to Cambridge, so they would view it together. Declan thought of his young sergeant. "McAfee's been to a post, right?"

Watkins nodded. "I took him with me last year to that body we pulled out of the river, and then again when you were on vacation in Connecticut and we had the suicide."

"How did he do?"

"You know drownings are never easy. He got a bit green at that one, but didn't embarrass himself. Did fine by the second one."

"Good to hear." He pulled into the drive and parked.

When the two detectives donned their gear and entered his autopsy suite, Charlie Borden was already suited. Bea Jones's corpse lay on his table. Her clothes had been removed and bagged. The bright overhead light made her pale skin appear almost translucent. Her mouth hung slightly open in a gentle smile, showing a hint of even white teeth. Charlie's diener stood nearby jotting notes. "Good morning, gentlemen. Right on time. You remember my assistant, Anna?"

The slender woman met their eyes over her mask and nodded.

"Let's get started, shall we? I've already had her X-rayed as I know you have to get to Cambridge." After he'd dictated Bea Jones' height and weight, Charlie started a visual examination of her body. Yesterday at Exeter he'd placed plastic bags on each of her hands, and now had Anna remove the bags one at a time to take scrapings from each nail. "Hallo, what's this?"

Anna handed him a hemostat. Charlie picked at the end of one of Bea's fingers. "There's something snagged in a fingernail here." He held the clamp up to the light while Anna opened a small evidence bag. Once he was satisfied his find was in the bag, he smoothed it closed, and Anna initialed and dated the label.

"What did you find?" Declan asked.

Charlie held the bag under the light for the detectives to see. "A white fiber, cotton at my first guess." He handed the bag back to Anna, who put it on a side table to send to the lab. "We'll see what the lab makes of that. But look here—" he pointed to the shoulders. "Now that a bit of time has passed, you can see bruising coming up on the front of the shoulders. These would have to have been done perimortem to have blood flow."

Both detectives peered at the areas Charlie indicated. Watkins asked, "Fingertips from a push?"

"Possibly. Probably. I'll ask forensics examining her clothes if it's possible to obtain any prints from those areas. Her shirt was cotton; might have impressions. The Scots have done great things with vacuum metal deposition, but I don't know if we're doing that here. Anyway, with our budget, don't hold your breath."

Continuing his physical exam, Charlie dictated his findings into the overhead microphone. He noted X-ray confirmation of fractures to the neck, right arm, both lower legs, and pelvis. He lingered at her breasts and examined them closely.

"Something there, Charlie?" Declan knew Charlie well enough to know his interest wasn't prurient.

"Something I need to confirm."

Anna helped him turn the dead woman's body over, and Charlie began the same intense scrutiny of her back. He worked his way through her scalp and down to her neck, where he stopped to have Anna take several close-up photos of her nape. He also paused near Bea's waist for more photos, and had Anna measure from her waist to Bea's heels. He reached her toes, and after checking between them, stood up.

"The bruising on the back of her neck I'd mentioned before is more visible. See here." He moved his huge hanging magnifier light closer to Bea's neck.

Declan leaned in to see the thin line of purple that showed up clearly with the light. He moved aside for Watkins to examine it. "Only on the back of the neck, so your original thought of having a chain yanked off her neck stands."

"Yes. With the time lapse, now we have this line here." Charlie pointed to a faint waist-high bruise in a straight line. "I had the SOCO measure from the height of the railing on that stairwell to the floor. If these match up, as I expect them to, I'd say the rail bit into her back as she fell over."

Declan met his sergeant's eyes.

"Which with the bruises on the shoulders, points to a push and fall backwards, rather than a forward-facing jump or slip," Watkins said.

"Exactly." Charlie had Anna help him turn the body over. He picked up a scalpel that glinted under the bright light in preparation for the Y incision. "Let's see what else this young woman's body can tell us."

Declan backed away slightly from the table, Watkins following his move. This part was usually engrossing, despite the odors, if he kept a bit of distance. The colors of the interior of the human body fascinated him, and he tried not to picture Bea Jones alive and laughing.

Half an hour later, the heart, lungs, liver, spleen, and stomach were noted as "unremarkable" and showed no signs of incipient disease. "She was never a smoker," the pathologist noted, and showed the detectives healthy pink lung tissue. Anna weighed each organ and took samples. Charlie paused after removing and opening the woman's uterus.

"Now, this confirms my suspicions." He murmured into the microphone: "Uterine size and cervical neck both enlarged," and handed the reproductive organs off to Anna for weighing. He looked up at Declan and motioned for him and Watkins to step back in closer. "I noted darkening of the areolas around her nipples." He pointed to several shiny stripes on the abdomen. "These are resolving stretch marks." Charlie stood and looked at Declan. "At some point, likely in the past year, this young lady has borne a child."

CHAPTER EIGHTEEN

11:10 AM

Nora shoved Sean's buggy over the uneven cobblestones inside the Covered Market. There might have been another person on that landing when Bea fell, and she felt frustrated by not being able to help Declan in the hunt.

Nora fought back a sigh and supposed her job today revolved around doing her best to keep Claire occupied and her thoughts of Bea at bay. At the same time, Nora would keep her eyes and ears open for anything else her sister might recall that would help Declan. Distraction for Claire headed her list. "I know you've been here, but did you know the market has been here since the late 18th century, to rid Oxford of its foul-smelling street markets? Can you picture fishmongers and butchers with their wares out in the open? This building was rebuilt and roofed over in Victorian times."

"No wonder it feels like a step back in time." Claire held Typo's leash as they walked. The little beagle nosed the walkway and people's shoes. They passed Nora's favorite hat shop, several shoe stores, grocers, florists, and the butcher with turkeys and sides of beef hanging.

They stopped in front of a bakery, which reminded Nora of the case where she'd met Declan. A young boy who worked here had been a key witness at that time, and every time she was here, Nora wondered where Davey Haskitt was now. She bought a crusty loaf of bread and they moved on to the pie seller.

"If you'll wait here, I'll run in and get a few pies for tonight's dinner, to have with the soup and a salad." She had started a butternut squash soup this morning that would simmer all day in the Aga.

"Sure." Claire knelt down to Sean's level, holding Typo's leash away from the center aisle of foot traffic. The puppy jumped on his hind legs to lick Sean's face, while Claire pulled the puppy down and made him sit. The boy giggled in delight and clapped his hands.

Nora stood in line in the shop and watched Claire pull Typo down and rub his soft ears in compensation. When it was her turn, she chose two large pies, one with pork and the other filled with roasted veggies. She passed on the haggis. As she held out her hand for her change, she noticed a slender young man had stopped to talk to Claire, who gesticulated to Nora inside the shop. His high cheekbones and dark skin glowed with good health, but there was no mistaking the sorrow on his face as they spoke. Another friend of Bea's, Nora decided, as she left the shop and studied the man's red-rimmed eyes.

Claire introduced them. "Nora, this is our Shakespeare don, Chad Brown."

Chad shook hands with Nora. "I understand from Claire that your fiancé is looking into what happened to Bea." He had a light Caribbean lilt to his speech. "I was under the impression she had a terrible fall."

"Declan Barnes and his team. I believe he's on his way to Cambridge right now to visit her parents."

A shadow crossed the man's handsome face. "Good luck to him. Her mother's a shrew." His jaw set in a tense line; he knelt down to rub Typo under the chin.

Nora's instincts twigged. "You've met Bea's parents?"

Brown's smooth forehead creased. "At a reception during Bea's first year. Her mother asked me for a refill of her champagne, then looked at me as if she didn't believe Bea when she corrected her mum's impression that I was a waiter. Not her idea of a don, I suppose."

Nora picked up on suppressed anger as Claire said, "I'm sorry that happened."

"Not your fault." He stood up and looked away as his chin trembled and his emotions looked to be on the brink of spilling over.

"I'll let you know if I hear anything about a funeral or memorial," Claire said. "Although I have the impression there won't be anything formal until the investigation is over."

"Even for a fall?" His shoulders slumped. He thrust his hands in the pocket of his waxed jacket.

"They have to be certain," Nora explained, wondering how much she should say about police procedures, and if he realized there would be an inquest. "I'm sure the college will put up a notice once decisions have been made."

"We'll see about that." His voice broke as he looked off into the distance.

Nora thought that an odd statement and took a chance. "Does the name Verity mean anything to you?"

Brown jerked back a step as if stung by a bee. "Who told you about Verity?"

Claire rushed in. "That's the name of the child Bea took care of on weekends as a nanny."

Brown's startled gaze roved between them both. "Sorry, I need to go now. Nice to meet you." He left quickly, disappearing into the crowd.

Nora watched his retreating back and frowned. It wasn't her

imagination that Chad Brown had run when the name Verity had been introduced. But then, how could Bea's nanny job be connected to her death? And what did Chad Brown know about it? She was convinced more than ever that Verity was mixed up in Bea's death.

She stowed her package in the back of the stroller. "Good don?"

"Knows Shakespeare inside and out," Claire said. "Very popular. He makes his classes entertaining."

"He looked very upset, but I suppose anyone who knew Bea will be." Nora tucked Chad Brown's response away to consider later. There was definitely something there that needed looking into. Her fingers itched for the little notebook she always carried in her backpack.

They started out the back door onto Market Street where it crossed Turl Street, and the stone fence surrounding Exeter's grounds. "I should probably check my mail while we're here," Claire said.

"Of course." They walked on the narrow pavement outside the college wall, made more cramped by racks of chained bicycles, until they came to the main entrance by the Porter's Lodge. Nora bumped the buggy over the deep sill of the ancient door, and pulled dog and child out of the way to one side to wait as Claire checked her cubbyhole for messages and mail.

A middle-aged man came into the lodge from inside the college and stepped up to his own box. He noticed Claire and touched her shoulder. "All right, Claire?"

He looked familiar, and Nora realized she'd seen him yesterday, leaning against the wall, watching over Bea Jones's body. She had her thought confirmed when Claire spoke to the man.

"Hello, Dr. Hamilton." Claire shrugged. "Better today, I suppose."

"Laura sends her best regards. We're both still in disbelief. Come and see us for tea tomorrow?"

"Thanks." Claire pointed to Nora. "I'm staying with my sister, Nora Tierney, for a few days just now."

"Good idea." Hamilton ambled over to Nora to shake hands. "Peter Hamilton, Claire's tutor." He knelt down to Sean. "And who's this young chap?"

"Typo!" Sean chortled.

"This is Sean," Nora explained. "Typo is the puppy."

Typo had thrown himself at the man's feet, legs splayed open, waiting for a belly rub. Hamilton obliged. "We do love our pets."

"They become a part of our family."

"Agreed. Nora Tierney, I suspect you are one busy lady." His knees creaked as he stood up. "Come with Claire to tea tomorrow, say four o'clock? My wife Laura makes incredible scones."

"Thank you. I'd like that. I'll leave the puppy home," Nora promised.

"But not Sean. Laura loves the littles. See you tomorrow." He waved to Claire, told the porter to have a good afternoon, and re-entered the grounds.

Claire returned with one airmail envelope, and a small stack of slips she flipped through. "Messages from other students in our program who heard about Bea and knew we were friends."

Nora pointed her chin in Hamilton's direction "He's friendly."

Claire brightened. "Tea will be fun. His wife Laura is a powerhouse; you'll like her." She tucked her mail into her backpack and helped Nora lift the buggy over the high threshold.

They set off toward home.

"Mail from Connecticut?" Nora asked.

"My dad writes every week, lets me in on what's happening in Ridgefield. He hates email, says it's good for me to see his familiar handwriting."

Nora smiled. "He's a good man. My mom is lucky to have found him." At times she still missed her father with a pang, but there was no question Roger Scott and Amelia Tierney were happy together.

"They're lucky to have found each other," Claire said. "What are the chances?"

Nora clarified Claire's question. "Chances of finding a second love?"

"Think about it, Nora. There are so many people who cross our paths. Then we meet someone, and there's a connection, maybe a chemistry, that makes them different from all the others. You met Declan during a case. Dad met your mom at a widowed spouse support group. It turns to love, or something else entirely. How can you anticipate that? How do you know?"

"Are you saying you never know when love will cross your path?"

"Maybe love. Or maybe someone who'll love you to death."

CHAPTER NINETEEN

Cambridge

12:50 PM

Declan had worried about parking in Cambridge as they neared the town, but when Watkins called the local station on Bluetooth as a courtesy to inform them of their presence, the duty sergeant said he would call ahead to Christ's College.

"Stop at the main entrance. Phil Cook in the Porter's Lodge will give you a pass to park inside the gate in their car park. There are places to eat across the road in a shopping area or around the corner, too."

Watkins thanked the man for his assistance.

"No worries, glad to help. Shame about the Jones girl. You headed there now?"

Declan glanced at the satnav. "Five minutes out."

"I'll have Cook meet you at the door then."

Christ's College was on a one way, and Declan maneuvered the car to the main door on a sharp curve. A tall man with short hair and crinkly laugh lines around his eyes stepped out of the wooden door set between two stone turrets with the college arms picked out in gold, red, and white paint. He brandished a placard. "Oxford? We don't bite, promise. Follow the curve straight down Hobson to the first gate on the right, and turn in." He handed Declan the pass. "Put this on your dash, and here's a map of the college. I've circled Dr. Jones's rooms."

Declan took them both. "Very helpful, thanks."

Cook smiled broadly. "Don't thank me. You're the ones have

to deal with Maggie Hyphen Smythe. Make sure you put the 'y' in Smith or Mrs. Jones will have your guts for garters." He tapped the roof of the car and shooed them down Hobson Street.

Declan turned into the gate and found parking under the trees inside the area on the side of the college. "Sounds like Bea's mother is a piece of work." He climbed out of the low-slung car and straightened his tie.

"Notice he called her Maggie Smith, like the actress? And Dr. Jones for the father. Makes you wonder if she hyphenated her name after marriage and changed the spelling to go upscale."

"Bereaved parents, Watkins. Tread carefully."

"Cross my heart."

They took the walkways indicated on the map that bordered a large treed lawn to the far side of Christ's grounds and the Fellows' Building.

"Having McAfee set up a murder room today was a good idea," Watkins said. "We can hit the ground running after the inquest."

"Glad you approve. It will be interesting Monday to see if Bea registered a birth certificate."

An arched opening in the center of one of the stone buildings gave them a glimpse of the large peaceful garden beyond it.

"There's a swimming pool at the end of that garden." Watkins drew Declan's attention to the icon on one corner of the map.

"Nice place to go to school." Declan pointed to the ancient building opposite them and consulted the map. "The Master's Lodge is part of the original college from the early 16th century."

"Let's hope the plumbing is newer than that, poor sod." Watkins snorted as they found the correct door on a corner and rang the bell. An engraved brass plate over the bell read:

Dr. and Mrs. E. Smythe-Jones.

"Let's get this over with." Declan shot his cuffs.

The door was jerked open by a middle-aged woman wearing a tailored suit in a ghastly shade of purple, relieved only slightly by a cream silk blouse. Declan remembered his mother saying that purple, along with black and grey, was considered a mourning color. The woman was well-built and held herself upright in a rigid posture that reminded Declan of his super's military bearing, but that man's easy smile was absent from this woman's face, and her lips were set in a thin line of disapproval. Hair that had once been auburn had turned a mousy brown streaked with grey as she aged; she wore it styled in a stiffly-sprayed helmeted bob.

"It's about time." She stood aside to allow the men to enter.

Declan pointedly consulted his watch. 1:04 PM. Hardly late for a one o'clock appointment. He introduced them before entering. "Detective Inspector Declan Barnes, and this is my sergeant, Trevor Watkins."

The woman merely inclined her head, then pointed to the interior. They moved past her, and found Ernest in the living room, hands in his pockets, staring out the windows at the Master's Garden.

He turned at the sound of their entrance and came forward to shake their hands. "Inspector, good of you to come all this way. And Sergeant Watkins, please, have a seat. Margaret, is the tea ready? I'm sure after their long ride these gentlemen would appreciate some refreshment."

He and Watkins took seats in two chairs placed opposite a couch. The parents should want to sit next to each other—at least in normal circumstances.

"Lovely grounds, sir." Watkins jutted his chin toward the windows and the view as they waited.

"Yes, we're very fortunate to have such a nice flat. And so convenient for the classes I teach, plus so near the chapel for rehearsals and performances." Ernest looked at Declan. "Sorry, I jabber when I get nervous."

Declan met the bereaved father's eyes and hoped he conveyed his understanding. "There's no correct way to be in this kind of situation, Ernest."

His wife returned, carrying a silver tray with a tea set and fragile china cups.

"Ah, thank you, Margaret." Ernest frowned when he saw the delicate cups. "Excuse me a moment."

He scurried to the kitchen as his wife offered the men linen napkins. Ernest returned, holding three large mugs. "Here you go, gentlemen. These are better suited for a nice big drink after the drive you've had."

He added the mugs to the tray and ignored his wife's dark look. Years of practice, Declan suspected. Two could play her game.

"Thank you, Ernest. That's very thoughtful." Declan turned to Margaret. "When we met in Oxford, your husband insisted we call him by his first name."

Margaret busied herself pouring their tea, and sending 'round a plate of surprisingly good lemon drizzle cake. He couldn't help wondering if she'd made it herself, and suspected someone from the church had dropped it off for the bereaved parents. There was no comment from her, and no invitation to call her by her first name.

"I wanted to express our condolences again to both of you."

Declan nodded to each one of them in turn. "I'm sorry to have to put you through this, but I have several questions for you. Let's start with what you can tell me about Beatrice's weekend job."

Margaret answered before Ernest could. "My daughter was in line for her master's degree next week, Inspector, and as such, was a highly valued tutor for the undergraduates. She spent her weekends working with them in the Radcliffe Camera, showing them how to conduct the research they'd need for their coursework in ensuing terms."

"I see. Therefore, you didn't see her most weekends?"

Ernest opened his mouth but once again his wife got there first. "We saw her at the start of the semester for a weekend after her return from Wales in early October, and again in November on a Sunday. Since then she's been working, as I've just told you."

"Can either of you think of any reason Bea would have told her fellow students she was coming home to Cambridge to work as a nanny each weekend, and wasn't seen around Oxford until Monday morning classes?"

In the brief silence that followed this pronouncement, Declan saw a tour pass by outside, and heard the voices of the cluster of tourists speaking Japanese that floated in through the open window.

"That's impossible!" Margaret finally exploded, while her face turned red in consternation.

Declan turned to Bea's father. "Ernest?"

The man frowned. "I admit I thought it odd we didn't see Bea more, but after her being gone so long in Wales, we'd become used to seeing less of her. She is—was an adult, of course."

"She was in Wales for what period?"

Ernest spoke up. "Bea left right after Christmas last year and was there until the end of September, not too long before the new term started."

"A resident fellowship?"

Margaret found her voice. "In Roald Dahl's hometown, Swansea, a lovely seaport. It was an honor to be chosen." Her chin rose.

"Wouldn't a fellowship of this type be for the Hilary term? If it included Trinity, that would still have been completed by the end of June, yet you say she didn't return until just as Michaelmas term was starting?"

Ernest said, "We only know what Bea told us. She was writing his biography, you see."

Margaret gave him a cold look. "There must have been a special provision for her. She was quite brilliant."

Declan continued. "Neither of you have any idea why Bea gave you one explanation for her subsequent weekends, and another to her colleagues at Exeter?"

Ernest looked perplexed and shook his head.

"I don't understand these questions." Margaret's face was even redder, if that was possible. Knowing the further revelations to come, Declan hoped she didn't have high blood pressure.

"Does the name Verity mean anything to either of you?"

Husband and wife exchanged looks. "I don't know anyone of that name, do you, dear?" Ernest asked.

Margaret shook her head. "Why do you ask?"

"It's come up in our investigation." Declan turned to Ernest. "When we saw you at the mortuary yesterday, you indicated Bea wore a necklace she didn't take off, a gold chain with a heart charm. This wasn't found with her or in the initial search of her room. Any idea of its significance?"

"You searched her room?" Margaret sat up straighter, ready to protest.

"Margaret, let the detectives do their work." Ernest tried to take her hand.

She pulled away and sniffed. "We didn't give any necklace to her."

"It appears that shortly before she died, this necklace or something similar, was torn off your daughter's neck, so it's of importance to us. There is also a witness who feels Bea wasn't alone on the landing when she fell."

Declan braced himself for the parents' reaction to this, watching as it sunk in.

Ernest got there first. "Are you saying Bea was pushed to her death?"

Margaret's eyes opened wide. "Beatrice was *murdered*?" Her voice rose on the last word to end in a shriek. The red color rapidly left her face.

"It's a possibility we have to consider. There will be an inquest next week, which I fully expect to be adjourned to allow us to continue our investigation. The coroner's family liaison will be in touch once that date is firmed up, and you will be invited to attend to hear the evidence."

Ernest nodded and met Declan's eyes. "The coroner's office already called and explained again that we couldn't have Bea back for her funeral until after the inquest and investigation. She also offered us a family liaison officer, which Margaret refused."

"We certainly don't need strangers around us." Margaret bristled and lifted her chin.

"What did the autopsy show?" Ernest asked.

"Ernest!" Margaret's dismay was acute. She searched her skirt pocket and brought out an embroidered hankie she pressed to her face.

Declan swallowed. "I'm afraid Bea's fall caused several limbs to fracture. It was likely the fracture to her neck and skull that resulted in her death."

Ernest sucked in a breath.

Margaret moaned. "You had to know, didn't you?"

This time when Ernest reached out, he grabbed her hand. "There's no point in not knowing what killed our girl. She's gone, Maggie."

His wife jerked her hand away. "Don't call me that!"

Declan looked at Watkins, who grimaced. Might as well get it over. "The autopsy also showed that Bea had borne a child in the past year."

Ernest picked up his head. "What? There's no question? But—"

At a loud thump, everyone turned as Margaret slid to the floor.

After checking she was breathing, Declan sent Ernest to fetch a glass of water for his wife, while he and Watkins sat the woman up as she came around. They helped her onto the couch, where Declan put several cushions under her feet to elevate them as Ernest ran back with the water glass and a damp cloth.

He helped his wife take a few sips, and laid the cloth across her forehead, then sat by her feet.

Declan stood over the woman. "I'm sorry to have upset you,

Mrs. Smythe-Jones, but I agreed yesterday with your husband to share any information on Bea and her death when it came to light."

She whimpered and waved him away.

Declan had a flash of empathy for the woman who had lost her daughter and was now learning Bea's secrets. He turned to Ernest. "The pathologist saw evidence that Bea had delivered a child. Whether it was alive or not we can't ascertain. We'll be looking for any birth certificate she might have registered."

"Thank you. If you'd please keep me aware of what you find, I'd be grateful. If there's nothing else of importance today, I think I should call our GP for Margaret."

"I'll be in touch if there are any further developments."

As Ernest walked the detectives to the door, Margaret called out: "Find my grandchild."

CHAPTER TWENTY

7:28 PM

Nora checked the oven where she'd put bread she'd cut into small squares to toast for croutons. "Declan, could you bring the soup tureen to the table? There's a trivet and ladle out already." She wiped her hands on a dishtowel she'd bought the first time she'd visited Oxford while in college and kept as a talisman that she would return. It displayed the crests of the main Oxford colleges and had softened from many washes. Nora had grown to love the adopted city she'd made her home. That feeling was reinforced as she looked around the kitchen at Declan, Claire, and Val's partner, Sophie Jordan, sitting at the table. From upstairs came the low rumble of Val's voice, reading a book to Sean.

Declan carried the heavy-lidded tureen to the table, while Nora cut the warmed pies into serving slices and arranged them on a platter. "Anything else before we eat?" he asked. "How about I take Typo for a garden run so he'll behave at the table."

"Perfect." She blew him a kiss and he took the beagle outside.

Val and Sophie had arrived earlier when Nora was cleaning Sean's face after his dinner. They'd insisted on giving him his bath. "Godmother's prerogative," Val had said.

After bringing a pajama-clad Sean downstairs for goodnight kisses, hair combed and smelling of baby shampoo, Val had said she would do the nightly book duties and put him to bed, leaving Nora to get the adults' dinner on the table.

Sophie sat with Claire at the dining table, talking quietly over glasses of pinot noir. Nora was happy Claire had someone else to talk to, and listened in as she finished making the dressing for the salad.

"I'd love to give you a tour. How's Monday, say around 10?" Sophie worked for Oxford University Press as an archivist. "I'm very sorry to hear about your friend." She tucked her dark shoulder-length hair behind an ear, her brown eyes warm with concern.

"I'm still in shock, I think," Claire said. She launched into a description of Bea Jones, her kind attitude, and her work in children's lit.

Declan returned with Typo and gave him a chew toy. The puppy settled down under the table, and Declan took a seat and poured himself a glass of wine.

"I'm a huge Dahl fan. Bea sounds absolutely lovely, Claire." Sophie touched Claire's hand briefly.

Nora noticed Declan taking in Claire's conversation.

"She was lovely. I'd brought her to Val's cooperative this fall. We had the best time taking a break from school and browsing through everyone's specialties. I bought these that day." She touched her earrings, delicate swirls of silver. "It's so difficult to talk about Bea in the past tense when we'd been at a concert Thursday night, and only a few hours later, she was dead."

Sophie sighed and nodded. "I was with my Nan when she died, and still remember watching the light go out of her eyes. There was this huge absence I swear I could feel, as if she'd suddenly become lighter."

Claire nodded. "I saw that nothingness in Bea's eyes, too. It's sobering to think we're here one moment and suddenly gone in the next."

"Incomprehensible." Nora brought the salad to the table, then put the toasted cubes into a bowl and added it to the table as she took her seat. “When I saw my father’s body the day he died, I remember thinking he looked peaceful and so much younger.”

Declan filled her glass and raised his own. “To Bea.”

Footsteps on the stairs heralded Val’s return. At the sight of raised glasses, she ran to take her place at the table. “What are we toasting?”

“Who,” Nora said. “Claire’s friend, Bea.”

“To Bea.” Val raised her glass and they all sipped. “I just saw her last week.” Val’s unusual golden eyes glowed with mischief that matched her pixie haircut.

“At the cooperative?” Nora ladled out bowls of the thick creamy squash soup. She added garlic croutons and the heady aromas of cumin and basil spread across the table while she handed the bowls around. “Careful, it’s still very hot.”

“Yup.” Val helped herself to a slice of pie. “Thanks for getting veggie, Nora.”

“Thanks for getting meat, Nora.” Sophie helped herself to a healthy slice of pork pie.

Val elbowed Sophie. “Philistine.” She tasted her soup and waved her spoon at Nora. “Delicious. Bea came to pick up a gift for Claire.”

Claire stopped with her spoon halfway to her mouth. “For me?”

Val put her spoon down. “I suppose you might as well have it now.” She leaned over and brought out a shopping bag she’d placed next to her chair. “You’d admired this when you were at the cooperative together. Bea paid for it and asked me to ship it to you at Christmas. I thought you might like to have it now.” She took out an item wrapped in tissue and handed it to Sophie, who passed it to Claire.

"I had no idea—" Claire's face lit up when she saw what the package contained. "It's that vest you made! We had a whole discussion over you guys calling it a waistcoat." She shook off the tissue and held up a vest made of colorful vintage ribbons. Embroidered flowers, laces, and narrow velvets had been sewn together and made into a vest backed in pale green watered silk. Claire gulped and swallowed at the bittersweet gift.

"It's beautiful, Claire." Nora met Val's eyes, signaling for help to decrease the maudlin moment.

Val jumped right in. "Before you get too cocky about gifts, I have something for Declan, too." She reached into her bag and brought out a small tissue-wrapped parcel.

"Sadly, this isn't a Val Rogan original." Sophie handed the package over to Declan. "Mrs. Tink found this behind the refrigerator in your flat, which we are enjoying, by the way. I had it dry-cleaned."

Declan raised an eyebrow as he unwrapped a navy silk tie with gold crests. "My favorite tie! Bless Mrs. Tink. Now how did that get behind the fridge?"

Nora recalled all too well the night the tie had been wrenched off and impetuously thrown in the air to celebrate her return to Oxford. Val had taken Sean for the night, and there had been a huge bottle of champagne involved. She kept her thoughts to herself, and instead winked at her friend. "I notice everyone has a present but me."

"Yankee!" Val pointed her fork at herself. "I'm the one who found you this house, remember? Best gift of all."

Declan laughed and brightened the mood. "I told you she'd never let us forget that."

CHAPTER TWENTY

After the dishwasher was loaded, Declan lit a fire to ward off the chilly evening and the women moved to gather round it. He observed that Claire had better color in her face tonight. Having Val and Sophie over had been a good idea. He'd been unable to discern any reason why Claire had been involved in Bea's death and felt relieved. It would take a while for her to get over the way her friend had died, but it helped to talk with people who knew Bea, even if tangentially.

"Try on your waistcoat, Claire," Sophie urged, and Claire acquiesced, strutting around and making a turn in the colorful garment like a model. "Looks wonderful with your turtleneck and jeans. I can picture it at the holidays with a silky blouse and dress pants, too."

"This was so thoughtful of Bea." Claire took off the vest and carefully rewrapped it in its tissue.

Declan asked Val about Bea's stop at the cooperative to purchase the waistcoat. "Was she alone?"

Val sat near the hearth, rubbing Typo's ears, and thought back. "Hmm. She was definitely in a hurry, so I had the impression someone waited for her outside, but I can't see the street from that basement."

Nora piped up. "She didn't mention the name Verity, did she?"

"Nope. Who's Verity?"

"That's a charming old-fashioned name," Sophie said.

"She's a child Bea was a nanny for, at weekends," Claire said.

Maybe, Declan thought. He had a suspicion Verity was Bea's child. Now all he needed was evidence to support that hypothesis.

Typo ran to the back door and hit the bells Nora had used to train him. He rose to let the dog outside, and while the puppy nosed around his corner, Declan stood in the doorway and looked up at the night sky. It was cool, with a few scudding clouds. Stars glittered through and the contrail of a plane spread across the sky. Next door, a light was on in the attic room their neighbor Neil Welch used for his writing. In the distance, Declan heard a siren racing away from the city, growing fainter as the noise died on the breeze.

Talk of the dead woman filled his head. He made a pact with every murder victim to do his best to bring their killer to justice; when there was an unsolved killing, he found it difficult to leave his case at the station. Having Nora's sister find the young woman made it more pressing. He took out his phone and used his Notes app to make a list of calls he wanted to make tomorrow, Sunday or not. He'd wait to see if there was any forensic news before deciding whether to go into the station. He would also need to decide if he should have the other students' rooms searched for the missing necklace, but he would make that determination after the inquest.

He pocketed his phone and felt a pair of arms encircle his waist.

"Communing with the moon?" Nora leaned her head on his back.

He reached behind and pulled her in front of him, locking his arms around her as they studied the half-moon, the dark and light halves a yin and yang in the sky.

"Waiting for the pup to do his business." He looked around.

She chuckled and he caught a whiff of her perfume. "He's inside already. That's when I saw you on your phone."

"Guilty as charged." He looked back over his shoulder through the window to the living room, where the three women had their heads together in rapt discussion. "What's up in there?"

"They started in on the pros and cons of veggie versus meat eaters. I decided to leave them to it."

He squeezed her arms. "By the way, I did remember how that tie found its way behind the fridge. I suppose there's no way we could sneak past them and go upstairs?"

"Not a chance. But I could put out coffee and dessert."

"Only if you think they won't feel we're hoping they'll leave."

"We are!" Nora grew thoughtful in his embrace. "Declan, do you think Verity is the key to Bea's death?"

He took a moment to gather his thoughts. "I think, like her necklace, that Verity may be the heart of the matter."

CHAPTER TWENTY-ONE

Somerville

Fall 1992

Jim Robson watched Dora playing with the baby in the garden of their Somerville home. The sandpit had been a huge hit this summer, so much so that they'd had a hard time getting the boy out of it at times. His shovel seemed glued to his little hands, and Jim had nicknamed him "Digger," which made Dora laugh. She laughed a lot these days. Over the past months, he'd convinced himself he'd been right to bring the baby to a home where he was safe, cared for, and loved. The tyke was an easy child on top of it, with a cheery smile for all. He'd been a bit clingy when first brought to his new home, but if Digger had memories of his months near Bowness, they didn't appear to surface, seemingly consigned to the dirty playpen left behind.

The few neighbors they knew all accepted their little family as a unit when they'd moved into their rental house, and they kept mainly to themselves as they settled in. He liked the neighborhood in North Oxford, an easy drive to his company's headquarters in Headington. He was on the road less, too, the hospitals on his territory closer, a boon with the child at home. The transfer saw him supervising newer salesmen now. More paperwork, and he didn't have the freedom he once had to roam and set his own hours some days, but he found himself anxious to leave work to head home and see what the progress of the day had been.

Digger picked up things quickly, and with proper nutrition and care, soon toddled over the garden on unsteady feet, making noises. He waved to people from his buggy on their evening neighborhood walks. The only ones who knew he'd been "adopted" were Dora's sister and her husband. With Dora's fair hair and Scottish background, the baby's coloring resembled her well enough that anyone they met accepted him as their son. It was none of their business to know more.

And the boy was as good as their own, Jim decided, for all the attention they lavished on him. He felt pleased to have his little family finally complete. The change in Dora had been miraculous. He thought she would faint the first time Digger called her "Mama." Her face had glowed with a happiness he hadn't seen since their wedding day. Last week she'd been coaching the boy, so that when Jim walked in the door, Digger reached for him as he had that day in the playpen, and chirped, "Da-da." He'd cried a little then, happy tears.

Dora tickled the baby, which elicited high-squealed laughter. Jim looked at her joyful face and reassured himself. She'd lost weight before he brought the child home, and while she struggled to regain it, her cheeks were ruddy with fresh air and optimism. She'd never been more contented, she told him, and she'd never asked too many questions, either. The unspoken agreement between them was that Jim had saved her sanity, and with it, their marriage. With his hospital contacts, he'd even managed to wrangle a new birth certificate with their names on it, well worth the hundred-pound note passed across the counter. If the seal on their copy was a bit smudged, it passed muster with the local pediatrician they'd chosen after the move.

Now with the news that Dora's sister and her husband were moving down from Scotland and would live nearby, his wife was blissful. They hadn't seen much of Deirdre since their move to

Cumbria after they married. Dora had found it difficult not to show her envy when Deirdre had her little boy last year. The sisters kept in touch by phone, and Dora blamed the distance and Jim's work hours for staying away, except for the boy's christening. In any case, Deirdre had never questioned the story that Dora and Jim's long-awaited adoption had come through.

And if his thoughts about what he'd done kept him awake at times, well, that was the price he'd pay to give the boy a secure home and have his wife back.

Just last month a new couple had moved into the attached house next door, a bit older than them, warm and friendly, without children of their own. They seemed over the moon if asked to babysit if he and Dora wanted to have a meal out or catch a new movie. It really was the perfect situation.

Life couldn't get much better. He just hoped he'd soon start to sleep better.

CHAPTER TWENTY-TWO

Oxford

Sunday, 3rd December

12:30 PM

Nora sat in the kitchen with Claire, while Sean and Sam Welch played on an old comforter she'd thrown on the floor. They had a set of building blocks Typo kept trying to steal. It was a chilly and drizzly December day, too cool to play outside. Nora made notes of antics her fairies could get up to in Provence, while Claire pecked away at her laptop, reading and revising her final essay, asking Nora for better word choices here and there. Declan was up in his study making work calls, and he told her when she and Claire left later for tea at Exeter with the Hamiltons, depending on the outcome of his calls, he might pop into the station for an hour.

Nora put down her pen and stretched, thinking a cup of tea all around was in order, when Sally Welch knocked on the back door, standing under a bright blue umbrella. Emblazoned around its perimeter was a phrase picked out in gold Old English font: "Blessed are the flexible, for they shall not get all bent out of shape." Today's shirt was a bright plum that set off Sally's round cheeks over her priestly collar. Her curls frizzed in the dampness. After Nora opened the door, she introduced Sally to Claire, then put the kettle on. "Earl Grey, Sally?"

Sally folded the umbrella and left it by the door, then shook off her mac and draped it over an empty chair. "Tea would be lovely. That rain goes right through me." She rubbed her arms.

"Thank goodness the meeting didn't last as long as I'd thought."

"No worries," Nora said. "My turn to have Sam here for a while anyway."

"I like your umbrella," Claire said.

"Me, too. It was last year's fundraiser for the Young People's Fellowship." Sam ran to his mother and put his arms up. "Hello, love." She put him on her lap. "I had a mighty difficult time convincing them to go with this phrase instead of the one they wanted."

"Should I even ask?" Claire smirked.

Sally hugged Sam. "They were quite keen on 'Cremation is your last chance for a smoking hot body.' I convinced them sales would be low in the older part of the congregation, including the Bishop." When Nora and Claire laughed, she turned her attention to Sam. "Have you behaved yourself, young man?"

Sean put his arms around Typo as the pup tried to scamper over to Sally; the boy peered up at her from the blanket.

"Sean, I am not here to take your puppy." Sally smiled. "One aging shepherd is enough."

Nora set out three mugs. "Sean thinks Sally will take Typo home with her." She spoke to her son. "It's all right, lovey, really. Typo just recognizes Sally and wants to say hello."

Sean finally released his hold on the squirming pup, who ran to Sally for petting.

"How's the little guy treating you? Housebreaking holding?"

"We have to watch his chewing, but most days he's brilliant." Nora filled the mugs and brought a loaded tray over to the table. "Boys, would you like apple juice?"

"Jooz!" Sean crowed and clapped his hands.

"What do you say, Sam?" Sally whispered.

"Yes, peas."

Everyone laughed while Nora fixed two sippy cups and gave one to each child. Sally put Sam back on the blanket with Sean. Typo settled down between them with a chew toy. Nora put out a plate of biscuits from last night's dessert, and took her seat.

"Goodness, Nora, I almost forgot." Sally got up to root around in the various pockets of her mac. "A piece of your mail was stuck between the pages of a clerical journal I get. It's here somewhere."

"Probably a confirmation of my next freelance assignment for *People and Places* magazine."

"A new assignment?" Claire asked.

"I bet this is confirmation of my February article. The head editor is an older gent who backs up emails in writing. He doesn't trust computers completely." Nora didn't add that Jenkins didn't trust many people, either, but he had a soft spot for Nora. The articles helped her extend her visa to stay in England. Once she and Declan married, she'd apply for permanent resident status. Having a child with dual citizenship would help the process. "I have to find a cultural spot I like, and introduce American readers to it."

"Here we are!" Sally handed over a damp blue envelope.

Nora recognized the handwriting. "My mother. She usually emails me." Nora opened the soggy paper and a Visa gift card fell out. She scanned the note that accompanied it. "I guess this makes sense. She wants me to find several gifts from her and Roger to put under our tree. She can't bring everything in her luggage, and the post is so expensive." Nora scanned the note's contents.

"Who do you have to find things for?" Claire asked. "I can give you suggestions!"

"She says she ordered monogrammed slippers for Declan ages

ago after seeing the state of his in October, and those are being shipped directly here." Nora looked up. "Trust my mother to notice that." She kept reading. "I'm to get something small for Val and Sophie, and yes, for you, Claire, and also myself—I'm to be generous with myself and 'get something totally impractical.' That sounds like fun."

"Especially when someone else is paying for it," Sally said, and all three women laughed.

Nora slotted the note and card back inside the envelope and set it aside. "How did your sermon go over, Sally?"

Sally stirred sugar into her tea. "The rain kept people from hovering at the door, but several stayed inside to say they found it 'invigorating.' Whether that's a good or bad thing I haven't decided." She shrugged. "At least I made them think."

"It must be so difficult to have to write an essay every week," Claire said. "I have enough trouble writing several a term on topics I like."

Sally turned to Claire. "They don't have to be as long as yours, fortunately. I always run across a topic I easily warm to. The difficult part in today's age is to not sound preachy when that is exactly what it's called."

Nora watched the interplay between the two women and sat back, which Sally took as a signal to take over the conversation.

"I understand a friend of yours died tragically on Friday. I'm very sorry for your loss," Sally said.

"Thank you, um, Reverend—"

"Sally is fine."

Claire breathed out. "Sally then. It's taken getting used to, losing a friend. I can't imagine what her parents and brother are going through."

"I expect not. Was there a boyfriend in her life, too?"

Nora's ears perked up at this. This was an aspect she'd not heard Claire address before. Had Declan thought of this? She chided herself. Of course he had, and at the interviews yesterday that was probably one of the questions the students were asked. He couldn't share all the details he knew with her. He had told her there was some discrepancy about the nanny job, with Bea's parents thinking she was tutoring.

"I used to think so, but she was always on the go and didn't mention anyone special, which was odd as she was so lovely. I never saw anyone sneaking up to her room, either."

Sally smiled. "Does that happen often?"

"Maybe less than you'd think. We're all here for a result and pretty narrow-minded about work, I suppose. Some more than others. Not that we don't indulge in a bit of fun from time to time." She threw Nora a sheepish look.

"Hey, I was your age once upon a time." Nora thought of what Declan would want her to ask. A different perspective on the other students might be helpful. "Does that include the undergrads?"

Claire nodded. "Jack and Patti are both better students than they like to give off. Jack is a chess champ, his big outlet from what I see. Patti might be a hardcore feminist, but she's a dedicated Shakespeare fan. Of all of us, she's the one who can have a late night and still look good the next day. Nicola's a natural student, very bright, also Shakespeare. Obsessed with the Bard. She's spending the term break at The Globe."

While Sally asked more questions and let Claire talk about Bea's kindness and expertise on Roald Dahl, Nora stirred her tea absent-mindedly. She discreetly consulted her phone and clicked on the calendar to check the upcoming week. Tomorrow was a nursery day, and Sally's turn to take the boys home and give them lunch afterward. An idea formed and she waited for a lull in Sally's conversation with Claire to jump in.

" … and I wear purple or plum shirts right now for Advent." Sally finished explaining and sat back to drain her tea.

Here was Nora's chance to change the subject from clerical dress. "Sally, are we still good for you to give the boys lunch tomorrow?"

She nodded. "I'll bring Sean back at nap time. Neil said he has research to do at the Bodleian so the boys won't bother him. He claims he's at a very important part. I suspect he doesn't know where to go next, and hopes browsing through historic newspapers will give him a pathway."

"I call that the muddled middle," Nora said.

"What's his novel about?" Claire asked.

"It's a fictionalized account of Wilkie Collins' relationship with Charles Dickens, particularly their trip to Paris together. He's been consulting an autobiography Collins' mother wrote, and digesting his letters. At times it consumes him."

"Sounds interesting compared to contrasting Wordsworth with Emily Dickinson. That's what my current essay is about."

Nora made another attempt to settle her plans. "What about you, Claire? Any thoughts about tomorrow afternoon? Mr. Tink will be here, but he takes care of himself."

"Sophie is giving me a tour of the OUP archives in the morning. I thought I'd finish work on my essay after that. I can handle Sean for his nap if you need to go out."

Perfect. Child care sorted and a few hours to herself. Now to plan how to use her precious time. "I just might take you up on that."

CHAPTER TWENTY-THREE

2:10 PM

Declan enjoyed working in the study at the end of the upstairs hall, in what had probably been called a box room when the house was built.

The snug space had a set of built-in bookshelves, room for his desk, and a small filing cabinet. Best of all, when closed, the thick door kept noises from downstairs at bay and allowed him to work from home and make calls without interruption.

He'd taken time to read over the rest of the reports that had been uploaded from his team and learned Dr. Hamilton had arrived on the scene almost immediately after Bea's fall. Also, it had been confirmed that the scout had indeed called in sick the day before with an undisclosed ailment. Lily George had clarified with the university that Bea Jones did not hold any kind of employment or tutor position at the Radcliffe Camera.

He worked diligently, adding to the Home Office Large Major Enquiry System, where his actions and their rationale allowed any member of his team to see decisions, and to share their own progress. With a murder investigation, which this likely would be deemed at the inquest, HOLMES2 was used, a national system. He'd had McAfee set up a major incident room, which his team colloquially called "the murder room." This administrative center would coordinate further actions and as the senior investigating officer, he could direct and control the course of the enquiry. The computer program contained a Dynamic Reasoning Engine, known as DRE, which made it possible to combine the skills and experiences of his team with their input to identify new lines of enquiry. It was time-consuming but necessary, and once that was done, he felt organized.

After his chat with Nora, he'd decided he would tell Morris he'd take the DCI position tomorrow. He would have to wait for a board to approve his promotion and that of Watkins to DI in his spot, but with Morris recommending them both, he knew this would be more of a formality. Nora had considered the decision as seriously as he had, and in the end, she'd insisted he was the best person for the job. At the bottom of it all, he felt a real tie to his team and to this area and couldn't bear the thought of leaving it to be run by someone else.

His phone rang and he saw it was Charlie Borden.

"Don't tell me you gave up your Saturday and now you're at work on Sunday, too?" Declan could hear shouts of children in the background.

"At the park with the kids. But I just had a call from the weekend morgue assistant and I thought I'd better pass it along."

Declan sat up straighter, on alert. Charlie wouldn't have called him unless he deemed it important. "I'm all ears."

"A man called and wanted to know what he'd have to do to set up a view on one of our bodies currently inhouse, if they'd already had a formal ID from another family member."

"Did he say who he wanted to see?"

"No, and once the attendant explained that if the ID had been completed, he was welcome to a viewing but would need to bring along proof of his relationship, he rang off—hey! Let your sister have a turn on that slide!" Charlie huffed into the phone. "Kids. Wait 'til you have another and they fight like cats and dogs."

"I'll bear that in mind. Who do you have in the morgue who have already had IDs accomplished?"

"There are three right now: a male overdose, an elder who had a stroke at home and was found when her son brought her groceries, and your Beatrice Jones."

Declan's mind stirred with interest. "I see. No definitive way to pin down who this guy wanted to see?"

"Sorry. But this call was unusual enough for me to be notified. Most families stay as far away from the morgue as possible once the ID has been completed. Extra viewings are fairly rare."

"Who identified the others?"

"The parents did for the young man, rotten shame. The son who'd found his elderly mother had already seen her dead, but he came along to do the honors formally."

"I already know the father and brother of Bea have been there."

"It was definitely a man who called."

"You thinking what I'm thinking, Charlie?"

"The father of Bea's child? Perhaps. Maybe he doesn't have a way to prove he's related and rang off."

"Or maybe he does, but it's not at hand."

"You're thinking a birth certificate that names him as the father?"

"Yes. Keep me notified if he calls again or shows up."

"Have a good one."

Charlie rang off and Declan made a note on his iPad. He felt a glimmer of intuition that he and Charlie had figured it correctly: Bea Jones was the intended visit. He hoped the man would show up or call again. He turned his attention to making a list of things for his team to accomplish tomorrow. The scout might know about Bea's personal life. To have been pregnant and delivered a child meant there had to have been someone special to Bea.

He'd told Nora he might go into the station today, but there wouldn't be a need now that he'd seen there were no new forensic reports and he'd caught up on his paperwork. He would let Watkins know about Charlie's call, and he could check if his sergeant had reached Benedick Jones to ask what story he'd been told about Bea's weekend job.

"I'm assuming there's no baby news or you'd have texted me," he said when Watkins answered.

"None. We're enjoying our last days of freedom alone. We slept in and had a nice brunch out."

"Savor it. You may not sleep in again soon unless the little one's at a grandparents' house overnight, but you can still go out to brunch as long as you bring enough equipment to fill the back of that car you still need to buy—oh, and you'll become a dab hand at changing nappies in the back of said vehicle."

"As if. And thanks for the cheery outlook."

"You'll be smitten. Look, I won't take up a lot of your time now."

"No worries. Julie's taking a nap."

Declan detailed the call from Charlie Borden, and they discussed if the man who'd called had wanted to see Bea Jones. "It seemed most likely to Charlie; he'll be on alert if anyone shows up."

"This could be a big break for us."

"Let's hope so. Did you see the inquest is set for Tuesday? And how did you get on with Benedick Jones?"

"Yeah, saw that about the inquest. Unsatisfied with Brother Ben. I called this morning, but he was in services and whatever they have after that. Took his time getting back to me, too."

"Coffee hour, I suspect, when the congregation chats

informally with the vicars. Fellowship, Watkins."

"Whatever. Julie's Church of England but I'm not much of anything. When he finally returned my call, he sounded distant and very uncomfortable down the line. Tried to hurry me off the phone. When I said we could easily visit Cambridge again, he became a tad more cooperative."

"Good. What did he say about his sister's weekends?"

"He admitted he knew she wasn't doing tutoring, but was taking care of this Verity, and not in Cambridge."

Declan whistled. "Interesting. Why didn't she—or he—tell her parents that?"

"He mumbled his mother wouldn't have understood. Maybe she'd think that kind of job beneath her daughter? But I feel there's more to it. He kept hesitating and pausing."

"What about the baby she'd had?" The importance of the hunt for a birth certificate tomorrow became stronger.

"That's when he said there was the sanctity of confession to remember, and he needed to get advice about that. I had no idea Anglicans even did confession. Then he suddenly remembered a meeting and rang off, said he would get back to me tomorrow. He's definitely hiding something."

"Never underestimate a copper's feelings."

"Yeah, but if my instincts are so good, why don't I know if we're having a boy or a girl?"

"Different set of parameters." Declan reminded Watkins of how helpless he'd felt when Sean had been kidnapped 10 weeks ago. His copper's senses had felt muddied, and he'd had a difficult time knowing if he could trust his feelings. "All bets are off when it's your family."

"I'll take your word for that."

Declan brought Watkins up to speed on Denys Curshik and the missing boy case. "McAfee took the file home for the weekend. There's a copy on my desk if you're so inclined. I haven't logged it into HOLMES just yet."

"I'll check it out tomorrow. I have Lily George set to check the birth registry tomorrow for any birth Bea might have posted." If anyone could find it, the civilian analyst assigned to their team would sort it. "Should we visit the scout for that stairwell and get background on our suspects? And Bea's boyfriend or lack thereof? Phone or in person?"

"Let's try to meet with him or her tomorrow. Scouts keep their eyes and ears open, and their mouths closed. They might give up more in person than they would on the phone."

"I'll set that up. See you at the office for the morning briefing."

Declan clicked his phone off. He and Watkins might need a second trip to Cambridge to see Bea's brother. He thought of what he'd told Watkins about people giving up more face-to-face than over the telephone.

They also found it more difficult to lie.

CHAPTER TWENTY-FOUR

3:30 PM

While the rain had stopped, the sky was still leaden and dark by the time Nora was ready to head out with Claire to Exeter for tea with the Hamiltons. Sean woke from his nap fussy and drooling, and Nora gave him a packet of Nelsons granules for teething babies while deciding whether she should stay home with him. She wanted to hear what the don who knew Bea so well would say, but her mother's instincts told her the boy would be miserable for the next few hours, and it wasn't fair to inflict that on the Hamiltons, nor to take Sean out and expect him to behave when he was clearly uncomfortable.

But when she brought Sean downstairs and told Declan she thought she should send Claire off alone, he urged her to leave him behind and go with her sister. "She might enjoy having you to herself for a few hours. We have plenty of leftovers here for the two of us, between soup and pies. I'm good at distracting him."

Claire came downstairs then, ready to go.

Nora placed a bottle of sherry for the don and his wife into a decorative bag. "If you're sure. Just in case, *Yellow Submarine* is already in the DVD player." Nora chose her trench coat after kissing her men goodbye. She inhaled the lingering scent of Declan's woody aftershave and felt a wave of warmth expand in her chest. Still, she dithered on the stoop. "There's a cold teether in the freezer for him. And sometimes a bottle is better than a sippy cup."

"Partners, remember? I can handle him for a few hours. Claire, take her and get going." Declan handed Nora an umbrella and shooed them out the door.

The women followed the route Nora and Declan had rushed along only Friday morning. It didn't feel like only two days ago she'd received the frantic call from Claire. Nora glanced at her sister, who tailored her longer stride to match Nora's. She hoped it wasn't too soon for Claire to return to Exeter.

"At least the traffic is lighter on a Sunday afternoon," Nora said as they crossed the wide road of St. Giles in front of the Martyr's Memorial, a statue that commemorated Latimer, Ridley and Cranmer, all burned during the English Reformation for heresy for their Protestant beliefs. The sun was already low in the sky, and it would be dark when they came home.

"I keep thinking of Bea's last moments, Nora." Claire's brow furrowed. "She must have been terrified. I do all right during the day, but when I'm trying to fall asleep at night, I think about her terror, and flash back to when I looked over the rail and saw her crumpled on the stairs."

"That's a natural reaction, Claire. Would you like to try something to help you sleep?" Nora felt badly that she hadn't suggested this earlier.

Claire considered this. "Let me try on my own for a few more nights."

"It doesn't have to be a sleeping pill. There are herbals around."

"Let's check that out when we get home."

They turned onto Broad Street and entered Exeter through the main entrance off Turl Street. Claire nodded to the porter, the same fellow Nora had seen yesterday. They followed the slate walk around the Front Quad, past the Undercroft Bar. Nora wondered if Bea had ever trodden on the perfect grass. Even at this time of year, while not as lush as in the summer, the hallowed square remained neatly manicured, in contrast to the meandering ivy that climbed most walls of the ancient buildings. They passed the back of the chapel and the Rector's Lodgings.

"The next staircase is where Dr. Hamilton has his rooms," Claire said. "The Hamiltons have a house in Jericho, near the canal."

"I always connect Jericho with Inspector Morse." Nora was happy they wouldn't have to go into the area where Bea had fallen.

"I know." Claire pointed the way. "Mrs. Hamilton is head of the rehab center in Headington. Every other Sunday they attend chapel at Exeter and invite a student in for afternoon tea. This will be my second visit." Her eyes flicked ahead through the portico where Bea had died.

"They sound nice."

"They are." Claire opened a heavy arched wooden door, covered in the ubiquitous ivy. They ascended to a long hall and stopped at the first door. At Claire's knock, Peter Hamilton opened it and ushered them inside.

The first time Nora had seen the tutor he'd been in running clothes; yesterday in the Porter's Lodge, he'd been in casual attire. Today Hamilton was dressed in a three-piece tweed suit, every inch an Oxford don to her eye.

"Come in, please. Where's the little lad?" Hamilton's blue eyes twinkled while he ushered them into an expansive room with high ceilings and thick woodwork. There were book-lined shelves on either side of the windows at the front, which gave a view of the back of the chapel, where the late afternoon sun glimmered through the tall stained-glass windows.

"I'm afraid he's teething and I've left him home with my

fiancé," Nora said, handing him the sherry.

"What a shame. I hope he feels better soon." His eyes lit up as he took the gift. "This was kind of you."

A petite woman with curly hair and sparkling eyes came in from the second room, carrying a tray. "That's too bad. I hear he's adorable." She put the tray on a low table between two couches and shook hands with Nora. "Laura Hamilton. Hello, Claire. Please, take a seat and I'll pour."

While Laura served teas all around, her husband offered a plate of warm scones. "Plenty here, help yourselves." He stirred his tea. "How are you feeling, Claire?"

Nora was pleased Hamilton was direct. It stopped her from having to cast around for a discreet way to bring Bea into the conversation. At the same moment, she realized that Hamilton himself could have been the culprit, even if she couldn't see a motive for him to be involved yet. He was right on the scene when Bea fell, and it was only her impression that he'd been returning from his run. She tucked this thought away to examine later, but she'd keep her ears open for now. No one could really be eliminated, as far as she was concerned, except Claire.

"I've just told Nora I'm having trouble falling asleep. I keep seeing Bea on those stairs." Claire shuddered.

"Not an easy image to forget, Claire." Hamilton leaned over and spoke earnestly. "But if for even a moment she was aware of you as she faded out, you can take comfort in knowing you were there with her, holding her hand."

Claire sat up straighter. "I hadn't thought of that. Thank you."

"I have some melatonin I'll send home with you," Laura said. "See if that helps, with a cup of chamomile tea."

Claire nodded. "Thanks. Nora and I were talking about

looking into an herbal remedy. I'll try that."

This was Nora's chance before they moved off topic. "I didn't know Bea, but I understand she was very bright and kind."

"Kindness personified," Laura agreed. "She literally wouldn't hurt a fly. Once I was coming here after work and saw her leaning out her window, shooing a spider out of her room."

"Smart, too." Hamilton helped himself to two scones.

Nora broke off a buttery piece of her scone. "That was an unusual fellowship she had in Wales."

He agreed. "Not one I'd heard of, but Bea found it herself, and was willing to graduate a semester later to experience Dahl's home while she wrote his story. She was keen to connect his background to his writings to see if something in his childhood contributed to his anti-Semitism, or if he'd developed those feelings as an adult. The fellowship covered two terms and she stayed the summer, too. Remarkable when you think of it. Not many students would embrace their topic as fully. The end result showed it was worth her time and commitment."

Nora smiled. "You must wish all your students were so dedicated."

Everyone laughed and Hamilton pointed to Claire. "This one has a bit of that streak, too much work and not enough play at times."

"For all her hard work, Bea liked to escape Oxford at the weekends." Nora kept her tone casual as she helped herself to a finger sandwich.

"Very close to the family she worked with, apparently. Kept her work up, though. Brilliant book." Hamilton set his tea cup back on the tray. "I plan to get in touch with her family after a decent interval and ask if I can try to have OUP publish it posthumously."

Claire's eyes shone. "That would be wonderful."

"I can't imagine her family wouldn't agree. Sad business, though." He looked around. "I believe I need something stronger."

"I wonder if Bea had a boyfriend, or someone she was close to, who might have helped her with her research." Nora took a second scone. "These are delicious, Laura."

Hamilton rose and helped himself to a decanter that sat on a side table. He poured a measure into a rocks glass. "Bourbon for anyone? Or some of Nora's sherry?" At the women's blanket refusal, he sat back down and savored the scent of his drink before tasting it. "I thought she and Chad Brown had a thing for each other last year, but it seemed to fizzle out. They avoided each other this fall."

Nora's ears perked up. This would have been before Claire came to Oxford. "They were an item last year?" That would explain why the Shakespeare tutor appeared so distraught over Bea's death.

"Last Michaelmas." Hamilton sipped his bourbon appreciatively. "But then he was on sabbatical for Hilary and Trinity terms when Bea was in Wales, and I assumed they'd grown apart."

"Hmm. Brown. I wonder if his mother could be a hairdresser I used to see in Cowley." Nora pulled that out of her imagination's hat.

"Look at that gorgeous color." Hamilton raised his glass to the light. "No, wrong direction. Brown lives in Woodstock, in the shadow of Blenheim Palace."

"Now, tell me about this little boy who's teething, Nora," Laura asked. "Peter said you have a puppy, too?"

While Nora launched into a recitation of Sean and Typo's

antics, half of her mind was active elsewhere. Her years in journalism had taught her people had a habit of hiding in plain sight.

Even as she answered Laura Hamilton, Nora knew exactly what she would do with her hours off tomorrow.

CHAPTER TWENTY-FIVE

Monday, 4th December
8:50 AM

Declan went over the case with the team in the major incident room set up for Bea's case. If her death was deemed murder at the inquest tomorrow, things would ramp up quickly. After talking with Charlie Borden at the autopsy, the verdict seemed inevitable and he didn't want to waste time. He looked at the sea of alert faces whose attention he held. He wondered if he'd miss this when he handed these briefings over to Watkins?

Probably not. He didn't need to be the center of attention. His need was to restore justice to those who'd been hurt; that's what drove him. He couldn't do anything for Bea Jones, but he might bring that sense of order to her brother and parents. And to the father of her child, if he was still in the picture, as that phone call suggested he might well be.

He felt a tinge of guilt about not telling Watkins about their probable promotions yet, but first he had to speak to Morris and accept the offer of the DCI position, and clarify that the superintendent would back him on Watkins for DI. He would mention it to his sergeant and friend only after that was assured, while they waited for the formal review boards to meet sometime in the New Year.

He brought his attention to the civilian analyst, Lily George, whose job today would be researching a birth certificate for Bea's child. "George, a thought. If you don't find anything in England, expand your search to Wales." He saw Watkins nod in agreement, and then pointed to McAfee.

"McAfee will lead on a secondary case we've been handed." Several people moaned, not for McAfee, but for another case piled on. Having a suspicious death would take the bulk of their time without the thought of running a second active case. Declan explained about the young man who was convinced he was the missing boy from Cumbria. "Anyone recall that case?"

Lily George raised her hand. "I do, guv. Young boy snatched from his playpen behind a pub, mum a drug addict?"

"That's the one."

"My aunt lives in Windermere. I believe the boy's mother died of an overdose a few years later. That kidnapping was all my aunt would talk about when she'd call my mum. Made a big impression on me when I was just a child."

"You were never a child, George," someone called out, and everyone had a laugh. The young woman took her position seriously and handled the good-natured ribbing of the mostly male team in her stride. Declan never let it slide into harassment or bullying.

"Settle down, folks." Declan saw McAfee pecking away at his tablet. "Good background, George, thank you. Not exactly a cold case at the moment, but close. Cumbria has sent down the file."

Someone in the back raised a hand. "This chap thinks he's the missing boy?"

"Blimey," someone else said. "Good luck on that one, McAfee!"

Declan continued. "Watkins and I will be out interviewing the scout from stairwell 10. Anybody have anything else?"

McAfee raised his head from his tablet. "Forensics just sent through an analysis of that white thread found on the victim, guv. Egyptian cotton, nothing else special about it."

"All right, people. The inquest is set for tomorrow and will likely be adjourned. We'll ramp this case up, so get your actions from McAfee and HOLMES2. Let's see if we can't find out what happened to this young woman." The team lined up by McAfee to gather their assignments, except for Watkins. "Do we have a name for this scout, Watkins?"

"Sheila O'Connor." His forehead creased. "The porter's office was to send me an email with her address if she hasn't returned to work today. Forensics has released that stairwell."

Declan checked his watch. Morris would certainly be in by now. "Right. See where we're headed and I'll come find you in a few minutes."

Watkins threaded his way to his desk and computer, and Declan took the stairs up to the super's office. He stood outside for a minute in the quiet hallway to gather his thoughts, nodding to a civilian who passed. He was comfortable as a detective inspector and reminded himself of the huge responsibility as DCI. If something went wrong, his name would be the one the papers would seize on.

Last night after Nora's breathing had evened as she slept, he'd lain awake and gone over his list of pros and cons one last time before firmly deciding to accept Morris's offer, and included Nora's inheritance. While he wanted to support their family, pride wasn't the biggest factor. They would always have a cushion with Nora's money in the bank, but more than that, its presence represented a sense of security for her in addition to his life insurance if something should happen to him. He remembered how his mother had struggled financially when his father had died suddenly in an accident at work.

He hadn't mentioned this aspect to Nora. His mother was

gone for years now and Nora had never met her. Yet every police officer had to confront the thought that evil people accomplished evil deeds, and that made his work hazardous at times.

At one point later in the night, he'd woken to find the bed empty beside him. He thought Nora was in the bathroom, but the door was open and the light off. Then he heard her soft voice on the monitor, comforting Sean. Their little family was her priority, but she also had her writing. How she juggled it all with a puppy and new house, he didn't understand, but he knew his life wouldn't be the same without Nora in it, or Sean for that matter. He had to protect them.

He thought of Watkins, and how the promotion would give him a leg up, too, as he started his own family. The man's detective skills were solid. He would be a great DI and they could continue to work together. Watkin's wry sense of humor would hold the team together.

Most of all, he thought of Nora telling him she was behind him and her firm belief he was the best person for the job. He didn't have the ego to need this promotion, but he did have the conviction that it would allow him more latitude to achieve that sense of justice that drove him.

Declan inhaled deeply. He ran his hand through his thick hair, too long over his collar. A cut was in order before Nora's American family arrived for the holidays, and he needed to think about a Christmas gift for his fiancée.

Enough stalling. Declan cleared his throat, stood up straighter, and turned the doorknob to enter the next step in his career.

8:54 AM

On her brief walk around the hedge to the nursery with Sean, Nora tried to avoid tracking the buggy's wheels through several large puddles on the sidewalk after last night's rain had picked up in earnest.

In the middle of the night, she'd roused to the sound of the heavy rain outside, then realized the baby's mewling on the monitor had woken her. She'd felt disappointed to cancel her sleuthing today—not fair to leave a fractious child with Sally Welch. After she gave Sean more Nelsons granules, she rubbed numbing gel on his sore gums, then rocked him back to sleep, soothing him with a low rendition of the lullaby Billy Joel wrote for his daughter, "Goodnight, My Angel," while she rubbed his back.

To her surprise, he'd woken a few hours later in his usual cheery mood. When she investigated with a clean finger, she could feel the edge of the new molars had erupted through the gum, relieving the painful pressure. She called Sally anyway, who told her to go ahead with her plans but pack Nelson's granules and numbing gel just in case they were needed.

Nora left the stroller in the undercroft, along with Sean's restocked bag. She prayed his good mood would hold for Sally as she took off his coat and kissed him. She waved at one of the young caretakers, who scooped him up and brought Sean inside, plopped him down in the opening circle next to Sam. Sally caught her eye and gave her a thumb's up. Today her shirt was bright violet. With Claire set to be home by the time Sally brought Sean back for his afternoon nap, everything was in alignment for her to have this time to herself.

CHAPTER TWENTY-FIVE

Declan had his instincts about detecting, but Nora had her own feelings about people she brought to the table. Her promise to Claire to get to the bottom of things, both to clear her as a suspect and to find out what had happened to Bea, were made with resolve. Nora knew she needed to do what she was good at: ferreting out the truth about people.

Nora was on the sidewalk leading to her drive when a cyclist flew past close to the kerb, riding through the edge of a huge puddle, and sending muddy spray all over her mac and jeans.

"Hey!" she shouted at the biker's retreating back. He had the cheek to raise one hand in a salute behind him as he rode away without slowing down. "Was that supposed to be an apology?" She looked down at her clothes. With the mac hanging open, even her shirt had mud streaks down the front.

Nora stomped up her drive, muttering to herself, and met Mr. Tink coming out of his truck toward the house, carrying clean brushes.

"Whoa! Looks like you had a mud fight and lost."

"Cyclist plowed right through a huge puddle, as if he couldn't see it. It must have splattered his legs, too, but he didn't care."

"Always in a hurry these days." Mr. Tink held the front door for her and shook his head. He whistled "Happy Days Are Here Again" as he disappeared into the library.

Nora shook off her wet mac and left it in the hall, then climbed the stairs to change her clothes. She didn't want to spend a frustrating day in a grouchy mood when she needed to keep her wits and all of her investigative skills about her. She could wear her nicer trench coat, and that thought tamped down her irritation. This was supposed to be a relief day for her, a respite of stress-free hours. She opened the closet door in the master bedroom to peruse her choices.

She'd heard Sally say patience came with deep breaths and a change of focus; when life gives you lemons and all that. Maybe getting muddied up would be a good thing. Instead of reaching for another pair of jeans, Nora chose to change her look entirely.

By the time she came downstairs and threw in a load of wash that included the muddied clothing, she wore dress slacks and boots with a crisp patterned blouse. She'd added a string of green vintage beads Val had given her for her birthday, ones Declan swore brought out the color of her eyes. Coming back into the hall for her trench coat, Mr. Tink called out to her.

"Before I get too far, how do you like that radish inside the bookshelves?"

Nora stepped into the library and inspected the first bookcase. The back wall was now a bright raspberry color. "I think it's grand. Thank you." She explained Claire would be home later to put Sean down for his nap and that she would see Mr. Tink had lunch if he wanted.

"Mrs. Tink is coming by this afternoon, with the wall color the paint store had to mix so I can keep going. She'll help out."

Nora thanked him. This was the first time since the kidnapping she was leaving Sean with someone else. Reassured that between Claire and Mrs. Tink they would manage, Nora left the house for the bus stop that would take her into Woodstock. She didn't often bother to dress up and felt pleased with her appearance. With her mother's card and list in her backpack, she had a legitimate excuse for her outing.

She just hoped her afternoon would turn up something useful, something to explain the mystery of Bea Jones.

CHAPTER TWENTY-SIX

9:46 AM

DS Douglas McAfee had enjoyed his bacon sarnie after the briefing, but now it was time to get to work. Denys Curshik had returned to the station with an envelope of photographs of himself as a child, including several taken with his parents. McAfee introduced himself and explained DI Barnes had asked him to personally shepherd the case.

Chuffed at handling this, McAfee showed Denys to an interview room and sat across from him. After the morning's briefing, he'd handed out the actions to the team that HOLMES2 had thrown up. Then he'd confirmed that Donnie Walsh's mother had died of an overdose four years after her child had been kidnapped, although her DNA was on record from the time the child had been taken. He'd added that information to his file. He didn't mind being left at the station, not when he'd been named to lead the team actions and this other case. He was determined to show his senior officer he could handle it all.

Denys insisted McAfee call him by his first name. He tipped the envelope out and spread several photos on the table between them, turning them to face McAfee. He tapped each one as he described the approximate date and the people in each one while McAfee took notes.

"This one here has the date on the back, December 1992, so that must be right after we moved from Scotland to Oxford, based on what my mum told me. I would have been just shy of two years old then. Mum said she wanted to be near her sister."

Denys raised his head. The man's fair hair fell over his forehead. In the photo he was a sturdy toddler. "That's if what she told me was the truth. I hate that I'm doubting her."

"And these?" McAfee took in the young parents, the father with the fair hair his son possessed. His mother had reddish-blonde hair cut in the short style Princess Diana made popular in those years. McAfee picked up that one with a rush of connection. His own mother had worn her hair the same way for years.

"They're all a bit later. You can see I'm taller in that one." Denys pointed. "That rose bush, I recall my father planting it for my mother's birthday at the Headington house when I was about four, and here it's grown a bit, so I must have been five or so; that would make it 1996 or thereabouts."

McAfee nodded. "You told DI Barnes you don't have any earlier photos of yourself, and none as an infant, is that correct?"

"Nothing at all, and believe me, we've been through the entire house, cleaning it out and painting every room." Deny brushed at his hair again, a habit McAfee thought would be solved if the man would get a decent haircut. "I brought a copy of this." He withdrew a folded paper from the envelope. "It's my birth certificate. See, right here it says DUPLICATE."

McAfee noted the stamp in the corner. It registered the birth for Denys Marek Curshik on February 7, 1991, at the Glasgow Royal Maternity Hospital, and noted the mother as Deirdre Stewart Curshik and the father as Marek Antony Curshik. "I'll check with the hospital."

"This copy is yours. I'd like the photos back eventually." Denys carefully stowed everything back in the envelope and handed it over.

"Promise I'll take good care of them." McAfee consulted his

notes. "I've been over the file from Bowness. They do have DNA from the bottle left behind in the playpen. Once we have yours, we can compare them. I'm afraid that will take a while."

Denys nodded. "Any idea how long?"

"Several weeks probably. DNA testing is faster than it used to be, but never as fast as you see on telly. Sit tight, and if you think of anything else or find anything that might move your case up the ladder, feel free to get back to me before I contact you." McAfee handed him one of his cards, then paged through his file to the copy of the Bowness file. "One last thing. I've confirmed that Donnie's mother died several years after his kidnapping. His birth certificate doesn't name the father, I'm afraid, so no help there."

Denys nodded. "That's it for now then." He stood up. "I need to get back to work. Thanks for your help with this."

McAfee showed the man out of the building, and on the way back, crossed paths with Lily George on her way to the canteen. McAfee, who had just cleared the height requirement for the police, enjoyed being around the tiny woman who always made him feel taller. He'd thought of asking her out, but his natural reticence and lack of success with other women kept him from ruining a good working relationship.

"Fancy a tea or coffee, Douglas? I'm on my way for elevenses."

McAfee perked up as he accompanied Lily downstairs to the canteen, trying not to focus on her slim hips, or her light brown ponytail that swayed with each step. He realized she was the only person who called him Douglas. He liked it.

Once they had their drinks, he thanked her for telling him about Donnie Walsh's mother dying. "I checked it out and you were right." He detailed the interview that he'd later enter into the HOLMES case log. "No father listed on the birth certificate, either."

"What happens now?"

"I'm going to add two of the photos Curshik brought today to the DNA search. They may have his mother's DNA on them and we can see if they match, as a second confirmation. Then we have to wait for the comparison results, which will take ages, I suppose."

Lily arched one perfect eyebrow. "Maybe. Unless someone you know has a friend in that department and could call in a favor."

McAfee would hardly believe his luck. First Lily wanted to have a coffee with him, and now if he was reading the signals right, she was flirting with him. Vastly different from Patti Phillips, too. He swallowed hard and tried to think how Declan Barnes would handle this. He sat back and tried to appear nonchalant. "Just what would it take to have you call in that favor?"

Lily sipped her tea and looked at him through her lashes over the rim of the cup. She had the most extraordinary dark brown eyes he'd ever seen, like velvet. "Oh, I don't know. Maybe once we have a night off, a drink after work?"

She *was* flirting with him. Lily broke a shortbread cookie in two and offered him half.

He took it and his fingers brushed hers. "It's a deal."

CHAPTER TWENTY-SEVEN

10:39 AM

Declan rode away from St. Aldate's station through a complicated pattern of one way streets and "bus only" streets that would take them back to Exeter and the glowing spires of the center of town.

"We should have walked, cold or not." Watkins had become grumpy in the last hour.

"Bad night?" Declan maneuvered through traffic, at ease behind the wheel. "Your mood has swiftly deteriorated."

"Sorry, Dec. Lots of tossing and turning on Julie's side of the bed, trying to get comfortable. Every time she got up to pee, I thought this was it."

"Like waiting for the other shoe to drop." Declan realized he'd missed all of that with Nora. He'd met her in the early stages of her pregnancy, but she lived in Cumbria when Sean was born.

"Suppose so. That, and knowing that when it does fall, all hell will break loose. And then there's this ridiculousness today."

Declan wasn't certain he understood what Watkins found absurd. "Meaning what, exactly?"

"This whole business of scouts. Feudal, if you ask me. Some of these kids have been packed off to boarding schools from their youth, where they've been expected to make their beds and empty their garbage. Then they enter Oxford, and suddenly they need to have servants do that?"

"Not every student is from a wealthy family, Watkins, with more than a few on scholarships. But I grant you the practice smacks of 'Downton Abbey.' Oxford is big on tradition, don't forget, and it's an ancient practice."

"So are public hangings, and we got rid of those in the 1860s."

Declan reached Exeter and parked on the double yellow line, half on the sidewalk outside the main entrance on Turl Street. "Public, yes, but we still hung people for 100 years after that. Change is slow, Watkins." He propped his police card on the dash and the two men extricated themselves from the low-slung car, then stepped over the high sill of the arched wooden door to speak with the porter.

Watkins had established that Sheila O'Connor, the scout for Stairwell 10, had returned to work. The porter texted her, and while they waited for her response, Declan inspected the announcement board. Amongst several notices of club meetings, he spied one for the Chess Club competition that had passed and not been removed; another noted an outing to Stratford-upon-Avon's Swan Theatre to see the Royal Shakespeare Company perform "The Taming of the Shrew" on the following weekend. The flyer had "CANCELLED" written across it on an angle in red pen.

The porter interrupted his thoughts. "Detectives, Mrs. O'Connor will see you in the second-floor pantry of Stairwell 10." He described where they would find the pantry.

They thanked him and entered the college grounds.

The men rounded the first corner of the grass quad by the Undercroft Bar, where noisy conversation and the sound of chinking glasses floated out.

"Early lunch?" Watkins asked.

"Or late breakfast if you've been up half the night revising."

"Or drinking. And expect your scout to make your bed and clean up your sick. I hope my kid doesn't want to go to a uni like this." Watkins exhaled a deep sigh.

"Relax. It's only Oxford, Cambridge, and I think Durham that still do scouts. I think Cambridge and Durham call them 'bedders' instead of scouts."

"Bloody hell. I don't want to know where that came from."

Behind the chapel, they passed under the archway to the scene of Beatrice Jones' final moments. After walking up two sets of stairs, the men passed Nicola Morton's door, shut tight with a note: *Do Not Disturb.* Across the hall Watkins knocked on the door behind the shower room as directed.

The door was opened by a lean brunette whose pixie haircut was streaked with grey. She wore a navy pinafore over a three-button shirt and jeans, and a brace on her left hand. Tortoiseshell glasses hung from a beaded chain around her neck and clanked against a lanyard that held a bunch of keys.

Declan introduced them, and O'Connor told them to call her Sheila.

"Mrs. O'Connor's my mother-in-law, the old battle-axe." She grinned, her Irish origins evident in the hills and valleys of her speech. "Come in; just in time for elevenses."

The room was long and narrow, with windows that let in light and the same view of the far side of the chapel as Claire Scott's room. Rows of shelving held clean linens, garbage bags, toilet paper rolls, and cleaning supplies. They stepped around a vacuum cleaner to the rear, where a rolling cart held a microwave, fixings for tea, and two folding chairs.

She looked at the chairs and at the two men. "This is about Bea, yeah?" At their dual nods, Sheila crooked her finger at Watkins. "You, come with me." Watkins dutifully followed her to Claire's room.

Declan turned in the doorway to watch O'Connor pull the

clutch of keys from the lanyard on a retractable line. She chose one and unlocked Claire's door.

"This one's away for a few days. Won't mind a borrow." She pointed inside the room, and Watkins carried a sturdy wooden chair back to Sheila's den, while she carefully relocked the door.

Back in her pantry, she said, "I have Barry's and PG tips." She put a Barry's teabag into a large mug and poured in bottled water. "No tap for me even if I don't have a hob. Have to keep my standards, don't I?" She grinned, crinkling the laugh lines at the corners of her eyes.

Declan thought the lines around her mouth begged for a cigarette. "Thanks, we'll pass." He sat on the flimsy folding chair and hoped it would hold him, while the more robust Watkins took the wooden chair.

"Biscuit then?" She held out an open roll of Hobnobs cookies.

"You go ahead please." Declan saw Watkins' flicker of disappointment and decided he'd buy his sergeant a decent lunch after this interview. "We know you're on a tight schedule and appreciate your time."

But Sheila had seen the flash in his sergeant's eyes and shook the roll of biscuits at him. "Go on, then, have one. No harm done."

Watkins thanked her and obliged, juggling his pen, notebook, and cookie. Despite the use of tablets in the office, Watkins preferred, as Declan did, to handwrite his notes and observations in the field and transfer them to the tablet back in the office.

The microwave dinged and Sheila prepared her tea and sat down. "Right then, now I'm like the queen on her throne, what'll I tell you?"

Declan plunged in. "We understand you were off work on

Friday?"

She held up her left hand. "This eejit wrist. Had an appointment with the ortho finally, after waiting months. Carpy tunnel. Needs a fix, but prob'ly not 'til first of the year." She waved the offending wrist at them. "Still, works most times." She arched an eyebrow and dictated to Watkins: "Mr. McNab, Nuffield Ortho Centre, Headington."

Declan thanked her for the information to check on her appointment. Wise woman. He chose his words carefully. "We'd like to ask about Beatrice Jones and the other students on this stair. I know in your position you see and notice things. We need to have a sense of all the personalities, and their relationships, both personal and with each other." He hoped he'd phrased that well enough to get beyond any reservations she might hold about what she deemed gossip.

Sheila gave a sharp dip of her head. "You want the craic, their secrets, too? Fine line we scouts walk, you know. Some resent us, see us as an invasion of their privacy. Others are polite and grateful. We do our work, get in, get out. After a while, we get to know which students will be up early—that American lass whose chair I borrowed, she's one up sooner. Always at her desk when I knock, even if she's not proper dressed yet."

Declan decided not to share that he knew Claire Scott; he caught Watkins' eye to get him on board. "What can you tell me about her?"

"Polite, always thanks me. At first, she was embarrassed to have me vacuum weekly and change out her tea things every day. Now she's used to me, will ask about my wrist."

"And her relationship with Bea Jones?"

"Friendly. Had lunch together most days, but then I don't often see any of them late in the day, so they might have spent time together after class or in the evenings. I also cover the middle common room, though, and neither hung out there much from what I could tell."

"What about the young man, Jack Soong?

"Likes to sleep late at times. Hides his smarts, not a gobdaw, just shy, unless you get him talking chess. Confides in me when I'm changing his sheets."

"A woman he likes?" Watkins ventured.

Sheila hesitated. Declan assured her any information she shared of a personal nature wouldn't be used unless it had direct bearing on the case.

"He likes women *and* men, but hasn't come to terms with that, nor told his parents, and agonizes over telling them someday, poor boy. Afraid he'll be disowned. He wants to do well here so they can be proud of him for that. I'm like an agony aunt to some, ya know?"

"But no partner you've seen?"

"Not around Exeter, at least, nor to his room. He hangs out mostly with Patti, that's the Phillips gal." Sheila drained her mug and checked her watch. "Maybe time for a topoff." She refilled her cup and talked over the noise of the microwave. "Them two upstairs, Jack and Patti. Different as chalk and cheese, her with that gruff exterior, but for all her feistiness, Patti's good to Jack. Keeps him under her wing, so to speak, so he's not alone all the time. She's another one who hides her smarts. Abused when she were a child, I think; reason she hates men."

Declan raised his eyebrows. "You're quite the armchair psychologist."

The scout shrugged. "Over 30 years I bin doing this job. Ya

get to know people, see the signs. There's some scut of a useless sod out there she's wearing those heavy boots for, wanting to kick his bollocks."

"All right then." Declan was not about to argue with Sheila's opinions. He needed her observations.

"And what about Jack and Patti's relationship with Bea Jones?"

"Not a deep one, I'd say, but friendly, as you would with people living in close proximity. Different degree years. Never saw them eating together or going out with her, which Claire and Bea did a lot."

Declan reflected on a woman who could use "bollocks" and "proximity" in the same conversation. "What about Nicola Morton? I noticed the sign on her door."

The microwave dinged and Sheila made her second cup of tea. She handed Watkins a second biscuit. "Likes things a certain way, that one. Never seen her leave her room without full makeup." She lowered her voice, as if Nicola could hear them across the hallway. "Boyfriends, that kind of thing you want to know?" At Declan's nod she continued. "I used to think she liked women because of her posters. Who cares, right? She's got Marlene Dietrich and Marilyn Monroe, Judy Collins and Kate Bush posters Blu-Tacked to her walls. But that's just retro celebs she favors. She has a boyfriend but keeps him secret. Mind you, I've not found him in her bed of a morning, but no one spends on lacy thongs and undies like that one does and leaves them lying around unless they're trying to impress someone. She works weekends at Boots to buy her fancy makeup and knickers. And she keeps her hanging clothes closet locked."

Declan wanted to ask how Sheila knew this but she got there ahead of him.

"Knocked and came in a few times to see her shutting the doors real fast. Turned the key right in front of me." She shrugged. "Not necessary. I never go into their personal things."

"You are clearly observant. What about her relationship with Bea Jones?"

"Something there. More of a competition, leastways from Nicola's side. Always ready to put Bea down when I was around, even though they were different degrees, too. 'Some of us don't have the tutor's ear,' that kind of thing. Haughty, kind of, ya know? Could just be she's a scholarship student and Bea clearly came from money." She sipped her tea. "'Course, Nicola were runner-up for Miss Pre-Teen Jamaica before emigrating, and that'll make a gal's head swell, so she mighta been like that with all and sundry."

Watkins wiped crumbs off his shirt and scribbled furiously. "How did Bea Jones react to her?"

"Pretended she didn't notice." Her face filled with sadness. "She were that kind of gal, kind and sweet-natured. You saw those quotables in her room?" At Declan's nod, she continued. "'Course there were two sides to her, too."

This was the first Declan had heard this said about Bea. He encouraged her to elaborate. "Please, go on."

"Not bad either side, no. Just that when she were here working, she were all business. Worked at her desk, headed out to the library, in her room at night working more, based on what she told me. Shared an occasional glass of wine with Claire Scott. And then Thursday afternoons she were out of here like a flash, never looked back, never saw her until Monday mornings, and her bed not slept in all weekend. That were different from last Michaelmas, before the Wales thing, so I asked her what she got up to all weekend. She told me she was with her heart's love, and that's all she would say. But the others told me she had a nanny job back home in Cambridge."

That nanny story again. "Did you notice a necklace Bea wore? Maybe a locket?"

"Ah, sure. She were wearing that when she came back from Wales. Never took it off. A delicate gold heart with a tiny amethyst."

"Any idea where it came from?"

Sheila shook her head. "A memento of her time in Wales. She said those months were the highlight of her life."

"Before that, last year before she left for Wales, any sign of a relationship then?"

Sheila was clearly uncomfortable now. She avoided looking at either of them as she made a show of clearing up, dumping her tea bag, twisting the packet of biscuits closed and shoving it into a tin. "Mighta been."

"Someone in her room then?"

"No, not that, just—"

It dawned on Declan what Sheila's reticence might be down to. "Sheila, we've had to do a post mortem on Bea." He let that thought settle between them all.

Sheila sighed. "Then you'll know she were hiding a pregnancy when she left for Wales."

"Yes, we do know. Any idea who the father was, and if she carried the baby to full term?"

"No and yes. Don't know who the father was, but yes, she had the child. It were one reason she went away to Wales, so her family wouldn't know about it. She wouldn't give me the details and I didn't push." She stood to stow her biscuit tin and wiped out her mug. "Hard to hide a pregnancy from someone cleaning your room, especially in the early days, although she tried at first. I have to say, she wasn't upset, in fact, she was more like jubilant, especially when her fellowship came through. She only told me the father was the love of her life. When she saw I kept her confidence she told me that much and begged me to secrecy. When she came back, and I asked her where she went all weekend, she said it was better if I didn't know for now, but that she'd be celebrating at graduation. The others thought the nanny job took her away." She shrugged. "Not my secret to tell."

"So no current boyfriend?"

"Not that I've seen."

"So the next question is: where is this baby?"

At this, Sheila O'Connor shook her head. "She wouldn't talk about it when she returned, but I figured she went to Wales each weekend to see the father and her baby. That's just supposition, though. In reality? I have no fecking idea."

CHAPTER TWENTY-EIGHT

11:53 AM

Nora's feet started to hurt. She'd taken the Route 7 bus from Keble Road, near St. Giles, to the Marlborough Arms stop in Woodstock, passing Blenheim Palace on the way. The birthplace of Winston Churchill was a true grand palace, and would be beautifully decorated for the holidays, even if touring its gardens and extensive grounds would have to wait until the spring for the open season and nicer weather. It would make a delightful place to take her mom and Roger between Christmas and New Years.

When she'd arrived in town, she'd walked down the High Street, eyes alert for any signs of Chad Brown, her quarry for the day. He wasn't listed in the phone book, but then perhaps they didn't have a house phone, as so many used their mobiles exclusively. The street had quaint shops the locals used, but she didn't see his distinctive visage. Long shot, anyway, she decided. She'd have to get more creative. Her excuse to be here was holiday shopping as her mother directed, and a little for herself. While she truly wanted to accomplish some of that, she also wanted to see how Brown connected to Verity and to Bea. His reaction to the name Verity was too distinct not to think there was a connection.

Nora reached the end of the street where it connected with the square at Market Street, with the Town Hall at its apex. The glove shop next to the hall belonged to the town's history; it had been gloves that had driven some of its former prosperity. She scrutinized their offerings and bought her mother a pair of cherry-red leather gloves lined in soft faux fur. One gift down.

She tucked the package in her backpack and considered her options. She could walk left down Park Street, but her stomach rumbled and she chose instead to cross to The Star Inn for sustenance and an investigative chat.

The dark beamed ceiling was offset by bright salmon-colored walls interspersed between runs of stone. Vintage furnishings added to the ambience.

Once she was seated and decided on her lunch, Nora drank her water with lemon, and tried to think how she could broach the subject with her waitress, a woman she'd pegged as a local after hearing her talk with a couple at the bar about an upcoming carol sing in town at St. Mary Magdalene's. Her name tag read "Janna," and when she brought Nora's meal, Nora hoped she came across as casual when Janna asked if there was anything else.

"Since you asked, a friend of mine who teaches at Exeter, Chad Brown, lives here. I thought I'd pop in to see him but I don't remember his address."

Janna's face lit up. "Lovely man, isn't he? Always trying to get us to Stratford for a play, but my Davey isn't keen on men in tights." She looked into the distance. "I know he lives right around here, not exactly which house." She snapped her fingers. "Wait—his mum works up the square, at Antiques at Heritage. He and Alvita share a house."

"Thanks. I'll pop over after I finish eating."

Bingo. Now she had his mother's name, and had learned they lived together, information she could use. Nora attacked her chicken salad wrap and, after paying and leaving Janna a nice tip, left the inn and turned left up Market Street in the direction Janna had pointed out. Right next door to the inn, a large antiques store displayed a tall Georgian armoire in its window, although the name wasn't the one Janna mentioned. Some of the connected buildings were from the 17th century. Shops mingled with others still used as residences. Nora passed an art gallery, and a few more homes, then stopped at a vine-covered shop with two large mullioned windows decked out in cranberry paint. They contrasted nicely with royal blue doors. Gold printing on cranberry banners at the top of each window proclaimed *Antiques at Heritage.*

This was it. Nora hoped the shop wasn't closed for lunch, and lights inside convinced her it was open. Before trying the door, she peered in the left window, artfully displayed with antique tables, silver, and paintings. Through the right window, she saw porcelain dishes and figurines, leather-bound books, and stacked vintage luggage. She could see several glass-fronted display cases that must hold jewelry and other smaller items deeper into the shop. She would shop here and try to get information at the same time. Perfect.

She pushed open the blue door; a bell chimed in the back of the shop. Nora inhaled the scent of old paper, wood, and leather, overlaid with a balsam candle that reminded her it was winter. A collection of shiny glass Christmas ornaments that showed wear but were still beautiful stood in a bowl on the corner of the main counter, which had been festooned with greenery draped with clutches of red berries. She could happily lose herself here for hours without a toddler in a buggy if she didn't have a different agenda.

A tall woman with dark wavy hair pushed aside the curtain from the back and approached the counter. "Chris Breen. How may I help?"

Nora was happy she'd dressed nicely; the woman wouldn't question whether she could afford the pricey items in here. She brought out her mother's shopping list. It might be best to butter the woman up before plunging into her quest. "I need to browse around for several gifts." That was the truth, at least. She might as well accomplish two things at once.

"Certainly. Let me know if you need a locked case opened."

This was the kind of place she and Val liked to forage in before their days of babies and relationships, drooling over things they couldn't afford, gaining decorating ideas, sometimes purchasing a tiny bauble. Someone with a good eye for design had arranged the displayed items. There was a sense of wonder and discovery for Nora that most of these objects had all been used and loved by others. She toyed with the Tiffany watch her father had given her for her 16th birthday that had the name "Judy" engraved on the back. She wore it every day in his memory, despite having the time on her phone. She and Val had once spent an entire evening over a bottle of wine creating stories about Judy.

With Val on her mind, Nora spied an old hatbox crammed full of vintage ribbons and laces. Beside it, a cut-glass lidded jar held a selection of antique buttons. These would be perfect for Val, from her and Declan, and from her mom. Heartened, she brought them to the counter.

The woman looked up from an account book and smiled. "Great finds already?" She noticed Nora's necklace. "Those are beautiful malachite beads."

Nora pointed to the hatbox and jar. "These are for the friend who gave them to me. She's a textile artist."

"Lucky you. She'll love these."

"I'll just leave these here and keep shopping, all right?" Nora wandered, reaching the back of the store down one side, and coming up the other, her eyes peeled for gifts. She soon added a pair of tortoiseshell combs for her mom to give Sophie. Nora had already ordered a pair of tickets for a play Sophie had mentioned she wanted to see, so she was done, too.

She spied a collection of driving caps and chose a Harris tweed flat cap for Roger she hoped would fit. Then she lost herself browsing through the shelves of rare books for Claire and couldn't decide between a first edition of a biography of Wordsworth or a three-book collection of Emily Dickinson's letters. In the end, she put both on the counter, deciding her mother and Roger could choose which one to give Claire; she and Declan would give her the other. She might pick up a scarf to go with the vest Bea had gifted her sister, too, as she'd noticed Claire liked scarves.

Satisfied she had made good headway on her mother's list and her own, Nora remembered she needed a gift for Declan. While she tried to think of a natural way to ask for Alvita, she gazed at the contents of a locked case that held estate jewelry. She strained her ears to listen for noise from the back office.

Perhaps a pair of cufflinks Declan could wear at their wedding, and afterwards with the French-cuffed shirts he favored for dress? She looked over the choices available while she thought of blatantly asking if Alvita was at work that day, but if she said she was a friend, and the woman came out of the back office, it would immediately be obvious they didn't know one another.

Then Nora spied a silver bar pin, engraved along either end and its perimeter. In the middle, the name NORA stood out in raised letters. This might be not only the perfect gift from her mother, but also a natural way to engage the owner in conversation.

"Excuse me, could I see a few things in this case?"

"Certainly." The woman strode over and selected a key from a bunch she withdrew from her pants pocket.

"Those engraved cufflinks, please, and that silver pin."

The woman withdrew both items. "These cufflinks are Art Deco shields, a mix of yellow gold and platinum, etched with a latticework design. Very nice and in excellent condition."

"They are lovely. Let's keep those out." Nora chanced a question. "I don't suppose you have a gold heart locket with an amethyst?"

The woman shook her head. "The only locket I have is this oval one." She pointed to another shelf.

"No, that's all right. What can you tell me about this pin?"

It was the right tactic to take. The woman glowed as she launched into a description. "Very rare. Victorian sterling, and instead of the name being etched into the silver, each letter has been cut out separately in that font and applied." She handed the pin to Nora for her inspection. "Do you know a Nora?"

"I'm Nora, and shopping for my mother's gift to me. She's coming over from America and has me choosing my own gift."

"Smart lady. She'll be able to fit clothes in her suitcase. If you're Nora, then this is your pin. I have vintage boxes for both of these, and I can gift wrap anything you'd like."

Nora thought of Val's stepmother, who's favorite saying was, "Wrap it up!" "I'll take both of these, and let you wrap them, please. Keep prying eyes away. I'll wrap the rest myself."

"Wonderful." Clearly pleased by the largesse of Nora's purchases, the woman brought the jewelry to the main counter.

Nora followed, and sat in the chair placed next to the counter. She watched the woman find leather boxes stamped with gold filigree for the jewelry and put tissue around the other gifts.

She helped herself to a hard candy from a cut glass bowl on the counter and launched her plan. "I believe my friend from Exeter, Chad Brown, said his mother Alvita works here?" Nora watched the woman wrap the jewelry boxes in cheery green foil.

The woman's face lit up. "She does, part time, mostly Friday and Saturday when we're busier." The woman added red satin bows to each box. "She's our jewelry guru. She could tell you all about the healing properties of your beads."

"Oh, that's a shame she's off today then. I'd love to meet her and thank her for Chad pointing me in your direction." Nora laughed. "I've managed to get most of my Christmas shopping done in one fell swoop."

"Yes, you have a nice pile there." The woman totaled her purchases and slid the bill toward Nora.

Nuts; that hadn't cut it. She handed over the Visa gift card and her own credit card for the pieces she'd purchased. "Chad said he and Alvita live near here?" Nora held her breath. Maybe knowing he lived with his mother would do the trick.

"Right down Park Street in the terrace. Montague House. So convenient for Alvita to walk to work, and she says they have a cute little garden out back." She handed Nora her credit cards back. "Still a bit of a balance on this gift card."

Nora nodded as she put the cards back in her wallet. "Romeo and Juliet. Of course, Chad's specialty is Shakespeare."

"Alvita says Chad's a real romantic." She put Nora's purchases into a large shopping bag with sturdy handles that had the shop's name emblazoned on the side. "There you go. I do hope you've found what you came for."

Nora thanked her and took the bag. "I believe I have. Merry Christmas."

CHAPTER TWENTY-NINE

Cambridge

1:06 PM

Ben Jones rolled down his shirt sleeves and buttoned his cuffs before knocking on the door of his tutor at Ridley Hall. The brass plate on the door read: *Rev'd Dr. J-M Crothers, Academic Dean.*

The summons to see Rev. Mike, as he had his students call him, had felt like God's hand reaching out with an offering. When Ben had seen the dean at yesterday's services, Rev. Mike told him to stop by, then sent a message to his room this morning to see him after lunch. How did the priest know Ben was floundering?

At his knock, Rev. Mike called for him to enter, and when Ben opened the door, the priest had already risen from his desk. He came around it to clasp Ben's hand and patted him on the shoulder. "Ben, thanks for coming." He leaned on the corner of his desk and pointed to one of the two leather chairs that stood in front of it. "Make yourself comfortable."

Ben took the proffered chair and tried to relax. He admired Rev. Mike and had found his counsel in the past to be wise.

"How are you managing? I can't imagine the loss of a sibling, much less a twin. You must be gutted."

Trust Rev. Mike to cut to the heart of the matter. "I am. I know I should trust in God's plan, but sometimes it's tough to see what that could possibly be." Ben's eyes filled with tears he tried to keep from brimming over, even as a burst of anger tore through him and caught in his throat.

Rev. Mike pushed a box of tissues on his desk toward Ben.

"I'm not certain God's plan was for Bea to have this tragic fall. Accidents do happen after all. It's how those Bea left behind handle her loss that concerns me."

Ben gave a sharp nod of his head as he collected himself. At least his dean hadn't told Ben that Bea was in the arms of God, the same God he'd pledged to give his life to, and with whom he was currently furious. "It's possible her fall wasn't an accident. There's an inquest tomorrow. My parents and I will attend to hear what they've found so far and about her state of mind."

Rev. Mike pursed his lips. "How was her state of mind?"

Ben raised his eyes. "Bea was so happy! On the brink of everything she'd been working toward in so many areas of her life." He shook his head. "She wouldn't have taken her life; I'm convinced of that." He inhaled a shaky breath. "I'm concerned someone pushed her."

The priest's eyes widened; he cocked his head to one side. "Is there evidence of that?"

Ben lifted a shoulder. "A necklace she always wore had been ripped off and is missing. I won't know 'til tomorrow if there's more."

"That's really tough, Ben. I wish I had more encouraging words right now." He frowned. "I only met Bea a few times. She was so pleasant, not the sort of person who would attract enemies."

"She was lovely," Ben choked out. "I hate talking about her in the past tense." His tears finally fell fast and hot, splashing his shirt.

Rev. Mike went behind his desk to grab a bottle of water from a tray on the credenza. He twisted it open as Ben cried, then handed him the bottle once he'd gulped his tears back and blown his nose. "It's acceptable to show emotion, Ben, especially grief."

"I know." He chugged half the bottle and wiped his mouth with a clean tissue. "Phew."

"Releasing those feelings does help." The priest took a seat in the chair opposite. "I remember when we talked before about your questions regarding keeping Bea's confidences. These were not under the sacrament of confession, but you had your reasons when she was alive. However, with her death you can't lie under oath if you're asked a direct question, Ben. In any case, I'm not certain those confidences should be kept now, if you feel they might have bearing on the way she died."

"It's all I can think about, wondering if they did—well, that and knowing I'll never hear her laugh, or share special moments with her again. Today I should have called back one of the detectives I put off yesterday, but he'll be there tomorrow. I want to help, I do. I just don't know if what I know about her life has any bearing on her death."

"It's a tough decision, I get that. You'll have to feel your way. My feeling is that being open now may be best for everyone." He leaned forward. "Keep Bea alive in your memories, Ben. A poor substitute, I know, but try to find the joy you shared when you do think of her, once the acute sadness passes." He sat back and crossed his legs. "Now, how are your parents holding up?"

"My father loses himself in his music. He's almost frantic, listening to pieces as a distraction, trying to pick those Bea would have liked for her funeral." Ben explained how his mother at first refused to believe Bea was gone, until he and his father had traveled to Oxford and seen her lying in the morgue.

"That must have been a very difficult moment."

"The worst. Now Mum's found out Bea had a child, she's gone quiet, almost numb. Totally not what I would have expected."

Rev. Mike raised his eyebrows at this news. "I see. So that's one secret out of the bag already." At Ben's nod and miserable expression, he asked: "How did you expect your mum to react?"

"For her to be livid, yelling about how Bea let our side down, things like that. If she only knew all the details ..."

"And you do?"

"Oh, yes." Ben looked at the calluses and sores on his fingers from the guitar he'd sought refuge in all weekend, playing Bea's favorites until his fingers bled. "I know everything."

1:36 PM

McAfee stood up from his desk, then sat down again. He didn't want to crowd Lily, but he wanted to know if she had contacted her friend in the DNA lab. He looked over the open-plan office to her desk, where she was focused on her computer, her fingers flying over the keys as she did data input on the cold case. Whether Denys Curshik was Donnie Walsh or not remained to be seen. McAfee hoped he would be the one to get to the bottom of it all.

His computer dinged with an incoming email. He clicked on it and read that the tech had taken Bea's phone to the morgue and used her index finger to unlock it. His report noted that while Bea Jones had closed or inactivated her accounts on most social media, she did have an active text messaging with someone she listed as "Luv." When the contacts listing was accessed, "Luv" was only identified by that nickname and a phone number. McAfee would apply to have the owner identified, but the phone company would probably require a warrant before they'd release that information.

McAfee read through the most recent texts from Thursday night that the tech had transcribed, which revolved around weekend events Bea hadn't lived to see.

> Luv: How was concert? xx
> Bea: Fun! Stress relief! All good by you? xx
> Luv: We missed you (string of heart emojis)
> Bea: Me, too. You'll appreciate me more! Xx (kissing emoji)
> Luv: Never. Want you always. Xxxxx
> Bea: Edits DONE! Free at last! Xx
> Luv: Calls for celebration! (champagne bottle emoji) Staycation picnic Sat?
> Bea: With our fave peep, brilliant. See you first thing AM (sleep emoji). Hang tight. Almost there (hearts emojis of varied colors)
> Luv: Best is yet to come (more heart/kissing emojis) Excited! Xxx

The tech said he would send previous texts if needed, but McAfee thought he would ask Declan if that was warranted before the inquest. It was evident to McAfee that Bea Jones had been in a close relationship with this "Luv" person and had planned on being alive on the weekend. He logged the information into the system.

The coroner would want to see this information, too, as it established the victim's state of mind, and he forwarded the email to Declan and Watkins, and then to Lily for the team's input. His computer dinged again, and this time it was an email from Lily in her professional guise sent to the team:

Nothing with birth certificate Eng/Scot. Wales registry closed today, computer maintenance. Left email: should hear tomorrow.

When he looked up to seek her out, Lily sent a smile across the room. He gave her thumbs up and mouthed, "Thanks." As she bent her head to her work, McAfee decided she blushed.

CHAPTER THIRTY

1:38 PM

Nora balanced her backpack on one shoulder with her laden shopping bag on her other side. She retraced her steps down Market Street, past The Star Inn, and kept walking. Several shops, including a wine merchant, mixed with the homes here, too. When the road curved to the right, it became Park Street, and more residential. Most of the terraced houses were built of creamy Cotswold stone, and she checked for house names as she strolled, all while she planned her approach to Alvita Brown.

Then she realized Alvita might not even be home. She could be off doing her own holiday shopping or a myriad of other chores outside the home. Nora felt foolish. Why would anyone share secrets with a total stranger? She wasn't seeking to interview a celebrity with her magazine credentials, someone who would welcome an article that gave them free promotion.

And what if Chad Brown opened the door? He would recognize her after meeting her in the Covered Market. She needed a concrete strategy. She decided to use her beads as an excuse to worm her way in to see Alvita. Chad represented another matter. Nora paused near one of several trees planted on this road, and scrutinized the next house, where a bright spot of color caught her attention between its very tall windows. A vibrant tile hung over the top of its pale blue door, pink and blue flowers with black scrollwork in a Venetian design on a white ground with fancy lettering: **Montague House.**

Shakespeare. That would be another way in for her. She rooted around in a side pocket of her backpack for the stack of business cards she kept there. Her freelancing would be come to the rescue.

Now that she had a fixed scheme, Nora stepped boldly to the door of Montague House and rang the bell. Her heart sped up as she heard footsteps approach. Someone was home.

The door was opened partway by a wary, attractive Black woman with closely cropped salt-and-pepper hair. Her armful of bangle bracelets clinked against the door as she spoke in a melodic voice. A hint of classical music, turned low, floated out to Nora. "Thank you, but whatever you're selling, we don't need it." She started to close the door. Nora spoke up.

"Alvita?" She brandished her shopping bag as the woman stalled closing the door. "I've just come from Antiques at Heritage. The owner said you could tell me about my beads." She pointed to her necklace and rushed on. "I have a few questions for Chad, too, about Stratford. My sister is a master's student at Exeter and introduced us." Nora took a breath. "My name is Nora Tierney." She held out her card, with her name, phone, and email that announced she was a freelance and children's book writer.

Alvita inspected the details on the card. "Nora Tierney. Your name is familiar to me." Her eyes shifted to Nora's necklace as she scrutinized the beads. "Malachite. Do you know where they're from?" She opened the door wider.

"They were a gift from my friend who runs the artists cooperative in Oxford, so I have no idea." Nora gave her most winning smile.

Alvita bobbed her head in recognition. "You write about fairies from the Lake District, yes?"

"Yes, those are my children's books." Nora nodded eagerly, pleased her name struck a chord, as she remembered her excuse in case Chad was home. "And I freelance for "People and Places" magazine and wanted to ask Chad about an article I'm writing on Stratford." Nora picked up signs of strain on the woman's face in the deep grooves next to her mouth and between her brows.

Alvita checked her watch. "Chad's not home yet. I have about 15 minutes. I suppose I can tell you about those beads if you like." She opened the door all the way and the music became a bit louder. "Come in, child, don't stand on that doorstep letting the chill in."

Nora thanked her and followed the woman's swaying hips and clanking bangles into the first room on the right, a sitting room with a worn brown leather sofa and two chairs grouped on either side of a fireplace. A book was laid face down on a side table, which also held a lit candle that emitted the soft fragrance of green tea and lavender; the music was a soothing Bach air Nora recognized. The room's wallpaper, a William Morris pattern Nora had in Haven Cottage, had a navy ground with pairs of birds and fruited vines. The space felt relaxing. "Strawberry Thief—that's one of my favorite Morris designs." She didn't have to fake her enthusiasm. "I papered a wall in my guest room with it."

"It makes me happy." Alvita shoved a colorful item under a tapestry pillow, and sat on the sofa with the pillow at her back. She patted the cushion next to her. "He based that on the thrushes that used to steal strawberries from his kitchen garden at Kelmscott Manor."

"I didn't know that. It's a place I keep meaning to visit." Nora shrugged her backpack to the floor and put her shopping bag down next to it before taking her seat. "Perhaps I'll take my mother there when she comes over for Christmas." Amelia Tierney Scott was becoming quite the conversation piece. She'd have to tell her mother that.

"I'm sure she'd enjoy that." Alvita leaned forward and pointed to Nora's beads. "May I?"

This close, Nora could smell the woman's perfume, a light floral scent with a hint of spice. "Here you are." She removed the beads and handed the long necklace over. Gold spacers separated the beads of dark green swirled with lighter green bands, all polished to a high sheen.

Alvita examined them closely. "Malachite is the stone of transformation, keeps evil spirits at bay. These could be from the Congo, Russia, or even the US, no way of knowing." She let the beads run through her fingers, weighing them in her hand. "Some people in the islands wear them daily to balance their highs and lows. These are also the stone associated with St. Francis of Assisi and a love of animals. Back home, the elders put chunks of malachite in a crib to help babies sleep."

"Where is home?"

"Born in London, but lived my married life in Jamaica. I was a literature teacher there."

"That must be where Chad gets his love of Shakespeare." Alvita was certainly a woman of many talents and interests.

Chad's mother smiled. "I like to think I've had an influence on several of the children from our little town. I have two adopted children. One does study literature; the other is a car mechanic. Didn't rub off on him at all! I taught here, too, but now I'm retired. I work at Heritage on weekends and get to play with old things I adore, especially jewelry." She handed Nora her necklace.

Nora liked this woman more and more. "Me, too. I have a vintage pin collection and just bought one at your store."

Alvita clapped her hands. "The 'Nora' pin—perfect! It should be yours!"

"I've a weakness for vintage creamers and platters, too, that my fiancé doesn't understand but tolerates." Nora looped the beads over her head.

"Malachite also opens your heart in relationships. Maybe you need to wear these around him more often." Alvita checked her watch again. "I'll tell Chad you stopped by but it might take a few days for him to contact you."

"Could you ask him to email me when he gets a chance? No rush. My article is geared for American visitors to Stratford, and I hoped he had ideas for off-the-beaten-track sights I could include." Nora ran her eyes around the room in her precious remaining seconds, looking for any clues that would help her. The backs of the armchairs had bright throws draped over them. The mantel held an assortment of carved wooden figures, one a woman balancing a basket on her head. A bookshelf held a row of volumes. Nora drew in a breath when she saw a pile of slim volumes on the lower shelf that looked like children's books. "If you have my book here, I'm happy to sign it for you."

For the first time, Alvita looked uncomfortable. "Perhaps another time. I don't think I can put my finger on it at this moment." She stood, indicating Nora's time was up.

Nora moved to the door. She heard a creak overhead. Was someone hiding up there? "Thank you very much for your time." The women shook hands on the doorstep. "I had no idea malachite had such an interesting history."

"You're welcome. I'll pass your message and card on to Chad. It may take him a few days to get back to you." The music faded as she closed the door.

Nora stepped away from the house. She felt watched, and glanced back at the building and its blue door. Motion at an upstairs window drew her gaze upward.

Through the gauzy curtain at the long window, Nora saw the outline of what she convinced herself were the rails of a crib. A small head with springy light curls peered above it.

5:43 PM

Declan stood at the whiteboard that had been set up in the major crime room. He glanced over his shoulder at the team members logging off computers. There was no overtime allotted for this case until the inquest. He wanted everyone well rested, as they would be down a man once Julie delivered and Watkins went out on family leave.

The uncovered texts made it clear that Bea was in a relationship. Whether it was with the father of her child remained to be seen. They would pursue that line of investigation in earnest immediately after the inquest.

"Heading out, guv?" Watkins stood in the doorway.

"Just the man I was thinking of." Declan pointed to the list of names scrawled on the board. Watkins looked tired, and Declan would let him get home soon. He asked one last question. "Do we have background checks on any of these yet?"

"Most of them. Lily was logging them in this afternoon. Want me to pull them up?"

Declan shook his head. "I'm beat, too. Just give me the short form."

Watkins joined him at the board and pointed to the names written there. "Peter Hamilton, respected don, several books published, as well as multiple articles on poetry and literature and their effects on children. Nothing in his history stuck out except one student, a few years ago now, lodged a complaint against him."

"Any idea what the complaint was about?" Had something with Bea's tutor been unearthed?

"Complaint dismissed and record cleared. Only blemish after years of teaching, first at a private school, then here for a decade now."

"Still, we may need to chase that down after the inquest."

Watkins continued down the list. "Jack Soong, youngest son of wealthy parents in Surrey. First in his class; chess champ. No priors." He moved on to Patti Phillips. "This one's from Chelsea, here on scholarship. One older sister, lives in Australia now. Parents divorced when Patti was 12. Father a drinker, several arrests for domestic abuse. Mother finally threw him out."

"Wonder how he treated his daughters? Any whiff of the abuse Sheila O'Connor reckoned?"

"Wouldn't show up if his abuse extended to the children unless one of them brought charges against him or the mother had him arrested."

Declan considered this. "True. Interesting though that Patti may have witnessed the father abusing her mother. That could affect her attitude toward men." At Watkins' nod, he continued. "And Nicola Morton?"

"Local gal. Emigrated with her brother a decade ago." Watkins frowned and stroked his chin. "Nothing there—except something that stuck out to me in her formal statement."

Declan raised an eyebrow. "Which is?"

"I'll have to go back over my notes. I could swear she told me Bea Jones sent her a note when her mother was ill."

Declan sensed Watkins was disturbed, and couldn't fathom why this would be an issue. "And?"

"Her mother died when she was 10."

8:15 PM

Nora checked Sean. The boy slept on his back, his reddish curls, lighter than her own, framing his chubby cheeks. She felt a wave of tenderness for her child, safely clad in a blanket sleeper with his favorite bunny tucked under one arm. She closed his door after making certain his monitor was on and went back downstairs where Claire and Declan had poured glasses of wine.

They settled themselves in front of the lit fireplace in what was becoming their usual places: Claire in the wing chair, Nora and Declan on the sofa. As she sipped her red wine, Nora thought back to her arrival home with her full shopping bag. While Claire had enjoyed Sophie's tour of the OUP archives, and said Sean had gone down for his nap without a fuss, she appeared distressed. As the person who'd found Bea's body, Claire had received an email telling her to appear as a witness at tomorrow's hastily arranged inquest and had confessed her dismay.

"Declan, Claire's nervous about the inquest tomorrow. Anything you can tell her to ease her mind?"

Declan put his glass down and looked over at Claire. "Claire, an inquest is an inquiry into a death to register it when its cause is unclear. I expect this inquest to be adjourned as Charlie's post mortem report will indicate suspicious circumstances. The coroner can open and adjourn an inquest immediately, pending an investigation. In this case, he's putting a few preliminary key witness statements in the record. You'll be sworn in, asked to describe what you heard and saw, and how you acted, and that's it. It should go fairly quickly."

Claire seemed reassured, if still unhappy. "Nora's going to come with me. That will help."

"I expect you couldn't keep Nora away." Declan put his arm around Nora's shoulder.

Nora decided to distract Claire from thinking about taking the stand tomorrow by describing her day in Woodstock and running her impressions by Declan. "I had a nice few hours of holiday shopping in Woodstock today, and ran into someone you might know, Claire." That the running into had been deliberate on her part she didn't mention.

Claire perked up. "Really? Who was it?"

"Chad Brown's mother, Alvita. They share a house there, and she works at one of the antique stores on town."

Claire shook her head. "Never met her, but I remember Bea saying she was a delightful character."

"Bea knew her?" Nora caught Declan's eye to see if he was taking this in. He gave a sharp nod to indicate he'd duly noted this bit of information.

"She must have," Claire said. "I remember her saying Mrs. Brown was the kind of supportive mother she wished she'd had. 'You don't have to fight against every little thing with a mum like that.' I don't recall anything else."

"What's so special about this, Nora?" Declan asked.

"You know me too well." She sat up and looked at him.

He smiled. "Only when you decide to wear your sleuth hat. What gives?"

"It's just that when I was leaving their house—"

It was Declan's turn to sit up. "Wait, you were at their house?"

"Just for a few minutes. Alvita told me about the malachite beads I wore today, you know, the ones Val gave me for my birthday."

"Don't change the subject, Nora."

Uh-oh. "She invited me in," Nora protested.

Declan arched an eyebrow and Nora hurried on.

"Anyway, as I was leaving, I saw movement at an upstairs window. I could swear I saw a child staring down at me, over the bars of a crib." She saw the look that passed between Declan and Claire. "Really. The windows are very tall. And if the child was standing up in a crib …"

"How much of this is wishful thinking?" Declan asked.

Claire cocked her head. "What *are* you thinking, Nora?"

Nora took a deep breath. "I think the child is Bea's baby Verity, and Chad Brown is her father."

Both Declan and Claire gaped at Nora at this pronouncement.

"That's quite a leap, Nora." Declan shook his head. "How did you get there?"

Nora had a moment of doubt. Was it really a child's head behind that curtain, or did she simply want it to be one? Were those crib railings, or the back of a chair?

Maybe Alvita kept children's books for visitors. For that matter, she didn't know if Chad had siblings. Maybe there were other grandchildren. "Dr. Hamilton said Bea and Chad seemed attracted to each other last year, then kept their distance this term. A couple trying to hide their relationship would do that."

"She might be onto something, Declan." Claire's agreement surprised Nora. "Straight out of a Shakespearean play."

"Don't let her be a bad influence on you, Claire." Declan laughed.

He wasn't angry, but Nora felt a surge of annoyance. "Listen, Alvita said she had one of my books on hand, and there were plenty of children's books on her shelves. She looked distinctly uncomfortable when I offered to sign her copy. Maybe she didn't want me to notice the amount of kiddie lit there."

"Maybe by then she just wanted to get you out of her house." Declan twitched a smile to soften his words.

"Wait, there's more. When she invited me into her living room, she hid something behind a pillow at her back. It bet it was a child's doll or toy."

"Or a bag of cookies she didn't want to share." Claire's eyes twinkled.

"You're definitely reaching, love." Declan pulled her to him and kissed the tip of Nora's nose. "One of the hallmarks of good detecting is to follow the evidence, not fabricate it."

"That's exactly what I did do, followed the evidence. I can't help if you don't believe me."

"I believe you want it to mean that."

"Do you think you should follow up on Nora's hunch?" Claire asked Declan.

"Maybe after the inquest."

That seemed to satisfy her sister, to Nora's chagrin, and Claire changed the subject by asking what gifts Nora had bought. She decided it didn't make sense to be upset with either one of them until she could muster up more conclusive information, which she intended to do.

In bed later, spooning comfortably, Declan told Nora he had a feeling Bea's mother might have pushed for the inquest to include witnesses before what would likely be an adjournment. "She's related to the deputy chief constable, who already called Morris once to drive our investigation. I can see her pressing for this to get a move on, as if we're not."

"She's not a fan of the police?" With Declan's arms wrapped around her from behind, his sturdy warmth her solace, Nora heard his grunt and let go of her exasperation with him from earlier.

"I'd say Margaret Smythe-Jones is not a fan of anybody. Too many exacting standards for most to fall short of." He explained that when Maggie Smith married Ernest Jones, she immediately changed the spelling of her name and hyphenated it, although the twins both used their father's name. "I suppose that's trendy in some circles, the hyphen thing. Changing the spelling to appear more regal certainly isn't."

Nora smiled into her pillow. "Why do I get the distinct feeling the dislike is mutual."

Declan kissed the back of her neck. "I admit she rubbed me up the wrong way. Her husband says she's prone to depression; he overlooks her behavior. Lord knows the death of her daughter is enough to make anyone cranky and depressed."

As his breathing slowed and he dozed off, Nora ran back over what she'd seen today.

There was no question the shape she saw upstairs at Montague House was distorted by the gauzy curtain material. Some sleuth she was, second-guessing her discovery. Nora decided until she had more concrete evidence, what Declan might call an inspired guess only muddied his waters. Mind made up, Nora snuggled deeper under the down comforter, and hoped tomorrow's inquest would be easy for Claire, while it gave them all better insights into what might have happened to Beatrice Jones.

CHAPTER THIRTY-ONE

Tuesday, 5th December

9:28 AM

Seated next to Claire on the right-hand section inside the Oxford Coroner's Court, Nora shifted on the hard wood bench in the second row. The building looked like a miniature castle outside with its castellated facade, while its interior remained shabby and dated. It retained many features of a classic English courtroom, with stairs that led to the gaol cells from a square elevated prisoner's dock that faced the judge's seat, although the building was only used now for inquests.

She'd been here before, when Val's partner had been murdered and Val was briefly a suspect. Declan had indicated he didn't see Claire as being a viable suspect, so that was one relief. Nora's presence today in the courtroom brought her back to that time when, newly pregnant and worried for her friend, her efforts had been focused on convincing the detective on the case that Val was innocent. Now she lived with and loved that same detective.

Outside the high windows, the wind howled and dark clouds added to the gloomy atmosphere, a portent of the changing December weather.

Declan sat in front of them in the first row, bookended by Watkins on one side and Charlie Borden at the other. Declan looked handsome in one of his dark suits, worn today in deference for the proceedings. He had told her he'd signal her when Bea's parents arrived.

Nora recognized several local press representatives, phones

ready to tape the proceedings, some augmenting their tapes with steno pads for handwritten notes of observations. A handful of other people sat behind them, talking quietly. Tourists or nosy locals, she first supposed, until she saw Peter Hamilton among them.

Nora checked the time on her phone and scrolled to the settings to put it on airplane mode. With Sean at the creche, she had two hours until pick-up time. She doubted this inquest would take long.

Claire nudged her with an elbow. “Declan wants your attention.”

Nora saw him turned slightly toward her in his seat. His eyes slid meaningfully to the left. He turned to the front again while she watched a middle-aged couple accompanied by a younger man pass, and then pause at the front left row. The men waited to allow the woman to be seated before filing in after her. Dressed in a severe black suit with a lilac blouse, Margaret Smythe-Jones held her head stiff and high. Her face was a tight mask, with a glazed look from medication, and her eyes were slack with the dullness of grief. Her husband slid in next to her, a tall man whose shoulders drooped as much as his facial features.

At the end of the row, Bea’s brother Ben took his seat, looking every inch an ordinand in his black suit with a large cross silver on his black shirt, leaving no doubt he was associated with a religious vocation, despite the lack of a clerical collar. To Nora, he also looked the most uncomfortable. He leaned forward with his hands dangling between his knees, and pursed his lips.

Claire leaned over and spoke quietly. “I never met Bea’s twin. He has that auburn hair from his mom. Bea’s was fair like her father's." She lowered her voice to a whisper. "Seminarian, she told me."

Nora studied Ben Jones. "His appearance reminds me of the first vicar in 'Grantchester.'"

The bailiff stood. "All rise for Her Majesty's Coroner, the Honourable Mr. Gardiner." The coroner entered from the right, behind the judge's bench, and stepped up to the elevated seat under a canopy. He wore a suit and carried a folder. Nora recognized him from her prior visit, perhaps with more grey hair, but his air of brisk seriousness remained unchanged.

"Detective Inspector Barnes," the bailiff called. Shuffling in the seats stopped as Declan eased into the tiny witness box, ignoring the narrow bench and standing upright as he was sworn in.

He confirmed his rank and described the events following his notification of the death of Beatrice Jones. "The area was controlled by constables to outsiders immediately; paramedics agreed soon after that life was extinguished."

Nora saw all three members of Bea's family wince at this description.

Declan continued. "The medical examiner attended, and a forensics team was called out." Mr. Gardiner clarified a few minor points and Declan was dismissed.

"Claire Scott." At the bailiff's summons, Nora squeezed Claire's hand as her sister stood and walked to the witness box. She'd worn a pair of dark slacks with a navy blouse and had pulled her wavy hair back in a neat bun. Her face looked pale but composed.

Claire was sworn in and also stood in the box. She explained she'd been asleep when noises that might have been whispering outside her room had woken her, followed shortly by a scream. "When I rushed out, several of the other students had heard the scream, but I was the one who looked over the rail and saw Bea lying at the bottom of the stairwell." She inhaled, the tension evident on her face, then continued stoically. "I had one of the other students call 999, and ran down the steps to Bea. I couldn't find a pulse." Her eyes welled with unshed tears as Claire added that her tutor, Peter Hamilton, had shown up shortly after that, and stood guard over the entrances until police arrived. "Then I held her hand until the medics made me leave her."

She blew out a breath when the coroner thanked her and dismissed her. As she made her way back to Nora, the pathologist was called. Charlie Borden chose to balance on the narrow seat so he could refer to a slim file he'd brought. He described arriving at the scene, then consulted and read from a report on his visual and the post-mortem findings.

Gardiner had the most questions for Charlie. "What did these bruises suggest to you?"

"Under external and microscopic examination, one on the cervical area looked like a chain, and I'm having enlargements made of the design. The family mentioned a necklace the victim wore at all times that was not found on the body or at the scene."

Bea's mother dropped her head as if the details were too difficult to hear. Ernest hung on Charlie's every word. Nora found it interesting that Ben mirrored his mother, head dropped low, but one knee bounced.

Charlie continued to expound. "There are multiple bruises on the extremities that likely occurred during the fall. However, there are also small marks on each shoulder that are consistent with fingertips. Also, an external bruise across the victim's waist in a straight line, at a height consistent with the stairwell railing. This indicates at one point before death the victim's back was pressed firmly against the rigid metal railing."

"Facing away from the stairs," Gardiner clarified.

"Yes. The rest of the exam was unremarkable except for two white threads found caught under one of the victim's fingernails, which were sent for analysis and proved to be white cotton. If we eventually have something to compare them to, it could be significant, but not at this time."

When he detailed the specific injuries that caused Bea's death, her mother started to quietly cry. Ben's face became ashen; Ernest Jones's head remained high while his lips thinned.

"Any incidental findings of note?" the coroner asked.

"The victim had been pregnant and likely delivered a child in the past year."

Bea's mother flinched at this. Interesting to Nora was that Ben now raised his head and took on the same stoic look as his father.

The door to the back of the courtroom opened, and Nora turned to see who entered. She leaned forward to tap Declan's shoulder. When he turned his head, she pointed her chin over one shoulder and saw Declan's eyes watch the newcomer take a seat in the last row of the courtroom. She mouthed a name to him.

Several other people turned at the thud of the closing door. Nora caught the expression of surprise on Benedick Jones' face when he saw Chad Brown sit down.

CHAPTER THIRTY-TWO

Somerville

Winter 1992

The mild weather had turned cooler midway through the month, and today's rain had turned to sleet. Dora Robson blamed the changes in temperature as the reason she couldn't rid herself of the cough that lingered after her summer cold, when her weight loss became noticeable. Jim had been at her for months now to see their GP, but she kept ignoring him, too wrapped up with Digger to take care of herself.

Dora was pleased with her new figure and joked with Jim that she'd "lost her baby weight." It was as if she'd grown to believe the child was theirs, right from the start. She rubbed her arms and pulled her cardigan tightly around her and, at the sounds of stirring, went to fetch Digger from his nap.

Jim was warm enough; their little home felt toasty with the fire on. He looked around at their older furniture, mixed with newer baby equipment in most rooms. Dora had a knack for sewing and had made the curtains at the windows in bright cheery patterns that made the rooms feel inviting. Even more than that, it felt like a home where a real family lived, two parents with their much-loved son.

The passing months had settled into a routine. Jim slept better at night and stopped having heart palpitations every time a panda car raced past their house, blue lights blazing and siren blaring. He convinced himself this was meant to be.

The couple next door continued to help with babysitting when needed and doted on the boy they knew as Jim and Dora's son.

They were only a few years older than him and Dora, though childless, and he knew the pangs that had caused in his own marriage. The couple seemed solid though, and very caring. Digger filled a hole in so many lives; he was a real joy to them all.

Jim was well-liked at his job, too, and had settled well into his new supervisory role. He rarely thought of his old travel routine or the days in Cumbria. Really, life was close to perfect.

This day, Jim sat watching a replay of Michael Schumacher's first Grand Prix win from earlier in the Formula One season. He would be one to watch, that blonde German driver. Dora came in, carrying Digger, all rosy-cheeked and sweet-smelling after a nap.

"Jim, I want to talk to you about something."

"Oh no, here it goes. That lad has enough toys, Dora." He softened this with a laugh. She'd been talking about them putting a jungle gym in the back garden next spring for Digger. She must be ramping up her timeline.

Dora sat next to him on the couch. "What would you think if after the holidays, I looked for part-time work? Maybe nearby, in an Oxford shop." She held Digger on her lap as she said this and kissed his rounded cheek. "Be good for him to be around others, and I can start a fund with my earnings."

Jim opened his mouth to complain, then stopped to consider what she said. He hadn't thought Dora would tire of being home. "I'm surprised you'd want to leave him." He put out his hand, and Digger grabbed his finger. A warm glow spread over him.

He had lost the majority of his misgivings to the happiness they'd found in their little family, in just this small kind of gesture.

He'd also stopped the subscription to the Cumbrian paper

he'd had forwarded to their new home. He chose not to hear if the Bowness kidnapping case was still active.

"It's not that I want to leave him, not really. But I want Digger to have anything he needs, and he's so smart, I know he'll go to university. He'll need a car and living money. He could have a semester in a different country, too. That's expensive."

What Dora said made a certain sense. While Jim earned enough for this house and an occasional night out, dinner and a movie, university would be more difficult on his salary, especially if Digger needed a car and if there was travel involved, the costs would soar even if the tuition was covered. There would be books and living expenses, too. "Who would watch him while you're gone?"

"Carol and Peter next door. They're so good with him when we go out for an evening. Digger already knows them and he's comfortable there."

Jim was surprised. "Not your sister? He'd have her boy to play with."

"Yes, but Deirdre and Marek have only just moved down, and there's something not right there. They left Glasgow in such a hurry. I'm happy she's nearby, but two babies so close in age would try any woman's patience, and we know which one would come first." Dora smiled. "I want our son to have his caretaker's undivided attention, to be the center of their world as he is ours. He'd get that next door. What do you think?"

He leaned over and kissed her lightly. "I think I have a very smart wife."

Dora beamed. "I'll just go call—" A raspy cough cut her off mid-sentence. This turned into a shuddering jag, deep and croupy, and she left the room to get a tissue.

She returned and finally had the spell under control when Jim heard her small moan.

When he looked up, he saw her frown and heard the distress in her voice. “Probably nothing.”

He saw her tissue, where she’d coughed up a glob of bright red blood.

He knew in that instant it was a very big something.

CHAPTER THIRTY-THREE

Oxford

10:15 AM

Declan felt Nora tap his shoulder, and put his arm along the back of the bench so he could casually turn his head to her.

She used her chin to point out a new arrival at the back and mouthed "Chad Brown." Declan sat forward and watched Ben Jones turn as the door thudded shut. He could see the young man's eyes widen when Brown took a seat at the rear of the courtroom.

The coroner dismissed Charlie Borden. As the pathologist made his way out of the witness box, Declan's phone vibrated. He stole a glance at a text from Lily George, telling him Wales had been in touch, and to check his email. When he pulled it up, he saw two attachments from the Wales registry he opened. One was a copy of the birth certificate filed there for Bea's child, plus another document none of them expected. Declan handed his phone to Watkins, who scanned both, then raised his eyebrows as he handed it back. Declan suspected the next moments would shock the room.

He gave Nora a look with raised eyebrows that said, "Watch this."

The bailiff called the next witness: "Chad Brown."

Declan saw Nora and Claire turn their heads in surprise; he watched Bea's family carefully. Maggie and Ernest clearly had no idea who Chad Brown was, but Ben put his head in his hands. The young don made his way to the witness stand, holding an envelope, and stood upright to give his oath.

"Thank you for contacting me, Mr. Brown," Gardiner said. "You said you had knowledge of the child the victim bore, and its whereabouts?"

Declan observed Maggie and Ernest, as both leaned forward at this question. Maggie frowned. Ben avoided looking at either of them.

"Yes. This is a copy of my daughter's birth certificate, naming me as her father." He withdrew a sheet from the envelope and handed Gardiner the copy. "The child lives with me and her grandmother, and is well cared for."

Maggie's indrawn breath could be heard throughout the courtroom.

Gardiner examined the paper. "A daughter?"

Declan could feel Nora shift in her seat behind him. He should have known her instincts were solid.

"Yes, Verity." Chad was clearly grief-stricken; his voice cracked as he struggled with his composure.

Declan saw the shock on Maggie Smythe-Jones's face. Ernest looked confused, while Ben looked miserable.

Chad turned to the coroner and raised his chin. "You see, Bea had everything to live for, and taking her own life is an impossibility."

Gardiner nodded. "I see."

Chad handed over a second sheet from his envelope as he continued. "I took a two-term sabbatical earlier this year. We married in Wales, where we stayed for the birth of our daughter, and while Bea completed her thesis. I felt I couldn't come forward until I could prove I was her husband. I had to arrange for a copy of our marriage license as Bea has it tucked somewhere." He closed his eyes when he realized he'd used the present tense.

"I'd like to visit the morgue to see my wife."

"Certainly." The courtroom fell silent while Gardiner examined the marriage certificate. This time it was the coroner's eyebrows that rose. "You were married by her brother?"

Maggie Smythe-Jones's mouth gaped open. She stood and practically threw herself over her husband and son, then stormed out of the courtroom.

10:44 AM

At Chad Brown's pronouncement, an abrupt silence fell on the courtroom, broken only by the slam of the door as Bea's mother stalked out. Nora raised her eyebrows to Claire at the news that Bea's brother had married her to Chad. The coroner asked Chad another question that was lost in the noise as the reporters spoke urgently into their phones and amongst themselves while scribbling notes or typing on tablets, sending texts Nora knew would be tonight's local headlines. The reporters flurry of noise forced the coroner to bring his gavel down to restore order. When she looked to the front of the courthouse, Chad Brown was ready to answer Gardiner's question.

"Yes, we had the proper 28-day waiting period for a marriage certificate. My wife contacted the registry office after we learned the marriage had to be conducted by or in the presence of a person authorized to register the marriage in that district. As Bea's brother is not ordained yet, he was allowed to conduct the ceremony in her presence." Brown had composed himself with the recitation of dry facts. "Bea toured the maternity facility and found a local doctor when she went for her fellowship interview. She was on top of everything. Bea was amazing." His voice filled with pride.

Nora met Claire's eyes as the story unfolded. She knew Chad Brown had just added his name to the suspect list. The poor man. No wonder he'd been so upset when they'd met in the Covered Market. If she ran across him again, she would have to apologize for startling him with Verity's name. Claire looked astonished. They watched the bailiff hand Chad a bottle of water as he continued.

"Ben helped us move the weekend of the wedding. Ben and my mother were there when Verity was born, and my mother stayed a week to help. Ben or my mother would occasionally manage a visit after that. It was a wonderful spring and summer with our daughter while Bea worked on her thesis." His sorrow threatened to overwhelm him again, and he reached for the water and gulped some down, then wiped his mouth and took a deep breath.

The coroner nodded. "A very pragmatic young woman, I can see. May I ask why the need for secrecy? She was of age to marry without parental consent."

Chad's eyes settled on Ben. "My wife felt that due to my race, her mother wouldn't approve of our marriage. She was insistent we follow this plan."

Nora watched Ernest's face fall at the veracity of this statement. Ben put a hand on his father's shoulder. As the truth of the situation was revealed, Ben's relief grew, and he sat up straighter.

"Bea planned to introduce me and Verity to her parents with her degree in hand. She hoped once they saw their grandchild, her mother would yield, soften a bit …" His voice trailed off. Nora felt his embarrassment. No wonder Bea had told Claire she wished her own mother had been more like Claire's.

"I see." Gardiner made a note. "Thank you for these copies and for coming forward. The bailiff will call ahead, and text you the address so you may visit your wife immediately."

"I'll go there right now."

Gardiner dipped his head. "You may step down." He closed his file and sat up. "Right then. Based on the evidence given by the witnesses and taking into account the forensic findings of the pathologist of the suspicious circumstances surrounding this death, I am adjourning this inquest to allow for further investigation and gathering of evidence."

He left as the bailiff shouted: "All rise! Court is adjourned."

Nora and Claire stood and waited while Declan and Watkins conferred with Chad. The young father would have to answer their questions once he'd seen his wife. In the bustle of escaping reporters, Chad turned to Ben and his father as Declan spoke with Charlie Borden. Ernest was the first to put his hand out to shake Chad's, and they exchanged a few words. Ben gripped Chad's shoulder briefly, and the young father walked out of the courtroom, nodding to Claire as he left. The Jones men stepped across the aisle and Ernest spoke to Claire.

"Miss Scott, please accept my sincere thanks for staying with Bea as she passed from this life. That was a very brave thing to do." He shook Claire's hand and Ben moved beside him.

"I'll always be grateful to you." Ben clasped her hand in both of his.

Claire bowed her head. "Thank you both, but I didn't do anything Bea wouldn't have done for me," she said. "This is my sister, Nora Tierney. She's engaged to Detective Barnes."

Ernest nodded to Nora, who murmured, "Very sorry for your loss. Bea sounds like a wonderful woman."

"She was," Ben said. "Devoted to her daughter, too."

"I have a little boy, so I understand," Nora said, and Ben gave a half smile. "Today must have been so difficult for you both. It took a great deal of courage for Chad to contact the coroner and testify."

"I doubt my mother will see it that way." Ben shook his head. "Sorry I didn't tell you, Dad. Bea insisted on keeping this secret."

"Chad deserves to see Bea," Ernest said. "I can't believe this entire turn of events. You were right to keep your sister's confidence, Ben. I appreciate the difficult position you've been in. Hellish."

Declan and Watkins joined them as Charlie left the courtroom.

Ben exhaled a long sigh. "Bea really loved Chad. He's been wonderful to her and Verity, his mother, too." He turned to Watkins. "Sorry I never called you back. I needed to wrap my head around giving away Bea's confidences. Yesterday afternoon, Chad and I talked about how to handle the situation. He had decided it was time to set the record straight. No point hiding anything now that Bea is gone."

Watkins gave a sharp nod of his head. "I won't be arresting you for obstructing justice, but next time a detective asks you a direct question, be more forthcoming, please."

"I'm afraid we have more questions for you both, and also your wife," Declan said. "Tomorrow in Cambridge, Ernest, unless you'd rather come to St. Aldate's now?"

Ernest looked to the back of the room. "I think my wife might need time to get used to the, er, revelations. If you want to come up to Christ's tomorrow, I'll have my assistant cover me in the morning."

"That will be fine," Declan agreed. "Can you be there, too, Ben, around 10?"

Ben nodded. "If my mother will let me in the door."

Ernest scrubbed his face with a hand. "What a morning." He shook his head. "This is so bittersweet. I'd like to see my granddaughter, but since Chad is with Bea, we'll have to be in touch later. I assume you have his number?" he asked Ben.

Ben nodded. "We'll call him and set something up, Dad."

"All right. Let's go face the music together, son."

"I don't envy them," Watkins said after the two men walked away. "Formidable woman."

Declan's mouth twitched in the brief smile that tugged at Nora's heart.

"You shouldn't envy me," Declan said. "I have my own formidable woman, one who won't let me forget when she's right."

10:59 AM

Nora checked her phone and took it off airplane mode. She had half an hour to walk to the church to pick up Sean. The two detectives accompanied Nora and her sister as they moved through the high arched door to the stone steps outside, where Ben stood in conversation in the forecourt with his mother. Ernest moved away towards the limited parking area in front. Tall black iron lanterns stood on square stone pedestals by the entry gate. Margaret Smythe-Jones stood next to one, nostrils flared and face flushed, her mouth set in a stern line. She looked into the distance while Ben spoke to her.

"That's one for the books," Watkins said.

"Quite the revelation that Brown is the father of Bea's child," Declan agreed.

"And her husband," Nora said. "Don't think Maggie is pleased."

"That's a look of rage if I ever saw one." A frown puckered Claire's forehead. "Poor guy. I wouldn't want to be Ben on that car ride home."

"But is she upset she was left out of the loop, or because she knows her daughter knew her well enough to know she wouldn't approve of an interracial marriage?" Nora was thoughtful. Bea Jones must have been in a terrible position to feel this was the way to handle things, hiding from her father, swearing her brother to secrecy. Still, she didn't see how this situation would connect to Bea's death at Exeter. It didn't suggest a motive, unless Chad Brown was a very good actor. Bea's parents were in Cambridge without access to the Oxford college at that time of day. Or were they? She would need to ferret out if Maggie could have found her way into Exeter. Just how good an actress was this Maggie Smith?

"Speaking of car rides, I have a station car," Declan said to Nora. "You and Claire like a lift home? I know you have to pick up Sean soon."

Nora thought ahead to the afternoon and what she could accomplish. She needed to talk to Claire alone before they picked up Sean and convince her they should return to Exeter. The college seemed to be the heart of this investigation, and she needed to do her own interviews with the students who knew Bea best. Yes, Declan's team had interviewed them, but she brought her own brand of instincts to the investigation.

"Sure thing." Nora said. Watkins stayed with the women as a few other stragglers left. Ben and his mother walked toward the car Ernest had backed out, Margaret a few feet ahead of Ben, Declan a few paces behind.

A reporter ran in front of Margaret and snapped a photo of her grim façade. She brushed him aside with a wave of her arm and kept walking, refusing to answer his questions. Declan stepped up to the man, and after speaking with him, the reporter left.

"That will be all over the rag sheets tonight," Watkins said.

"I'm more interested in what Declan said to put him off." Nora turned to Watkins as they waited. "I meant to ask earlier how Julie's feeling."

He grimaced. "Besides waddling and miserable? She's ready to move on to the next part." He shook his head. "I thought for sure it was go time when she woke me in the middle of the night, but it turned out she wanted ice cream."

Claire laughed. "No pickle?"

Declan pulled the station car around the courtyard and Nora slid into the back seat with Claire, stepping on food wrappers discarded into the footwell. Declan pulled out after signaling to wend his way to Haven Cottage.

"Where are you two off to?" she asked. If she had to take a bet, she knew exactly where they were headed—Woodstock.

Declan met her eye in the rearview mirror. "Pub lunch, I think, since we know Brown's at the morgue. With the formal pronouncement and the inquest on hold pending our investigation, our case can ramp up, so we need a decent meal when we can get it. Then I think our priority will be a trip to Woodstock to see Alvita Brown, verify some of Chad Brown's information, and wait for his return."

"As I suspected. It's where I'd head."

"So glad I have your approval, Nora."

From the passenger seat, Watkins chortled. Declan cocked an eyebrow him. "For that, you're buying."

Nora turned to Claire. "Do you need to pick up anything from your room at Exeter?"

Claire hesitated. "I think it's time I went back to my room."

"Don't leave on my account," Declan said, as he negotiated a one-way street. "I'll be out all hours. Nora could use the company getting the house righted before the holidays, if you don't mind pitching in."

Nora leaned forward. "Stay a bit longer, Claire. It will be so lonely at college with the semester winding down and the other students leaving, and you said your work was done."

"I hit 'send' last night," she admitted. "If you're sure I'm not in the way."

"Not at all. That's settled." Nora sat back in satisfaction. Now she'd engineered a reasonable excuse to visit Exeter and snoop around. "We can take Sean for a walk and swing by your room."

"Sounds like a plan." Declan turned by St. Giles. "Just be careful."

Nora decided Declan knew exactly what she had planned. At least he didn't tell her not to go. They'd really come a long way in their relationship, she realized, and hid a smile.

"You can let us out at the end of the drive, Declan. Easier for you." He pulled over and Nora exited the car and tapped the driver's window. When he lowered it, she leaned in for a quick kiss. "That will have to hold the great detective for now."

"Watch it, Yankee." Watkins waved as Declan pulled away with a toot of the horn.

Claire put her hands on her hips. "What gives? I've been around you long enough to know you're up to something."

"Let's check on Mr. Tink first and I'll give you my thoughts." The women walked up the drive and Nora let them into the house, where the smell of fresh paint reached them, along with a happy Typo. Mr. Tink had thought he'd be done by Thursday. Then she could air out her library and sort her things. By the weekend she'd be up and running. They walked into the room, where two walls gleamed with the first coat of a soft pale green. "Looks great, Mr. Tink."

"That one's been napping in here." He pointed to the puppy. "Think he likes the smell of wet paint." The painter paused in his rolling and stood back to examine his handiwork. "Never thought I'd say this, but this green's set off nicely by that radish color in the back of the bookcases." He took off his glasses and wiped them on a rag he took from the back pocket of his splattered coverall. "However, you've created a monster, Nora Tierney."

"Whatever do you mean?" She could tell he teased her by the glint of mischief in the man's eye.

"Mrs. Tink saw those bookcases of yours yesterday; now she wants me to do ours like that. She's scrutinizing my swatches as we speak." He took off his cap and scratched the back of his head.

Claire laughed out loud. "Bit of a busman's holiday for you at home this weekend, Mr. Tink."

They left him to his work. Nora let Typo out and, after a rousing "good boy" when he ran over to his corner and squatted, she gave him a round of petting and roughhousing while she kept an eye on the clock. When he seemed tired out, she left him outside with a treat and chew toy.

"Here are my thoughts." She washed her hands as she spoke to Claire. She opened the pantry and chose a squeeze tube of cranberry applesauce, then grabbed a yogurt from the fridge, and a plastic spoon. "As much as we don't like what Bea felt she had to go through because of her mother's attitudes, it's unlikely Maggie was the person outside your room the morning of—um, when Bea died. The outside college doors would be closed and locked at that hour, right? How do you get in if the door is locked?"

"We have 'Bod Cards' the university gives us that we swipe. We use those to purchase food, and to use the washers and dryers, too."

Nora checked she had a packet of wet wipes in her backpack. "At that early hour of the morning, it's unlikely anyone not in the Oxford University system could have access to your stairwell."

Claire nodded. "Go on."

"You came out of your room quickly, and only saw the other three students on that stairwell. So our suspect pool, must include those three."

Claire's face fell. "I hate to think that, but I guess you must be right." She tilted her head to one side. "Or, it could have been someone else from the college who ran quickly down the stairs after Bea fell."

"You're thinking of Peter Hamilton. Yes, you don't know he was returning from his run just then. He could have pushed Bea, run down those stairs and out through the archway, then turned around and pretended to be arriving back from his run, conveniently out of breath."

"I suppose—but why?"

"No idea." Nora went into the mudroom and returned with an insulated pack. "That still narrows our suspects down to the three students and Dr. Hamilton, as nice as he appears."

"Yes, but you're forgetting one other person knew where Bea lived when at college and would have access to her."

Nora stowed Sean's lunch in the insulated pack. She emptied a juice box into a sippy cup, and zipped it closed. This bouncing ideas off someone else was helpful. She looked at Claire with interest. "Who's that?" As soon as she said it, Nora knew who Claire would say.

"Her husband."

CHAPTER THIRTY-FOUR

11:42 AM

Since leaving Oxford and the inquest, Ben had been talking nonstop from his perch as his father drove back to Cambridge. Crammed in the back seat of the car, his long legs meant his knees were bent high.

He couldn't wait to return to Ridley Hall and leave the oppression of the enclosed space, where his mother's frosty fury had given way to a sulky silence. The more he spoke, the less she listened, yet he knew in this enclosed space she had to hear every word he said.

"I understand it must have been a great shock to you both, but Bea insisted, and once she had taken me into her confidence, I didn't feel I could break it. I did counsel her that honesty was better, but she wouldn't budge." He looked out at the window at the rolling hills dressed in drab winter colors of browns and greys, and longed to be on his own in the quiet chapel, or walking beside the River Cam, watching the swirl of the current.

Ernest spoke up. "Bea could be stubborn like that, once her mind was made up about something."

His mother stirred to say: "You were always the weaker twin."

Ben clenched his fists and tamped down a nasty retort. He thanked God for the patience seminary was teaching him to practice and for his father's support. For a few moments back at the inquest, he'd been afraid he'd lost his father, too. "She told me she was tired of fighting for her corner, and always meeting disapproval." He was careful not to come right out and place the blame on his mother, despite her being the one who always expected to have things go her way. She knew how to make life miserable if that didn't happen. "Once I knew she was going ahead with the marriage, whether I approved or not, it seemed the best course to assist. At least she had one family member to support her, and her child would have married parents."

He paused to catch his breath, and decided he'd said enough. He left out that he had been to Wales every chance he could to see his little niece, a sweet baby with a sunny disposition. He wished he'd had his father drop him at the station to take the train back to Cambridge. His mother finally spoke again. The venom in her voice made his toes curl.

"I'm her *mother*. I should have known my daughter was pregnant and had a baby, not discovered I had a grandchild from some detective, nor learn at an inquest she was married and you were there!"

Ben bristled. "Can you even hear yourself? It's all about you, and what *you* should have had. You're forgetting that Bea didn't tell you because you wouldn't have approved of the man she loved."

"Are you insinuating I'm racist? I'll have you know I serve on committees at the chapel with many people of color."

"Yes? And how many have you invited into your home for a meal? Bea knew exactly the argument she'd face if she told you her husband and the father of her child was Jamaican."

His mother winced, then gave a false laugh. "Who are you hoping to convince, Benedick? Me, your father, or yourself?"

"That's unfair. I was right there when you demanded she study at Cambridge undergrad so she could live near home and be under your thumb, remember? Then you monitored and passed approval on every friend or date or activity she had at Downing

College. Bea had absolutely no freedom and no chance to grow. No wonder she did her post-graduate work at Oxford! Remember the fights about that?" He heard his voice rise and toned it down. "And that huge blowout about studying children's literature, how that would never get her anywhere?" He took a breath and tried to speak calmly. "I had it easier because you approved of my theology course, and Ridley Hall. But remember the arguments when I was deciding between theology and social work? You've never supported our choices, Mum, or listened to reason if what we wanted conflicted with your ideas of what was proper."

His mother shot back, "Your sister did things her way and look where that got her."

"Maggie!" Ernest shouted. "I can't believe you said that." Ben saw his father's hands shake on the wheel.

Good God, all they needed now was an accident. "Dad, pull over, let me drive, please." To his surprise, his father did pull over, but stayed in the driver's seat. He took deep breaths to compose himself.

Ernest never raised his voice. Ben took in his mother's look of shocked surprise as she turned to him. "Really, Ernest, I will not be shouted at!"

His father thumped the steering wheel. "And I will *not* sit here and listen to you talk about our daughter as if she got what was coming to her because she didn't do things the way you'd have liked." He turned in his seat to face his wife. "You must realize the awful position Ben was in. I'm happy he gave his sister the support she desperately needed since she didn't feel she could get it from her own parents. What does that say about us, Maggie?"

"Don't call me that!" she shrieked.

Ben struggled to keep his mouth shut but couldn't contain

himself. His anger at his mother made his words pop out before he could take them back. "Bea would have told you, Dad, but she didn't feel it was fair to put you in that position with Mum. She felt badly enough she confided in me, but she and Chad wanted her side of the family involved at some level."

His mother huffed. "What does that mean? I'm the evil one all around, is that it? Despite only wanting the best for my children."

Ben sat back and tried to recall his counseling courses. How would Reverend Neil advise him to handle this? "At a certain age, what is best for a person should be their own decision, not the one their mother wants." He opened the back window to let the cool air diffuse his resentment.

Ernest put the blinker on and the car in gear, and pulled out into traffic. "Well said, Ben." He glanced over at his wife. "There was a time you liked me to call you Maggie. I think it's Maggie I loved, not Margaret."

11:50 AM

After dropping Nora and Claire at home, Declan suggested Turl Street Kitchen for lunch. Since it was located down the street from Exeter, he and Watkins could easily walk to the lunch from the Porter's Lodge, after checking to see if Chad Brown had stopped in after the morgue viewing. Declan knew with Michaelmas term ending this week, undergraduate exams were underway. He didn't know what Brown's responsibilities would be after seeing his wife and didn't want the don to use that as an excuse to avoid talking to them. He had a sense of urgency to talk to the man, but the husband had the right to visit his wife first. And they needed sustenance.

At Exeter, the porter on duty said Chad Brown wasn't there, and that he didn't expect him to return to the college that day. Declan thanked him, and they walked down to the Kitchen, whose dining room was in a lovely Georgian building that had rooms and workspace to let on its upper floors. "By the time we eat and drive into Woodstock, Brown should have returned home. If he avoids us and says he had to be at college, we know otherwise."

The men took seats and ordered from the lunch pie menus, steak and ale for Watkins, chicken with wild mushrooms for Declan. Both had mushy peas and chips, and while Watkins ordered a Cotswold Cider Company offering called "Sideburns," Declan was driving and stuck to lemonade. The lunch rush was crowded and noisy.

Declan didn't think they'd be overheard in the din. Still, he kept his voice low while they waited for their food. "Expect Brown's mother stayed with Verity this morning."

"Guess so. What did you say to that reporter?" Watkins sipped his cider and issued a happy sigh of appreciation.

"I reminded him that Margaret was a grieving mother, and having her face plastered all over his broadsheet might put off more people than he'd like. I suggested instead he use a photo of the very photogenic victim, garner more sympathy, and told him our press officer had a good one for him. Of course, I can't control what he'll write in the article."

"Think he'll use one of Bea Jones?"

Declan had a taste of his lemonade and envied his sergeant.

"Whether he gets to make that call is anyone's guess. That angry mother photo makes good press. Out of our hands now."

Watkins tilted his head. "You don't want that woman's rage to be on display."

Their waitress approached and Declan waited to answer. He thanked the young woman as she put down their plates. The scent of pastry and gravy reached him. "Smells delicious." He poked his fork through the crust to cool off the filling. The rush of warm air brought the aroma of sherried mushrooms, and his stomach growled. "No matter our personal opinion of her, Margaret Smythe-Jones has lost her daughter, found out she has a grandchild, that Bea was married, and Ben was there, all in the space of a few days. She's probably furious at the world right now and deserved a bit of accommodation, regardless of her bulldog personality."

Watkins pointed his fork at Declan between bites. "It has to be a horrid thing, to spend all of that time and worry to raise a child, and then lose them too soon."

"Upsets the natural order of things, Watkins, when a child dies before its parents." He speared a chip and they ate in silence for a few moments. "Speaking of children, Julie still hot on ugly baby names?"

Watkins rolled his eyes. "Don't get me started. We've reached what she calls a compromise. We each listed two names we like, and when we see the baby, we'll decide based on which suits him better." He frowned. "I wrote down Evan, after my dad, and Graham, but Julie thinks his nickname at school would be 'cracker.' She won't be in favor of that no matter what or who he looks like."

"Too bad. Graham is a favorite of mine, too." He forked up a mouthful of chicken. "And if it's a girl?"

"Give me simple old-fashioned names, like Beth, or Alice. Julie still wants her maiden name, Beasley, and get this: Ramona! Did you ever? From some kids' book she likes. I don't think we even know anyone named Ramona. And there's her father's mother."

"What's her name?"

"Elsie."

Declan thought it wise not to comment in case one of Julie's choices won the day. "Nora said when she was pregnant with Sean, choosing his name drove her nutty, and she only had to please herself. Their name is the one thing we inflict on our kids for life, unless they change it. She eventually decided on Sean, after her father, and his middle name, McAllister, was her mother's maiden name." He wondered if he and Nora would have this same argument about names for their own baby someday. His mother's name had been Hattie, not a name he favored. "What's our plan of attack when we interview Chad Brown?"

His sergeant washed down a forkful of mushy peas with a chug of cider before answering. "Hmm. Only people with access cards could get into Exeter at that time of day, so that rules Brown right in, as far as I can see, and why we will visit him as soon as he's back from the morgue, even though in Ben's version of things he's been a stalwart husband and father."

Declan agreed, happy Watkins understood Brown had to be considered. "It's hard to see why he would want his wife dead if Ben is to be believed." Declan put down his fork on his empty plate and ticked off on his fingers. "He had help at home after a prolonged honeymoon in Wales—"

"If you can call adjusting to an infant a honeymoon," Watkins threw in.

"True. At home, maybe Bea was only there three full days a week, but his mother lived with them so he could work, and that was about to change next week. Then they would have been together full time."

"Maybe married life with a baby wasn't what he expected it to be? Still, I'd say we use the old 'asking questions to eliminate you from our enquiries' gambit to get his alibi, and then hit him with, 'why didn't you come forward immediately when Bea died,' and watch his reaction to that." Watkins drained his glass. "Maybe Momma Brown wasn't all that keen on Bea, for all we know."

"Good thought." Declan signaled for the waitress to bring their check. "And precisely the way I'd handle it.

12:31 PM

McAfee's stomach grumbled and he looked up at the clock. After a call from Watkins, he'd added the names Chad and Alvita Brown to the white board, alongside Bea's family, all the classmates who lived on Stairwell 10, and Dr. Hamilton. While Brown would have a university card that would allow him to enter Exeter whenever he wanted, his mother could have access to his card.

He looked over at Lily, intent on her computer, a tiny frown between her eyebrows as she concentrated. She must have felt his gaze, as she looked up unexpectedly and caught him looking at her. Even as he felt his face start to flush, instead of looking annoyed, Lily's face lit up with a big smile, and she pointed to the Apple watch she wore.

McAfee took that as encouragement and walked over to her desk.

Lily stood. "I'm ravenous. Want to grab lunch?"

He brightened. "Sure. Let's get out of here."

"Let me pop to the loo and I'll meet you outside in five minutes. We don't need these snoops knowing our business." Lily grabbed her purse and left.

McAfee wandered back to his own computer and checked his email before he followed her. He had a response from Exeter Administration to his query about the details of the complaint lodged against Dr. Hamilton.

After he read it, he sat back in his chair and wondered if Bea's death could have been a case of history repeating itself.

CHAPTER THIRTY-FIVE

12:42 PM

Nora lifted Sean's buggy over the high sill of the ancient door to Exeter, while Claire checked her mailbox. Nora could swear she caught a whiff of Declan's aftershave in the entryway. She reflected on how she used to call the buggy a stroller. Loo instead of toilet, boot instead of trunk, term instead of semester. It was all about adjusting to where she lived, especially since she planned to stay here. She'd never thought of herself as an 'expat,' but supposed that was her identity now.

With a stiff breeze blowing leaves in whorls on the sidewalk, she and Claire had worked out a minor strategy on their walk over, while Sean slurped his apple sauce from the squeeze tube. He had a habit of letting the empty drop on the sidewalk, so Nora kept a watchful eye. With his other hand he clutched Peter Rabbit.

The porter on duty nodded to Nora as she rescued the empty tube, wiped Sean's hands, and offered him his sippy cup.

"Jooz, Mummy!" He kicked his sneaker-clad feet on the footrest.

The porter watched with interest. He looked vaguely familiar, and came out from behind his desk toward her. She wracked her brain to recall how she knew him.

"Hello again." He bent down to chuck Sean under the chin. The boy responded with a toothy grin and offered his Peter Rabbit for inspection.

Nora checked his nametag as the man accepted the stuffed toy. Wilson. That rang a bell, too, as did his hint of Scottish brogue.

"The last time I saw you this little one was still in utero." Wilson made the toy dance to Sean's delight, and handed it back. "Here you go. Nice bunny." His knees cracked as he stood up. "Turned out to be a boy. Cute fellow."

With a start, Nora remembered the porter. She'd been pregnant when Val's partner had been murdered, and one day had pretended to be the niece of a don she wanted to interview. Now she cast around for something to say, as she had no idea whether Ted Wheeler still taught at Exeter.

"Thank you." Part of her ruse had been to say she'd found out the baby was a girl and wanted to tell her 'uncle' the good news. "The sonographer had it wrong after all." She gave a small laugh, aware of Claire's scrutiny.

"A right charmer. Your uncle enjoying his retirement?"

Nora could see confusion grow on Claire's face. "Oh yes, seems so." She hurried to change the topic. "This is my sister from my mother's side of the family, from America." She widened her eyes at Claire. *I'll explain later.*

"Well now, I didn't know Claire was a relation. Imagine that." Wilson went back around his side of the desk. "No wonder you chose Exeter, miss. Keep it in the family, so to speak."

Claire's answer was smooth. "Oh yes, Nora's uncle highly recommended I study here. Too bad he's retired." She gave Nora a pointed look.

She was good, Nora had to give Claire that. A student came into the small area, retrieved his mail, and left without a backward glance. Nora raised an eyebrow to Claire. *Go ahead.*

"Wilson, would you please let Sheila know I won't be back in college until Friday or Saturday? I'm staying with Nora for a few more days after Bea's death." Claire didn't have to fake her distress as she turned to Nora. "Sheila is the scout who covers my stairwell."

"Hullo again." Laura Hamilton stepped through the arch that led to the interior of the college. "Hullo, Wilson. I've come for that package for Peter." She turned to the women as he left for the storeroom. "Hi Nora. All right, Claire? How are you feeling?"

"I was just telling Wilson I'm going to stay the rest of the week at Nora's. Not sure I'm up to sleeping here so soon. We came to pick up a few things from my room. The tea and melatonin have been helping, so thanks for that."

"I understand. Peter is upset, too." She bent down as Sean waved his bunny at her. "Look who we have here, the infamous Sean, I take it. Molars come through?"

"Both sides." Nora watched Sean smile at the newcomer. Even after the kidnapping, he never met a stranger he didn't like.

Laura took the offered bunny and exclaimed over it. "What a handsome bunny! I love his blue coat."

"Boo." Sean parroted and held out his hand.

"Good sharing." Laura handed back the toy and Sean stroked the bunny's blue coat before slipping him under one protective arm. "Look, I'm off today, and this little guy would perk Peter up. Why don't I take him to our rooms, you two get what you need, and pick him up after? Easier than dragging him up three flights of stairs, and then trying to carry both him and Claire's things back down."

The image of a broken young woman at the bottom of the stairs hung unsaid between them. Nora hesitated. Leaving her son with someone she'd met once, nurse or not, brought back a flood of fear from his kidnapping. She felt her heart rate speed up. She wished she'd asked Declan about Hamilton after she'd toyed with the idea of him being implicated in Bea's death. Was she being foolish?

But then Nora looked at Laura's kind blue eyes, at the fact that Laura was a responsible nurse, and thought of Declan urging her not to hover over Sean. She couldn't smother him.

She needed to trust other people. Her gut feeling had been that Dr. Hamilton was a good man. "If you're sure he won't be a bother, that would be very kind. We won't be long."

"No bother at all. Let me start to walk him over, and you wait here to see how he reacts. If he screeches, come running!" She flashed a bright grin. "Take your time."

Wilson returned from the storeroom with a small box. "More books, I daresay."

Laura thanked him and stowed the carton under the buggy. "Thank you, Wilson." She spoke directly to the child. "Sean, let's go and see what Peter is up to, shall we? And show him your bunny named after him. Wave to Mummy."

Sean waved as Laura strolled off. Nora felt a moment of consternation he hadn't made a fuss. "I suppose I should be happy he's so friendly." It helped to know that when he'd been kidnapped the experience hadn't traumatized him. She turned to Claire. "Let's get your things."

"We'll see them shortly," Claire assured her. She turned back to Wilson. "Thanks for letting Sheila know I can't face sleeping here yet."

"Sure thing." Wilson looked subdued. "Tragic. Have to say I was right glad it was my day off last Friday. We've all been interviewed, and not one of us could think of anyone who would harm Bea Jones. Rotten shame."

"Yes, it is." Claire leaned into him. "Nora's fiancé is the lead detective on the case. We're all finding it difficult to figure out who would have wanted to harm Bea."

Wilson looked at Nora with new respect. "You dinae say! He was just here. Lovely young woman Bea was, not a bad side to her, none of that Miss Jones stuff. Insisted I call her Bea."

Nora knew she'd smelled Declan's distinctive aftershave. Now that Claire had laid the groundwork, Nora stepped closer to the desk. "There was no one at the college who didn't like her then?"

Wilson shook his head. "Not that I ever saw. Such lovely manners, and so thoughtful. Some have their heads together all the time, nattering away. I only see everyone coming and going, you know, but you can tell a lot about people by the way they stop to have a word, or take no notice of you altogether."

Nora smiled. "Wilson, I can't imagine anyone ignoring you. Surely not."

The porter shrugged. "You'd be surprised how many feel because they go to an Oxford college, they don't need to remember their elders with a simple 'hello' or 'good day.' My mam would've set them straight. They talk around you as if you're not there."

"Awful." Nora put a quizzical expression on her face and leapt right in. "Anyone from Stairwell 10?" Being rude didn't make one a killer. Still, Nora was interested in his thoughts.

Wilson hesitated. Nora decided he hovered on the edge of a confidence that fought with his predisposition to his job not to gossip. She needed to reassure him. "Anything you said to me would be held in the strictest confidence, except for the detectives, who would value the insider's look." She hoped that would soothe him and laid it on thick. "You could be a great help to the team working on Bea's death."

Before Wilson could answer, animated chat reached them

that stopped their conversation. The door opened to admit Patti Phillips, Jack Soong, and Nicola Morton. All three nodded to Claire and Nora, ignored Wilson, and swept through the arch into the quad, gone in an instant.

When Wilson spoke, he raised both eyebrows, and his eyes followed them out. "I really couldn't say, miss."

Woodstock

12:59

Declan found a parking spot on Park Street a block away from the Woodstock home Chad Brown shared with his mother and daughter.

"Think we gave him enough time to return from the morgue?" Watkins asked as they exited the car.

A gust of wind blew Declan's jacket open. "If not, we can talk to his mother first." He'd had Lily George run a quick background check on both Browns; neither had any criminal history.

They found Montague House with its tile plaque and pale blue door. Watkins rang the bell and they heard it echo inside. "Nice street to live on. You can walk to the shops."

"Yes, convenient. Feel of a village." Declan was about to ring again when they heard quick steps on a wooden floor and took out their warrant cards. The door was jerked open by a statuesque woman wearing a colorful caftan and an armload of bangle bracelets. Declan introduced them. "Alvita Brown? We have a few questions for you and your son, Chad."

The woman pursed her lips. "He's not here yet, but come in quickly. I've left my granddaughter in her high chair." She hurried down the hall to the kitchen at the back of the house, leaving them to shut the door and follow her.

Floor to ceiling sliding doors replaced the back wall that looked out on a compact garden and let in a huge amount of daylight, despite the grey day. Pulled up to the pine table, a little girl buckled into a high chair was absorbed in trying to pick up small pieces of cut up banana with her chubby fingers. A bib tied around her neck featured Peppa Pig.

Verity Brown had a halo of shiny blonde curls that contrasted with her light brown skin. She had inherited Bea's cornflower blue eyes and examined Declan with a solemn gaze. He had the feeling he was being sized up by the young child.

He changed his own expression to a welcoming hearty smile. "Hallo. You must be Verity."

The girl's face lit up with a blazing smile. She was beautiful.

Alvita's bangles clanged as she put her hands on her hips. "So the whole story's finally out. I'll put the kettle on." Her tense expression spoke to the strain she'd been under. She pointed to the table. "Take a seat. Chad should be here any minute. He's had a tough time of it. We all have, and even this little one knows something's wrong." She refilled the electric kettle and turned on the switch, then busied herself with a large teapot and strainer, her back to them as she worked.

Declan sat next to Verity, while Watkins took a seat on the other side of the table and pulled out his notebook. "It can't have been easy these past days."

Alvita turned to face him and leaned against the worktop. "No, it hasn't. Verity's become used to going days without seeing her Mum when Bea left for Exeter. Soon enough she'll start asking for her." The bracelets clacked as she crossed her arms. "Bea would leave here Monday morning and most weeks be back Thursday late afternoon. The semester flew by. I only had the baby alone during the day when Chad was teaching; otherwise, he took care of his daughter. Bea was also like a daughter to me, with all we shared."

"Can you tell me where Chad was last Thursday night into Friday morning?"

She narrowed her eyes and gave him a sharp glance. "Right here at home, taking care of his babe. Me, too. Too bad Verity doesn't talk yet, to tell you that's the God's honest truth. She's not been sleeping well and we took turns getting up with her. Babies are intuitive—she knows something's wrong. At one point I brought her in to her father and put her in bed with him. That must have been just before dawn. They both fell asleep for a while then."

"And Bea and Chad seemed happy, no arguments or misunderstandings recently?"

Alvita sighed. "I know you need to ask these questions, but it's clear you never met Bea. She and Chad were very happy together, and this little girl is their crowning glory." She shook her head. "No, inspector, they were over the moon to be together with their sweet child."

Declan didn't push her. "I understand you helped out in Wales after Verity was born?"

Alvita nodded. "I was there when she was born, and for the first week as they adjusted to a newborn. I came home after that, but I'd visit every few weeks. They were aces as parents, shared everything from feeds to nappy changes." The kettle clicked off.

Alvita rinsed the pot, put in the tea, and filled it with hot water. She brought the pot, covered with a quilted cozy, to the table to steep, and placed it well away from the child.

"Can you explain why Chad and Bea were so determined to hide their marriage and their child?" Declan could smell a woodsy scent from the teapot. Definitely not Earl Grey or PG tips.

Alvita let the water run at the sink and wet a washcloth. "This one needs a nap soon. Chad will want to see her, even if just for a moment, after what he'll have been through. I don't think I could do that. I want to remember Bea as she was, all warm and very alive." She wiped Verity's hands and face, and then the high chair tray as she spoke. "Hiding everything was at Bea's insistence. Her plan was to introduce Chad and Verity to her parents at her graduation, and have a small wedding reception after, whether her mother approved or not. She was even open to having another ceremony at her father's chapel, if he wanted that."

The woman's face grew pensive and she gazed into the distance. "It wasn't just her mother, though. She was concerned if they went public before graduation, there might be repercussions for Chad, having a relationship with a student, even one of age—Oxford can be a bit feudal like that—so they took pains to hide their marriage."

Watkins bobbed his head. "Look at their scout system."

"Exactly." Alvita flashed him a brief smile. "Knowing she was pregnant, when she learned she'd won that fellowship, Bea said it felt like the answer to her prayers. They moved their wedding to Wales, and she became even more firm that they wait until she'd graduated to bring her parents and the college into it." She rinsed out the cloth and took a cold teething ring from the freezer to put on the high chair tray, then sat at the table. Verity picked up the ring and chewed on it.

Declan recognized the teether as one in their own freezer. "But Ben knew."

"Yes, Ben was very close to Bea, and he helped with their ceremony, such as it was. I tried to convince her to tell her parents, both before and after Verity was born. While she said her father would be supportive, she didn't want more arguments with her mother. Bea felt like her childhood had been one long battle with the woman. I've never met her, but 'set in her racist ways' and 'obstinate as a mule' were phrases Bea used." She shrugged. "Course, Bea could be stubborn herself, but we often don't see our own failings, do we? Once her mind was made up, there was nothing I could do but follow along."

"Did you ever think of calling her parents, maybe her father, and cluing him in?" Declan asked, as Alvita poured tea for them. To his surprise, the tea was deep reddish color.

Alvita saw his look. "Rooibos, from South Africa. Caffeine free, full of antioxidants, and naturally sweet. Try it." She poured her own cup and recovered the teapot to keep it warm.

Declan sipped. She was right. The tea had a slightly nutty taste and was mildly sweet on its own. To his surprise, he didn't hate it. Watkins gamely tried it. He could see by his sergeant's face that rooibos wouldn't feature in his sergeant's pantry any time soon.

"I did think of that, but that would have betrayed Bea's trust, which I valued. I didn't know her mother, but she did. Bea was so sweet and kind otherwise. It wasn't as if they'd done anything illegal. It was their business, no matter my private thoughts."

She played with the golden curls on Verity's head, and the child leaned into her. "I confess I loved having Verity all to myself some days."

The front door slammed and Verity raised her head. Footsteps could be heard coming down the hall. Chad Brown pulled up short when he entered the kitchen. "What the hell are you doing here?"

CHAPTER THIRTY-SIX

Oxford

1:15 PM

Nora hurried Claire past the spot where Bea Jones had died, and up the stairs to her room. By the time she and Claire rounded three sides of the quad, Sean's buggy rested outside the door to the stairs where Dr. Hamilton had his rooms. Perhaps this meant Sean didn't have any bad memories from a few months ago and wouldn't be sitting in a therapist's chair two decades from now, suffering from anxiety about the time he'd been kidnapped as a baby. The kidnapper had given the child to a woman who took in children for social services, and she'd treated Sean well.

Nora sent Claire into her bedroom to gather what she needed, while Nora stayed by the door and raised her voice. "Bring any wash you have, too, Claire. Might as well get that done."

As she'd hoped, the door to Nicola Morton's room opened, and Patti and Jack emerged, while Nicola stayed in the doorway, leaning against the jamb.

"Hello." Nora walked over to them. "I'm Claire's sister, Nora. All finished with exams?"

"Thankfully." Jack flashed a grin full of white teeth.

"Hellish." Patti swiped at her platinum locks. "I may spray a 'V for Victory' into the back of this." She turned around and pointed to the cropped back. "A nice purple one, right here, no?"

Nicola laughed at Patti's antics. Nora hadn't realized the three were friends, but if they all shared classes with Chad Brown, it was natural they would be. She turned to Jack. "Any special end-of-term gestures for you?"

The young man furrowed his brow while he considered her question. "I believe I will play virtual chess games as my reward."

Patti sighed. "That's all you think about, Jack. Lighten up. There's more to life than chess and poetry, no matter how good you are at both."

"I doubt it." The solemn tone of his voice belied the chuckle that followed.

Nora made eye contact with Nicola. "Did you find the exam grim, too?"

Nicola lifted one graceful shoulder. "Chad is such a good teacher. I didn't find it as tough as these two. I keep telling them, if they do the work, the exams shouldn't faze them."

"That's because you're a master bullshitter when you write." Patti started up the stairs to her room. "I'm off for a nap to rest my weary brain. Then I think a few rounds at the King's Arms tonight. What do you say, Jack?"

"Sure. Text me 10 minutes before you want to leave." He cut Patti off and scampered around her up the stairs.

"That boy." Patti sighed in mock exasperation. She flounced away, calling back over her shoulder. "See you at seven, Nicola."

Nicola nodded. "Sounds good." She stayed in her doorway and locked on Nora's eyes. "Patti said your boyfriend is the detective on Bea's case."

Nora came closer. "Yes, my fiancé." While she wanted to talk to all three of the students, at least here was one willing to talk now. "He's the senior investigating officer on the case." Nora hoped Claire wouldn't appear until she had time to talk more with Nicola.

Nicola looked to the door to Bea's room, still closed off with crime scene tape. "Bea's death couldn't have been an accident?"

Nora shrugged. "I don't know what their thinking is. Declan doesn't discuss his cases at home." She knew better than to say she had any inside information on Declan's cases, and forged ahead. "Claire said everyone liked Bea, that she was very kind."

Nicola stood up straight. "Oh, yes. She was nice to everyone. Too nice, maybe." She shrugged. "She had her secrets. Everyone thinks someone so kind can do no wrong, but Bea wasn't quite as good as everyone thought."

Nora waited, knowing most people couldn't help filling a silence.

Nicola grimaced. "Sorry, not a nice thing to say about someone who's passed on."

"Some people have insights others don't see." Nora put on a sympathetic face. "You have a different impression from so many others—what did you see that gave you that feeling?" Was Nicola disappointed that Bea had secrets?

Oh, Bea was very kind, just not a saint." She sighed. "Forget I said anything. I just hate when someone dies and everyone puts them on a pedestal, instead of remembering they were human and real, you know?" Nicola turned to go back into her room.

Nora cast around for something to say to keep her talking. "Good luck with your results."

"Don't need luck. I've had the best teacher Exeter offers." She disappeared into her room and quietly closed the door.

1:21PM

Declan spoke first. "You must have realized we'd need to speak with you, Mr. Brown."

Chad shook his head. "The husband's always the prime suspect, right?"

His mother unstrapped Verity from her high chair. "That's not how I brought you up to speak to company, son. These men are trying to find out who killed your wife, and you need to convince them you had nothing to do with it so they can find the real culprit. And your daughter wants you." She brought the girl over to her father.

Chad wrapped his arms around his daughter, burying his face in her curls. When he raised her head, his eyes were shining. "Sorry. Rough few days. Today especially. Seeing Bea there—" Verity wrapped her chubby arms around her father's neck and yawned. "I think you need a nap, my dumpling." He kissed her forehead, each eye, her nose, each cheek. The girl giggled. "Gran will put you down for a nap, sweetheart." He handed the girl back to Alvita.

With a clink of her bracelets, Alvita carried Verity out of the room.

Declan sipped his tea while Chad composed himself. The widower opened a cabinet door and took out a mug, then removed the cozy and poured himself tea. As Chad added a teaspoon of sugar, Declan eased back into conversation. "I appreciate it can't be an easy time, Mr. Brown."

Chad waved his hand. "Chad is fine. Mr. Brown is lying in a grave in Portmore back in Jamaica, along with dozens of other Browns who died of rum disease." He sniffed his tea and took a sip. "Don't recall him much; the little I do I try to forget." He Jamaican lilt became more pronounced. "My mum was born in London, moved to Jamaica when she married my father. She's wanted to move back since I was little. Mommy was the stable one, brought us here when I was 12.

Watkins pushed his cup aside. "Us? I didn't think you had siblings."

"No siblings. Children who belonged to Mum's best friend. When their mother was dying, she made Mum their guardian." He looked at Watkins. "And before you ask about their father, more rum disease. We left Jamaica as soon as the paperwork all went through." He stirred his tea. "All legal emigrations, although I have dual citizenship. Mum taught for years in Jamaica. Most of her stuff transferred. She had to take a few classes when we arrived here, I remember that. She was an excellent teacher."

"You come by your talents naturally, then." Declan resumed his track. He needed information, but the man had just lost his wife. As he often told Watkins, tread carefully. "As painful as losing Bea has been, having your marriage and baby brought out in public at the inquest this morning can't have been pleasant, either."

"Nothing as bad as seeing Bea lying there, her lips blue, stone cold." He shook his head. "I'm proud of my wife and child. If it were up to me, we would have never hidden anything." Chad's face darkened. "Did you see that cow of a mother of hers stalk out? She should only know how much this is all her fault."

Declan sat up at his vehemence. "You think Bea's mother was involved in her death?"

Chad deflated. "Not really. I mean, not her fall. I meant that we had to hide our marriage and baby, hide our love." He looked at Declan with dull eyes. "Bea should have been living here with us full time instead of still at college. This should never have happened."

"When was the last time you saw Bea?"

Chad hesitated as he thought and rubbed a hand across his mouth. "Thursday around lunch. She had a concert date with Claire. I encouraged her to go. She'd been working so hard, and it had been her birthday a few days before. She deserved a night out." His shoulders drew up. "I keep thinking if she hadn't gone, she'd still be alive." He shook his head. "We had our whole lives in front of us."

"You were here Thursday night?"

"Yes, with Verity and my mum." He looked Declan in the eye. "I know you need more than that." He thought for a moment. "I spoke to a colleague about the finals schedule quite late. You can check with Dr. Peter Hamilton. He'll tell you I was here because Verity woke up and Mum called me away. You can check my phone, too."

"We'll do that. And all night into Friday morning?"

"Yes. Verity had a bad dream and was up and down all night. Mum will tell you. At one point she walked the floor with her. I finally let Verity into my bed just before dawn and we both had a few hours of sleep. Then I waited for Bea to show up, and when she didn't arrive by late morning, I thought she overslept. I finally went to the college but couldn't get to her room. I saw the police tape and the porter told me that 'Miss Jones' had fallen and died. I couldn't believe it! Can you imagine finding out your wife has died from the college porter?" He shook his head at the memory. "I wandered around town, trying to take it in, when Ben called me. He'd just found out and was on his way to pick up his father. We agreed they'd do the formal identification then as I had no proof at that point Bea and I were married."

Declan saw Watkins make a note and knew he would ask whoever interviewed the porters if Chad had shown up as he claimed. They could call Ben Jones for verification of Friday's calls, too. With Chad's story matching Alvita's, it seemed Chad was covered for the relevant time when Bea was pushed and his phone would verify his actions. "Would you like a family liaison officer assigned to you?"

Chad looked startled. "What? No, not at all. Mum and I can handle things—have been since we heard about Bea. Do you know anything more than I heard at the inquest?"

Declan shook his head. "Not yet. I promise you we have a team working on your wife's case. Chad, can you think of anyone who would want to harm Bea?"

He looked down at his cooling mug of tea. "Everyone loved Bea."

Declan kept his tone gentle. "That's what we hear, yet obviously one person didn't."

Two large tears ran down Chad's face. "I can't think of anyone who would want to do that to her. I feel like I'm in a nightmare and can't wake up." He wiped away the tears with the back of his hand. "We were so happy. Bea had me convinced that once her parents saw Verity, they'd come around. Ben has been wonderful, and Bea said her father is like him in his attitudes. I kept telling Bea we had at least two-thirds of her family who would support us, and if her mum didn't, so be it. That was easy enough for me to say when I've never lived with Maggie." He looked up then. "Bea and Ben used 'Jones' and that drove Maggie crazy."

"That was probably their intention." Declan thought of Nora

suddenly being taken from him and suppressed a shudder. He could only imagine the depth of the man's pain.

"What can you tell me about the necklace Bea always wore, a heart pendant her father said," Declan asked.

In a flash, Chad's look changed from sorrow to anger. "At the inquest I felt sick when I heard it was missing. I gave Bea that locket the day our daughter was born. It had a small amethyst set into it, Verity's birthstone." His voice broke. "Bea always said she wanted Verity to have it when she grew up. You think Bea's killer yanked it off her neck?"

Declan nodded. "That's one possibility. It wasn't at the scene, and not in her belongings. If it turns up, we'll get it back to you." Declan didn't elaborate that if the locket ever showed up and was deemed evidence needed for a murder trial, it might take months or longer to return it.

Watkins didn't have any questions to add. Declan wanted to better understand Bea's relationship with her mother. "You say your wife insisted Mrs. Jones wouldn't approve of your union, even if it brought her a grandchild?"

Chad drained his mug before answering. "It goes beyond Bea being convinced her mother simply wouldn't approve of our marriage. She had an irrational fear her mother would try to get custody of Verity. Bea decided Maggie would think she could give the child a more normal upbringing than interracial parents who would be subject to people's whispers and stares."

"But the child is mixed-race herself," Watkins burst out. "Surely not in today's world."

"I know, I know. Believe, I tried on many occasions to convince Bea this was the wrong way to go about things. Maggie would never get custody. I suppose she could make life miserable for us for a while. We're upstanding parents, I have a good job, and nothing in our past to worry about, but then I didn't grow up with that woman as my mother, thank God. There are years of history there, a track record if you will. Bea's fears were a big reason we married in Wales, instead of waiting until she graduated. She thought her mother would reject the child, yet she worried Maggie would try to take Verity from us. It didn't make sense. Maggie was Bea's blind spot." He looked down at his hands.

"It can't have been easy."

"Bea's experiences with her mother colored every decision she made. She told me I could never understand the depth of Maggie's need to control her."

Declan remembered how the shock of hearing Bea had borne a child had caused Maggie to faint. "I understand her mother suffers from depression at times."

Chad shrugged. "If you call it that. Bea said those jags always came on after Maggie didn't get her way." Chad sat forward and pushed his empty mug away. "Look, after months of hostile arguments, Bea finally agreed to stay at Cambridge for her undergrad work, but her mother was relentless. Maggie would turn up to Downing at all hours, supposedly to check Bea didn't need anything, when she really wanted to be certain Bea wasn't partying, or with a boyfriend she didn't consider good husband material." He picked up his head as Alvita's footsteps came down the stairs. "In her second year, her father found his strength and told Maggie she couldn't visit Bea at Downing. But Maggie's on several chapel committees at Christ's, so there was always a ready excuse for her to be floating around town. She'd find Bea in Downing's library and start grilling her. It's amazing Bea graduated with honors with her mother's interference. When her father supported Bea doing her master's here, Maggie didn't speak to him for weeks and took to her bed with one of her 'depressive' spells." He put air quotes around the phrase.

Alvita entered the kitchen. "That baby is so easy to put to sleep. Went right off after a book." She leaned against the sink. "Maggie? Smothering love instead of mothering love, I call that. It's a type of control, like the helicopter parents we used to see at school."

Declan wondered how a person who felt the need to exert that kind of dominance would feel if they found out they'd been mightily thwarted. "I was there when Bea's parents learned of her pregnancy. They seemed genuinely shocked."

Watkins agreed. "Maggie fainted."

Chad rolled his eyes. "She would."

Declan persisted. "Is there any chance Bea's mother could have found out about your marriage?"

"I don't see how." Chad tilted his head to one side in thought. "The only two people who knew were my mother and Bea's brother, Ben."

"As far as you know," Watkins pointed out.

"True. There's only one other person Bea might have trusted enough to tell, although she never told me she had."

Declan's eyes widened. "Who?"

"Peter Hamilton."

CHAPTER THIRTY-SEVEN

4:32 PM

Nora sat in the dining room at the long pine table, glancing up from her laptop to check on Sean and Claire, who played in the garden with Typo. Bundled up against the chilly day, they seemed to enjoy the fresh air. Claire tried to teach Sean how to throw a ball for the puppy. So far the one thing he'd mastered was yelling, "Fetch!"

She'd been happy to retrieve Sean from the Hamiltons and felt silly for worrying now. They were perfectly nice people and Laura Hamilton had been happy to watch Sean for the 20 minutes Nora and Claire had been away.

She decided to redirect her energy. She scrolled through websites to research Provence and look for a likely place for her fairies to visit. Several places appealed, and she added to the outline of a story for her next book from scribbled notes. Mr. Tink had told her he'd do touchups tomorrow, and she could start to move books into her library shelves soon after. She'd be at work at her desk in a few days.

Nora looked up as Neil Welch came through the gate in the side yard and stopped to talk with Claire. Sally must have told him about Claire and why she was staying at Nora's, as he put a hand briefly on Claire's shoulder. Typo scampered over, and Neil knelt down to roughhouse with the dog as Sean toddled over and grabbed Neil's knee to steady himself.

By the time he rose, Nora had the kitchen door open, and the lanky man loped over to her. "Come in."

He wiped his feet on the doormat and stepped inside.

"Tea?"

"No, thanks. Just finished a chapter and need to take over with Sam so Sally can head to a meeting, think it's the Altar Guild this time. I wanted to know if I emailed you the chapter, if you'd have time to give it a quick read sometime this week? I need to take a break from writing. This is harder than it looks."

"Why do you think I write children's books? Sure, send it on. I'll read it tomorrow and get back to you." She took in Neil's anxious expression. "I meant what I said about the last chapter I read, Neil. You've nailed the voices, kept Wilkie Collins and Charles Dickens distinct."

Neil beamed. "Thanks. It's hard when there's so much written about each man, but not much about their relationship together." He leaned against the doorframe. "Sally told me Claire's friend died tragically." He shook his head. "Tough situation."

"Claire's handling it well."

"One thing Sally's work has taught me is that people are multilayered. There's a lot beneath the surface we don't see." He checked his watch. "I'd better go. I'll send that chapter off to you later." He saluted her and left the way he came, waving to Claire and Sean.

Nora stood at the door and watched Claire play in the yard with Sean and Typo. The days were shorter, and it was already dusky outside with the light fading. She reflected on Neil's words. Maybe she needed to sift through the layers.

Claire took Sean's arm and tried to show him again how to throw the tennis ball for Typo. Having her sister here was a good thing, despite the horrific cause, and Claire had proved herself to be a worthy assistant in Nora's minor investigation.

The puppy leapt and ran after the ball when it rolled under

a rosemary bush. Nora leaned over the table, hit "Save," and closed her laptop. She stood at the sink and watched Sean clap his hands. A wave of dreariness washed over her.

Nora hated the feeling. She had always been able to compartmentalize parts of in her life, to distance herself to find resolutions to problems.

This business of settling her house, being a mum, working on a new book, all that she loved and embraced, should be plenty to keep her occupied. Most days it was, and she had a May wedding to plan, too. While it would be a small affair, she still needed to find a venue for the ceremony and reception that would work with the honeymoon they'd planned in Cornwall. Two friends had a thatched cottage called Strawtop they had offered the couple. They could travel somewhere exotic when Sean was older.

Plenty to do, especially with the holidays looming, so why did she feel so unsettled? Nora took out milk and cocoa to have ready for Sean and Claire when they came inside. As she stirred the cocoa into the milk in a pot on the stovetop, she understood her feelings with a clarity that surprised her. She was jealous of Declan and his ability to spend his days investigating.

Her years in journalism had kept her curiosity directed. The other cases she'd been involved in since writing the children's books had fed that part of her nature. Now here she was, with a death she needed to get to the bottom of for her sister's peace of mind and to remove her firmly from the suspect list, and she felt stymied and frustrated. Those layers spoke to her. Her intuition had served her well before, and with her strong writer's imagination, she'd had some surprising finds in other cases.

She needed to examine what she *could* accomplish, not what she couldn't.

She wasn't a real detective, so she couldn't insist people talk to her. On the other hand, that had never stopped her before, and look how she'd made progress discovering Verity. Her foray to Exeter today had left her with a few minutes of Nicola Morton's time, but she hadn't been able to talk long to Patti Phillips or Jack Soong. She was certain the culprit was someone Bea knew from college. People often knew more than they realized they did, many times missing a key point.

She needed to be more proactive. With a jolt of energy, Nora texted Declan to see what time he would be home.

He replied: *Late. Eat without me.*

Thought I might take Claire out for a bite after Sean's in bed.

Fine xx PS Who'll stay with him?

I'll find someone. You concentrate on work. Talk later, xx

Nora moved the cocoa to the edge of the hob and went in search of Mr. Tink. She found the painter cleaning his brushes. The walls gleamed with the green with a hint of blue, brought out by the pale color between the ceiling beams. "Teresa would be very pleased, Mr. Tink."

He took off his paint-dripped cap and scratched the back of his head. "No idea who comes up with these names—but looks nice, I'll give you that. Definitely finish in here tomorrow."

"While I'll miss having you around, I expect you'd like to rest up before Christmas. I wondered if Mrs. Tink has plans tonight? I'm looking for a babysitter for a few hours."

"Tonight's my dart night at the local. Give her a call. She's usually home on Tuesdays."

After speaking with Mrs. Tink, who agreed to stay with Sean as long as she could watch *Master Chef* on television that night, Nora called Claire inside. Sean's cheeks were very pink, and

Typo leapt around Nora in his excitement as she took her son's coat off and installed him in his high chair. "You two seemed to have a good time."

"Fetch!" Sean yelled, and the beagle jumped up to look for a ball.

"Say that only when you throw the ball, Sean," Nora explained. "But you did a very good job outside." She gave the puppy a biscuit and poured warm cocoa into a sippy cup for Sean, and into two mugs for Claire and herself. "Thanks for that time, Claire. I managed to get quite a bit done toward the outline of the new book. Now I need to let it percolate in my brain a while."

Claire rubbed her hands. "Thanks to you for this. Chilly out there."

Her sister's ruddy cheeks gave her an attractive glow. "Do you feel like going out for dinner? Declan will eat on the run, or rummage once he gets home. I have Mrs. Tink coming after Sean's had his bath and is in bed."

Claire drank from her mug. "Lovely. Sure, let's go out. What do you have in mind?"

"How about a bite and a pint at the King's Arms?"

5:23 PM

As they left Montague House, Declan received McAfee's text and immediately called Dr. Hamilton. He caught the man before he left for home. Hamilton agreed to wait for them in his rooms. Then he called McAfee and told him to have someone on the team verify with Ben Jones that he'd called Chad after he found out Bea died, and that the two men had agreed on their approach to let Ben and Ernest identify Bea while Chad looked for his marriage license. He also wanted someone to check Chad's phone log, which he'd given them access to, to see if he had called Dr. Hamilton the evening before Bea was killed, even though he planned to ask the man himself. Bea's husband seemed to be genuinely grieving for his wife, but Declan needed evidence to back up his instincts before completely eliminating Chad Brown in his wife's murder.

Declan explained to Watkins the nature of the complaint McAfee had unearthed as they drove back to Exeter. Could Hamilton have tried something with Bea, and been involved in her fall? He searched for parking until he finally put his police card on the dash and left the car bumped up on the sidewalk on Turl Street as he had earlier.

For the second time that day, the two detectives flashed their warrant cards as Watkins asked the evening porter for Dr. Hamilton's rooms. Once directed around the quad, they passed the Undercroft Bar again, where loud music and raucous laughter reached them at a frenetic pitch.

"Sounds like celebrating," Watkins said.

"Term ends Friday, and some are done already. Letting loose, I expect. Hilary term doesn't start until the second week in January."

"Nice for some. What did you think of Chad Brown?"

"I think he's devastated by his wife's death."

"I thought so, too." Watkins stopped in front of the ivy-covered door to Hamilton's rooms, and pushed it open. "Or else he's an accomplished actor."

"Let's see what this don has to say. You take over the questioning." Declan started up the staircase.

Watkins threw him a look. "I always jump in here and there; why take the lead now? This some sort of tryout?"

"Just want to be able to say you've had all the experience you need if the opportunity arises." Declan winked, and Watkins' smile broadened. He knocked, and the door opened almost immediately by the don, wearing chinos and a sweater vest over a pale blue Oxford shirt. "Dr. Hamilton? We saw you briefly last Friday, when I believe you spoke to my sergeant, Detective Watkins."

"Please come in. I'd offer you refreshments, but I was about to leave for home when you called. Have a seat. What can I do for you?" Hamilton sat in chintz armchair near the fireplace.

Declan chose a hard-backed chair that looked easier to climb out of than the soft leather sofa that swallowed Watkins. He took out his notebook, interested to see how Watkins would begin the interview.

Watkins cleared his throat. "I expect you heard at the inquest today about Bea Jones's marriage to Chad Brown and the birth of their daughter."

"Yes. Bit of a gut punch, although I realized after I shouldn't have been terribly surprised. I'd thought last year they had a relationship, yet this semester after Bea came back from Wales, they seemed distant. Brown was on sabbatical at the same time. Now I know why he wanted it then." He sighed and sat forward in his chair. "Terrible business."

"So you didn't know about Bea's wedding, nor her child?"

"I didn't, no. But after the inquest I spoke with my wife. Laura noticed last fall that Bea's face was rounder, and that Bea took to wearing flowing dresses last Michaelmas, before she left for Wales. I don't take much notice of my students apparel unless it's really outrageous. We see all sorts these days, from piercings to tattoos and the like. A few loose dresses wouldn't have been cause for me to notice. Neither of us had any idea of their marriage."

"Can you think back to last Thursday evening, sir, and confirm if you spoke with Chad Brown that night?"

"Oh yes, quite late. One of the invigilators took ill, and I'd just gotten a call about it. Hated to disturb him at that hour, must have been near 11. We were able to move some others around to cover and worked it out."

"And was it your impression Mr. Brown as at home during this call?"

"I assumed he was, as I heard his mother in the background say she needed him and we ended the call." He ran a finger around his collar, and Declan had the suspicion Hamilton knew the next topic Watkins' would raise.

"I need to ask you about a sexual harassment complaint brought against you last fall by a female student, referred to as 'DP' in the report."

Hamilton flinched and jerked back. "Denise Parsons. That idiocy was investigated thoroughly and completely dismissed. I've no idea why you're bringing it up now, or what those lies could possibly have to do with Bea's death."

"Covering all our bases, Dr. Hamilton. When complaints have been made, we look for patterns of behavior."

"Crawl out the woodwork, you mean." The man wagged a finger at Watkins. "Most students attend Oxford for an education, but for those fortunate to be admitted, there are always a few who like to party too much, and Parsons was one of those. We use programs to detect plagiarism in a student's work, detective, things like Turnitin and CbPD, Citation-based Plagiarism Detection." He shook his head. "Denise Parsons fabricated an essay on Spencer's 'Faerie Queen' by putting together bits and pieces of other works already published online.

"Every student is made aware their work will go through these programs, so I don't know if Parsons didn't bother to read the handbook that informs them of that, or simply thought she was above doing the work." His face reddened. "When it became obvious what she'd done, a disjointed effort at best, she retaliated with this spurious complaint, totally made up, saying I'd made sexually suggestive comments to her on multiple occasions." He scrubbed a hand across his face. "Never overheard, of course."

"You straightened this out to the college's satisfaction?" Watkins caught Declan's eye. He nodded to let him know he was doing fine.

"Absolutely. I'm careful to never be alone in my rooms with any student, and if I'm conducting a personal evaluation, it's in the library or other public place. We do have students here for teas on alternate Sundays, but my wife is always present. Once that was established, and in light of the clear plagiarism, Miss Parsons was sent down and the case closed." His color returning to normal, Hamilton added, "Sorry if I'm tense. I love teaching here, and most of my students are wonderful. This young lady threw away her chance of a great education, and then had the temerity to try to wriggle out of the consequences and tear me down with it. Unconscionable."

"I'm glad it worked out for you, sir." Watkins looked to Declan.

He gave nothing away, just returned the look with a steady gaze. Declan knew he could throw in a question of his own at any time, but he wanted Watkins to fully explore being the lead. The college report had cleared Hamilton. As far as he was concerned, Hamilton was off the list of suspects.

"If I might ask one more thing, Dr. Hamilton," Watkins continued. "Can you think of anyone how would have had a reason to harm Bea Jones?"

"Believe me, it's something I keep thinking about. The Broad Street entrance is kept locked, and that's the closest to that staircase. After 10 at night, the main entrance needs a Bod Card to gain admission, so the only people who should be here are either staff or students, or someone a student admitted." He bent his head, and suddenly looked tired. "I can't forget the sight when I came back from my run that morning and saw Bea lying there, that halo of blood all around her head …" He looked at Watkins and Declan in turn. "This young woman had a brilliant mind and a bright career ahead of her. Please find out who's responsible for this tragedy. Bea didn't deserve this."

7:40 PM

Nora walked with Claire to Park Road, and the corner that boasted the oldest pub in Oxford. They entered the pink building built in 1607 that housed the King's Arms on its ground floor, and ordered dinner at the bar, taking their drinks with them. She'd had the foresight this afternoon to call ahead and book a table, and they were shown to the back room, called The Office. Nora looked around the front room and the snug, searching for her quarry as they moved to the back. Their table was tucked in a corner; the three Exeter undergrads sat clustered with several other students around a larger table farther into the room.

Nora had spoken to Claire on their walk over. They agreed they would take their seats without drawing attention to themselves, preferring to have an unguarded look, if possible, at the students who had their interest. Nora would have to turn her head to see their targets, while Claire's view was more direct.

Claire's wavy hair, loose tonight, mirrored Nora's own, and she wondered if anyone would take them for sisters, despite being unrelated. She hoped returning to the place where Claire and Bea had had their last meal wouldn't be too upsetting for her sister. Nora thought of how Bea would never see Verity grow up. Life, so fragile, could change in an instant. It was a sobering thought.

She took a thirsty gulp of her cider, and put the glass down, then reached out to pat Claire's hand. "Thanks for coming with me to do this. It seems like a small thing, but you never know what nugget might tip someone's hand. I hope it's not too painful. You're a star."

Claire squeezed Nora's hand back. "I wanted to come, if it helps understand what happened to Bea. I like seeing you in action, too. I don't mind being your sidekick, as long as you don't start calling me Watson."

"Watkins is close enough, and he's Declan's. I like having you with us, Claire. It's been a chance to get to know each other better. I'm just sorry for the reason. We may not have blood between us, but it's nice to feel I have a sister."

"Me, too." Claire tilted her head. "We're sisters of the heart."

"Perfect. Sometimes family is who we choose to be around."

"Only a sister would try to prove me innocent of murder." She winked at Nora. "I've known all along I must be on the suspect list, as I was the one who found Bea. Even I read the occasional mystery."

Nora put up a hand. "Guilty as charged." She inclined her head toward the center of the room. "What do you see?"

"Patti Phillips is holding court—that's her braying laugh you hear—in the center of the table. Nicola Morton is talking to another student I don't know well. Think she's a first-year undergrad. Looks like Nicola's giving the girl a tutorial instead of letting her hair down. In the short time I've known her, she's never been a party animal."

"Too serious to play?"

"Maybe. Jack Soong is sitting up against the wall, staring at his phone and ignoring the gal next to him. She's one of Patti's acolytes, hangs on her every word. He could even be playing a game of chess on his phone."

"Why bother to come along then?"

Claire shrugged. "He's usually on the outside of things looking in, a fringe person. I don't think he knows where he belongs. Patti makes him come out, or he'd always hide in his room."

"Very astute. No girlfriend or boyfriend?"

"Not that I've seen."

Nora turned and stole a look at the trio. Patti slapped the table to punctuate a story she told, and several around the table erupted in laughter. Jack ignored the outburst. "Interesting. Jack's into his phone, and Nicola looks like she'd rather be anywhere else."

"Yes, but she has a need to be seen as part of the group, so she tags along and then makes it clear she's uncomfortable. I get the feeling she thinks she's better than the other undergrads."

Nora was impressed with Claire's acuity. "You have good insights."

Claire lifted a shoulder. "Minored in psychology as an undergrad, she says with modesty."

The women shared a laugh. A jeans-clad staff member appeared and put down their plates. Steam from Nora's salmon and prawn pie brought her a rich scent that made her stomach growl. "Guess I'm hungrier than I'd realized." She salted her chips and dug in.

Claire squeezed a pool of ketchup on her plate and ate a few of her own chips, then spread the chickpea and garlic mash that accompanied her Portobello mushroom burger on top of the bun. "Uh-oh, incoming."

Patti Phillips stopped by their table. "Look who's here. Where've you been hiding, Scott?"

Claire pointed to Nora. "Staying with my sister, Nora, for a few days."

"Restroom's always crowded anyway." Patti grabbed a chair from the table next to them and plopped down and scrutinized Nora. "So that dishy detective's your husband?"

"Almost. We're getting married this spring."

Patti stole a few chips from Claire's plate. "He can be fierce. Hope he's a lot more chill in bed." She waved a chip around. "Although, still waters and all that."

Nora tamped down feeling defensive. "Declan takes his work seriously."

Patti nodded. "Believe me, I could tell." She turned to Claire. "You moving out this weekend? Be good to get away from that stairwell."

Claire shook her head. "I had a vacation residence approved;

not going home for the holidays." She thrust her chin at Nora. "Our parents are coming over for Christmas."

"Cool." Patti swung one leg over the other, her heavy boot swinging as she stole more chips from Claire's plate.

"Help yourself." Claire pushed her plate closer. "I still can't believe Bea is gone. I keep trying to think who could have had a grudge against her."

Nora was glad Claire steered their talk back to Bea. "What about you, Patti? Know anyone who disliked Bea?"

"The Kindness Queen?" She shook her head. "Everyone loved her, not a bad vibe there. I still don't get what happened. Last person I'd think would tick someone off."

Nora agreed. "Yes, it would seem Bea didn't have enemies. How about you? Going home soon?"

The young woman wrinkled her nose, making the ring in her eyebrow dance. "Home? Not bloody likely with the new guy my mum fancies." Her face blazed with a happy smile. "My sister in Australia is having me over for the holiday break—can't wait."

"Australia! How wonderful. I've always wanted to visit there," Nora said with true enthusiasm.

"You and me both! Monday night, I'm out of here, and don't have to be back until Hilary term starts."

"You'll be gone quite a while," Nora clarified.

"Over three weeks, then I'll come right back here." Patti looked up as one of the students being ignored by Jack stopped on her way out and motioned smoking a cigarette. "Yeah, be right with you." She stood to leave and threw back over her shoulder: "Tell that almost-husband of yours to find out who did for Bea, all right?"

"That was interesting." Claire said when Patti was out of

earshot.

"I'll have to find out if Declan knows she won't be around for a while." Nora made a note on her phone and eyed her cider. She usually only had one, and wanted to make it last. At that moment, the staff member who had brought their meals stopped to ask if they needed anything. "Could we have two glasses of water, please?"

"Yes, I'll bring them over."

Claire stuffed a chip in her mouth. "Do you think it's suspicious Patti's leaving the country?"

Nora pursed her lips. "Probably not. A trip like that would have been in the works for a while, I'd think."

"True. Convenient, though."

"And here I thought I was the suspicious one."

On his way to delivering another tray, the staff member dropped off their waters. Nora sipped hers and wondered what excuse she could come up with to visit the other table. "What are the others doing?"

"Jack is still on his phone. Nicola and the other gal are deep in conversation—oh, wait, they're getting up to leave." Nicola walked out, talking to the other student. She nodded to Claire and kept going. "That leaves Jack with his head in his phone. I don't think he's even aware the others have left." Claire looked at the remaining chips on Nora's plate. "You going to eat those? Patti decimated mine."

Nora pushed the plate toward her. "All yours if you catch Jack's eye and wave him over."

Claire looked up from the plate in surprise. "And do what then?"

"Go ahead, you can do it. Put on a friendly smile, wave him over."

"What do I say once he gets here?"

"I'll take care of that." Nora watched Claire stare at Jack until he felt her eyes on him and looked up. Her sister smiled brightly and waved to him, then pointed to the chair Patti had left by their table.

"It worked. He's coming over," Claire hissed.

Jack Soong reached them and stood awkwardly, holding the back of Patti's abandoned chair.

"Jack, I think you've met my sister, Nora Tierney. Her fiancé is the lead detective on Bea's case."

Nora pointed to the chair. "Patti's gone for a smoke. Please, join us for a moment."

The young man hesitated, then pulled the chair out and sat down. "Think I'll be heading back soon."

"You're the chess champ Claire's been telling me about." Nora gave him all of her attention.

Claire beamed at Jack. "He's an amazing player."

"Any tournaments coming up?" Nora asked.

"Not until after the holidays." Jack shifted in his seat.

Not a conversationalist. Nora tried again. "You going home for the holidays, Jack?"

He sighed. "No getting out of that, I'm afraid."

"Too bad you can't arrange a trip like Patti's taking," Claire said.

His face brightened. "It's all she's talked about for weeks now. I told her I might hide in her luggage." He turned to Nora. "Those detectives the other day, that's who you mean?"

"The brown-haired one, Declan Barnes, is my fiancé. He's the senior investigating officer on Bea's case." Nora deliberately kept Bea's name in the conversation.

"We talked about her after our final today." Jack's face fell; his eyes lingered on hands he twisted in his lap. "I still can't believe Bea might have been deliberately killed. And to be married to Dr. Brown and have a baby! It was all over college by this afternoon. It's like we didn't really know her at all."

Nora leaned toward him. "Can you think of anyone who disliked Bea enough to hurt her, or who would have been upset at her secret family?"

Jack's head snapped up. "No! She was pure goodness, a really lovely, kind person." The force of his words had him lower his voice. "Sorry, I get upset thinking of her lying there." He looked at Claire. "You know, Claire—you saw her."

Claire nodded, while Nora said, "If everyone loved Bea, it makes it hard to figure out who would have wanted to hurt her."

"I don't know who would have, but let me tell you one thing." Jack's eyes blazed and his voice rose on those last words. "Bea must have had a very good reason for keeping her marriage and her baby secret. And if she needed to, it was no one else's right to bring that out or hurt her in the process."

Claire nodded. "I totally agree, Jack. It's a rotten shame."

Jack stood up, almost knocking over his chair. "I need to go now." He turned to Nora. "Nice to see you again."

He left quickly, and Nora reflected on the young man's face when talking about Bea.

"Was that helpful at all?"

"I'm not sure, Claire." Nora echoed Jack's words. "But I'll tell *you* one thing. Jack could have found out about Bea's marriage and baby and struck her out of jealousy if they argued that morning. I think Jack Soong was in love with Bea Jones."

11:23 PM

Declan sat on the side of the bed, tired after a long day, and realized there was an open space in their bedroom. "Where's the puppy's crate? For that matter, where's Typo?"

Nora put aside Neil Welch's pages. "He hasn't had an accident for a while. Remember I'd started to leave his crate door open?"

"That's right. I'd forgotten." His head had been in his work, and all of the housebreaking and training had been left to Nora. "I did notice he has the hang of hitting those bells you put on the door."

"Works like a charm. A few times this week I woke up and found him asleep under Sean's cot. I moved the crate into Sean's room. That crate is his safe place now to nap and sleep. Plus I can hear him on the monitor if he needs to go out."

"Reasonable. Gives us more privacy, even if it's just from the dog." He left his ratty slippers next to the bed and slid in beside Nora. "What's on your agenda tomorrow?"

"Mr. Tink said I can start to fill my shelves and get my books unpacked. I'll ask Claire to give me a hand. Sean has nursery in the morning, so we can work when he's out. After lunch, Sally and Neil are taking both boys to this kiddy art thing at Val's cooperative, where they paint on white T-shirts."

Declan plugged his phone into its charger. "Neil's taking a day off writing?"

"He said he needs a break to think. I've been reading his latest chapter, and he's really getting into his story now. Often you need to step away from writing to see the whole picture, though." Nora turned out the light on her side of the bed. "What about you?"

"Headed to Cambridge in the morning with Watkins. Then back to the station unless something else comes up. I'll miss Watkins when he's out on family leave."

"Assume you'd have told me if there was baby news."

"You'll know when I know." Declan put out his lamp and the darkness closed in, the red glow of the monitor and the dial on their bedside clock the only light. Nora rolled closer to him. "How was your dinner out?"

"I've been busy." Nora shared what she'd learned that afternoon, starting with Nicola Morton's adoration of Chad Brown, moving on to the evening, with Jack Soong and Patti Phillips.

He was surprised at how much Nora could ferret out of a brief conversation. "Nicola Morton does seem infatuated with Brown. I recall that from her statement to Watkins." Could Brown lead a double life, and be the secret lover Sheila O'Connor mentioned? Something there niggled at his mind.

"Did you know Patti Phillips is heading to Australia next week?" Nora's feet felt cold up against his leg.

"Hmm, I knew she had a sister there. I'll get McAfee to look into it tomorrow. She never mentioned it in her interview with him, but it might not have come up. That statement was done the day Bea fell, way before the inquest." He drew Nora closer, inhaling the lingering pear scent of her shampoo. "I see you're teaching Claire your bad habits. What else did you glean?"

Nora described Jack Soong and how he distanced himself from the others. "It's like he wasn't part of the group emotionally, he was just there physically." She snugged herself in under his arm and pulled the duvet up higher over them. "I think he had a crush on Bea."

"That's interesting." He kept to himself Sheila O'Connor's description of Soong's vacillation over his bisexuality. "Too much unrequited love around."

"If Jack found out about Bea's relationship with Chad Brown, there's potential for an argument between them that ended badly."

"It certainly bears looking into." Declan couldn't share the finer aspects of information on the case with Nora, yet she was trying to be helpful to his investigation.

She must have read his mind. "Don't worry, I know there are things you can't discuss with me." She turned her head and kissed him. "But there are other things we can share."

He pulled her to him and caressed her back as he returned her kiss. "Definitely."

CHAPTER THIRTY-EIGHT

Somerville

January 1993

Jim sat next to Dora in the oncologist's office, after weeks of tests and a recent biopsy. They'd had their first Christmas with Digger, his wonder at the bright ornaments and twinkling lights of their tree a distraction from their worry.

They'd helped him tear apart wrappings, only to watch him play with the boxes more than the toys on Christmas morning and the days after, when there were a few blessed days break from the ongoing tests. Jim carried around a feeling of dread that consumed him.

He held Dora's hand now as the doctor spoke, the man's face impassive, without a hint of a smile, and that telegraphed his news. He gave Jim the willies.

His brain almost shut down when the man uttered the words "advanced lung cancer," but Dora squeezed his hand so hard he thought she'd break his fingers, and that woke him out of his stupor. Still, he sat in a daze as snatches of their conversation sank through, with words like "metastasis" and "stage four" lingering. He couldn't look at Dora then, he just couldn't. He kept hold of her hand and stared at the hair growing out of the oncologist's ear.

The oncologist moved on to describe available treatment, several rounds of chemotherapy, with the usual side effects of nausea, hair loss, more weight loss, fatigue, as well as the option to "do nothing and let the disease take its course." This couldn't be happening.

Beside him, Dora ran her tongue over dry lips and croaked out, "How long?"

"With chemo, maybe six or seven months."

Dora's voice wavered. "And without?"

"Three to four. I'm terribly sorry."

A death sentence; whenever it came, Dora wouldn't last much beyond their son's second birthday. Jim looked at Dora, took in her white face, and saw resolve tighten her jaw as she spoke.

"If I choose not to have treatment, how sick will I be?"

"Dora! You must have the chemo." Jim couldn't handle this. He was going to lose his wife, and she was talking about speeding up the time she had left, to leave him alone with a toddler.

"It boils down to a quality of life decision, Mr. Robson. About half the patients with the same disease at the late stage as your wife choose not to have treatment." The doctor spoke directly to Dora. "You wouldn't feel very differently the first months, although your cough will increase. We can give you medicine for that. Then your fatigue will worsen as you lose your strength and appetite. Eventually you will stop eating and slip into a coma. We would send in hospice care, and give you medicine to keep you comfortable, even pain free until the end."

Jim burst out, "Sure, give her all the drugs you can throw at her when it won't make a hill of beans difference."

"Jim!" Dora's rebuke stung. "It's not the doctor's fault." She turned to the doctor. "We have a son at home who's not even two. If I take the treatment, I'll be sick for most of the little time I have left with him. To me, it doesn't make sense to do that for a matter of weeks I won't enjoy with him."

The doctor gave a brief shake of his head. "Why don't you take a day to think it over, Mrs. Robson. The nurse will give you pamphlets about the chemotherapy and hospice care on the way out to help you decide. Call my office tomorrow, once you've had a chance to talk more with your husband and think it through." He stood up.

"On to the next victim," Jim muttered.

Dora stood and thanked the man for his honesty. Jim stalked to the door and held it open for his wife.

The doctor stood behind his desk. "I'll support you in whatever decision you make, Mrs. Robson."

In the car heading home, Dora remained silent at first, reading the pamphlet on chemo while Jim drove, his heart thumping as he considered his future. Dora would be gone in a matter of weeks. That doctor could say three to four months, but that still boiled down to 12, 14, maybe 16 weeks. Too short. That time would fly by.

How would he care for Dora as she weakened, while he juggled work and cared for their son? How was he going to work and care for Digger alone after she was gone?

His vision clouded; life without Dora felt insurmountable. This must be a nightmare. The gods were making him pay because he'd taken the boy. But Digger had been given so much love and attention, proper food, clean clothes, and a good home with two loving parents. What would happen now? He only knew he couldn't do this alone.

Dora turned to him and patted his arm. "Jim, I know you think I should take the treatment, but I want what time I have left with both of you to be filled with more good days than bad. It's hard to wrap my head around thinking of not being here with you two."

She faced the front of the car and he could tell she struggled to hold back tears. "I'd have to leave him so many days to have treatments, and then be sick at home. I'm not vain about the hair loss, but what if he wouldn't recognize me, even with a wig? And for what? A few extra weeks of his mother throwing up, her appearance changing, unable to care for him, not being really present in his life? I want my last days with him—with you both—to be good ones." Dora looked out the window as the hills flashed by. "I want my last days with him to be great ones."

Jim's hand trembled on the steering wheel. Saliva built up in his mouth and he swallowed a few times. He had the sensation of things moving too quickly, an incoming tide he couldn't fight. He gulped in a breath. "I don't know what to say, Dora. I can't think straight. I don't know how you had the courage to ask the doctor all those questions."

"I think on some level I've known for a while it was bad." She took in a deep breath and gave his shoulder a little squeeze of comfort, as if he were the one who was ill. "We have a lot to think about, Jim. A lot to decide."

Oxford

Wednesday, 6th December

8:04 AM

At the morning briefing, Declan assigned team members to make contact by phone with all four Exeter students. While he knew of Claire's plans to stay at college and be at their house for the holidays, he'd let someone else document that.

They were to confirm the students' plans for the term break, while asking again if any of them noticed anyone recently who should not be at Exeter. "Whoever takes Jack Soong, see if there's any gossip about him and our victim. You might try a discreet ask around the Undercroft bar at the college."

"A pint might be in order, to fit in," Watkins added, garnering a few hoots and whistles from the team.

Declan assigned McAfee to Patti Phillips, with the chore of finding out when the young woman had made her travel plans. "Call her sister in Australia if you need to." Then he reminded the group that Watkins would be on family leave soon. "If any of you have outstanding paperwork you need to close out on older files, please get those sorted today or tomorrow." He ignored the groans. "No one likes paperwork, but it's the only way we build cases and leave a footprint of our work—and get paid." He consulted his list as McAfee said: "And we want that!" A few thumps on desks accompanied this pronouncement. "Settle down. Any reports come through we need to know about?"

Lily George raised her hand. "Sir, about that other case, the kidnapped boy? I heard back from Glasgow City Council about the duplicate birth certificate." She glanced down and read from her laptop. "The Scotland registrar has a note in the file, said the mother, Deirdre Curshik, requested a replacement as her original had been lost in a house fire. It was sent to an address in Somerville in August of 1992, the same house where Denys Curshik lives now."

"Thanks, George. McAfee, Curshik say anything to you about a house fire?"

McAfee shook his head. "No, guv, but he was young, might not remember. He told me he has scant memories of Scotland other than a few visits back as a youth."

Declan thought for a moment. "See if between you and George you can track down Denys Curshik's uncle in Glasgow. I seem to recall Denys told you in one of his interviews that his father's brother still lived there. Call Curshik to get the name, and if he remembers anything about a house fire. I'll want that phone number when Watkins and I get back from Cambridge at some point."

"On it, guv."

As the team broke up to have their assignments parceled out, Lily George caught Declan at the door, waving a slip of paper.

"This just came in, sir. It's the work address in Milton Keynes for Nicola Morton's brother. Do you want me to have Doug—um, McAfee call or visit him?"

Declan looked at the address and did a quick calculation. "No, thanks, he has enough here to go on with. Watkins and I will handle it on our way back from Cambridge."

Watkins joined them, holding two disposable coffee cups for the ride. "What are we handling after lunch?" They headed to the car park.

"A side trip to Milton Keynes on our way back from Cambridge, where Nicola Morton's brother works. Let's take my car today. We'll make better time. Want to drive?"

"That would be a resounding no. I'm a bigger car kind of guy."

"Still holding out for that Range Rover, I see." Declan slid behind the wheel of his MGB. "Hope this isn't a waste of time."

"If we're fairly certain the culprit is from the Exeter community, why *are* we going to see the parents again?"

"We only think all of Bea's secrets are out in the open. We need to see if she was hiding anything else, and while we're at it, if any other suspects might have occurred to her family. We also need to see their attitudes. But I agree; this should be our last trip up there. Then we hit Morton's brother on the way back in Milton Keynes, and try to eliminate her."

"After we stop for lunch?"

"Where we will find a place off the main road and have a quick lunch before we track down Nicola Morton's brother."

"Then a visit to Miss Nicola might be in order, depending on what he says. And the team will have done their bit with the others, so we'll have more information when we get back."

"Sounds like a plan."

Declan drove expertly through traffic; once settled on the M40, he relaxed. "Nora asked if you had any baby news. I told her she'd know when I know, and I'll know when you know."

"That's about it. Julie's so miserable at this point, I'll welcome the little bugger if he gets her good mood back. Mind if I put the radio on?" Watkins fiddled with the dial.

"As long as it's not reggae."

"Hey, it reminds me of a tropical vacation."

"How many of those have you been on?"

"Not enough, that's for sure."

Cambridge

10:15 AM

As Declan pulled into Cambridge, Watkins called ahead and asked Phil Cook, Christ's College porter, if they could access the parking again to meet with the Jones family. Cook told Watkins to text as they arrived and he'd run them out a pass.

The traffic grew heavier once they turned off from the outskirts into town. Declan was never happier he'd installed a modern satnav that updated twice a year.

"Cambridge is like Oxford, only smaller. Both have too many one-way and bus-only streets." Watkins tapped the satnav console. "We'd be lost without this guy. Only thing I don't understand: why do you have it set on a male accent?"

"It arrived already set to that, and I never bothered to change it. Nora told me to leave it; says it sounds like Daniel Craig."

"Julie likes him, too. I'd best text Phil Cook." Two minutes later they pulled up to Christ's College main entrance with its towers. Its painted coat of arms glinted in the morning sunlight.

Cook waited in the doorway and came forward when he saw the car. He leaned down to hand Declan the pass. "Good luck. Maggie's on the warpath."

"Now how would you know that?" Watkins asked.

The porter smiled and set his blue eyes dancing. "The chapel where Ernest hangs out is just beyond our office, perfect acoustics for shouting matches in these old buildings. Sounded yesterday like Maggie fell off her high horse." He tapped the MGB's ragtop. "Still counting on you to find the bastard who hurt Bea."

"Interesting," Watkins said as they drove away. "Guess Momma Bear didn't care for yesterday's revelations."

"I suspect Margaret Smythe-Jones has a difficult time not being in control of any situation. The fact her daughter would go behind her back in such a devious way for two important life milestones says volumes about how Bea felt about her mother." Declan parked and the men followed the pathways. "I expect that's all sinking in. It can't feel very good."

When he knocked, Margaret opened the door, her face stony, her lips pursed. She walked ahead of them into the main room. The gray suit she wore washed out any color from her face and vacant eyes. She didn't invite them to sit down. Instead, she stood near the window.

Declan looked around. "Is your husband held up? Your son was to meet with us, too. Is Ben on his way?"

"My husband and I are not on speaking terms at the moment." The woman's brittle tone matched her stiff posture. "You'll find Ernest in the chapel with Benedick after you're finished with me." She fiddled with a button on her jacket.

Declan thought if he touched her, Margaret would break into a thousand pieces. "Thank you." He cleared his throat. "After the revelations at the inquest, we need to know if you've been able to think of anyone who might have wished Bea harm in these new circumstances. This could be a long-standing grievance you're aware of and forgotten, or something new, even anything odd happening in the weeks leading up to her death. We don't know what might be significant."

Margaret turned to him and arched an eyebrow. "By odd, you mean other than my daughter marrying without telling me, or having me present? And having a child I only found out about after her … after she …" She faltered and turned back to the window. "Beatrice and I had little recent contact, as I told you before, except for a few brief visits home, and weekly calls where she couldn't get off the phone fast enough. She told me there would be plenty of time to visit when the term ended. Now I know why. I'm obviously the wrong person to ask about her private life."

In the bright light from the window, Declan saw deep lines etched between her brows. Margaret must have once been an attractive woman; now her grief and anger had worn her down.

He looked at Watkins, who gave a slight shake of his head. Nothing to add. "If you do think of anything at all that would be helpful, please call."

She stepped forward and handed him a slip of paper she took from her suit pocket. "This is where I'll be staying, with a cousin in Sussex. You have my number. I would like to be kept informed if you find out who did this terrible thing to my daughter." She stepped back to the window. "You can show yourselves out."

The detectives left the building to walk the short distance to the chapel. Watkins spoke before they reached its door. "Must have been very high."

"What's that?"

"That horse she fell off." Watkins scratched his head. "Have to admit, I feel kind of sorry for the old bird."

"I know. She doesn't know where to put her anger right now. I'd guess it's displaced to her son, husband, and Chad Brown. Shame." Declan pushed the door open to a vestibule that contained an ornate war memorial and a modern piece of sculpture. They turned right to the entrance of the narrow chapel, with high ceilings lined with wood darkened with age that reflected its Tudor era. White and black marble floor tiles, laid in an intricate design, echoed their steps. He looked up the long nave toward the altar, where a large paneled stained-glass window let in jewel-toned light. The carved wooden pews and choir stalls along each side appeared empty at first, until he saw two heads bent in prayer on his immediate left.

Declan motioned to Watkins to let the men be for the moment, and read a plaque about famous Christ's College alumni, who counted among them Milton, Darwin, and even Morse creator Colin Dexter. When Ernest crossed himself, the detectives advanced into the nave.

"Detectives. We were just praying for Bea." Ernest stood to shake the men's hands, as did Ben. "Have a seat." He motioned to the pew opposite so they could face each other.

"Thank you. We don't intend to take up a lot of your time." Declan sat with Watkins on the hard benches. "We've just come from seeing your wife."

Ernest remained standing. "I told Maggie to send you here." He closed his eyes briefly.

Declan felt resignation and grief emanate from the man. "I know this is a difficult time for you all."

Ben spoke up. "You have no idea, Inspector." He patted his father's hand.

Ernest cleared his throat and pointed to a portrait that hung on the back wall of the nave of a Tudor woman, hands clasped in prayer before an open Bible. "That's Lady Margaret Beaufort, Henry VII's mother, who endowed Christ's College in 1505 after it had been known as God's College for a century. I give you this potted history lesson to illustrate that while things may change the form they take, life continues, although not in the same way." He sat down. "After a long afternoon and even longer night, my wife and I have decided it's best we spend time apart."

"I'm sorry to hear that," Declan said. How like Margaret to say they weren't speaking and leave out a separation.

"Don't be," Ben said. "I'm learning there are toxic people we don't need in our lives. It's time my father had some peace."

Ernest looked at his son. "Very few people are all good or evil, Ben. Your mother's ... difficult streak became more pronounced as you and your sister matured, and she felt she had no purpose in life beyond her church meetings."

Ben shook his head. "You've always been so tolerant, Dad. She's been lucky to have you. I suppose when we were young, Bea and I were, too. But once we grew up, Mum should have enrolled in a course, or taken up painting, or done volunteer work to feel fulfilled, like hundreds of other women do. Instead, she tried to live her life through her children by controlling them and making everyone miserable in the process."

Declan observed the dialogue between father and son. He could almost feel Ben's struggle to deal with the pain and anger toward his mother in a mature way.

Ernest sighed. "That may all be true, Ben, yet you must still respect your mother."

"I will. I know it isn't easy being a parent. I don't hate her, Dad. Just please stop making excuses for her. She's responsible for her actions, just as she said Bea was. And if those actions have finally driven you away, I won't pretend to feel sorry for her. It wouldn't be honest of me. I'm tired of lies. I won't do that again." Ben looked directly at the detectives. "In the car on the ride back yesterday, my mother essentially told us that Bea caused her own death." He put his arm around his father. "Tell them what you fought about yesterday that brought things to a head."

Ernest picked his head up and looked across the aisle. "I decided we needed to reach out to Chad, to meet with him and our granddaughter. I'd told him at the inquest we'd be in touch. Maggie disagreed vehemently. When you first told us there had been a baby, an extension of Bea, she was amenable to see the child, even to have us care for it. But at the inquest she found out there was a father who would have legal claim and control our access." He shrugged. "We each refused to budge from our position. After listening all afternoon to her say vile things about our daughter, it was my proverbial last straw when she issued an ultimatum. Maggie said she would leave if I called Chad and made an appointment to see him. Suddenly, that didn't seem like a bad thing."

Declan couldn't say he was surprised. "I've seen how the murder of a child of any age can either bring parents together or drive them apart."

"Dad, you need to be straight with them." Ben's nostrils flared. "Mum called Verity a half-breed! Can you believe that? An innocent child, her own granddaughter!" He shook his head. "Bea was right, after all. Mum would never accept Bea's husband, or her baby, and would only make trouble for them."

Declan absorbed Ben's outrage. He looked at Watkins, who gave a slight nod. "I'm sorry, Ernest, I have to ask. Is there any way your wife could have found out before the inquest about the marriage, and traveled to Oxford to confront Bea?"

"No, Detective Barnes." Ernest shook his head emphatically. "You saw how shocked she was when we heard about Verity, and again at the inquest when she learned of Bea's wedding. Last Thursday evening, my wife and I were at a faculty end-of-term reception at the proctor's house. She wasn't out of my sight, and others there saw both of us. Friday she was in bed when I awoke early, and later she went to a church meeting after we got the call about Bea."

Best to cover all bases; worth a try. "Now that you've had time to mull it over, can either of you think of anyone who might have wanted to harm Bea, for any reason? It could be an older conflict or a recent one."

Ben answered first. "I promise, I've spent a lot of hours trying to think who might have had a grudge against Bea, and I haven't thought of anyone."

"I agree," his father said. "There's no incident I could think of, nor a person who would want to hurt Bea—yet obviously, someone did." Ernest checked his watch. "Sorry you wasted the drive up here."

"Part of the job." The detectives left their pew, and this time Watkins spoke.

"We want to remind you both, we can refer you to a grief counselor. As time passes, you may see that need more."

Ernest started to say "thank you" but before he could finish, the chapel door opened. Ben and Ernest stood up. Chad Brown walked in, holding Verity on his hip, her mocha skin a contrast with her hair, a nimbus cloud of gold. Verity recognized her uncle and smiled in delight. Her blue eyes glowed as she held out her arms to him.

Ben left the pew and scooped Verity from her father, kissed her cheek, and turned to his own father. "This is your granddaughter. This is Verity."

Declan saw the raw emotion that flew across the man's expressive face. Ernest was struck by the reality in front of him. He must have held himself in check to not overwhelm the girl.

Ernest spoke directly to the little girl. "It's very nice to meet you, Verity, and to see your father, too." He told Chad, "She's beautiful."

The young father agreed. "She's the best parts of both of us."

"Let's sit down a minute, and you can get to know your Grampa." Ben brought Verity to Ernest, and the two men sat down and talked quietly to the child.

"If we could have a moment of your time, Mr. Brown, you'd save us coming to Woodstock later today."

"If you must." Chad moved into the vestibule and kept an eye on Verity.

Declan needed to break through the man's defenses. "Your daughter is a charmer."

That brought the desired effect. Chad's smile reached his eyes this time. "She's her mother's daughter, so friendly to everyone, although she already knows Ben."

Watkins threw in a question. "Will you stay in Cambridge long today?"

"We're having lunch together. Small steps. With any luck, she'll nap the entire ride back." Chad tore his gaze from his daughter. "What do you need to ask?"

Declan gestured to Watkins to continue. "Had any thoughts of someone who would wish to harm your wife, anyone bearing her ill will, or someone we haven't talked about?"

Brown looked at the floor for a moment. "I know you didn't know Bea, but if you did, you'd realize how unlikely that would be." He shook his head. "No. Nothing has come to me, and believe me, when I can't sleep at night it's all I think about." He broke off as emotion overcame him and he turned away.

Declan gave Watkins a look that said: *Nothing here with Chad.* "All right. We're being thorough because we have to be. We'll keep you apprised as the case advances."

Chad grabbed Declan's arm. His grief was written in the haunted look he turned on Declan. "Please, find out who did this to my wife," he implored. His deep brown eyes held the same anguish as his voice. "Find who robbed Bea of our life together."

CHAPTER THIRTY-NINE

Oxford

1:21 PM

Nora kissed Sean goodbye and handed him off to Sally Welch. Claire gave Sean's car seat to Neil, along with a restocked diaper bag. When Sam saw Sean, he pointed at him and yelled "You!" in delight.

"I'm heading to the car with these two." Sally walked down the drive slowly so the boys could keep up. "Bye-bye Mummy." Sean walked off with a quick wave and kept going.

Nora tamped down feeling offended. "He's had his lunch, and a fresh diaper just on, Neil. There are snacks in there for them both, plus two juice boxes." Nora swiped her hair into a scrunchie she took off her wrist. "I can't believe you and Sally are going to surround yourselves with a room full of rowdy toddlers at this art thing."

"Blame your friend Val. She organized it through the creche, says it's important to have kiddies interested in arts and crafts from an early age. You've seen how these two can be entertained with blank paper and crayons."

"I think it's great they're such good friends already," Claire said.

Neil beamed. "We're both so happy for our new neighbors. It can be lonely being a vicar's husband, unless you want to bake cakes." The women laughed. "Nora, thanks for those comments on my chapter. I'll take a closer look tonight after Sam's asleep."

Nora waved him off. "There's not much there that needs revision, Neil. Maybe add more texture about Paris in that time period to solidify the setting. I've marked up several places where you could add a sentence or two to flesh it out without sounding like a travelogue."

"Splendid." The horn honked and he held up the car seat. "Better run. We'll keep Sean for naps afterwards and bring him home before dinner. Sam has a new play tent in the house we've packed with sleeping bags. Too cool to play outside today."

"Sounds like fun. Good luck, and thanks again." Nora closed the door and leaned against it with a sigh. "Phew."

"That's what you get for working like a dog all morning." Claire smiled. "At least you get a break now."

It had been a long morning while Sean was at the nursery. Nora and Claire opened box after box of books from storage. She'd had the foresight to mark them clearly to make re-shelving by genre easier when she'd packed up her Oxford flat to move to Cumbria. That seemed so long ago, although it had been less than two years.

"With Mr. Tink done, that room is almost in order." The painter had helped them move Nora's desk before he left. The remaining chore involved the boxes of files and supplies to be sorted into the cabinets under the bookshelves.

"Do you want to go back in there and sort those files?"

"Lord, no." Nora laughed at her sister. "We have a free afternoon, and I worked you too hard all morning. I want to play." She looked down at her jeans and sneakers. They would do. "Let me change my shirt for one less dusty."

"Me, too." Claire followed her up the stairs. "What do you have in mind?"

"Fancy a trip to Woodstock for Christmas shopping? I know a great antique store to poke around, and there are other shops we can check out." They stopped on the landing outside Nora's room. "I can drop off signed copies of my books at Montague House for Verity, too. I feel guilty about my last visit."

"So that you can see what else you can ferret out? How did I know Bea's case was still on your mind?" Claire swept Nora into a hug. "Thanks again for everything."

Milton Keynes

1:42 PM

Declan sat back with a contented sigh and motioned to the waiter for the check. He and Watkins had enjoyed their filling lunch, and as he looked around The Swan, he knew Nora would enjoy a visit to the rustic pub. From its thatched roof and whitewashed exterior, to the flagstone floors and low beams with a huge stone fireplace, it was the quintessential English pub.

They allowed dogs, too, so in warmer weather it would be a good family outing with Typo. Then he smiled that he had thought "family." Nora, Sean, and Typo really were his family. He was a lucky man.

He signed the check and slipped the receipt in his notebook. Lately he and Watkins had made time to eat, but that didn't always happen, and far too often lunches had been a bag of chips from the canteen machine. "Ready to go?"

The two men walked into the sunshine. Despite the cool breeze, fleecy clouds studded the sky, and it looked like rain would skip them today.

Watkins slid into the passenger seat. He set the satnav for Vintage Classic Cars, where Winston Morton, Nicola's brother, worked. "I wonder if new detectives understand how much of the job is rubbish interviews."

"TIE, Watkins, the cornerstone of detecting."

"Trace, interview, eliminate, get that. But what if you TIE everyone and there's no suspect left?"

Declan grinned. "Not like telly, is it? How many high-speed car chases, or suspects confessing due to your superb grilling skills have you had?"

"That would be none. Only the bad coffee is true." Watkins shifted his legs. "Take this Winston bloke. His sister lives on the same floor as Bea Jones, but what does that tell us?"

"People lie all the time to the police, or withhold information they don't deem significant. We won't know until we ask." Declan signaled and turned into the driveway of the auto restoration shop.

"New sign for our office: 'Leave no stone unturned.'"

Four bays each held a car being restored by mechanics sporting identical forest green jumpsuit in various stages of age and disrepair. Declan picked out a red Triumph roadster with a crushed wing, and a snazzy black Bentley S2 he knew was from the 60s. Several highly polished cars for sale stood on the forecourt to attract buyers. "That's a sweet one." He pointed to a small white convertible with a red leather interior. "Austin-Healy, 1958 if I'm not mistaken."

A man came out of the salesroom, clearly the manager, as he wore a suit and tie. Declan asked if they could speak to Winston Morton. As he and Watkins held out their warrant cards, he explained Morton was not in any trouble, but they needed background information on a witness in a case. "It would be helpful if he could meet with us briefly."

"One of my best mechanics." He called into the shop. "Winston! Take a break and talk to these chaps."

A mechanic poked his head out from under the hood of a burgundy Jaguar. "Be a sec."

After the manager went back inside, Watkins walked over to the Austin-Healy Declan had pointed out and whistled. "This little number you like is for sale for a mere 76,000 pounds—think Nora would go for it? When's your birthday again—want me to drop a bug in her ear?"

Declan chuckled as Winston Morton walked over to them, wiping his hands on a rag.

"What can I do for you gents? That MGB misfiring on you?" The mechanic bent down to look at the interior. "Nicely done. Gotta watch the petrol float reliability on these, though. They get loaded with fuel and your gauge will stick and go off."

"Not giving me trouble yet." Declan introduced himself and Watkins, and explained they were seeking background information on his sister, Nicola.

Morton put the rag into his back pocket. "What's my little sis done? Not in trouble, I hope."

"Does your sister often get into trouble?" Declan asked.

"Nah, she's the smart one." He grinned, showing a mouthful of white teeth that dazzled against his dark skin. "Me, I've always been into engines and cars, taking things apart and putting them back together. Share a flat with my girlfriend, don't get home often now. Nicola, she's all books and Shakespeare, all the time." He puffed up. "She's at Oxford."

"We're aware of that, Mr. Morton. A young woman who lived

on her floor died—"

"Yeah, saw that on the telly," he interjected. "Didn't know she lived near Nicola, though, but she's into exams now, so we haven't talked in a coupla weeks. Miss Alvita will be gutted if she doesn't do well."

Declan exchanged a glance with Watkins. "You mean Alvita Brown?"

"Sure. She's our adopted mommy, our guardian after ours died. That's how we came to England." He shrugged. "Guess you could say we were her wards, but she always treated us just like hers."

Watkins stepped in to clarify. "You're telling us you emigrated at the same time as Chad and Alvita Brown, correct?"

"Yeah. We four like a family, all through our teens lived with Miss Alvita. Haven't been together for a while, what with Nicola in school, Chad being on sabbatical and away all summer, Miss Alvita traveling and renovating the house. And I'm busy here."

Declan's mind raced with this new information as the mechanic continued.

Morton leaned on the MGB's front wing. "Miss Alvita was always so encouraging, say nothing's wrong with getting my hands in guts of cars if that's my passion. She big on following your passion. Nicola, she and Chad always the bookworms, but I love to tinker. Those two," he shook his head and the smile flashed again. "They fight like older brother and little sister, but Nicola, she has this big crush on Chad through the years, only one ever allowed to call her 'Nic,' decide she gonna marry him one day."

Declan remembered Sheila O'Connor telling him Nicola Morton had a secret boyfriend. It appeared the scout had the right instincts.

Woodstock

2:29 PM

Nora found parking on Park Street, a few doors from Chad and Alvita Brown's house. With an eye on the clock, she'd decided to forego the bus and had taken the Volvo. "Let's drop these books, and then we can browse the shops."

She and Claire approached the pale blue door of Montague House, and Nora rang the bell. A minute later the door opened to Chad Brown, holding Verity on his hip. The child smiled at the two women.

He recognized them and looked surprised but not upset. "Claire—and Nora, isn't it?"

"I've brought your daughter my books." Nora handed him the offering and shoved her hands in her jeans jacket, as a gust of wind blew down the street. "I spoke with your mother the other day, and she thought you might have one, but I didn't know which, so I've signed both of these to Verity."

"Her first autographed books—brilliant! Come in, come in. Too cool to be standing about." He turned and dropped the books on a console table and led the way to the kitchen at the back of the house. "I just put the kettle on. Have a seat."

Nora shrugged her shoulders and led Claire into the house. Chad had invited them, after all. It wasn't her nosiness that got them here. A little voice in her ear whispered: "*This time.*"

Verity squirmed when Chad tried to put her in her high chair, stiffening her legs. She clung to his shoulder. "Cheep-cheep,

Daddy," she implored, refusing to sit down.

He tousled her curls. "All right, dumpling, come on then." He grabbed her quilted jacket off the counter, where he'd thrown it amidst the mail, and jiggled her into it while he spoke to the women. "We're just back from Cambridge, and she's been cooped up in the car most of the day. She loves to watch the birds outside. We keep a playpen in the garden for her." Coat zipped, he opened the sliding door and took her out to the garden, disappearing off to one side. "Ten minutes," he told his daughter as he came back inside.

"She's adorable, Chad." Claire took the mugs he held out to the table while he made tea.

"She's a good girl, but she's missing her Mommy and doesn't understand." He shook his head. "Rough days ahead. I'm glad there's a break in the term."

Cambridge must mean he'd been to see the Joneses. Nora ventured asking, "You went to visit Bea's parents?"

"Yeah, no secrets anymore. Her father and brother. Verity knows Ben, so he was a familiar face, but she's very friendly to strangers. Ernest seemed thrilled to have a granddaughter." He swished hot water in the pot. "Bea's mum, not so much apparently. We didn't see Maggie at all, and I had the impression from things Ben said that we might not for a while." He shrugged. "Bea was afraid this might happen. I'm not going to beg the woman to get to know us. Shakespeare said, 'Then hate me when thou wilt; if ever, now …'"

"Let me guess," Claire said. "One of the sonnets?"

"High marks. Sonnet 90." He put the pot on the table to steep and took a creamer from the fridge to the table, where he pushed the sugar bowl toward them.

The front door slammed. “I’m home,” Alvita called out.

“In the kitchen,” Chad called back. “But that’s all right, because Verity has the best grandma right here.” Alvita came into the kitchen, and he hugged his mother. “This is Claire Scott and her sister, Nora Tierney.”

“I know Nora.” Alvita smiled. “No malachite today?”

“I brought my books for Verity. We’re doing holiday shopping next.”

Alvita nodded. “Early birds get the best picks.” She turned to Chad. “I dropped Nicola off after lunch to shop, too. She’ll meet us here later for dinner. She’s anxious to meet Verity, now that we can have her here again. I’ll call Winston later, too.”

Nora’s antennae quivered. “Nicola Morton?”

“Ah, tea made. Lovely.” Alvita poured for them all, her bangles jangling with each tip of the pot. “Mmm, you know my Nicola?”

Nora met Claire’s eyes, her thoughts in overdrive.

Chad answered. “Nic lives on the same floor as Claire at Exeter.”

Alvita pointed her finger at Chad. “You are the only one who could get away calling her that. Still, I managed to talk her around,” Alvita told Chad. “She seemed to accept Bea’s need for secrecy for a few weeks.” She added sugar to her mug.

Nora couldn’t contain herself. “You said, ‘my Nicola,’ Alvita?”

The woman’s eyes lit up. “I’m guardian to Nicola and her brother, Winston. They emigrated with us and have lived here since their teens.” She inhaled the fragrant tea. “Winston is a mechanic for vintage cars. He lives in Milton Keynes now. Always good with his hands, that boy.”

Could there be something here? This was information Nora needed to get to Declan. She had no way of knowing if he knew this. She directed her next question to Chad. "You and Nicola and Winston grew up together?"

He nodded. "But I was more like an older brother to them."

Alvita laughed, a joyous low sound. "That girl had a crush on you as big as a house until you left for uni."

Chad shook his head. "Nic's always been my little sis, nothing more, Mommy."

But did Nicola accept that? Nora decided a trip to the loo would allow her to discreetly text Declan.

Before she could ask to use the bathroom, Alvita asked Chad, "Where's Verity—still napping? How did Cambridge go?"

"No and fine enough. We'll talk later." He pointed at the sliding doors. "Verity napped the entire way back. She's in her playpen in the garden watching the birds."

"She calls them 'cheep-cheep.' She loves those birds." Alvita shook her head. "Is she in a wet nappy?"

"Relax, Mommy. I changed her when we came in."

Alvita glanced outside. "Those clouds look dark. Think I'd best get her in before the rain." Alvita pushed open the slider.

"She can't stand to be too long without that little girl," Chad said, his affection clear. "I don't know how I would have made it through this week without my mother."

"Chad, is there a loo down here?" Nora clenched her fingers around her phone in her jeans pocket.

"That door under the stairs."

But before Nora could leave the room, they heard Alvita shout. She raced back into the kitchen. "She's gone! Verity's gone!"

CHAPTER FORTY

Somerville

January 1993

When they pulled into the drive outside their house, Dora told Jim she'd head next door to pick up their son. Carol had urged them to leave Digger with her whenever Dora had a test. She was kind and would be a comfort to Dora about her negative results.

After taking off her seatbelt, Dora sat for a moment, looking at their house. She whispered: "I knew this was happening."

Jim looked over at her. How had he not seen the change in color of her skin? It already had a greyish cast from the disease eating her up. He swallowed a wave of nausea. "How do you mean?"

She lifted one shoulder. "Each test I had brought me closer to what I already recognized, deep down." She turned to look at him. "That's why I wasn't surprised. I've been gearing up for confirmation of what I already suspected."

He reached out for her hand. "Dora—I'm so very sorry."

"I know you are, Jim. And I know you can't take it all in, but we'll make a plan together, all right? I'll call my sister tonight and let her know, after we put Digger to bed. He's the most important thing now. We have to keep his world normal, even if ours isn't."

"All right." Even as he said the words, Jim felt his strength drain away.

She opened her door. "I expect I'll be a few minutes. Put the kettle on, would you?"

Jim watched her walk to the neighbor's door and ring the bell.

He unbuckled his seat belt and let himself into the home he'd thought of as their haven, moving sluggishly as if he were seeing everything through a cloudy lens. The house must have been the same as when they'd left it this morning, but to Jim it had changed dramatically. The bright curtains Dora had sewn looked tawdry, their cheeriness mocking him; their son's colorful basket of toys appeared bedraggled and dirty. The house seemed to be saying, "The life you thought you created was a lie."

Jim switched the kettle on, took out their mugs, then sat at the kitchen table, waiting. This would be his life now, each day filled with waiting. Waiting for Dora's disease to progress, waiting for her to die, waiting to be left alone with Digger, all the responsibility on him, on his shoulders alone. He'd never felt so helpless, nor so weak.

He had no one to talk to about this overwhelming feeling of brittle despair. His heart rate sped up, his chest tightened and made him feel as if he would choke. He was going to pass out if he didn't do something. Arms and legs quivering, he rose and rummaged in the back of a cabinet for the bottle of good scotch Dora's father had given them one Christmas before he died. They'd never opened it. Jim did now. He poured a dram into his mug with trembling hands as he tried to control his breathing.

The scotch's fiery warmth spread down his throat, then hit his stomach. The heat spread out to his limbs, and he plopped down into his seat. A bloody panic attack. He'd never had one, but he knew the symptoms. As his breathing returned to normal, he poured a second dram to sip more slowly, and left the bottle on the table. He was pathetic.

What a poor excuse he was for a husband, wallowing like a spineless coward. His wife was the one who was dying. Dora had to face the next months, knowing the end was coming, and with it, unknown pain before there was … nothing.

Jim thought of how it must feel to know you were soon to die, the knowledge there would be no more sunny days with flowers bringing new promise, or birds singing a chirpy song, not another Christmas certainly. And no way to watch their boy's milestones and see how he would turn out. There would be no awareness of anything at all. He broke out in a cold sweat, embarrassed at being unable to control his fragile emotions.

He reached for the cardigan he left hanging on the back of the kitchen chair, finding comfort in its warmth, and took a sip of the bracing scotch. Jim recognized that his alarm at Dora turning down the chemo was due to his own fear.

He finally understood Dora not wanting to take the chemo, not wanting to put herself through the rigors of treatment if it wouldn't change the outcome.

Hope. That's what the oncologist had taken from them. Hope.

There was no hope.

He swallowed back a surge of bile that rose in his throat and reburned it. This was no time to be ineffectual, to give in to his inadequacy. He'd been strong in Cumbria when he took that little boy, hadn't he? He could do this.

Dora needed him. He had to be resilient for her. He had to allow her to die the way she wanted to.

He resolved that during these next difficult months, he would do whatever he could to ease the way for her. She wanted to have a plan for the time she had left. They would figure one out together. He would see she had whatever she desired.

Then he didn't know what he would do.

CHAPTER FORTY

Woodstock

2:56 PM

Chad ran past Alvita to the garden to establish Verity was truly missing, then immediately called 999. Nora grabbed a tissue for Alvita and took control.

"Claire, you and Alvita scour the neighborhood. Check with the houses on either side first, find out if they saw anyone enter the back garden. Chad should stay here to talk to the police, and in case Verity's brought back." Nora grabbed her keys from the table.

"Good idea," Claire said. "Where are you going?"

"To Exeter." She ran to her car, thinking hard, certain Nicola Morton had taken Verity. Nicola had been driven to Woodstock by Alvita from Oxford after their lunch. It was too coincidental the child went missing when Nicola was in town, supposedly shopping. She had just found out the man she'd loved for years was married to someone else and they'd had a child together. In her mind it would have felt like a huge betrayal. It was the only thing that made sense.

Where could Nicola go but back to Exeter? She would need to take a bus or a ride to get anywhere. Nora drove past the bus stop and saw a few people lingering in the shelter. No Nicola and no Verity. A ride, then. If Nicola had money for shopping, she could pay for a taxi or Uber.

Nora called Declan on her Bluetooth and waited for him to pick up as she turned the Volvo toward Oxford. When he answered, she had to control herself not to shout. "Declan! Verity's been taken from Chad's garden. Nicola Morton was in town and I think she took her. She was one of the students Alvita brought to England, has had a crush on him for years." She paused to catch her breath as Declan answered.

"We know. She thought she was going to marry him. We're on our way back from interviewing Nicola's brother to see her, should be to Exeter in 10 minutes." She heard another phone ring in Declan's car. "How far out are you?"

Nora glanced at her satnav. "Seven minutes." She heard Watkins shout, "WHAT?"

"Listen Nora, do not go up to Nicola's room alone. Wait for me. Hold a sec."

She could hear Watkins' urgent tone as he said Julie's water had broken.

Declan came back to her. "Guess you heard that. Watkins will drop me at Exeter and take my car to bring Julie to the hospital. We'll call in now and have officers come to the college."

"I'll find parking and meet you by stairwell 10. That baby's life may be at stake."

"Nora, wait for me in the Porter's Lodge. I'm a few minutes behind you."

Nora bit her lip. "If I'm not there, come up to Nicola's room."

"Wait—" Declan's voice cut off when Nora disconnected. She waited for the inevitable call back, and when it came, ignored it. How could she wait for Declan when Verity might be in danger? If Nicola's jealousy prompted her to take the child, there was no way to predict what she might do to Verity. Nora wouldn't take that chance.

She sped down Woodstock Road, watching her speed. Nora

prayed she was wrong, that Nicola Morton hadn't stolen Verity. The little girl was only starting to walk. Yes, toddlers were great climbers, she knew that from Sean. Even if Verity had climbed over the side of her playpen and managed to wander off, she couldn't have gotten very far in the few minutes she'd been alone.

Nora hit the outskirts of Oxford, thinking about where she might find parking, and called Claire's number to check if there was any news in Woodstock.

Claire answered on the first ring. "Nothing yet. The police are here talking with Chad, taking a report. Alvita and I checked the neighbors, but no one's home. We're going to walk the neighborhood next." She lowered her voice, and Nora heard footsteps as her sister walked into another room. "You think Nicola took her?"

"It's the only thing that makes sense. Declan will be at Exeter soon. He and Watkins interviewed Nicola's brother, who said she had a crush on Chad to the point she thought he would marry her."

"Ugh. Chad is almost losing it and Alvita's not far behind. Find Verity, Nora."

Oxford

3:18 PM

Lily George was pleased as punch, as her grandmother used to say. She'd convinced her friend to push through the DNA testing on the Denys Curshik case, and the friend has just called to say she was emailing the results.

Lily hoped she and McAfee could soon they could have that drink after work. And if that drink turned into dinner, she would split the bill, no taking advantage here. It would be nice to get to know Douglas outside work.

She looked over at McAfee, working the phones. She liked the way his hair curled over his collar. She liked everything about the young sergeant, especially his name. Douglas. She tried that in her mind a few times. Everyone at work used their last names when they spoke to each other, but Lily had taken to calling him "Douglas" when they had their canteen visits, and he'd seemed pleased.

Her computer dinged. She pulled up the email from her friend, with a message she owed her a visit to the pub one of these days. Small price to pay for getting in with Douglas. Lily walked over to the printer to retrieve the report.

She returned to her desk, scanning the report as she went. Wouldn't it be something if that young man was the same child who'd been kidnapped from his playpen decades ago, and she and Douglas had helped to crack the case?

Lily frowned. What she read didn't make sense at all. She pulled up the report on her email attachment and compared the two. Her face flushed. She put the report in a folder and hid it in her desk until DI Barnes returned. Meanwhile, she needed to have a good think.

CHAPTER FORTY

Oxford

3:19 PM

Nora knew Declan wouldn't be pleased with her for not waiting, but he was only minutes behind her. She remembered the terror of those days when Sean was missing, and her heart sped up. Chad would be inconsolable, especially after losing Bea.

She found parking at one of the few metered spots on Broad Street, but couldn't get in that entrance, so she jogged quickly around the corner to Turl and the main entrance. A couple walking a Scottie dog wearing a jaunty tartan coar stood talking to Wilson, asking directions.

Nora rushed to the desk and pushed past the couple. "I'm so sorry to interrupt, but this is urgent. Wilson, did Nicola Morton go past here with a toddler in her arms? A little girl—"

Wilson was already nodding. "Yes, with blonde curly hair—"

"That's Bea's baby, Wilson. Call 999 and tell them that, and when Declan Barnes gets here, send him right up to her room."

Nora ran around the quad and approached Staircase 10. When she reached the spot where Bea Jones had died, Nora stopped and listened. With term finished, most students had left, and the area felt deserted. She started up the staircase, glad she wore trainers. She reached the turn in the landing before Claire's floor when she heard a young voice exclaim, "Daddy!"

Nora stayed put, her ears peeled. That meant Verity was alive and well. Listening carefully above the pounding of her heartbeat in her ears, she heard Nicola's voice rumbling, talking to the child. Should she approach, or wait here for Declan?

She took out her phone to lower the volume so it wouldn't alert Nicola to her presence, but on second thought, set it to record before she shoved it back into her jeans pocket. She might only have a video of the inside of her pocket, but at least the audio would record whatever happened next.

Then she heard a screech, and Nora's heart fell. Claire's casement window, without screens, had made the same sound when she'd opened it. She raced up the remaining stairs, her heart pounding furiously in her chest, and hoped Nicola's door wasn't locked. When she hit the upper landing, she saw Nicola's door was ajar, and Nora carefully eased it open.

A clothes cupboard to her right had its doors wide open, revealing photos stuck all over the insides of the doors. Nicola sat on the wide window ledge, pointing out the window to Verity, who sat complacently on her lap.

"… And in the spring, you can hear the birds right there in that tree."

"Cheep-cheep." Verity leaned out the window to look. Nora gasped. She took two careful steps into the room and risked a glance at the open cupboard. Photo collages held repeated images of Chad and Nicola, and in the center of one door, a blowup of Chad's smiling, handsome face was glued onto a large paper heart with handwritten inscriptions underneath.

Nicola sensed Nora's presence and turned. "Stop!" She leapt up from the wide sill, holding Verity on her hip. "What do you want?"

Nora stood still. At least Nicola wasn't leaning Verity out the window any longer. Now to get her to move away entirely. "I'm here because Chad is worried. He misses Verity."

Nicola tossed her elaborate braids, the beads clacking. "Then he shouldn't have left her out in that playpen alone. If he's so worried, why isn't he here?" She advanced around the bed, holding Verity so tightly the girl started to squirm. "He should've come himself to get his daughter. I thought he would at least do that. Leave us!" Nicola backed Nora out of her room onto the landing near Claire's door.

Nora's heart stuttered. What would happen if Nicola was left alone with the child? *Where was Declan?*

Nicola followed her to the landing and looked over the railing. Nora's breath caught. She gauged the distance. Could she leap up and crash into Nicola, bring her and Verity down to the floor, without hurting the child?

Before she could act, Nicola whirled around, her back to the railing. "He's not coming, is he?" Her face deflated. "I only wanted to explain to Chad, to ask his forgiveness." She buried her face in Verity's curls and started to cry softly. "It's all gone wrong."

Nora wondered if she slid down to the floor to sit, if Nicola would mirror her actions. But if she did that and Nicola tried to leap off the stairwell, could Nora get up in time to stop her? Her thoughts whirled. She broke out in a sweat. Best instead to keep Nicola talking until Declan arrived.

Nora kept her voice low and soothing. "Forgiveness for what, Nicola?"

"It wasn't supposed to be like this." Nicola's voice was despondent. Verity wriggled in her grasp. "I went home last weekend as a surprise, to see this big house renovation. I was a block away when I saw Bea and Chad leave the house, pushing a buggy. I couldn't believe my eyes! When I used my key and went into the house, there was a high chair in the kitchen, and a playpen in the yard." Her face glistened with wetness.

Verity's fidgeting increased. "Down!" she cried, her face

getting red. Nora knew tears weren't far behind.

Nicola struggled to hold onto the squirming girl. "Ssh, that's a good girl." She patted Verity's back to calm her. "It was a horrid week for me. I always thought Chad and I would be together. When I heard Bea leaving early last Friday, I had to confront her. I told her Chad was supposed to marry *me*!"

Nora saw movement out of the corner of her eye. *Declan.* He rose stealthily up the stairs below their landing. Nora kept her eyes fixed on Nicola so she wouldn't turn her head.

"You must have felt so distraught." Nora leaned back against Claire's door as if she had all the time in the world and this was a casual conversation.

"That's when Bea told me he was already married to *her* and the baby was theirs. She took out this locket she wore inside her shirt, with photos of them all."

Nora hoped her phone was still recording. "What happened, Nicola?"

"I grabbed that stupid locket and tore it off her neck! She came after me like a tiger, and I pushed her away, hard." She blinked. "One second she was there, and the next …" She blinked back tears, and begged Nora to believe her. "It was a stupid accident! I never meant for her to fall!"

Despite the quaking in her legs, Nora kept her voice calm. "I know you didn't."

"Before I could get back into my room, your sister came out. I pretended I'd just opened my door." She squeezed Verity tighter and the girl yelped. "This should be my child with Chad."

Declan's shoe scraped on a stair. Nicola whirled around and saw him. She staggered back but still hugged the rail. "Don't come any closer. I'll throw her over!"

He raised his hands in a show of supplication as he took the last step up to stand beside Nora. "I don't believe you want to hurt Verity, Nicola. You never wanted to hurt Bea, not really."

Nora knew they had to diffuse the situation. Verity began to hit Nicola's shoulder, oblivious to the drama playing out with her young life in jeopardy.

Declan's voice stayed reasonable. "Why don't you give Verity to Nora, and we can talk this whole thing over? Sounds to me like what happened the other morning was an accident."

"It *was*," Nicola wailed. "I never meant for that to happen," she moaned, while Verity wiggled to get down.

"I know, I know." Declan spoke soothingly as he took a step closer. He mouthed to Nora: *Get Verity*.

Nora gave a brief nod. Nicola was three steps away from them, leaning against the rail, sobbing as Verity writhed in her grasp.

Declan kept up his litany. "Give Verity to Nora, Nicola. You can have a cup of tea, and we'll talk this through."

Nora slowly edged forward into the gap until she was only a foot away from Nicola and Verity, Declan beside her.

Sensing the movement, Nicola raised her head, her eyes reddened and swollen. She turned toward the railing.

She's going to let her go. Nora launched herself forward and made a grab for Verity, catching her as she squirmed free from Nicola's arms. She clasped the child to her chest and skidded away as Declan tackled Nicola and brought her down.

Verity started to cry in earnest, just as Chad, followed by two uniformed officers, ran up the stairs. "Here's Daddy, Verity." Nora comforted the child until Chad took her and hugged her to his chest.

"It's all right, my dumpling, Daddy's here. Ssh, it's all right."

He looked around, wide-eyed, as if the answers to this mess would be found around him. "I need to call my mother." He took Verity into Nicola's room.

"Don't touch anything; just sit on the bed," Declan called after him.

Nora's heart thudded. She leaned against the wall and let out a long shuddering breath of relief. They had done it. Together, she and Declan had saved Verity, and kept Nicola from harming herself or the child.

One officer helped Declan up, while the other handcuffed a subdued Nicola, her eyes hollow. Her shoulders curled inward; she looked at the floor, the fight drained away.

"Bring her to St. Aldate's after she's been read her rights," Declan instructed. "I promised her a cup of tea." One officer escorted Nicola down the stairs. Declan instructed the other officer to bring up crime scene tape to cordon off Nicola's room before leaving.

Nora watched Nicola's braids sway as she disappeared down the stairs. That had been too close. Her hands shook as she stopped the phone recording.

Declan clasped Nora to him briefly. "Good job, even if you didn't wait for me at the Porter's Lodge."

"That was a tackle worthy of your rugby days." She laughed shakily, the adrenaline still pumping. "Wilson told me Nicola had a baby with her. I couldn't wait." She held up her phone. "I have it all recorded."

He put an arm around her. "That's my darling sleuth."

They walked into Nicola's room, where Chad sat on the bed, staring at the cupboard openmouthed. Verity had calmed down. She sat next to him, playing with his keys. "Look at these." He pointed to the photos taped onto both doors.

The collages of Nicola and Chad had been taken at various ages and event, laughing or making silly faces at the camera. A few posed shots included Alvita, along with a thin young man who must be Nicola's brother.

Nora looked at the inscriptions under the paper heart. "First she wrote, 'I would not wish any companion in the world but you.'"

Chad said, "The Tempest."

"She's put a line through that, and wrote, 'His unkindness may defeat my life, But never taint my love.'"

"'Othello.' A play about jealousy." Chad shook his head. "I had no idea she was still so infatuated with me. I went out of my way to treat her like all my other students. If I'd only known … "

"You can't blame yourself," Declan cautioned. "For what it's worth, I don't believe she set out to harm Bea. She'd become obsessed with the idea of you being together and confronted Bea. There was an altercation, she grabbed Bea's necklace, and when Bea fought her to reclaim it, Nicola pushed her away, and Bea fell over the railing."

Chad closed his eyes for a moment. "A senseless tragedy—one that has left my daughter without her mother, and me without my wife." He leaned down to kiss Verity's head. "Thank you both. My mother is relieved, too, but heartbroken."

"We'll arrange a duty solicitor for Nicola, and a psychiatric evaluation." He tapped in the station number.

Nora's heart finally slowed. She noticed a white toweling robe hanging on the back of the door and brought it to Declan's attention as Declan gave instructions to the desk sergeant. At the inquest, Charlie Borden had said he'd found white cotton fibers under one of Bea's fingers.

"I'm having the room sealed. Make sure they take the robe on the back of the door and the photos off the cupboard. Thanks."

"Look here." Nora pointed into the closet, where a side shelf held a shrine of sorts, set up with a pillar candle on a saucer, surrounded by more photos of Chad.

Declan took his handkerchief and reached in. From the saucer he lifted a broken chain that dangled a locket. It was a gold heart, etched with a swirl of leaves and flowers. Set into its center was a small amethyst.

CHAPTER FORTY-ONE

5:02 PM

Outside St. Aldate's, Declan leaned over in the front seat of the Volvo to give Nora a deep kiss. "You were spectacular back there, Nora. We make a great team. Things could have gone spectacularly wrong for young Verity today."

"As good as you and Watkins?" She arched an eyebrow.

"Different. I don't go home and sleep with Watkins." His comment achieved the desired smile from Nora, a wide grin that made his heart lurch.

"I hope Julie's doing all right."

"*I'm* hoping Watkins got there in time and Julie didn't deliver in my car."

Nora laughed. "I'd think a first baby will take a while."

"What's your plan?" Declan opened the window to wave to the traffic warden, who steadily approached their Volvo to move Nora along. "Won't be a minute." The warden recognized him, nodded, and walked off down the street.

"I have to drive back to Woodstock and pick up Claire. Poor thing's been with Alvita holding down the fort. Then we need to pick up Sean from the Welches."

"Right, the art thing. God bless Neil and Sally."

"Good neighbors, especially today." Nora frowned, the green in her eyes bright in a shaft of sunlight. "What will happen to Nicola, Declan?"

He bowed his head. "It's up to the Crown Prosecution Service to decide what charges will be brought. A lot will depend on what the psychiatrist says, and Nicola's willingness to admit what happened. With your taped confession, they should be able to avoid a trial."

"Speaking of which." Nora dug in her jeans pocket to retrieve her phone.

"Thanks. I'll get a certified copy of that recording made and return it to you tonight or—" he consulted the time on her phone. "Maybe tomorrow. How about a Chinese takeaway when we both get home, and maybe after you could drive me to the hospital to pick up my car?"

"If we wait until I put Sean to bed, Claire's around. We can sneak up to see how Julie's doing, wave that warrant card of yours around a bit?" Nora looked hopeful.

He laughed and kissed her again lightly. "How can I refuse you anything today?" He opened his door, then leaned back to say, "Love you," and closed the door.

"Love you, too." Nora tooted the horn and drove off.

Declan entered the station. He was a lucky man on so many levels.

Sergeant Damen hung up the phone. "Declan, forensics have been sent out, and McAfee's arranged for the on-call psych to come in tonight for an evaluation."

"Text forensics and make certain they print the necklace they find as top priority. How's our suspect?"

"She's in the bigger interview room with a PC, waiting for the duty solicitor. We gave her tea, and she asked for a pillow. When McAfee checked, she had her head on the table and was fast asleep."

"I imagine she's not slept much this past week." Declan was pleased McAfee was on top of things. "Any word from Watkins?"

"Last I heard, he texted upstairs to say Julie was in advanced labor. Said he'll keep us posted." Damen looked at the pad he kept in front of him. "Super wants to see you as soon as you return, and Lily George said it's urgent you speak with her before she leaves tonight."

"Thanks, Damen." Declan took the stairs on his way to see Morris. He met Lily George pacing at the top of the stairs.

"What's so urgent, George?"

The young woman's face was flushed. She gripped a plain folder. "I found the Glasgow number for Denys Curshik's uncle. It's in this folder. I have a friend in the lab who moved those DNA tests up the ladder to compare Curshik's to the missing boy."

"Tell me we've solved a decades-old case." Declan was puzzled by Lily's agitation as he took the file.

"It's a bit more complicated than that, sir."

He flipped open the folder and started to read. Declan's eyes grew wide. He jumped to the bottom line. "Phew. Who else knows about this?"

"No one. I thought it best to let you handle it."

Declan made a fast decision. "Think you can keep this under your hat until tomorrow? I have a few calls to make. Oh, and please have a certified copy of the last video recording on here made quickly, and see about having it transcribed." He handed her Nora's phone. "This is Nora's phone." He gave George the password to open it.

"I'll take care of setting that up right now." She turned to walked away.

Declan called after her. "Thanks. Good instincts, George. I might need you to do a bit more before you leave tonight." Declan slapped the folder against his thigh as he entered Superintendent

Morris's office, his mind racing.

Cat had her purse over her shoulder to leave for the day and motioned towards Morris's door. "Go right in." She gave him a wide smile and locked her desk. "Give Watkins and Julie my best when you speak to him. Let the night sergeant know when there's news, so we can organize the right gift."

"I'll do that." It had surprised Declan when he'd first entered the police how much the events of life were celebrated by members of the force. They really were like a second family. Declan knocked once and entered. Morris was rolling down his sleeves.

"There you are. Good result, Declan. Great team you've assembled. We have a duty solicitor assigned to the young woman?"

Declan nodded. "On the way, as well as a psych eval later. Once she's had that, she'll spend the night here under suicide watch. I'll interview her formally tomorrow, probably in the afternoon once some of the forensics are back and I've spoken to CPS." He explained about the taped confession of the accident that would be transcribed by then, plus Nicola's obsession with Chad Brown. "The victim's necklace was found in her room, too, and is being fingerprinted. Morton's bathrobe is being checked to see if it matches the thread found under Bea Jones' fingernail."

"That should be plenty for the CPS to offer her a plea deal, avoid the cost of a trial." He fastened his cuffs. "Just on my way out. Grandson's holiday concert tonight at the primary."

"Sounds nice, sir."

Morris shook a finger at him. "Paul, remember? In reality, it's horrid—all those squeaky violins and off-tune horns. You'd think it was The Royal Albert Hall the way my wife tears up when they sing, but they try hard and I wouldn't miss it. So much innocence at that age. We take everyone for ice cream after. I love it." His face creased in a broad smile. "Take a seat for just a second."

Both men sat as Morris continued. "This kind of quick result will go down well with the board towards your promotion. In the meantime, I'm authorized to raise you to acting DCI, with the accordant pay raise until the board review. That process will take a few months."

"Thank you. A tryout, then?"

"Pro forma with my recommendation, but never hurts to present even more reasons why you should move up. Let Watkins know that when he's back from family leave, he'll be elevated to acting DI, too."

"That's great, sir. I hope to see him tonight if I can talk my way into the maternity ward."

"Take Nora with you. She'll get you in." Morris rose from his chair and Declan stood. "That's sorted then. Congratulations." They shook hands.

Morris was a big fan of Nora after her exploits on previous cases. "Another thing has come up, if I may have a moment." Declan tried to signal he wouldn't keep Morris long. "The Denys Curshik case, the missing boy from Bowness?"

Morris barked a laugh. "Don't tell me you've a result on that already, too?"

Declan handed over the file. "In a manner of speaking. If you'll skip to the conclusion." He watched Morris read the last page and saw his eyes widen.

"Bloody hell. That's unexpected. Once you've notified everyone, call the press office tomorrow." He came around the desk. "This is exactly the kind of publicity they gobble up." He slapped Declan on the back. "You need to broaden your scope, Declan, start thinking like a DCI."

Declan nodded. The press would be all over their station once he set this in motion.

Morris must have read his mind. "Can't be helped, Declan. We need good publicity to balance the other. Handle this carefully, though." He handed the file back.

"I'm going to call Curshik's uncle for background right now, if I can reach him in Scotland. George will do extra research for me. Then I'll call everyone in tomorrow morning."

"Sound plan. Give my best to Watkins and his wife." He walked Declan to his door. "On second thought, text me if it's a boy or a girl. My wife eats that stuff up."

"Yes, um, Paul."

Morris laughed again. "You'll get used to it, son."

Woodstock

5:39 PM

Nora wasn't as lucky with parking at this hour, and had to drive down Park Street looking for an empty spot. She reached the end of the street by a school and turned to make her way back, just as a Ford Fiesta left a spot half a block away. The slots were angled, and she pulled the Volvo in, locked the car, and walked up to Montague House.

She felt badly she'd left Claire for hours with a woman she'd just met. When she knocked, Claire answered, and Nora was surprised to hear multiple voices from the living room.

"Everyone banded together when we went around looking for Verity. As people came home from work, they started to wait here until there was word." She shrugged off Nora's apology for keeping her there. "No bother. They're all nice people."

Nora entered the living room, where four women and two men of different ages sat in chairs, on the sofa, and on the deep windowsill, all talking at once, and with animation. They looked like a league of nations in what appeared to be a closely connected neighborhood. Plates with remains of biscuits and multiple tea cups were spread over the surface of the coffee table. Alvita sat on a chair clutching Verity on her lap. When Alvita saw Nora, she stood and clasped her close, mashing Verity between them until the little girl squirmed.

"Nora! You saved my Verity. Chad told us all about it." The others started talking again, a cacophony of noise.

Nora returned the hug. "Declan really called the shots, Alvita. I'm just glad she's all right." Alvita sat back in the chair, cuddling Verity. A man perched on the sill grabbed Nora's hand and pumped it, congratulating her.

Nora thanked him and looked about. "Chad's not here?" she asked Claire as the conversation picked up around them.

"The duty solicitor arrived and he went to meet her at the station," Claire whispered.

"Oh." Another neighbor shook Nora's hand, while a short woman offered her a plate of cookies that Nora politely refused. The doorbell rang, and Claire left to answer it.

Her sister had been at this long enough. "Alvita, you have plenty of company now. I'm going to take Claire and pick up my son."

"Of course." Alvita handed Verity to the short woman and walked with Nora into the hall. The couple Claire admitted carried a tray of sandwiches wrapped in cling film. "Thank you so much. In there, be right in."

The new arrivals entered to a chorus of welcome from the neighbors while Claire grabbed her shoulder bag.

Alvita took Nora's hand. "We will see you again. Our families are entwined now." She lowered her voice. "You have any news of my Nicola? I still can't believe it. She needs help, that child. Her brother will be here later tonight."

"Declan will make sure she's taken care of, Alvita. She'll get the care she needs." Nora didn't know what else to say.

"I won't abandon her, I told Winston that. It was an accident, plain and simple."

Nora nodded. "I don't think she really wanted to hurt Bea. She just lost it."

Alvita nodded. "She was always the one who would hold a grudge the longest. The boys would argue and 10 minutes later it was forgotten. Girls versus boys, I always thought. Who knew that a teenage crush would turn deadly." She shook her head. "I'll be praying for her, and for Bea. And this young sister of yours, she's been as good as gold all afternoon, scouring the streets with me. Then when we knew Verity was found, making tea and answering the door."

"She's golden, my sister."

"Chad told me about his visit to Cambridge. Bea's mother wouldn't go to meet her granddaughter." She rolled her eyes. "It's not for me to say; I won't judge. I will pray she comes around soon to the beauty of this child her daughter made."

"I hope it works out for all of you." Claire hugged Alvita and left, with Nora close behind.

Nora pointed out where her car was parked. "We'll hit traffic on the way back. A 20-minute ride might be twice as long. Want to drive or text Sally? We need to use your phone. Mine is being held captive." She explained about her phone and unlocked the door.

"Oh no, no Oxford driving for me. You drive. I'll text Sally."

As they left Woodstock and waited for a reply to Claire's text, Nora said, "Thanks for pitching in there, Claire."

"Hey, I was the one who asked you to find out what really happened to Bea." She checked her phone. "You missed seeing Alvita light up when Chad called to say Verity was safe. Then she really broke down when he told her Nicola had taken Verity. She feels if they had told Nicola right from the beginning about the wedding and the baby, she might have been angry, but she'd have eventually gotten over it. I'm not convinced."

"Any idea why they didn't?"

"Nicola worked weekends at Boots, and it was only a matter of weeks this semester, so Alvita acquiesced when Bea begged her to wait. Also, Chad felt it might be unfair to interfere with her work this term as it was only nine weeks. Nicola had so much riding on her grades, as he'd gotten her an apprenticeship at The Globe. I don't think he has a clue how obsessed Nicola really was with him."

"Love that's turned to obsession transforms to something else entirely."

"I remember you told me about the woman who loved Val, and killed her partner because she thought she deserved to be with Val."

Nora remembered that murder with a pang. It was how she

met Declan; it was also how Val had lost her first love. "I think Nicola probably kept her fixation in check until she discovered Verity was Chad's baby, and when she found out he was married, it put her over the edge of clear judgement when she confronted Bea."

"I suppose." Claire sighed. "What rotten luck for Bea, and for Chad."

"And Verity."

Claire's phone pinged with a text from Sally she read aloud: "Event huge success; lasted long. Boys still napping in tent. No rush."

"Great." Nora explained she would feed and bathe Sean, and Declan would bring a takeaway. "After I'll need to run Declan up to the hospital to get his car."

"That's fine." Claire yawned. "I'll stay with Sean while you get the car. Text me baby news. I'm for an early night after the drama of today."

"If you're sure you won't mind. I don't want to take advantage of your goodness to babysit. If Sean's had a late nap, he might not go down until later."

"No worries. I know the perfect movie we can watch."

The sisters said in unison: "'Yellow Submarine,'" and shared a laugh.

Nora said, "I promise to take you Christmas shopping another day."

"That's fine." Claire added: "But maybe not to Woodstock."

CHAPTER FORTY-TWO

Somerville
April 1993

Jim sat on a lawn chair in the back yard next to Dora, watching Digger play with several of the neighborhood children. It was his second birthday, and clutches of blue, yellow, and green balloons tied to the fence blew in the breeze. He might be young, but Digger understood that ice cream and cake were treats, and that the toys, paints, and puzzles he tore the paper off were for him.

Dora lay covered with a blanket on a chaise lounge watching the children, while the other adults sat at a picnic table, finishing their cake. In addition to the neighbors next door, who had become a vital part of Dora and Jim's plan, Dora's sister, husband, and son were there.

Deirdre's boy, Denys, was only a month older than Digger. At one time Jim and Dora thought they would grow up being close, "cousins" of a sort, even though there was no blood relationship. When Deirdre learned in January of Dora's plan to allow the couple next door to adopt Digger, she'd been offended, and they hadn't seen that wing of the family until today.

That had been down to Jim. He'd called Deirdre, told her Dora was failing, and that she had to put her anger aside and show up for Dora. This was too important to her. Dora had been holding on to survive until Digger's second birthday. Jim needed Deirdre to mend fences and be there for her sister.

He glanced over at Dora. She'd lost more weight as her disease progressed and her appetite waned. Her skin stretched tautly over the bones in her face, giving her a skeletal appearance. Her grey coloring had become more pronounced, too, her stick arms and bloated belly hidden by the blanket. Her pupils were constricted, little dots of black in the center of her eyes that told him her pain pills were working. The hospice nurses the oncologist had arranged came every day now.

Back in January when he and Dora had devised their plan, he'd seen the firm set of Dora's mouth and knew he'd never talk her round her idea to allow the neighbors to adopt Digger. He'd been ashamed at first of his inability to care for his son alone, but Dora hadn't blinked. "You can't work and take care of him at the same time, Jim. It won't do. He needs to be somewhere he can feel safe, not handed off to babysitters and day care. He's had too many disruptions in his short life." She'd looked him straight in the eye then. "You did this for me. This has been the happiest year of my life. I know you care for him, but it's not the same for you, if you'll be honest. He's so young now, you can become Uncle Jim from next door and still see him, but you won't have the worry and the work."

He'd been relieved she felt that way, and didn't offer much of an argument. "Won't your sister feel he should go to a relative?"

"Remember what I said when I thought I was going to find work? I don't want Digger to be an afterthought, a poor relation who had to come to live with them. I want him to always feel he's the center of attention, no matter where he lives. Too bad if she's annoyed. He's not a carnival prize for the highest bidder."

Now he watched as Deirdre walked over to Dora and sat by her legs on the lounger. He kept his eyes on the children and his ears on the sisters' conversation.

"How are you feeling, Dora?"

"Like I'm dying of cancer."

Deirdre flinched. "I'm sorry about that, you know I am. I just wanted to be certain you hadn't changed your mind—"

Dora cut her off. "It's all arranged, Deirdre. We've been to a lawyer, and the adoption was final yesterday. Starting tonight, Digger will be sleeping next door with Carol and Peter. I'm sorry you don't approve, but I really don't care. Last wishes, and all that."

Deirdre sat up straighter. "All right." She lifted her chin. "Marek and I are moving. We've found a house we like in Headington. Marek's always been keen on real estate, says it's a good investment. We'll keep the Somerville house and rent it out. I wanted you to know."

"You should always do what's best for your family, Deirdre, just as I've done what's best for mine."

Oxford

5:44 PM

Declan stopped by the interview room to see Nicola Morton before he headed to his office to call Denys Curshik's uncle in Glasgow.

He quietly opened the door where Nicola slept soundly, her head turned to one side on the pillow she clasped as it rested in front of her on the table. A blanket was wrapped around her shoulders. She lightly snored.

The officer sitting in the corner bounced up and stowed his phone. Declan motioned the young man outside the door; they kept their voices low.

"Give you any trouble?"

"None at all. Asked for the pillow and blanket, drank her tea, and put her head down. She fell into a deep sleep a few minutes later."

Through the door's window, Declan cast his eye over Nicola's clothes. Her ankle-length dress didn't have a belt; her shoes were flat slip-ons.

The officer noted Declan's look. "Nothing she can harm herself with. I checked carefully, and had her take out her earrings and leave those in her purse at the desk."

"Good man. Sergeant Damen says the on-call shrink should be here shortly. Let her sleep until then, and be certain to have someone take her to the restroom before he gets started."

"Chad Brown is meeting with the duty solicitor next door."

"All right. I'll leave them be for now. I should be here for another half hour, and after that on my phone."

"Yes, sir. And may I offer my congratulations."

Declan didn't know if this was for apprehending Nicola Morton, or if Cat had allowed news of the promotions to get around the station. It wouldn't be the first time. It helped with morale to know there was someone at the top, running things. "Thanks for your help. I know these kinds of duties are boring, but they're important. If this drags on, ask the night sergeant to have another officer relieve you for a break."

"Thank you, sir." The young man opened the door and took up his post.

Declan stared through the window at Nicola. She lifted her head; her cool, dark eyes assessed him for a moment. Then put her head back down on the pillow facing the other way.

CHAPTER FORTY-TWO

He'd decided Nicola's actions today were all too human when they revolved around obsession. Jealousy mixed with love—age-old reasons people would behave in ways they couldn't reconcile with their normal lives. Nicola's shove at Bea ended in tragedy, and accidental as that may have been, led to her wanting to possess the child to get Chad's attention, even for a brief moment of time.

He shook his head and left. On his way to his desk, he met Lily George bouncing down the stairs, talking with McAfee. "Sir! Watkins just texted. It's a girl! We're headed to the pub to raise a glass."

"Have one for me."

Back at his desk, Declan remembered to text Paul Morris the baby news, then scanned the file Lily George had given him, and pulled up the statements McAfee had taken from Denys Curshik. He made note of several questions he wanted to ask and dialed the Glasgow number.

"Hullo."

"This is Detective Inspector Declan Barnes from Thames Valley police, trying to reach Stefan Curshik."

"Speaking."

"Mr. Curshik, I'd like to ask you a few questions about your brother's family. Do you have a moment to speak now? I can give you the number here at the station in Oxford to verify who I am."

The man sighed. "I wondered if you'd ever get around to me after all these years. I didn't mean to do it, you know." The man's voice had an unusual mix of Scottish brogue with a Polish accent.

Declan was taken aback. Could this man be confessing to kidnapping Donnie Walsh? "Exactly what didn't you mean to do, Mr. Curshik?"

"Set that fire. I know it was rash, but nobody got hurt and I paid for the damage. Wait a sec. Marek's long gone, Deirdre, too. Did she leave a tell-all note for Denys? Is the boy trying to press charges this late in the game?"

Declan felt totally confused. "Mr. Curshik, please start at the beginning. I fear we're talking at cross purposes here. Let's get a few things straight, all right?"

"Fine. You's the one called me."

"Denys Curshik is your nephew, correct?"

"That's right. By my brother, Marek, and his wife Deirdre. Say, nothing's happened to the boy? I know I'm terrible about keeping in touch—"

"No, no, Denys is fine. I saw him earlier this week."

"That's all right, then."

"Denys is the biological son of your brother and sister-in-law. No adoption?"

"Naw, that was Deirdre's sister, Dora. She and her hubby, Jim wasn't it? They couldn't have kids. Lived in Bowness. Then right after they moved south, they adopted a little boy, can't think of his name."

"Can you tell me their last name, please?"

"I'll ask my wife. She'll remember." He yelled out: "Rhona! What was Dora Stewart's married name?"

In the background, Declan heard a woman's voice become louder as she came closer to the phone. "Ended with son. Upson, maybe? Who's asking?"

"Oxford copper. Not Upson, but that's close."

"Robson, that's it—Jim and Dora Robson," Rhona said.

Declan scribbled. He'd get these names to Lily George and see what she could find. "What can you tell me about Jim Robson?"

"Let's see," Stefan said. "Didn't know them well. It was Deirdre I knew."

Declan heard Rhona Curshik's snort. "That's one way of putting it."

"That was all over by the time we married," Stefan huffed.

"Who did you say was asking questions? Give me that phone." A woman's voice came on the line. "Who is this?"

The formidable woman made him try out his new title. Declan did his best to sound official yet polite. "This is Acting Detective Chief Inspector Declan Barnes, of the Thames Valley Police. Whom do I have the pleasure of speaking with?"

"This here's Rhona Curshik, and I'm married to Stefan. What's this you want to know about Deirdre's sister?"

In a few questions, Declan elicited that Rhona Curshik had grown up locally, knew all about the Stewart family, and kept track of local gossip. Deirdre was well-liked and popular. Dora had been years younger and spoiled by their parents, "a bit of a princess who usually got her own way," Rhona said.

Deirdre had been dating Stefan when his brother, Marek, had stolen her away. Despite standing up at their 1990 wedding, Stefan had a difficult time losing the young woman to his brother. His jealous feelings worsened when their son, Denys, was born the next year. One day when the child was 18 months old, Stefan entered their rented home, gathered all of the young family's photographs and albums in the center of their dining table, and set them on fire.

"Deirdre and the boy were out at the shops," Rhona said. "Marek came home first and put the fire out, but the table and sideboard were gone, the ceiling scorched, and their personal papers stored there burned to a crisp."

Declan made a note. That explained why there were no baby photos of Denys, and why his birth certificate had to be replaced.

Rhona continued. "Stefan bought new furniture and had the room and ceiling repainted. Marek agreed not to press charges—he must have felt badly taking his brother's girlfriend—still, they upped sticks and moved down south a few months later. Marek eventually said he forgave Stefan, but kept his distance. He would write Stefan with news a few times a year, but rarely visited. Bloody foolish if you ask me."

"No one asked you. Give me that phone back." Stefan came on the line. "I admit it was a lousy thing to do. I was that hung up on Deirdre at the time. Things were never the same between us." He coughed. "Silly obsession, but I got over it. A year after they moved, I met Rhona and never looked back, and we have our own life. Two sons, one married with his own little girl now."

"I see." Declan consulted his notes. "Any idea what happened to Dora and Jim Robson?"

"Dora died about six months after Deirdre moved near her."

"And this Jim Robson, know where he might be now?" Declan felt so close to getting answers. He heard Stefan relay his question to Rhona.

"That's right. Rhona says he was in hospital supply sales in Cumbria before they transferred near Oxford. After Dora died, Jim emigrated to Australia. She heard he died out there."

Declan decided having contacts with hospital personnel would have helped Jim Robson forge a birth certificate that would pass muster. But Australia? "One last question, and thank you both for your patience. The boy the Robsons adopted—any idea what happened to him? Did the father take him to Australia?"

Declan imagined he could see Stefan's shrug on the other

end of the line. "Marek told us after Dora passed, Jim wanted to leave everything here behind him. Wait, Rhona wants to say something, says it's important. She's picking up the extension."

The phone clicked in Declan's ear. "Stefan, remember Marek wrote in a letter that Dora told Deirdre she had her hands too full with Denys so young to take on two little boys. Me, I think Dora just wanted theirs to be the center of attention. Dora arranged for the people who babysat for them to adopt the boy when she passed, all proper and legal like. Never knew their name, though."

Now he was getting somewhere. "And Jim Robson went along with this?"

"Apparently. Marek said Jim was gutted when Dora died, couldn't get away fast enough. Now what was that child's name?" She sighed. "Nope, sorry, can't recall it."

"Thank you, Mrs. Curshik. You've both been very helpful."

"Inspector, can I ask what this is all about?"

Declan felt badly. "I need to have a few more pieces of information to sort this out properly. In a few days, you might want to give your nephew Denys a call. He and his wife are expecting a child, and he's keen to reconnect with family. He'll be able to explain it all then."

"A baby, how lovely. A cousin for our little grandbaby. Family is everything, you know. I'll make sure Stefan calls Denys."

Declan had no doubt Rhona Curshik would make certain her husband would do just that. Now he had one more important phone call to make, to set up a morning meeting.

8:53 PM

Nora and Declan entered the Women's Centre at the John Radcliffe, talking about his promotion.

"I'm so proud of you, Declan. And for Watkins, a new baby and a promotion in one day." Nora felt excited. They took the elevator to the labor and delivery department. They'd agreed not to bring flowers today, and instead bring a gift to the house after the baby came home. An officious receptionist sat behind the desk.

"Visiting hours are over," she said without looking up.

Declan flashed his warrant card. "Need to see my sergeant, 10 minutes, tops. Trevor Watkins and his wife, Julie."

Nora hoped the receptionist wouldn't hassle them. A nurse wearing scrubs stopped to check the computer and looked at the card.

"He's the real deal. Mrs. Watkins' husband is a detective sergeant. Better let them in before he arrests you." She met Nora's eye and gave her a wink. "I'll take you down to your sergeant. Follow me."

Nora's excitement grew. She didn't feel badly at all about elbowing their way in here with Declan's credentials. She could hear the high-pitched sounds of a newborn's wail behind one of the doors as they followed the nurse until she stopped at a door farther down the hall and opened it.

Julie sat up in bed, looking exhausted but serene, with a grin of happy surprise when she saw who was there. Watkins sat in an armchair next to the bed, wearing a pair of scrubs. He held a bundle wrapped in a pink receiving blanket and gazed at his daughter. A huge bouquet of flowers with "It's a Girl!" balloons sprouting from it rested on the windowsill.

"Look who I found wandering the halls trying to get in, Sergeant." The nurse nodded to the sink in the room. "Wash your hands, both of you. Five minutes, please. The new mother needs her rest." She pulled the door closed behind her as she left.

Nora washed her hands and made room for Declan at the sink as she rushed to hug Julie. "Congratulations! How are you feeling?"

Julie laughed. "Tired, sore, joyous. You just missed the new grandparents, all four of them. Look at those flowers! Thought they'd never leave." She turned to her husband. "Trevor, let Nora hold the baby."

Watkins looked at them properly then, his eyes glazed with happiness. "Sure." He stood up to let Nora settle in the chair, and carefully handed her the baby. The infant slept soundly, eyes closed, minute lashes splayed out against her cheeks. Her warm body was swaddled tightly. Only her head, covered in a striped cotton hat, peeked out.

"She's gorgeous." Nora tried to recall Sean this tiny as she inhaled the scent of a newborn. The room had subdued lighting and an aromatherapy gadget that scented the air with relaxing lavender.

"Isn't she the prettiest baby you've ever seen?" Clearly, Watkins was already besotted.

"I think she has Trevor's lips and my nose," Julie said.

"Thank God for that." Declan clapped Watkins on the back, and the men shook hands. "Wonderful. Job well done, Julie."

Watkins sat on the end of Julie's bed. "McAfee texted me about the result: Morton arrested. Blew me away."

While Declan caught Watkins up on what he'd missed that

afternoon, Nora talked with Julie about her delivery.

"Everyone was so surprised she came out so quickly. They thought I'd be in labor for hours yet, but I kept telling them, the baby's coming—and she was!"

"Home tomorrow?" Nora asked.

"Yes. Our parents will go spare if they can't get their hands on her longer. My mum and Trevor's are already planning our meals for the next week. Any excuse to take turns visiting."

Declan looked at the baby over Nora's shoulder. "Very sweet. What's this little darling to be called?"

Julie's laugh was merry. "I really gave Trev a hard time, didn't I? The best part of my pregnancy, besides feeling the baby move, was coming up with horrid names to terrorize him. I do want my maiden name for her middle, but she's going to be called Alice."

Nora looked down at the sleeping infant. "Alice—perfect for an Oxford baby. Alice Beasley Watkins is lovely."

"I think so. Trevor loves it, too."

"Trevor is thrilled," Watkins said.

Julie looked to her husband. "Trev, don't you have something to ask Declan?"

"What? Oh yeah, sure." Watkins had a sheepish look. "Julie's sister's going to be godmother, but not having a brother, we'd like you to be Alice's godfather."

Nora saw Declan's face light up.

"I'd be honored, thank you. She'll have everyone at St. Aldate's to protect her."

Everyone laughed and Nora checked the clock over the door. She handed Alice to Julie. "We should go. She had a busy day, too."

Declan held out his hand. "Need my car keys, if you haven't

lost them in the mad dash here."

Watkins rummaged in the pocket of the suit jacket that hung on the back of the door. "My parents will bring ours up tomorrow with the car seat." He threw them to Declan, who caught them in one hand.

He dangled the set. "Hope you didn't have too much trouble getting in that roadster, Julie."

"I wasn't in a position to be choosy," she said.

"Not as good as a Range Rover, I know." Declan pocketed the keys.

"As if that's on the cards," Watkins said.

"I don't know," Declan said. "Maybe on a detective inspector's salary."

Watkins stared at Declan while the penny dropped. Declan held out his hand for the second time. "Congratulations again. When Alice's dad returns from leave, he'll be Acting Detective Inspector Watkins."

CHAPTER FORTY-THREE

Oxford

Thursday, 7th December

10:23 AM

Declan spoke with the CPS prosecutor, explaining the forensics on the case. "Threads from Nicola Morton's robe are being compared to the ones caught in Bea Jones' fingernail; they should have that result later today, but Miss Morton's prints have been identified on the victim's locket. No surprise there considering she says she tore it off Bea Jones."

"Yes, I read a transcript of her taped confession," the woman said. "I've spoken with Morton's solicitor, and with the victim's husband. We are in agreement there is no evidence of intent or premeditation. Miss Morton has no previous convictions, and is showing remorse, as well as willingness to have therapy. The psychiatrist's evaluation agrees this appears accidental, borne out of Miss Morton's obsession. The forensics will back up that she is the perpetrator. It's likely a plea agreement is in order."

"I agree. I overheard the confession myself. She didn't see herself as kidnapping the child; that didn't occur to her. This was the child of the man she loved, and she wanted to use the child to bring him to her to confess about his wife's accident. Whether she would have ended up hurting the child is something I can't speculate on."

"Her judgement was obviously clouded. We'll plan to offer a charge of involuntary manslaughter by reason of diminished responsibility while under a disturbance of her mind. Anything else would have prison time, which the husband wants to avoid. Miss Morton would need to agree to inpatient therapy for at least nine months to a year and to outpatient therapy for another two years."

Declan knew of cases where fines were levied, but the CPS prosecutor said she wouldn't seek that, but would instead tack on community service once Nicola was released from inpatient care. "A student on scholarship hasn't the means to pay a fine. Mr. Brown told me he and his wife had taken out life insurance on each other when his daughter was born. That payout will be substantial, as there was a double indemnity clause for accidents. He plans to put those proceeds in trust for his daughter's education and is in agreement with this plea deal without a fine or prison time. He said his wife was very concerned with kindness toward others, and this second chance is what she would have wanted."

Declan thanked the woman for her swift response and decision.

"Don't thank me. Thank the husband. We've been on the phone all morning, and he met with the duty solicitor yesterday. He feels strongly that a quick resolution would be best for all concerned. He explained the woman's relationship as a ward of his family. Sad case."

She ended the call, and Declan pondered the brief life of Beatrice Jones. The young woman's kindness had certainly rubbed off on her husband, and on those around her. If only Nicola Morton had been able to see beyond her obsession to the goodness of Bea Jones. Indeed, Nicola would now be the recipient of that kindness with this plea deal.

Declan rubbed his knees, sore after tackling Nicola yesterday. The bruises would fade; if only the effects of Nicola's actions could be erased as quickly. He knew the Brown and Morton families were in for a rough time over the next years.

His office phone rang. Sergeant Damen announced Declan's visitors had arrived. As arranged, they were on their way up to his office, escorted by Lily George. When he arrived that morning, he'd asked her to bring two more chairs to his office, and those stood at the ready. He had a long story to tell. George had asked to sit in on the interview, and after the research she had done for him, he'd agreed.

At George's knock, Declan opened his office door and ushered the couple inside. He had met them at the Police Ball and greeted them again. "You've met Miss George, who has been instrumental in bringing today about." He shut the door behind them. "Thank you for dropping everything to come in and meet with me today." He showed them to the chairs arranged around his desk, then called down to Sgt. Damen to let him know he didn't want to be disturbed unless it was something truly urgent.

Carol and Peter McAfee were a pleasant middle-aged couple. Peter was taller than Carol, who had a cheery smile. It was Douglas's mother who spoke up.

"We're happy to help with anything that has to do with Douglas. You said last night on the phone it wasn't terrible news, just might come as a shock. We've been trying hard since then to figure out what you meant."

"Yes, sorry to be obtuse, Mrs. McAfee. If you'll bear with me, I promise to explain everything, once I ask for a few details on how you came to adopt Douglas."

Peter McAfee tipped his head to one side. "I assure you that was all above-board, detective."

"I'm sure it was. It's how you came to find Douglas in particular

I'm interested in. He didn't come to you through an adoption agency, for instance?"

Carol McAfee shifted in her chair. "No, that wasn't it at all. He was the son of neighbors in our terrace. We had applied to several adoption agencies and were waiting for news when the Robsons moved in. We often babysat for Douglas when he was a toddler. When his mother knew she was dying of lung cancer, Dora Robson asked us to adopt Douglas." The woman reached for her husband's hand. "We weren't able to have children, you see, and this felt like the answer to our prayers. We'd come to love Douglas, and readily agreed. It was what Dora and Jim both wanted."

"We went to a lawyer and had a private adoption done," her husband said. "We even have a birth certificate for Douglas, listing us as his parents. Jim insisted on that as part of the adoption."

Declan met George's eye. Robson would have wanted that. Another piece of the puzzle, one that would help erase all traces of Robson's kidnapping. "Mr. Robson didn't feel he could adequately care for Douglas on his own?"

"He didn't have family to fall back on," Carol McAfee said. "He worried about working and caring for Douglas, Digger we called him when he was young. Dora didn't want him to go to her sister, who had her own little boy almost the same age. Jim said he couldn't picture going on without Dora, working and caring for him as a single parent. He was depressed, reasonably so. At first, I was concerned he meant to commit suicide after she died, remember Peter?"

Peter McAfee nodded and picked up the thread. "Dora lived to see Douglas turn two. I think that's what she held on for—that birthday as her last good memory. She had refused all treatments, and was quite ill by that time, really hanging on by a thread. She stopped eating altogether after that."

"Douglas came to stay with us after his party," Carol said. "He was used to us and didn't bat an eye. We'd had overnighters once Dora took ill, and he had his own cot and familiar toys at our house. Jim brought over the rest of his things soon after. Dora didn't want him to see her deteriorate at the end." Her eyes teared up. "She really loved that boy."

"Dora died 10 days later," Peter said. "The first few weeks, Jim came by in the evenings to see Douglas, but soon came less and less. I saw he was packing up the house. When I went to speak with him, he said he'd decided to move, that it would be better for Douglas if he came to know us as his parents and he was out of the picture. It might be too confusing for the boy as to who to call Dad."

"Any idea where he moved?" Declan already knew from Lily's research just how good Rhona Curshik's gossip line had been, but it would be confirmation.

"Oh, yes." Carol nodded. "About three months after Dora died, Jim came to our door with a cheque. He said he wanted us to have Dora's life insurance for Douglas, that the house had sold and he was emigrating to Australia." Her eyes wide, Carol added, "We heard from him a few months after, a postcard with his new address, but when I sent a Christmas card that year, it was returned. Peter made enquiries and we learned Jim had been killed in a car accident just before the holidays."

Declan glanced at George, who sat transfixed, listening to the story. "Miss George here is an excellent researcher. Mr. Robson hit an overpass in his car and was killed instantly."

Carol inhaled sharply, her hand going to her mouth. "That poor man. After all he went through."

When George had brought him what she'd found, Declan wondered if Jim Robson might have fallen asleep at the wheel, and his death was truly an accident, as the Sydney police decided, or if Robson's guilty conscience had gotten to him. Perhaps he'd just been careless, or become depressed around the holidays, as so many others did. They would never know for certain.

But there was one thing Declan was certain about. "George, ask Douglas to join us, please." As he filled in the McAfees, he watched their eyes widen.

10:57 AM

Douglas McAfee finished filling the carton that held the photos and paper evidence gathered in the Beatrice Jones case. He'd cleaned the white board, ready for the next major crime case, and wondered when the budget at St. Aldate's would lend itself to one of the newer glass boards. Too fancy by half. He put the lid on the carton and made certain it was properly marked with the case number and name. Another life reduced to a box of papers and crime scene photos.

Lily had certainly been in the DI's wake yesterday and today. He'd barely seen her, and when they'd gone with the others to the pub to toast Watkin's daughter, she'd left early, pleading a headache. Maybe he could convince her to have lunch with him, if she ever came back to her desk.

He looked up, and there she was before him, a serious look on her face.

"Douglas, come with me, please. Barnes wants to see you."

"Sure." He gestured to the carton. "Let me just—"

"Leave it." Her sharp interruption surprised them both. "It can wait," she said in a softer tone. She left the office, and while McAfee saw a few of the others raise their eyebrows, he shrugged his shoulders eloquently, and left with her.

Once on the staircase, he grabbed Lily's arm. "What's going on, Lil? I'm not for the chop, am I?" He struggled to think what he might have done to put himself in the boss's bad favor. He thought he'd handled this case rather well, holding down the fort at the station, directing the team and the other civilians, while looking into the Curshik business, too.

Lily stopped just outside Barnes' office. " Of course not, silly." She looked both ways and stepped up on tiptoe to kiss him lightly, to his surprise. "Just remember, whatever happens in there, you're still the same person, and I'm with you all the way."

She smiled and squeezed his hand, and McAfee thought he could handle anything.

He walked behind her into the office, shocked to see his parents sitting in front of his boss's desk. His mother had been crying and held a crumpled tissue. Bad news then. A grandparent?

Barnes stood and motioned him into the open chair next to his mother. Lily sat beside him. "Mum? What's happened?"

"My fault, McAfee," Barnes said. "I wanted to prepare your parents and answer a few questions before I sprang this on you. Have a seat. Sorry for the mystery, but I had to have my facts straight."

His mother patted his arm. "It's all right, Douglas.

Everything's fine."

He sat as directed. His father's face looked white. What was happening?

Barnes launched into his explanation. "McAfee, you recall when you took over the Curshik case and interviewed Denys Curshik? He brought in photographs at one point. You touched at least one of them."

McAfee thought back to earlier in the week. He remembered he'd picked up one of the photos Deny had brought in, the one with Curshik's mother wearing her hair the way his own mother had worn it for years.

"George sent those photos, along with the DNA sample from Curshik, to the lab to be compared to the missing boy from Bowness, Donnie Walsh. Denys is who he thought he was growing up. Being in the police, your DNA is on file. When the lab checked DNA they found on the photos, yours matched that of Donnie Walsh."

For a moment no one in the office breathed. McAfee couldn't make sense of what his boss had said. "You mean …?"

Peter McAfee took over. "Son, it seems the couple we adopted you from weren't your biological parents. The father kidnapped you as a child."

McAfee sat back and exhaled. This was certainly not what he'd thought he'd been called in here about. "You mean, I'm that little boy from the newspapers?"

Barnes nodded and explained the series of events. "Jim Robson and his wife Dora lived in Cumbria then. We surmise he saw you left alone in your playpen and took you into his home. When his wife took ill, he allowed the McAfees to adopt you, and emigrated to Australia, where he died a few months later.

Unfortunately, regarding your true biological parents, your father is unknown. We've established your mother died of an overdose."

Lily reached out for his hand, gave it a gentle squeeze. McAfee remembered her saying a moment ago that she was with him, and that nothing had changed.

But everything had changed.

He cleared his throat. "I think I need some time to process this."

"Certainly." Barnes stood. "Why don't you take your parents to lunch. Maybe George would accompany you, as she knows all the background, and can answer your questions."

McAfee nodded. His thoughts whirled. He'd known Peter and Carol weren't his biological parents, but they'd raised him well, shown him love, and he loved them back. He couldn't have asked for better parents. Maybe that was what mattered.

"Just remember one thing, McAfee," Barnes added. "Our family is who we surround ourselves with, who we choose to love. Your parents are sitting right here."

Tuesday, 26th December

2:33 PM

Nora thought Haven Cottage had never looked better, filled on Boxing Day with the people she loved, as well as new friends. Their tree shimmered with lights and shiny ornaments; a fire glowed under the mantel decorated with her woodland animals, where stockings hung. This morning she'd had time to neaten up the unwrapped gifts beneath the tree, and now moved between clusters of people with a tray of nibbles, while Declan topped up glasses of wine and sparkling cider.

Christmas Eve and Day had been delightful. Harry and Muriel Pembroke, Sean's paternal grandparents, sat at the dining table with her mother and Claire's father, the men sharing golf stories, renewing the friendship that had sprung up after meeting at the Pembroke's Cornwall estate for Sean's first birthday two months ago. Amelia and Roger Scott arrived a few days before Christmas and helped wrap gifts and cook meals. Everyone had gone to St. Giles for the Christmas Eve service Sally Welch officiated.

Claire, along with Val and Sophie, filled out their holiday table yesterday, a huge prime rib meal prepared with help from Nora's mother, right down to Yorkshire puddings. They'd laughed over their Christmas crackers, which Roger and Amelia had never seen. Nora took photos of everyone wearing their silly paper crowns and vowed to frame one of her mother and Roger with Sean that had come out particularly well for her library shelves. She'd send her mom a copy, too, once Amelia returned to Connecticut, to thank her for her help.

Everyone was happy with the gifts Nora had chosen. Amelia told Nora she could shop for her every year. Declan had surprised Nora with a pair of sapphire and emerald earrings that matched her vintage engagement ring, and she wore those today with pride. She had no idea when he'd found the time to shop and thought Val might have had a hand in it. Declan told her he would wear his new cufflinks at Alice's christening and definitely when they married.

Val and Sophie sat in a circle in the living room with Neil and

Sally Welch and talked books. Sally ditched liturgical clothes today and wore a soft paisley dress. The Tinks had come and gone already, off to visit other friends.

The Browns had been happy to attend the Boxing Day Open House, all except Winston, who had gone to his girlfriend's family. Alvita had visited Nicola yesterday at the facility the psychiatrist had recommended. Alvita told Nora that Nicola, who was medicated and tearful, profusely apologized for the accident with Bea, and for putting Verity in danger. She also said the young woman knew she needed help.

"That's an important step, Alvita." Nora had consoled her, seeing the shadow in Alvita's eyes. It would take a while for them all to become used to their new normal, and perhaps for Chad to visit Nicola, but that was to be expected.

Nora invited the Jones family, too, and Ernest and Ben were in the kitchen with Chad, Alvita, and Claire at the moment. Claire looked resplendent, wearing the vest Bea had left for her. She sat at the kitchen table with Ben, keeping a watchful eye on Sam and Sean, who sat on the banquette side-by-side, and scribbled with crayons in new coloring books. To Nora's eye, Ben had spent a long time chatting to Claire when they'd first arrived. Verity sat in Sean's high chair with a teething biscuit and bib over her green smocked dress, with Chad by her side. Typo waited under the high chair, living in hope for a tidbit of biscuit to fall.

When Declan handed Chad a small box that held Bea's locket, he opened it to find Declan had had the chain fixed before returning it. Nora's love for Declan grew with this kind and meaningful gesture, and she leaned against the cabinets and watched as Chad sat down for a moment to gather himself, while

Alvita squealed in joy when she saw the locket.

She showed it to Ernest as she spoke to Declan. "This was a true gift of love. Thank you for returning it." She opened the locket to display a tiny photo of Bea and Chad on one side, and on the other, Bea holding Verity. Then she brought the locket over to the table to show Nora's parents and the Pembrokes.

Chad brushed his eyes with his shirt sleeve. "You don't know what this means to me. I will keep this safe for my daughter, and she will have it when she is older."

Alvita returned the box to Chad and gave Declan a hug. "I think you are a very kind man."

Nora felt a glow fall on her that had nothing to do with her glass of wine.

From the dining room table, Nora's mother called out: "Nothing beats being a grandparent, Ernest!"

At her pronouncement, the Pembrokes raised their glasses, and Harvey stood up. "A toast: To Bea and to Verity!"

As the adults toasted, the little girl continued to munch her biscuit, unfazed by a room full of adults calling her name.

A few minutes later, Alvita and Ernest's conversation caught Nora's attention as she refilled her tray with deviled eggs. They stood by the door to the garden where she could overhear them; the two grandparents spoke of Verity's unique beauty.

"I must ask Chad how he and Bea came to choose her name. I know Verity means 'truth' and think it's lovely," Ernest said.

"Between her name and her appearance, she will always stand out in a crowd," Alvita said. "No chance of your wife coming today to see her?"

Leave Alvita to get to the heart of the matter, Nora thought, adding some stuffed grape tomatoes to her platter.

Ernest shook his head. "The longer we're apart, the less I miss her, I'm sorry to say. I don't see her returning from Sussex. We'll both be happier."

Alvita's bracelets slid down her arm as she patted Ernest on his shoulder. "Sometimes change is good. A new chapter for you, too. Your granddaughter will need you, and you and Ben are welcome in our home any time. We're family now."

Ernest thanked her, and Nora saw him glance at Ben, who overheard the exchange and gave a wide smile. "We intend to take you up on that."

Nora believed the two families would find comfort in the caring and support of the people around them as they helped raise Verity.

Declan came into the kitchen just then and took her tray to do the rounds, dropping a kiss on her temple. "You make a great party, Almost-Mrs. Barnes."

She whispered in his ear. "That's Almost-Mrs. Tierney-Barnes to you, if you please." At his look of surprise, she burst out laughing and waved him off to show she was teasing.

"Pulling a Julie on me, Nora?" He kissed her quick and hard on the lips and left to circle with the tray.

Nora paused to take in the gathering as the conversations rose. She thought of what Declan had told her about Douglas McAfee, adjusting to his own new normal, and to Watkins and Julie, sleep deprived but over the moon with their little Alice.

She thought of how families could be created and recreated. Just look at her own family, a mix of friends and relatives. She'd learned family was who she surrounded herself with, not necessarily those who were tied to her by blood. She realized that while they might be a disparate crew from many backgrounds and guises, one thing they all had in common was their ability to be kind to each other.

Sally might have better words to explain that the way we treat each other mattered. In life, there would always be heartache mixed with joy. But to have people you could count on who you knew loved you, that was life's great gift.

Nora wished she could explain to Maggie Smythe that Bea's kindness had rubbed off on all who'd met her, and her daughter would never be forgotten because of it.

Kindness was a vastly underrated trait, but one that was necessary for the world to survive. She remembered the photo of the quotes from Bea's room that Declan had showed her, a gift from Chad early on in their relationship. As Roald Dahl put it,

> "Kindness—that simple word. To be kind—it covers
> Everything, to my mind. If you're kind, that's it."

THE END

ACKNOWLEDGMENTS

This is a book about obsession; about how a person can allow that passion to rule and influence their thoughts and actions, from arson to kidnapping to death. My sincere appreciation to authors Nicola Upson, Margaret Murphy, and Anne Cleeland for taking time away from their own writing to read and give advance comments on *The Evening's Amethyst*.

While Exeter College, Oxford and Christ's College, Cambridge are closely as described, Nora's Haven Cottage is fictional, set on what is the back garden of The Old Parsonage, my favorite place in Oxford to have afternoon tea. Similarly, St. Giles Church and its graveyard are where I've sited them, but there is no rectory, while all of the places described in Woodstock can be visited except Montague House.

Beth Cole is responsible for the grand cover and layout design; Becky Brown for the copyediting. Both are a delight to work with, and my great thanks to these talented women for their time and efforts. My writing workshop colleagues, Melissa Westemeier, Lauren Small, and Mariana Damon, gave early critique feedback and later workshopped the entire manuscript. We have been working together for 17 years and I depend on their honest critiques to make all of my books better. Special thanks to Lauren Small for Bridle Path Press. Beta readers who gave their opinions and answered my questions for this book were: Joyce McLennan and Philippa Hood in the U.K.; and

Barbara Jancovic, Anne Jacobs, Deb Wells, Betsy McDonald, and Dorothy Halmstead in the U.S. Arthur Graff reads my first and last drafts and comments on both. Thank you all, and an extra nod to Philippa and her David, and to Joyce, for answering specific questions as they arose.

Author Patti Phillips won a naming rights auction for literacy at Bouchercon Raleigh and appears here in a vastly different version of herself. Laura and Peter Hamilton are long time dear Long Island friends; Laura is indeed a nurse who runs a rehab unit. The Hamilton family have lent their names to minor characters, too. It was great fun to include them in this, and to have Peter, a wonderful writer in his own right, appear as a murder suspect.

Despite writing their own fine mysteries, when Cambridge friends Nicola Upson and Mandy Morton said they'd love to be involved in my next murder, Nicola Morton was created. Neither exhibit my Nicola's obsessive leanings, unless you count cats. Phil Cook really is a porter at Christ's College, Cambridge, a lovely gentleman who was helpful on my research trip when Arthur and I stayed at the college. I promised him he'd appear in my next book and here you are, Phil, helping out with parking once again.

It takes many people to assist with questions I have when writing, especially as this series is set in the U.K. Any mistakes are entirely my own, and some may even be deliberate for the plot, such as siting the Welch family in a rectory at St. Giles to give Nora's family a neighbor. Never underestimate an author's ability to bend the truth to fit her story.

Sincere thanks to those who willingly gave of their expertise or memories of Oxford and include in no particular order: Susan

Gayle Todd; Katie Brill; Helen Mochrie; Louisa Maher, media officer, Thames Valley Police; Andy Lamb, Cumbria CID; Rev. Ian Adams, chaplain, Ridley Hall, Cambridge; Fr. John Michael Crothers. Distinct liberties have been taken with St. Aldate's staffing and Declan's team to suit the story. Close readers will note Ben Jones's mentor is named after Fr. Crothers, an Episcopal priest I knew as a teen and found in retirement the year before he died. We had a lovely reunion via letters and email, and he contributed to those scenes between Ben and his dean.

Writing is such a solitary pursuit that completing a book during COVID-19 quarantine wasn't very different. However, crafting this story provided a welcome solace when my husband and I went through cancer treatment at the same time. Arthur is my rock, my mainstay, and my biggest fan. I'm so grateful to have him by my side. We are each other's best champions; he is indeed "my strength and stay."

What will be different with this book is my ability to reach people without a book tour or live appearances in its early days. If you are reading this book, thank you for doing so, and thanks, too, to all the librarians and bloggers and repeat readers who have come to support Nora Tierney and her adventures. I do this for you and each one of you matters to me.

This book is dedicated to my husband of 30 years, and to the treasured Chiswick friends we frequently stayed with, Averil and Martin Freeth. Thank you for the great meals, the theatre and Proms trips, the rides to and from Heathrow. You are greatly missed.

About the Author

Marni Graff is the award-winning author of The Nora Tierney English Mysteries and The Trudy Genova Manhattan Mysteries. *The Evening's Amethyst* is the fifth in the Nora Tierney series. Her short story "Quiche Alain" is in the Agatha-winning Malice Domestic Anthology, *Murder Most Edible*.

CPSIA information can be obtained
at www.ICGtesting.com
Printed in the USA
FSHW010858011021
85158FS